Praise for *New York Times* bestselling author Carla Neggers

"Only a writer as gifted as Carla Neggers could use so few words to convey so much action and emotional depth."
—*New York Times* bestselling author Sandra Brown

"Neggers captures readers' attention with her usual flair and brilliance and gives us a romance, a mystery and a lesson in history."
—*RT Book Reviews*, Top Pick, on *Secrets of the Lost Summer*

"[Neggers] forces her characters to confront issues of humanity, integrity and the multifaceted aspects of love without slowing the ever-quickening pace."
—*Publishers Weekly*

Praise for Cathy Gillen Thacker

"A lovely, emotional story that brings to life that Christmas feeling."
—*RT Book Reviews* on *Lone Star Christmas*

"[Cathy Gillen] Thacker's tale jumps off the page with lively banter between her characters. *The Texas Rancher's Marriage* is a good, heartwarming, fast read sure to attract and win new fans…with its memorable cast."
—*Fresh Fiction*

Carla Neggers is the *New York Times* bestselling author of more than sixty novels of contemporary romance and romantic suspense, including her popular Sharpe & Donovan and Swift River Valley series. Her books have been translated into twenty-four languages and sold in over thirty countries. Carla is always plotting her next adventure—whether in life or for one of her novels. A frequent traveler to Ireland, she lives with her family in New England. Visit carlaneggers.com for more on Carla and her books.

Cathy Gillen Thacker is married and a mother of three. She and her husband spent eighteen years in Texas and now reside in North Carolina. Her mysteries, romantic comedies and heartwarming family stories have made numerous appearances on bestseller lists, but her best reward, she says, is knowing one of her books made someone's day a little brighter. A popular Harlequin American Romance author for many years, she loves telling passionate stories with happy endings, and thinks nothing beats a good romance and a hot cup of tea! You can visit Cathy's website, cathygillenthacker.com, for more information on her upcoming and previously published books, recipes and a list of her favorite things.

New York Times Bestselling Author

CARLA NEGGERS

THE GROOM
WHO (ALMOST) GOT AWAY

HARLEQUIN®BESTSELLING AUTHOR COLLECTION

ISBN-13: 978-0-373-01020-2

The Groom Who (Almost) Got Away
Copyright © 2015 by Harlequin Books S.A.

The publisher acknowledges the copyright holders of the individual works as follows:

The Groom Who (Almost) Got Away
Copyright © 1996 by Carla Neggers

The Texas Rancher's Marriage
Copyright © 2012 by Cathy Gillen Thacker

Recycling programs for this product may not exist in your area.

HARLEQUIN®
™ www.Harlequin.com

Printed in U.S.A.

CONTENTS

THE GROOM WHO (ALMOST) GOT AWAY

Carla Neggers

To Joan Johnston

Prologue

Christopher Slade was eleven years old and convinced no one understood him. No one would care if he died. No one believed he had any feelings at all.

He ducked into one of the storage rooms in the old stone stable his grandfather had built decades ago. It wasn't used for much of anything anymore. Christopher quietly shut the door behind him. His little brothers wouldn't miss him. Jimmy wouldn't notice he was gone until he didn't show up for supper. Even Max wouldn't notice.

He could rot out in the stable before anybody noticed he wasn't around.

Big, fat tears rolled down his cheeks as he sat on the cold floor and leaned against a huge old trunk, his bony knees tucked up under his chin. He would never be as strong as Max, he thought. He'd never seen his older brother cry. Oh, Max had said it was okay for Christopher and his little brothers to cry; crying didn't make anybody weak. But Christopher had never seen Max shed a tear.

He squeezed his eyes shut, but still the tears came.

Four years ago today, Christopher thought. Four years and nobody but him remembered. He'd just been seven. A little kid. He'd hardly known what was happening.

A sob escaped despite his best efforts to keep his mouth clamped shut.

He missed his mom and dad. Max said that was normal; of course he would miss them. It was a sign, Max said, of how much they'd all meant to each other. He'd also said that Christopher shouldn't worry so much about getting over the loss of his parents, but of going on with his own life knowing that their loss was a part of who he was. Christopher thought he understood. And most of the time he got along just fine and laughed and messed around and just lived his life on Black Creek Ranch. But not always. Sometimes he just started thinking about his parents and couldn't stop.

His mom had had white blond hair and green eyes, and he could remember every detail of her smile and the way she would ruffle his hair and tell him not to worry so much. He was her cowboy poet, she would say. And his dad, lots older than his mom, had always said nothing in his life, nothing was more important than his boys—meaning the three young ones, not Max. Never meaning Max. Even at seven, Christopher had known that. In a way, Max wasn't like his father's son at all.

They'd died four years ago today, his mom and dad. Max had left New York and come home to Wyoming to take care of his three little half brothers and tend the family ranch. They'd done all right together, Max and Christopher and Timothy and Wynne, with Jimmy there to keep up the house and grumble and make sure the boys had baths. But Christopher wished he could see his parents again, even for just five minutes to tell them goodbye—to hear them say he would be all right without them. He wrote poems about them. He hadn't shown them to anyone, not even Max.

He brushed away his tears, feeling better just for thinking about his parents and the night they'd died. Wynne was only six and hardly remembered them. Timothy was nine and didn't like talking about them. Sometimes Christopher just didn't know what to say or think or anything, because nobody understood how he felt, and he couldn't explain even if he'd wanted Ωto.

Getting to his feet, he pulled the string that dangled from the naked lightbulb, which was screwed into a socket on the low ceiling, casting the small, crowded room into shadows and dim light. He seldom came in here, just when he and Timothy and Wynne were playing hide-and-seek. One whole wall was shelves, lined with old books and bundles of papers, iron boxes and junk from the ranch, some rotting hats, a pair of spurs. There were a couple of old wooden chairs and a roll-top desk shoved up against another wall, and just the one trunk.

Maybe there was treasure in it, Christopher thought. Gold, silver, secrets. He remembered how his mom used to send him out on scavenger hunts.

The top of the trunk was wooden and flat, functional, a little soft with age, nothing at all like the ornate, antique trunk his mother had bought for the study at the house. It creaked when he raised the lid.

Inside, however, was no treasure, not that he'd really expected any. He'd just wanted to do something to help him stop thinking.

Christopher squinted in the dim light, making out textbooks on finance and economics, the annual report of some company with a picture of New York City on the front and a couple of photo albums. A thin one with a burgundy cover was on top. Christopher flipped it open without taking it from the trunk.

Pictures of Max. A whole page of them. Pictures Christopher had never seen before.

Intrigued, he dragged the album out and laid it on the desk in the best light. In one picture, Max and a dark-haired woman in glasses were standing on an enormous set of stairs in front of a huge, columned building definitely not located in Wyoming.

Christopher had never seen the dark-haired woman before. She was smiling. He thought she was kind of pretty.

And Max was smiling in a way Christopher couldn't remember seeing him smile. Not since he'd come back to Wyoming, anyway. He looked carefree. Happy. As if he couldn't imagine being happier.

Obviously, Christopher thought, the picture had been taken before his parents' accident.

He turned the page. There were more pictures of his older brother and the dark-haired woman, but Christopher's attention was drawn to a couple of folded sheets of white paper tucked between the pages of the photo album. He opened them up carefully, his heart pounding. Max would have his hide for snooping.

The top page was dated four years ago to the day.

Dear Calley,

I don't know where to begin, or how…

The next words were smudged, the paper mottled, as if it had been wet and then dried. Christopher turned to the next page. Same date, same uneven handwriting.

Dear Calley,
I'll get right to the point. My father and his wife were killed today in a car accident in Wyoming. They have three little boys, my brothers, who need me. I have to go home to them. They have no one else. I'm too confused myself, and I know you, and I can't ask you to come home with me. It would be selfish, no matter how much I want you to be with me. I can't…

The letter ended there, midsentence. Some of the words were blurred. Whatever had spilled on the first letter must have spilled on this one, too, he thought.

Christopher could hear someone hollering for him. Max.

He quickly refolded the letters and put them back where he'd found them, shutting the photo album, then the lid to the trunk. He pulled the string on the light-bulb and slipped out of the dark room into the cool, crisp air of the Wyoming spring.

"There you are," Max said, coming around the corner of the small stable.

He didn't look like the man in the pictures Christopher had just seen. This Max Slade looked so much older and harder, as if he would never be as happy as he'd been that day on the steps with the dark-haired woman. He didn't even wear the same clothes. In the picture, he'd had on a suit and tie. Now he wore dusty old jeans and scruffy boots and a flannel shirt with frayed elbows, not because he couldn't afford a new one, but because he didn't care. He would say this one still had life left in it. His hair, darker than that of his little half brothers because his mother had been part Sioux, was longer, messier, and his face had more lines in it, and his smile—well, it wasn't at all like his smile in the picture.

"What's up, buddy?" Max asked.

Christopher brushed his fingers across his cheeks, just in case there was any trace of his tears. "Nothing."

But Max's dark eyes lingered on him, and Christopher knew he knew. "Your brothers are up at the house with Jimmy," Max said. "I think they're trying to get him to let them keep a snake they found. He won't do it, of course. Jimmy's not much on snakes in the house."

"I can go on up and talk to them—"

"No," Max said. Without warning, he touched one finger to Christopher's cheek. His voice softened. "They don't know what day it is, Christopher. It's not that they've forgotten. They just don't know."

Christopher nodded, ashamed at the tears welling in his eyes. He wished they would go away. He wished he would never cry again. He hated feeling so empty; he hated aching.

Max didn't question him. He looked out toward the main stables. "I thought we could saddle up a couple horses and take a ride down along the creek. Just the two of us. What do you think?"

"I guess—I guess that'd be okay."

He started to ask Max about the woman in the picture, about Calley, but he stopped himself. He knew Max wouldn't tell him. Max never talked about his life in New York before he'd come home to Wyoming to raise his orphaned half brothers. If he wanted to know about Calley, Christopher realized, he would have to find out on his own.

He promised himself he would. Somehow, some way, he was going to see his big brother smile as he had in those old pictures.

The key, he thought, was finding out who the dark-haired woman in the glasses was.

Calley. He had her first name.

But Calley who? How would he find her? And what would he tell her when he did?

Had she and Max been—

Christopher blushed, unable to finish the thought. He was still figuring out about girls and stuff.

Max glanced at him. "You okay?"

"Yep."

He would have to talk to his brothers. Together, they would come up with a plan.

Her name was Calley Hastings of New York, New York, and Christopher had her personal email address. Next to horses, he was best at computers. Max had gotten him and his two little brothers a new computer for Christmas. Christopher figured if he worked at it, he could find anyone in the whole world.

Calley Hastings had been easy. He'd ventured back

to the trunk in the storage room several more times, learning as much about her as he could.

Now he was ready. Timothy and Wynne were up in his room with him, hovering over the computer. Christopher had been careful with what he told them. Wynne especially had a big mouth.

He had to be careful with what he told Calley Hastings, too. If he said the wrong thing, he could scare her off. From what he'd gathered after sifting through the trunk, Max hadn't explained to her why he'd left New York. That was four years ago, but Calley Hastings might still hold a grudge. So, Christopher thought, he probably shouldn't pretend to be Max. And what if she were married? What if she had another boyfriend?

Christopher knew he was counting on Calley Hastings being just as unattached as his older brother, just as needful of smiling again as she had in the pictures in the trunk.

He wanted Calley Hastings to come to Wyoming.

But how would he get her here?

She would never come all the way to Wyoming to visit an eleven-year-old.

What to do?

"You going to stare at that computer all night?" Timothy asked impatiently.

Christopher sighed. He would type his message and think about it before sending it. That made sense to him. His poetry teacher had always told him to trust his instincts.

He shut his eyes, thinking.

Then he typed.

My name's Jill Baxter. I live on a ranch in Wyoming. I've been dreaming about New York

since I was a little kid. I love the idea of all those
tall buildings and all those people. I've always
wanted to ride a subway.

Timothy squirmed next to him. "How come you're
pretending to be a girl?"

Wynne screwed up his face as if he couldn't imagine such a thing.

Christopher shrugged. "It just feels right."

He continued, going with his instincts. He needed
a cover story, a real tearjerker, if he had any hope of
getting Calley Hastings to come out west.

I don't know if I'll ever get to New York. My husband died a few months ago. I'm here alone with
the five kids and my grandmother. She's not well.
The ranch takes up a lot of time and energy. Anyway, I don't want to burden you with my troubles.
Can you tell me about New York City? Please.
Tell me everything.

Christopher read back his work. It sounded pretty
good to him. He would have to make the grandmother
really sick, but he would wait until Calley Hastings
wrote back. He didn't want to lay it on too thick right
now, or she might get suspicious. In the meantime, he
would have to think of a dramatic way for the husband
to have died—maybe he would do something with trac-
tors—and he would have to come up with ages for the
five kids.

He hoped five kids weren't too many.

"Think it'll work?" Timothy asked.

Christopher grinned at his two brothers. "Trust me. Women love this stuff. It'll work."

"But she's a New Yorker."

"Yeah," Wynne said, as if he knew anything about the subject.

"Don't worry," Christopher said. "New Yorkers don't know anything about Wyoming."

Before long, though, he would have Calley Hastings on her way to Wyoming. He knew it.

Chapter 1

Calley Hastings grimaced as she dumped her luggage at her feet just outside the Jackson Hole airport terminal. In another hour or so, she would be on a place called Black Creek Ranch. Her ride should be coming any minute. Her flight had been on time, but because she hadn't checked any luggage she didn't have to waste time at baggage claim. She had packed an efficient wardrobe into two carry-on bags, with the intention her stay in Wyoming not involve things like roping steer and sucking rattlesnake venom out of her bloodstream.

There was no turning back now. She had her pride. Before leaving New York, she'd learned the entire floor of her office building had a pool going for just how long she would last in Wyoming. Nobody, apparently, wanted to bet on the whole two weeks she'd arranged to be gone. If she'd been staying at a resort hotel in Jackson, maybe. But not out on some ranch. It was common knowledge that Calley Hastings liked concrete under her feet, doormen at her disposal, take-out gourmet in a pinch and Bergdorf Goodman's anytime. If she felt the urge for fresh air and a view, she could have croissants on her building's rooftop deck. If she felt the urge for a taste of wildlife, she could head to the Bronx Zoo or go watch the pigeons in Central Park. She didn't have to fly all the way to Wyoming.

So why in blue blazes *had* she?

Hard to explain. Maybe impossible. But here she was.

The Grand Teton Mountains loomed all around her, the airport actually located on national parkland. She'd read about the Tetons in the Wyoming guidebook she'd picked up at a bookstore near her office. They were, she had to admit, stunningly beautiful, especially now that she'd landed safely in their midst. The small plane to which she'd transferred in Salt Lake City had tilted and dipped as if squeezing itself between the tall peaks, before coming to an abrupt halt on the short runway.

Calley liked big planes and big airports.

"It's a good thing I'm intrepid," she muttered to herself, as if saying the words would make it so.

Intrepid in New York was one thing. She knew her way around New York. Intrepid in Wyoming was another thing altogether. She'd noticed a stuffed cougar on display in the airport. It didn't bode well.

She didn't do cougars.

Although she'd been flying all day, the two-hour time difference between the East Coast and Wyoming meant it was just about sunset. The air was cool and dry, a refreshing break from the steamy Manhattan summer heat.

A dusty red pickup truck pulled up to the curb. Calley thought it might be her ride, someone dispatched from the ranch to pick her up. Jill Baxter surely couldn't travel. She had the five kids, the year-old twins were still too weak to leave home and her grandmother's Alzheimer's was worse. It wasn't easy for a young widow to run a Wyoming ranch on her own. Five kids and a dying grandmother didn't make the job any easier.

A tall man climbed from the truck, a dusty black cowboy hat hiding his face. He wore a blue denim shirt with the sleeves rolled up to the elbow, battered jeans and scarred cowboy boots, and the way he walked reminded Calley of Clint Eastwood in *The Good, the Bad and the Ugly,* which was as close as she'd ever gotten to the so-called Wild West.

The remaining light hit his face, and she gasped. *Max.*

No. That was ridiculous. It couldn't be. Max Slade was more urban than she was. When he'd vanished, he'd vanished to Los Angeles or Miami or Chicago, even Paris. Not to Wyoming. Never mind the resemblance— the angular features, that straight line of a mouth—this guy looked as if he'd just been out hunting buffalo.

Calley was quite confident that all Max Slade had ever hunted were women.

While she struggled to control her shock, the man in the black cowboy hat—whoever he was—disappeared inside the terminal.

Calley jumped off the sidewalk and checked the license plate of the red truck. It featured a cowboy on a bucking bronco.

Definitely Wyoming plates.

The truck was too beat-up to be rented. She noticed a distinct weakening of her knees at the thought, however absurd, of seeing the man who'd left her high and dry four years ago. No one had ever hurt her as deeply as Max Slade.

Or ever would again.

She returned to her luggage, wondering where her ride was and trying to forget about the man in the black cowboy hat and his startling resemblance to that rat of her life, Max Slade.

The man emerged from the terminal two minutes later. Really, Calley thought, he couldn't be Max. This guy was more muscular, probably taller, and his was one grim mouth. Max Slade had liked to laugh. She had to give him that much.

He'd probably had a good laugh the day he'd squeegeed her out of his life.

The man removed his hat, an impatient hiss escaping that uncompromising, hard line of a mouth.

"Holy cow," Calley breathed.

He *was* Max Slade.

He turned. His eyes raked her from head to toe. He swore under his breath.

"Well, if it isn't Max Slade," Calley said with a small, utterly fake laugh. "Fancy meeting you here."

"It took some fancy doing, I'll say that." His voice sounded deeper, raspier than it had four years ago, and none too pleased. He nodded to his truck. "You can toss your stuff in back. We'll sort this thing out later."

Calley didn't move. She would grow roots and finish

her days at the Jackson Hole airport before she tossed anything into the back of any truck owned by Max Slade. "I think you've made a mistake. There's nothing to sort out. I'm waiting for a ride—"

"I'm it."

"I don't think so."

"Calley, you've been had. I've been had. I'm your ride. Now, get in."

She shook her head. There had to be a Jill Baxter, a Black Creek Ranch, five kids, a dead husband, a dying grandmother. If Calley was anything, she was not gullible. Not after five months with Max Slade and seven years in New York. No, gullible was the *last* thing anyone would call Calley Hastings.

But a gnawing pain deep in the pit of her stomach suggested the possibility—the slim, awful chance—that he was telling the truth and she might indeed have been had.

Her only reasonable choice, however, was to blunder on. Every other choice involved trusting Max Slade, and that was unthinkable.

"Look, Max, I don't know what you're thinking, and I don't particularly care, but obviously you're mistaken. I'm waiting for a ride from someone from the Black Creek Ranch."

"I know."

His words—his arrogant tone—went right up her spine. "You always were a know-it-all, Slade. Well, this time you're wrong. I'm staying with a woman named Jill Baxter. She's a young widow who's always wanted to see New York, but she's stranded out here in the wilds with five kids and a dying grandmother—"

"Calley, there is no Jill Baxter."

She bristled. No. Forget it. Even if she *had* been had, she would stick to her story of a Jill Baxter and a Black Creek Ranch. Max didn't have to know how idiotic she'd been. He couldn't possibly know anything about what had brought her to Wyoming. After all, he must be here playing rancher himself at some dude ranch, participating in some urban-cowboy fantasy. She didn't know. She didn't *care*. She just wanted him on his way and herself back to New York.

"You could never admit to a mistake." She grabbed up a suitcase to channel some of her restless, unfocused energy. "I don't know what weird set of coincidences brought us here at the same time and place, but *I'm* here to visit a friend and see her ranch—"

"Calley, I own Black Creek Ranch."

She stared at him, speechless for perhaps the first time in her life. Even four years ago, when Max Slade had slithered out of her life for good, she hadn't been rendered speechless. Oh, indeed not. Anyone within earshot—even some who by no means should have been—had heard what she thought of him. As she recalled, she'd been articulate and inventive. Anger had been the only way she could protect her broken heart.

It was getting very dark. She was surrounded by mountains. She was on unfamiliar ground. Her state of affairs was getting worse by the minute. She had indeed, it seemed, succumbed to some kind of low, despicable scheme to lure her to Wyoming.

"You did this?" she managed to ask.

If possible, he looked even grimmer. "No."

"But you're telling me the truth? There's no Jill Baxter, no five kids, no dying grandmother? No dead husband?"

"Correct."

"But Black Creek Ranch—"

"It's real."

Her shoulders slumped.

"Look, you don't have much choice," Max said, not ungently. "It's tourist season here. You won't find a room, not this late. You might as well come on back to the ranch with me, and we'll sort this thing out."

"No way, Slade. I'm not going anywhere with you."

He shrugged. "Suit yourself."

Without another word, he went around to the driver's side of his truck, climbed in and started the engine.

Calley exhaled up at the sky. Lots of mountains. Lots of stars. Had *Max* cooked up Jill Baxter and the five kids and the dying grandmother and the horses Jill couldn't leave? She'd sounded so real, so believable. So lonely and desperate.

No, Max couldn't be behind the email correspondence that had lured her out west. Max Slade could never pull off lonely and desperate.

So who had?

Even before she acknowledged what she was doing, Calley had hoisted up one of her overnight bags and heaved it into the back of Max Slade's truck. She grabbed the second one without hesitation, without thinking. If she *were* thinking, she would go back into the terminal, sleep on the floor and beg, borrow or steal her way onto the next flight out of Wyoming. It didn't even matter where it was headed. *Anywhere* that was flying distance away from Max Slade was fine with her.

But she flung open the passenger door and climbed up into his truck, refusing to look at Max as she more or less tripped up onto the seat. "I hate trucks," she said, staring straight ahead.

"Ever been in one?"

She gave him a cool look, repressing the outrageous, instantaneous, uncontrollable, *stupid* physical attraction she felt toward him. It had to be biological, she decided. Some chemical reaction. Like moths. "You know nothing about me, Max Slade. Nothing. So don't make assumptions."

He gave her a grudging smile that in no way reached his eyes. They were slate eyes, she remembered. Slate with flecks of black. Now they were lost in the night, in the shadows of his hat. "You always were such a bundle of sweetness and light. Relax. I'll have you in a warm bed in another hour or two." He paused, his smile vanishing. "Your own warm bed, of course."

Calley felt her throat go dry. She swallowed. It didn't help. Finally, she said, "Max, do you know what's going on?"

"Not exactly, but I have a feeling I know who does."

"Who?"

But he didn't answer her as he headed out into country she'd only seen in *National Geographic* and movies. She decided not to push Max for answers. Not right now. She was on his turf. In his *truck,* for heaven's sake. He was hardly a stranger, and even after four years and the horrible way he'd left her, she trusted him not to hurt her. But he wouldn't necessarily be above tossing her fanny out on the side of the road and letting her fend for herself if she annoyed him.

She glanced over at him. He was staring straight ahead, still grim faced. Well, the office pool back in New York couldn't have come up with this particular scenario as an option. She wasn't sure she believed it herself. Maybe she wasn't really here. Maybe she was back in New York and somebody had slipped something into her morning coffee and she was hallucinating.

Really, she thought. Max Slade in a cowboy hat. Max Slade living on a Wyoming ranch. Max Slade within two feet of her.

She *had* to be hallucinating.

But when he turned his gaze slightly from the straight, dark road and met her eyes, she knew she wasn't hallucinating or dreaming. Max Slade was real, and she was riding into the wilds of Wyoming with him.

Chapter 2

They arrived at the ranch just before midnight. Max didn't try to put a better face on what had happened; he just let Calley Hastings adjust to her surroundings.

If that were possible, he thought, not optimistic.

Even with the array of stars overhead—nothing like she would ever see in New York—it was a dark night, none of the wild beauty of his corner of Wyoming visible. There were no streetlights out on Black Creek Ranch, no taxis to flag down should Calley change her mind about staying.

She climbed stiffly from the truck, not saying a word. If she were nervous, Max knew she wouldn't show it. He got one of her bags out of the back. She got the other. An owl hooted in the distance. He thought he saw her grimace.

Four years hadn't changed Calley Hastings a bit. She

was still pretty and smart and of the opinion that life as she knew it ended west of the Hudson River, a city girl right down to her expensive imported undies. She didn't belong in Wyoming. Max had known that four years ago. That was why he'd left her in New York. His brothers—who had to be responsible for her presence— would see it the minute they laid eyes on her. Max still didn't know for sure how they'd lured Calley Hastings west. She wasn't talking. He suspected, however, it had something to do with the computer he'd bought them and their vivid imaginations.

Widows, dying grandmothers, a passel of kids. Max wasn't surprised Calley wasn't talking. She would hate having to admit she'd fallen for a sob story. Of course, he hadn't known a thing about any of it until he'd seen Calley Hastings standing at the airport.

He led her up onto the big front porch; all the old furniture—the rockers and swing and wicker settees— were no comfort, he suspected, to a woman accustomed to looking out at tall buildings. She wouldn't even be able to imagine the spectacular sunsets that spread out across the horizon beyond the porch, the wildlife that would amble through the meadows across the creek.

As he pushed open the front door, the light caught her face and shone on the intense blue eyes behind the stylish glasses. She didn't look afraid, he noted, or worried or particularly embarrassed. Instead, he thought she looked remarkably annoyed for a woman in her position.

Now *that,* he thought, was the Calley Hastings he'd known and maybe loved four years ago. She'd always grown irritated in the face of embarrassment, worry and even fear, and she was never, *ever* one to suffer fools gladly, including when she was the one who was the fool.

Jimmy Baxter was waiting up in the living room, the biggest area in the rambling house. It had a huge stone fireplace, an old player piano and lots of clunky, comfortable furniture. Lissa Slade, the boys' mother, had planned to redecorate the place. She'd never gotten the chance. So long as the furnishings didn't get too tattered and remained vermin free, Max didn't care. Decorating had been the least of his worries these past four years.

Jimmy struggled to his feet. He had been a cowboy most of his life, until a fall from a horse six years ago—an ignominy he hated to acknowledge—had left him with a permanent limp. Now he pretty much ran the Slade household. He scanned Calley, his bushy eyebrows rising as his dark, alert eyes turned to Max. In that instant, Max knew, Jimmy had put the pieces together and figured everything out—or at least as much as he needed to know.

"Welcome," he said to Calley.

She nodded, her jaw clenched too tight for her to get any words out. Max made the appropriate introductions, his own tone just this side of surly. What was he going to do with Calley Hastings?

Get her back to New York as fast as he could.

"Once I figured out something was up, I set up the downstairs bedroom," Jimmy told her. "It's got its own bath. Figured you'd be more comfortable away from the rest of the house. Anyway, I checked around for spiders and snakes and the like, put clean towels in the bathroom, so it's all set."

"Thank you," Calley said dryly.

"What about the boys?" Max asked.

Jimmy snorted. He was sinewy and well under six feet, not a hint of Mary Poppins about him. "Those rascals—they're up in bed."

Calley narrowed her eyes. "Boys?"

Max grimaced. "Three boys. Christopher, Timothy and Wynne. They're the ones responsible for your being here."

She was blinking rapidly, not understanding. And Calley Hastings was a woman who liked to understand, who prided herself on not diving headfirst into anything before she'd checked it out with her remarkable thoroughness and astuteness.

But she'd dived into this one, Max thought. No getting around it. No matter what kind of story the boys had cooked up, Calley couldn't claim to have been thorough or astute. If she had been, she would still be in New York.

"Are they—" She cleared her throat. "Are they yours?"

Max frowned. His what? Then Jimmy snorted, and Max knew. "Oh. No, they're not my sons. They're my brothers. Christopher's eleven, Timothy's nine and Wynne's six. I'm their legal guardian. They—" He sighed. He hadn't explained four years ago, and he couldn't now, not with Calley's very blue, very suspicious and distrusting eyes narrowed on him, not with Jimmy Baxter standing right there. "It's a long story."

Jimmy mercifully intervened. "Warned you not to get those boys that damned computer, Max. They managed to order up a woman. Who knows what'll be next?"

Calley inhaled, saying nothing. Max understood.

Nobody ordered up Calley Hastings. She was not just some woman to be manipulated, to have her sympathies played upon. No way. Calley was an individual to be taken seriously.

Max knew all about Calley Hastings's attitudes.

Jimmy continued to grumble, in no better mood than the Slade household's "surprise" guest. On a good day, Jimmy Baxter hated to be duped. This wasn't a good day. The boys hadn't just manipulated Calley Hastings; they'd also manipulated Max and even Jimmy. While the old cowboy was off running errands, the boys had grabbed Max and told him Jimmy needed a package picked up at the airport, saying that the shipping company was charging extra to have it driven out to the ranch. The request was unusual, but not unheard of.

With Jimmy not around for verification, Max had set off. He'd enjoyed the ride to Jackson. It had been a beautiful evening, the kind that had forced him to make peace with his life many long months ago. He'd finally accepted that he couldn't go back to New York. Even without the responsibility of Christopher, Timothy and Wynne, he couldn't go back. He wasn't the same man he'd been four years ago. Not just his life had changed. He had changed.

On that leisurely, pretty ride, he had never once considered that his bratty little brothers had conjured up one of his former love interests. They couldn't possibly have realized that of all the women he'd known, Calley Hastings was the most likely to skin him alive if she ever saw him again.

But when he'd seen her standing at the airport, a fish out of water, he'd guessed that was exactly what had happened. The rascals had lured Calley out to Wyoming. He would take their little deed up with them himself.

Right now, he had to deal with the immediate problem of Calley Hastings in his living room, but he knew there was nothing to be done tonight.

"Jimmy can show you to your room," he told her. "I'll see you in the morning. We'll figure out what to do then."

"Thank you. Good night."

Stiff. Formal. Max tried to smile. "Sleep well."

She gave him a look that suggested nothing would be as impossible as her sleeping well under his roof. But she went with Jimmy toward the back of the house, with Jimmy insisting, of course, on carrying both her bags, limp or no limp. Calley argued. Calley, Max remembered, *always* argued.

Max headed up the staircase off the front hall. As big as the house was, each boy had his own room. Jimmy had a small suite on the other side of the kitchen from Calley's room. Max and his brothers had the entire upstairs to themselves.

Feeling the fatigue of a long, bizarre day, he checked on them one by one, Wynne, the youngest, being first. He was snoring away, his army of stuffed animals tucked in around him. Max brushed his soft cheek.

Six years old and on his own. Hell, life just wasn't fair.

But he didn't dwell on the thought. He moved down the hall to Timothy's room. He had his covers kicked off, all sprawling arms and legs; he wasn't a chubby five-year-old anymore. He was nine and growing up fast.

Max felt his throat tighten. Time hadn't stopped the

day their parents were killed. It kept marching along, one day after another, the little boys who'd been orphaned that horrible day vanishing, transforming, their loss and pain inexorably acting upon who they would become. Max ached for them. What would have become of them if their mother and father had lived? But Lissa and Ernest Slade were dead, and there was nothing Max could do to change that awful fact, nothing he could do to erase the effects of that tragedy from their children's lives.

He drew Timothy's blanket up over his skinny body. It was a cool night, quiet. Max tried not to imagine Calley Hastings downstairs, muttering to herself, trying to sort out what idiocy, what deviousness, had gotten her into this mess.

He wondered if she would go to bed before she'd double-checked every corner of her room for spiders and snakes.

Down the hall, Max stopped in Christopher's doorway. He was a serious boy, sensitive, introspective. He felt deeply the responsibility of passing on to his two younger brothers the memory of their parents. He could be as big a hellion as either Timothy or Wynne, no question of that, but his mischief was designed more to entertain and amuse, to distract, never to deliberately hurt.

He was trying for all the world to look as if he were dead to it, but Max knew better.

"A widow with five kids and a dying grandmother?" he asked.

Christopher stirred, opening his eyes. "Two of the kids are twins, just a year old. They were injured in the accident that killed the husband."

"What kind of accident?"

"Truck. They hit a moose."

"You're an imaginative kid, Chris, I'll say that. I can't believe Calley Hastings of all people bought such a sob story. Maybe you should be a writer when you grow up."

His eleven-year-old half brother brightened. "Then you're not mad?"

"Oh, *I'm* not mad," he said. "But before you breathe your sigh of relief, I suggest you wait until you meet Calley Hastings face-to-face."

Calley dreamed of rattlesnakes, big furry spiders and Max Slade, finally awakening to the pale light of dawn filtering through the muslin curtains and calamitous goings-on in the nearby kitchen. Three little boys. *What* was Max doing with three little brothers? How had he become their legal guardian? From the sounds coming through her door, she would have guessed an army of boys was in the kitchen, not just three.

She groaned, lying on her back. She hated morning. One eye focused on the old-fashioned clock on the chestnut washstand by her four-poster double bed. The little hand was on the five and the big was on the seven. By her calculations, that made the time five thirty-five and, therefore, still the middle of the night.

She exhaled at the ceiling. It was as if she were trapped in some bizarre mix of "My Three Sons" and "Bonanza." The entire all-male Slade household seemed to be up and at it at the crack of dawn. She heard voices. She heard a dog bark. She heard Jimmy Baxter growling and grumbling. She *might* have heard a rooster crowing. She was in Wyoming. She was not about to discount anything.

She smelled coffee. Surprisingly, her stomach growled. She hadn't eaten much on her trip west. She'd been too concerned with deciding how to greet the young widow who'd connected with her through an online service. What would they say to each other? How would they react face-to-face? Two women from two different worlds.

Not to worry, Calley thought. There was no widow, only Slades. Lucky her.

Well, the sooner up, the sooner out. With any luck, she would be back in New York by nightfall.

She threw back her covers, which consisted of two hand-stitched quilts, and crawled stiffly from the bed. The guest room was spacious and airy, with antique furnishings, cream-colored walls and two windows that looked out on God-knew-what. Calley padded across the thickly braided rug and pulled open the curtains.

The view was glorious. Utterly breathtaking. Better than "Bonanza" reruns, she thought. Rolling pastures, a winding creek, clusters of trees, grazing horses and huge mountain peaks rising up all around the narrow valley. It was just the sort of view she'd imagined when she'd encountered "Jill Baxter's" first email message and found herself captivated by the very idea of Wyoming, and by how very different Jill Baxter's life must be from her own.

"So," she muttered under her breath. "Yesterday wasn't some weird dream."

She felt like Dorothy waking up way the hell over the rainbow. And like Dorothy, pretty as Wyoming was, it wasn't home. Not hers, anyway. It was Max Slade's home, strange as that idea was. She had to get straight in her head the simple fact that the man she'd met last night was the same Max Slade who'd exited from her life without a note, a phone call, an email, even a message left with her doorman. This Max Slade came with a cowboy hat, scruffy cowboy boots, a ranch and three small boys. Her Max Slade had been the ultimate urban male. But the two men were one and the same.

Perhaps it was reasonable after all, Calley decided, to find him living among rattlesnakes.

She quickly retreated to the adjoining bathroom, done completely in white and not as old-fashioned as the bedroom, but hardly new. A small window looked out on a barn of some sort. Postcard country. She felt an unexpected tug of regret at not being able to explore it. Well, there was nothing to be done about it. She didn't want to stay in the same city as Max Slade, much less the same house. She would pick up a few postcards at the airport on her way back east.

Nobody back in New York needed to know she'd encountered her ex-lover instead of a lonely young widow with fantasies of life in New York.

Calley showered and changed into a plain white T-shirt, jeans that had nothing of the West in their cut and her New York Knicks sweatshirt. No pretending *she* wasn't from the Big Apple.

Taking a deep breath, she opened the door to the hall.

A little boy of about six was standing practically on the threshold, his unexpected presence giving Calley a start. She didn't scream. Years of negotiating the New York subway system had taught her to stay on the alert and not overreact, screaming only when she had good reason to scream. Presumably a six-year-old wasn't good reason.

He had tawny hair that needed cutting, huge blue eyes and two missing baby teeth. He wore shorts and a Spiderman sweatshirt, no shoes. Optimistic about the weather, it seemed. A scrawny, threadbare, stuffed golden retriever puppy was slung over one shoulder, and he had a plastic cup in one hand.

Max was this child's legal guardian, she thought. How? Why? She shook off the rush of questions. Answers would have to come later, if ever. What had become of Max Slade was simply none of her business. He'd seen to that.

Calley peered into the cup, noting the contents looked suspiciously like dead flies. "What's that?" she asked.

"Dead flies."

She made a face. "Charming."

He grinned, delighted with her reaction. At that moment, Max came up behind him. In the pale light of morning, he looked rugged and very Clint Eastwood. "They're not real," he said.

"Oh." Calley manufactured a smile. "I knew that."

"This is my brother Wynne. Wynne, this is Calley Hastings. She's from New York City." As if that explained any peculiarities the boy might notice about her.

"Nice to meet you," Wynne Slade said, racing down the hall before Calley could respond.

Max glanced after him. "Wait'll you see his rubber snake collection."

"Cute kid," Calley said, tongue in cheek.

"He loves practical jokes and has a hell of a temper. Too used to getting his own way, I guess. Don't let him fool you, he's a mushball inside. Doesn't go anywhere without his puppy." Max's searing slate eyes turned back to her. "You look like you could use a pot or two of coffee. Come on. Jimmy's cooking breakfast."

Despite her years in New York as a professional, Calley had to admit to her uneasiness as she followed Max into a huge country kitchen, where an entourage of dogs and boys seemed to be competing for volume. So far as she could tell, Jimmy Baxter made no distinction between dogs and boys, yelling at them all in the same gruff way as he flipped pancakes on a griddle and waved his spatula in mock warning.

The oldest boy was setting the table, a long, rectangular slab of pine situated in front of a double window overlooking the backyard. He eyed Calley with a mixture of curiosity and nervousness, his cheeks flushed. Max introduced him as Christopher Slade. He just gave her an embarrassed smile in greeting. Calley guessed he'd been the mastermind of the sob story that had successfully lured her to Wyoming. She wondered if he had any idea he'd accomplished no small feat or simply assumed she was a gullible, idiotic New Yorker, no match for a determined eleven-year-old Westerner with a vivid imagination.

The middle boy—lanky and probably a lot cuter than any nine-year-old male would want to admit being—was obeying Jimmy's command to let the dogs out before he threw them on the griddle, too.

"That's Timothy," Max said. "From what I can gather, the year-old twins were his contribution to the Jill Baxter tale. Wynne helped think up their names."

Alex and Jason, as Calley recalled. She didn't mention the little stuffed mice she'd tucked in her suitcase for them. She would prefer Max not know just how oblivious she'd been to his brothers' hoax. Talk about walking into the lion's mouth.

Duped by three boys, never mind that they were Slades. It was mortifying. She prided herself on being savvy and sophisticated, wise to every trick in the book, and here she'd fallen for a loony story off the internet, one worthy of convicted con men. What had the little monsters been thinking? A dying grandmother. Five kids. A widow. What lurid imaginations.

"I've already had breakfast," Max told her, his tone brusque, his eyes not reaching hers. He seemed even more distant and grim than he had the night before. "I need to get some work done before I drive you back into Jackson. There's a flight out around noon. I checked."

The three Slade boys grew silent. Calley nodded, not sure what she should say. On the one hand, she didn't want to get the boys into any more hot water than they must already be in. On the other hand, she couldn't wait to beat a path out of Max Slade's presence.

He retreated out the back door with the last of the dogs.

"Let's eat," Jimmy said.

He served up platters of pancakes and ham, and produced a pitcher of hot maple syrup, his gruff manner a welcome counter to the awkwardness of the moment. He pointed out the coffeepot and open shelf where he kept the mugs, and Calley gratefully helped herself. She was aware of three sets of Slade eyes on her. They were assessing her, waiting, trying to predict what she might do.

Finally, Jimmy sighed, muttering something about having eaten with Max, and made his exit, too.

"We had to lie," Christopher Slade announced once Jimmy was safely out of earshot.

Timothy concurred. "We knew you'd never come if we didn't."

"Yeah," Wynne said, as if he understood what his older brothers were talking about. He'd set his cup of "dead flies" next to his plate of pancakes, which he was drowning in syrup.

Calley sat at the long, scarred pine table with her mug of steaming coffee. Really, having to think at this hour was beyond the call of duty. "I'm sure you meant well."

Actually, she wasn't. They were Slades, after all, and who knew how young a Slade started with his nefarious ways? For all she knew, scheming was a genetic thing with them.

Christopher hadn't touched the pancakes and ham he'd heaped onto his plate. He seemed more serious than the other two, his eyes nearly as penetrating as his older brother's. "Max dumped you because of us."

"Is that what you think?" Calley asked.

"It's true."

"No, it's not true. Max dumped me because he's a—"

She stopped herself. She'd intended to say "heel." It was more restrained than most of the names she'd come up with in the past four years to describe Max Slade. But these were his brothers. They must look up to him. He was responsible for them. She bought herself a few seconds by forking a couple of pancakes onto her plate. Jimmy Baxter had fixed more than three boys and one woman could consume in a week, never mind one morning. Suddenly, she was ravenous.

But she made herself explain. "Your brother and

I went our separate ways quite some time ago. It had nothing to do with you."

"It did," Christopher said, his tone grave for an eleven-year-old. "Max left New York and came back here to take care of us when our parents were killed."

Calley nearly dropped the platter of ham. She glanced at Wynne, who was digging into his pancakes, disengaging himself from the conversation. Her throat had tightened. It was all making sense. These boys were orphans. Their mother and father were dead. Max had mentioned none of this last night on the drive to the Slade ranch.

Christopher and Timothy were studying her closely, as if they dared not anticipate what she might do. She was a woman, a New Yorker, and for the past six weeks, they'd had her believing in a character worthy of a daytime drama. The conniving little rats. They'd been so believable.

What was she supposed to say to three orphans?

She was a financial planner. She knew money, not little boys. Nevertheless, they had to know how wrong they were. Max hadn't abandoned her because of their parents' deaths. He'd abandoned her because he was a womanizing bastard afraid of commitment. He and Calley had started talking around, if not actually *about,* a life together—marriage, an apartment on Central Park—then he'd bailed out.

That was what had happened.

But none of her scenarios for how the notorious Max Slade had ended up after their affair remotely put him on a Wyoming horse ranch raising three orphaned half brothers. In the pits of hell, yes. Staked to a hill of fire ants, absolutely. Hopelessly in love with a woman who wouldn't give him the time of day, by all means. But not in Wyoming with three kids.

"Look," Calley said, trying not to get too far ahead of herself, "I'm not angry with you. I'm sure you had your reasons for doing what you did. I'm surprised I fell for your story, that's all. I'm not known for being gullible—"

"What's gullible?" Wynne asked.

"A sucker," Christopher said.

Calley made a face. Well, why mince words? "Anyway, obviously I fell for your story hook, line and sinker. I guess I must have been bored, ready for an adventure—I don't know. I should have checked out this Jill Baxter. I really don't know why I didn't. But I didn't, and now here I am. It's just one of those things."

None of the boys responded. Calley tried her pancakes, which to her surprise were multigrain. Jimmy Baxter perhaps wasn't as oblivious to good nutrition as she'd anticipated. And the syrup was sweet, heavenly.

Timothy fastened his especially intense blue eyes on her. "Then you're leaving for sure?"

"For sure," she said.

Wynne pushed out his lower lip, looking even younger than six. "I want you to stay."

Christopher leaned back in his chair, his eyes narrowed, his feelings unreadable. *He* looked older than his eleven years, that know-it-all expression all too reminiscent of his older brother's. The Slade genes at work. "If there's nothing between you and Max, why can't you stay?"

"Because I'm here under false pretenses—"

"Not anymore."

She swallowed a mouthful of pancakes. Explaining

the nuances of her relationship with Max to his kid brothers was out of the question. She did have some dignity left. "I can't stay."

"You bought a round-trip ticket. You said so in your last e-mail."

As if she needed reminding. It was embarrassing to think how much these kids knew about her, things *she'd* told *them.* "I can change it."

Wynne's shoulders drooped. "I want you to stay," he repeated as if he were well accustomed to getting what he wanted. Calley had no illusions he'd become attached to her in the past half hour; he was just a sociable little kid who liked having company. Her arrival probably broke up the monotony of life on a Wyoming ranch.

"What will you do in New York?" Timothy asked.

"This is your vacation," Christopher added.

Calley was well aware she had taken two weeks of her vacation to visit a trapped, lonely woman who'd always wanted to come to New York and, Jill Baxter's circumstances being what they were, likely never would. Something in their weeks-long computer correspondence had touched a nerve with her. She couldn't precisely say what it was, but she wasn't ready to dismiss it. Had the younger Slade brothers revealed some of their own yearnings in their messages to her? Or were Christopher, Timothy and Wynne Slade so devious they could fake the emotion that finally had prompted her to book a flight to Wyoming?

She would be wise, she knew, not to project any emotions or motivations onto anyone with Slade blood running in his veins. Wariness was in order.

Yet the boys' desire to have her stay seemed sincere,

regardless of its motivation. They'd gone through a lot of trouble to get her here. Clearly they'd misunderstood her relationship with their older brother and guardian, creating their own fantasy of why it had ended. Perhaps if she stayed, at least for a day or two, they could see for themselves the reality of her and Max Slade. The truth was, even if he'd dumped her because of the tragic turn of events in his half brothers' lives, he could have gotten word to her. He could have told her what had happened. Instead, he'd used the tragedy as an excuse to rid her from his life and had left her without so much as a goodbye.

It wasn't Max who'd lured her to Wyoming, either. It was his brothers. Something she definitely needed to remember. Max Slade no more wanted her back in his life than she wanted to be in it.

But she found herself saying, "I'll pour myself another cup of coffee, and you boys can show me around. Then I'll make up my mind." She studied each boy in turn. Good-looking kids, trying to figure her out the same way she was trying to figure them out. She had to remember to remain on her guard. "Just one thing. Keep me away from anything that crawls or slithers."

Wynne's expressive eyes widened. "What's that mean?"

Chris grinned. "It means she doesn't want to see Fred."

Fred? Who the hell was Fred?

More to the point, *what* was he?

But none of the boys was talking. Calley refilled her mug. Yep, these rascals were Slades. Best to stay on her toes at all times, no matter how long she stayed.

Chapter 3

Max didn't need to do as much as he did on the ranch. He had plenty of help and plenty of money to hire more if he needed it. Black Creek was not a struggling ranch. The Slades hadn't been poor in over a century. But work set an example for his younger brothers, and it helped keep his own demons at bay.

Out on the land, he could forget the dreams he'd had as an eleven-year-old like Christopher, because the land had never been the problem, never the reason he'd wanted to leave Wyoming at the first opportunity.

Out on the land he could remember that he belonged here, with Christopher, Timothy and Wynne. He could remember that this was his home. This was what held meaning in his life. Not New York, not even the woman he'd loved and left there. That was something his brothers needed to understand, Calley Hastings or no Calley Hastings. He'd made his decision four years ago. It was the most painful decision he'd ever made in his life, but it had been the right one.

Regardless, there was no going back.

When he returned to the house, he spotted Calley. He started to call to her, but stopped when he realized she was standing rock still. He expected a rattlesnake, something dangerous and unfamiliar to her, and approached her carefully, not wanting to spook her or whatever had her white-faced and scared. It could just be Fred, the boys' "pet" snake, but Fred was nonpoisonous. Still, Calley might not know that. She was a New Yorker, after all. She knew her roaches, rats, pigeons, not necessarily her snakes.

He brushed the dust off his denim shirt, felt his fatigue despite the early hour. It had been four years since he'd loved and lost his smart, high-strung, blue-eyed Calley Hastings. It seemed more like ten years ago, a hundred even. He felt so much older, so much more experienced, so damned different.

His gaze fell to her rounded bottom, encased in what appeared to be brand-new jeans. He smiled. Then again, it could have been just yesterday that he'd had Calley Hasting in bed with him.

She had to have heard his approach. But she didn't turn around. Didn't, so far as he could see, move a muscle.

He glanced around the lawn and the dirt driveway, but saw no snake, poisonous or otherwise. "What's the matter, has Wyoming frozen you to the ground?"

"Shh," she hissed, still not moving.

"Calley—"

Then he saw. Lucky, the household pet turkey, stood

in the shade of the henhouse about three yards off, his beady eyes pinned on the Slade household's new guest. The fowl had her in a standoff. She didn't move. He didn't move.

Max held back a howl of laughter.

"Does he bite?" Calley asked, her voice just above a whisper. *She* wasn't about to laugh.

"He never has, but he doesn't see that many New Yorkers." Max went up beside her, noting that she kept her eyes on the bird. He suppressed a smile. "Lucky, meet Calley Hastings. Calley, meet Lucky."

"He's harmless?"

"Utterly."

Her rigid body went slack. "Well, I'm not about to shake hands or whatever with some stupid turkey. He can just go on his way or do whatever it is turkeys do. I'm not—" She broke off, making a face. "I suppose I'll have to brush up on my barnyard etiquette."

Max laughed, clapping his hands a couple of times. Lucky got the message and strutted off as if he owned the place, something no one on Black Creek Ranch would bother arguing. "Never figured a wily New Yorker like you would be afraid of a turkey."

"Turkeys can be mean."

"How do you know?"

"I read it somewhere."

Or she'd made it up. Calley Hastings wasn't above making up facts to win an argument or avoid humiliation. Max decided not to press her for details. "Well, Lucky's not mean. He's just wary of strangers. I don't think he'd hurt you."

"What're you doing with a pet turkey?"

"He was destined for the oven a couple Thanksgivings ago, but the boys protested, and I relented. Now he's part of the family."

Calley eyed him dubiously. "The dogs don't bother him?"

"Nobody bothers Lucky."

"Kids and animals." She sighed, regaining her composure now that the "crisis" had passed. "I don't know what I'm doing here. I gather Lucky has the run of the place?"

"Not as much as he thinks. Jimmy and I both balked at letting him in the house. He likes playing Frisbee with the boys. He's gotten pretty good at catching it. Better than Wynne, actually."

Calley turned and faced him, her arms folded under her breasts. She still had on her Knicks sweatshirt, despite the fast-rising temperature. Her expression, at best, was highly dubious. "A Frisbee-playing turkey? Right. Very funny. Well, you're not going to have *that* laugh at my expense. I'm not falling for that one."

"He goes sledding with the boys in the winter, too. He likes being the last one aboard."

She snorted in disbelief.

"It's true," Max said.

"Well, I gotta tell you, Max, after what you Slade boys pulled on me, I'm not going to believe anything that comes out of the mouth of a single one of you without tangible proof. You get a Frisbee and toss it to the turkey. If the turkey catches it, then I'll believe you."

He shrugged. "Okay. Maybe the boys'll be up for a game before you go."

"Oh." Her cheeks colored suddenly, very unlike Calley Hastings, who could hold her own in any office on

Wall Street. "Then you haven't talked to them. They—we—I decided to stay on awhile. A few days, anyway."

Max narrowed his eyes on her. She seemed sincere, even ill at ease. "They come up with another sob story?"

"No."

"Then what? You can't *want* to stay, not with me here."

There wasn't a hint of self-pity in his tone. He was simply stating the facts. He'd seen Calley's face when she'd recognized him at the airport last night. She'd thought she'd landed in hell instead of Jackson Hole, Wyoming. He knew he'd done her wrong four years ago. Without doubt, so did she. And Calley Hastings wasn't known for forgiving and forgetting.

"I wouldn't want to stay in the same state with you, Max Slade," she went on. "But that's not the point. Or maybe it is the point. Your brothers went through a great deal of trouble to find me and get me here. They need to see that we're not suited for each other. They need to understand we wouldn't have worked out whether or not they'd been orphaned. Right now, they're convinced we'd be happily married or something if only you hadn't had to come out here to raise them. They blame themselves for what happened between us four years ago."

"It's not their fault."

"Oh, I know that." She gave him a cool look, nothing in her expression indicating she had any doubt her opinion of him needed revising. "I think if I stay on here for a few days, they'll know it, too."

Max shook his head. "No, Calley. You're leaving today. What those boys think or don't think is no concern of yours. I'm not going to fight with you for the next two weeks just to prove to my brothers they aren't responsible for what happened between us."

"I never said I'd stay the entire two weeks. At the rate we're going, they'll see our point in about forty-eight hours." She dropped her arms to her sides, the morning sun glistening on her dark, shiny hair. "Anyway, I'm not suggesting we have to fight to make them see what we felt for each other four years ago can't be reignited. We can be civil and accomplish that. I mean, even three boys under the age of thirteen ought to be able to see there're no sparks between us."

Max regarded her a long moment. "No sparks whatsoever?"

"Correct. None."

She pushed her glasses up, her eyes, intense and very blue, on him. Max didn't know if what he was feeling was a "spark," but it damned sure was something. Would the boys see it? Would Calley? He shook off the thought. Who saw what, what he felt—it was all irrelevant. She was leaving. He would drive her to Jackson, put her on a plane and wave goodbye to her forever.

"I know you'd like to think I've been languishing in your absence the past four years, Max," she said airily. "But the fact is, I haven't been. Not at all."

Max wondered if she was protesting too much, *knew* he'd hurt her. But Calley had never been one to like admitting to being hurt.

"Christopher assured me you're unattached. He says you confided as much in your messages to him."

She sniffed, possibly in an attempt to hide her embarrassment over what else she might have confided to his half brothers. "'Unattached' doesn't mean desperate, and I'd have to be desperate to want you back in my life."

Max grinned. "Wish old Lucky knew how tough you are. He'd never have tried to intimidate you."

"Don't make fun of me, Max Slade. And don't stand there and pretend you want me in your life any more than I want you in mine, because you don't. You're just—well, I guess you don't see many women out here in the wilds of Wyoming, and you're just responding accordingly to one in your presence."

That much he couldn't deny. She was a woman in his midst, and he was definitely responding.

She thrust her hands onto her hips. "But don't go thinking I'm going to mistake lust for anything but lust. I did that once with you and lived to regret it. It won't happen again."

In that instant, Max saw the consequences of what he'd done four years ago. The choice he'd made—the only one he'd been capable of making at the time—had had a lasting effect on her. Because of him, Calley Hastings would never easily trust her judgment of a man again, if at all.

"Do you regret what we had together, Calley?" he asked softly, suddenly serious.

He watched her throat as she swallowed, her icy blue eyes on him. She didn't answer at once. The light breeze caught her hair as fresh color brightened her cheeks. Finally, she shook her head. "No. I don't regret what I *thought* we had. I guess I don't even regret what we did have. I learned from it. I'm not the same woman I was four years ago, Max." She swallowed again, biting down on her lower lip. "Forget that at your own peril."

"Understood."

"I'll go pack," she said, and marched back toward the house.

Max didn't stop her. She should pack. He should drive her to the airport so she could catch the noon flight out. Then he could sit down with Christopher, Timothy and Wynne and explain to them that while he and Calley Hastings had once loved each other, that love was in the past. It was a conditional love, the kind that could go away. It wasn't like the unconditional love he had for them, the kind that could never go away. He would explain, and eventually, they would understand.

But Calley Hastings would be gone.

And suddenly, he wasn't sure he could bear that, not twice in one lifetime.

Max loomed in the guest-room doorway as Calley zipped her leather suitcase shut on the quilt-covered double bed. She wasn't looking at him, but she knew he was there.

"All right," he said. "You can stay."

She whipped around and glared at him, wishing she didn't notice every damned thing there was to notice about him, from his sun-washed dark hair to his scruffy, sexy cowboy boots. Earlier, when she'd caught him out of the corner of her eye, looking all dusty and rugged, she'd almost reacted, which would have surely incited the turkey. But she'd come to her senses since then. She was getting out of Wyoming. It had been madness to think she could stay.

"I have no intention of staying," she told him.

He frowned. "You just said—"

"I must have had some kind of lapse facing down that turkey. Staying out here in the wilds with you one *hour* longer than I have to is—well, it's crazy." She hefted her suitcase off the bed and dropped it to the floor. "But mercifully, I've come to my senses."

His eyes narrowed on her, as if he knew more about what she was thinking than she did. "So there are still sparks between us."

"Let's just say I'm not neutral on the subject of Max Slade and probably never will be."

Crossing his arms on his chest, he leaned against the doorjamb, one knee bent, eyes still narrowed. Calley shuddered inwardly. Nope. She was definitely not neutral when it came to Max Slade. If she stayed, his brothers would see that. There would be no pretense of bygones being bygones. It wasn't that her feelings for Max could be reignited. It was that they were still smoldering, hot embers buried deep inside her that she couldn't quite stomp out. She could feel them threatening to explode into an uncontrollable wildfire, their flames consuming her and all she'd become in the past four years.

Best to head back to New York.

"All the more reason you should stay," Max said finally.

She blinked at him. "Beg your pardon?"

"Your lack of neutrality on me is getting in your way. You need to get me out of your system so you can move on with your life."

"Get you out of my system—move on—where did you ever—"

She gulped for air, sputtering. Nobody had ever, ever jerked her chain the way Max Slade did. He could take her from calm, cool and collected to enraged in seconds.

And not just enraged.

But she couldn't think about that right now.

"Of all the arrogance," she said. "I *have* moved on with my life."

"Then why are you here?"

"Because I'm a sap. Because I've been working too hard and was ripe for an adventure. Believe me, if I knew I'd find you on the western horizon, I'd never have boarded the plane yesterday."

He shook his head knowingly. "You're here, Calley, because there's a hole in your life that you were hoping this trip would fill."

"There are no holes in my life. I love New York. I love my job. I have great friends. I have a great apartment. I'm happy. I'm here because I fell for your brothers' elaborate sob story and because Wyoming sounded like a good place for a summer vacation. That's *it*."

Max was unmoved. "You've got plenty of money. You could have booked a room at one of the nice hotels in Jackson. You could have done Wyoming without the widow, the five kids or the dying grandmother."

"Well, so you've seen my soft side. You might not remember me this way, Max, but I'm a nice person. At least, I try to be."

"Stay, Calley."

His voice was quiet, deep, irresistible. If she let it, it could knock her off her feet. It could make her remember what Max Slade had once meant to her. His humor, his steadiness, his confidence.

She shook her head adamantly. She *had* to go.

Max frowned. "You'd decided to stay. What changed your mind?"

"Going eyeball to eyeball with a turkey, I guess."

He smiled, not buying her answer. "I don't think so."

"Oh, and you know my mind better than I do?"

"I didn't say that. I just don't think you're being honest with yourself. Or me. Lucky had nothing to do with changing your mind, and you know it."

Calley grabbed both suitcases. Maybe Jimmy Baxter could drive her to the airport. Maybe she wouldn't have to go with Max. He didn't budge from the doorway, never mind that she couldn't get through with both suitcases.

"Admit it, Calley," he said.

"Admit what?"

"It wasn't Lucky that changed your mind."

She let the suitcases drop to the floor. "All right. I admit it. It wasn't Lucky. It was simply an assault of common sense."

He drew away from the door, walking toward her in that young Clint Eastwood way of his. Using one heel, he gently kicked the door shut behind him, not slackening his pace. Calley tried to look nonchalant. What did she care if Max Slade shut the door and was moving in on her? He was nothing to her. All that stuff about hot embers and wildfires was just an overreaction. So he was as physically attractive as ever. More so, even. So what? That was just lust. She'd learned not to succumb to lust. Her emotions, her *soul,* had to be involved. And they weren't, not with Max Slade. Not anymore.

He stopped right in front of her, the toes of his boots not two inches from the toes of her sneakers. She could see the fine lines at the corners of his eyes, no doubt from the Wyoming wind and sun and, perhaps, the responsibility of raising his three small brothers. His skin was tanned, more weather-beaten than it had been in

New York. The muscles in his chest and arms looked more developed, hardened by physical work, not hours in the gym. She noticed scars and calluses and a roughness that hadn't been there four years ago. He wasn't the same man who'd brought her flowers and silly gifts, who'd loved the pulse of New York as much as she did. She'd come to love that Max Slade, then to hate him.

But he'd changed, hardened, and maybe she didn't know this Max Slade at all.

He touched one finger to the corner of her mouth. She didn't draw back. Instead, she stood rock still and let the effects of his touch spin right down to her toes. She remembered the dozens—the hundreds— of dreams she'd had about feeling Max Slade's touch again, feeling his mouth on her, his body inside her.

Everything had changed when he'd disappeared. Everything. It didn't matter why.

"It wasn't an assault of common sense that changed your mind, either," he said softly. "It was more like an assault of all your senses."

"Max…"

"Wasn't it, Calley?"

She swallowed, shutting her eyes. His lips followed where his finger had been, just at the corner of her mouth, a kiss so feathery and light she wondered if she might possibly be imagining it. But she inhaled, her lips parting slightly, and his mouth came down full on hers, deepening their kiss, ending any doubt that it might just be her imagination. She had to pull away.

But she didn't. This was the Max she remembered, the Max she'd once loved. However he had changed, he was still the same man.

"Tell me the truth," Max whispered against her mouth. "Tell yourself."

"The truth. Right."

Her body was awash in sensations she hadn't felt in a long time, maybe too long. No one had ever made her feel the way Max Slade did. He made her ache for him, want him, need him. They were feelings she'd learned to distrust. Aching, wanting, needing. They weren't emotions she wanted to feel.

She pushed herself away from him, nearly tripping over a suitcase. "The truth is, I've lost my damned mind."

Something she couldn't read flashed in those searing slate eyes. Then it was gone, even faster than it had appeared. In someone else, it might have been disappointment. In Max Slade, it could be anything. She wouldn't even try to guess what was going on in his mind.

His expression turned hard, pragmatic. "I'll get the truck started and meet you out front."

"Oh, no, you don't. I'm staying."

He gritted his teeth. "That's it, Calley. I'm staking you out for the cougars. There's no making sense of you."

She ignored him, hoisting up first one suitcase and then the other back onto the bed. It was all so very clear to her now. She knew exactly what she was doing. "I'm not going back to New York with you thinking I'm running from you. Hell, no. I'm staying here and *proving* to you, Max Slade, that you don't mean a damned thing to me anymore. And I'm not leaving until you admit there's one woman on the face of the earth that doesn't give a rat's hind end about you. And that woman is me."

"Well," he said with surprising equanimity, "suit yourself."

"I will."

"Okay. Lunch is at noon. I'll tell Jimmy to set you a place."

"Fine."

"In the meantime, might as well make yourself at home."

"Oh, sure," she grumbled under her breath. "That ought to be easy. Kids, turkeys, horses, cowboys, mountains. Just what I'm used to."

Max regarded her with amusement. "It's going to be a fun two weeks, Calley."

"Two weeks? Who said anything about two weeks? This is a day-by-day thing."

"No, it's not."

"The devil—"

He started to leave, his back to her. "It's two weeks, Calley, just like it says on your ticket. I've got work to do. I can't be wondering every day if you're leaving or staying. You made your decision. You're staying." He turned back to her, his eyes unreadable. "I'm off for the afternoon. I'll see you when I see you."

She folded her arms under her breasts. "Makes no difference to me when I see you."

"I remain to be convinced."

Chapter 4

"Is Max very different from when you knew him?"
Christopher Slade asked as he and Calley walked up a
dirt path behind the stable.

She gave a small, evasive shrug, pleading ignorance. It was a warm afternoon, the temperature having climbed considerably since morning, but the dry
air kept her from feeling the heat. Timothy and Wynne
had long abandoned them on her whirlwind tour of
Black Creek Ranch—or at least what they could get to
on foot. Evidently, its acreage included far more than
a couple hours of wandering could take in. But what
Calley had seen surpassed even her highest hopes of
raw Western majesty and beauty.

Either that or she was so fresh out of a dirty Manhattan subway she simply didn't see the region's physical
shortcomings. Its social shortcomings were obvious:

only Slades, hired hands, Jimmy Baxter, assorted dogs, horses, chickens, wild animals and one Frisbee-playing turkey for company. In short, there wasn't a thing to do on Black Creek Ranch that didn't involve the elements or wildlife. She hadn't dared ask for the location of the nearest movie theater.

Given Christopher's heroic, if underhanded, efforts to get her to come west, Calley decided she owed him a direct answer. "I haven't seen enough of Max to know if he's any different."

"I think he is."

"Why's that?"

He thought a moment. His eyes were lost beneath his San Francisco Giants baseball cap. Now San Francisco, Calley thought, was her idea of life west of the Mississippi. Christopher had mentioned that Max promised to take him to a game before the end of the season. She suspected the oldest of Max Slade's three half brothers had a sensitivity to the world around him that wouldn't always make life easy for him on Black Creek Ranch.

On their afternoon walk, he'd pointed out things Timothy and Wynne had bypassed. It wasn't a matter of age, but of sensibility. A flowering tree their mother had planted now grown to maturity, a colt whose birth he and Max and Jimmy Baxter had overseen one cold, dark night, a hawk on the horizon. They were what Christopher Slade noticed. He was a good-looking kid, strong for his age, and Calley would bet he would do just fine with the junior-high girls come September. His sensitivity didn't make him less of a Slade.

"I found some pictures of you and Max." He walked ahead of her, not glancing back as he spoke. "They're what got me looking for you. He seemed happier then."

"Well, he was younger."

"Not that much."

Calley followed him into the shade of a huge oak at the corner of the main stable, an impressive structure of stone and wood. "You've got to be the first eleven-year-old I've ever met who doesn't think thirty's ancient."

Not that she knew many eleven-year-olds. None, in fact. Her life in New York didn't put her in touch with many kids. But she wasn't going to tell Christopher, lest he get any fresh ideas about throwing her ignorance up in her face and manipulating her into doing something else stupid. So far, she had a poor record. Coming to Wyoming had been yesterday's stupidity. Kissing Max Slade had been today's.

"Were you and Max happy?" Christopher asked, briefly glancing back at her in the shade of the oak. Her lame attempt at levity hadn't produced any sign of humor or amusement in him. "I mean, do you think you'd be together still if he'd stayed in New York?"

Calley sighed. There was nothing to do but be straight up with the kid. "When we were seeing each other, yes, I guess you could say we were happy. But that was quite a while ago. We went our separate ways four years ago, Christopher."

"Because of us."

"Not because of you. If Max and I were meant to be together, he would have told me about your parents. Anyway, it doesn't matter why we're not together, not anymore. We're not, and we've both gone on with our lives. Maybe when you're older, you'll understand—"

Christopher stopped, turning to her in the middle of the dirt path. "I understand now."

Caught, she thought. She'd patronized him, and he'd

just called her on it. She'd hated being reminded she was a kid at age eleven, too. "I'm sorry. It's just not easy for me to discuss private matters."

He gave her a small, self-deprecating grin. "You mean it's none of my business?"

She smiled. "You're a smart kid, Christopher Slade."

"Yep," he said.

"Then you know you can't make two people feel what they don't feel."

He shook his head, not so much in disagreement, Calley thought, as amazement that she just didn't get it. She had the feeling he thought he was dealing with a complete moron. "Max left New York for us. He left you for us. He hasn't had any other girlfriends in four years. I want— He deserves—" But Christopher stopped in frustration, his age catching up with him. "I can't explain."

A sensitive kid, Calley thought. Christopher Slade saw and understood more than his eleven-year-old mind could yet articulate. She said softly, "You want to give Max his life back."

He nodded, his eyes shining. "Yeah. That's it. He's done so much for my brothers and me."

"It was his choice, Christopher. I can't imagine he'd want you to feel this burden. To be frank with you, Max has known where to find me these past four years. If he'd wanted to, he could have gotten in touch."

"He wouldn't do that."

"I know."

"It's not why you think. He just—he couldn't—" He broke off again, unable to put into words what he so desperately felt he knew. "You know him. You know how he is."

"No, Christopher. I really don't know him. Maybe that's the whole point."

"But I— You can't—" He screwed up his face, turning red. "Oh, never mind." Then he abruptly shot down a narrow path that intersected with the one they were on.

Calley, suddenly feeling jet lagged and dehydrated from the dry Western air, followed at a slower pace. She hoped she hadn't blown it with Christopher. But Max happier with her? Not likely. Even at their best, they'd been far from an ideal couple. Too many sparks, too much fire, too much heat. If he hadn't trotted off to parts unknown, they would have burned each other out.

No, she thought, Christopher was just projecting his own preadolescent confusion onto his older brother and guardian.

As she came to the back of the sprawling Slade house, Calley took a quick, furtive look around for Lucky. She wasn't convinced he was a harmless bird, but he didn't seem to be around. Perhaps off playing Frisbee with Wynne or Timothy or one of the hands, something she still had to see for herself before she'd believe it. Max Slade wasn't above telling her a tall tale just to show her how out of place she was. But he didn't need further proof of her gullibility. Her presence in Wyoming was proof enough.

She hesitated a few moments, studying the house, shaded with oak and evergreen, in as pretty a setting as she'd ever seen. It was perhaps seventy-five years old, painted dark brown, surrounded by shrubs and a prosaic yard. Calley could picture an herb garden just outside the kitchen door, climbing roses and perennial gardens. New Yorker that she was, she could appreciate gardens. There was a huge wooden swing set, complete with a climbing rope and trapeze and a platform covered by a bright orange tarp.

If someone had told her two weeks ago she would find Max Slade within five miles of a swing set, she would have laughed herself silly.

Maybe Christopher was just trying to reconcile the Max he knew with the one she'd known. Maybe she was doing the same. The Max of four years ago had loved city life and was in no hurry for kids, and he'd exhibited no interest in ranches or horses or cowboy hats. They'd had fun together, walking through Central Park, taking in museums, discovering new restaurants. But had she really known him? She hadn't even realized he had brothers, never mind that they were so young that in the event of their parents' death he'd become their legal guardian.

Well, it didn't matter if she'd really known Max Slade four years ago or not. He did not belong in her life.

And she was quite confident that whoever he was, the Max Slade who'd kissed her that morning regretted it.

Jimmy Baxter was pulling together dinner in the large, sunny kitchen. He grunted at Calley in what passed for a greeting. The Slade household seemed to operate on a loose set of ground rules, with everyone looking after everyone else. Six-year-old Wynne might *appear* to be on his own, but he never went unsupervised. Calley had noted that Christopher, although the eldest, wasn't expected to look after his younger brother unless it was clearly spelled out. He was free to be a kid himself.

If, she thought, he would let himself.

She found Timothy and Wynne in the large front room, banging on the old upright piano. She gritted her teeth at the racket. "You boys ever have piano lessons?"

Wynne looked at her as if he'd never heard of such a thing. Timothy shook his head. Calley sighed. Their "playing" would give her a headache in another thirty seconds. She had them make room for her on the bench. Wynne complained that he was half off and climbed up on her lap as if it came naturally to him. He was no lightweight, and he smelled like dirt and sweat. Kid smells, she told herself.

It had been ages since she'd played. She didn't have a piano in her apartment in New York. What did she remember? A couple of études and sonatas. They would go over big. What might these rascals know that she also knew?

"You boys ever see *The Sound of Music?*"

Wynne nodded eagerly. Timothy said, "Yep. Max hates it, though."

He would, Calley thought. Judiciously, however, she kept her mouth shut. Taking a moment to focus, she adjusted Wynne on her lap so that she could get her arms around him, then started to play.

She made a few mistakes and hesitated a couple of times, and once nearly dumped Wynne off her lap, but all in all she thought she did a respectable version of "Do-re-mi."

When she finished, Wynne said, "Wow, awesome."

"Cool," Timothy said.

Calley laughed. "I'll take those as compliments."

Wynne slid off her lap, and Calley turned around on the wooden piano bench, only to find Max standing just inside the front door. She inhaled at the sight of him. She hoped Timothy, still beside her, didn't notice. She hoped *Max* didn't notice. He looked hard edged and exhausted, the humor and near-charm of this morning gone. His slate eyes penetrated her with an intensity she couldn't define. She had no idea if he were pleased to find her playing piano with his little brothers, annoyed, neutral, or even if he'd realized that was what she'd been doing. He was completely unreadable.

"Dinner's ready," he said. He glanced at his brothers. "You boys wash up."

Timothy and Wynne immediately scooted up the stairs.

Calley got to her feet. "Well, hello to you, too."

Max's gaze dropped back to her. "Jimmy's waiting."

He turned and headed for the kitchen. Calley scowled. Two weeks. Heck, she'd sure made *her* deal with the devil.

But she wasn't going to let Max Slade scare her off. No way. She would not be intimidated or put off by his deliberate surliness. If he wanted her gone, he could kick her out.

It was, she thought, a distinct possibility.

By her third evening at Black Creek Ranch, Max still hadn't kicked her out. He hadn't even hinted he wanted her to leave. He had simply, it seemed, done his level best to pretend she wasn't there. He would absent himself from her company at every opportunity.

It was, Calley supposed, easier that way for them both.

A magnificent sunset of reds and oranges and vi-

brant lavenders drew her outside after a barbecue of
sorts. Dinners at the Slade household tended to be sub-
stantial but uncomplicated. Tonight Jimmy and Max
had thrown chicken and corn on the cob on the grill
while the boys played Frisbee with Lucky. The idiotic bird really could catch a Frisbee. He even seemed
peeved when the boys switched to baseball. They'd
pressed Calley into pitching. She'd tried to pretend she
didn't feel Max's gaze on her, and hoped the boys didn't
notice either of them. She wasn't sure what Jimmy Baxter noticed, not that it mattered. He was decidedly the
type to keep his mouth shut and mind his own business.

With the sun setting and the boys inside watching a
video, Calley walked with one of the big dogs down to
the wide, rolling meadow that paralleled Black Creek.
Horses, mostly Appaloosa, grazed among the grass and
wildflowers. She leaned against the fence, its design
the picturesque "buck and rail" common to the region.
She breathed in the clean air.

"Pretty, isn't it?"

Max came up beside her, his slate eyes taking in
the sunset from beneath the brim of his dusty hat. She
briefly wondered if such a hat would have looked right
on him when he was in New York. Now it looked almost a part of him.

"Yes," she said. "Very pretty."

"I used to like watching the sunset from the roof of
my building in New York. There was a deck up there."

"I remember," she said.

He acknowledged her words with a small nod, still
not looking at her. They'd had wine together on his
rooftop deck. Morning coffee. Long talks. They'd imagined their future together. Or at least, Calley thought,

she had. She no longer knew what Max really had been thinking—what he'd wanted, what he'd feared—during their months together.

"It was relaxing after a wild day on Wall Street," he went on, pensive. "I felt as if I were above the fray, removed from it at least for a while. It restored my spirits."

"You never seemed too troubled by life in New York."

"Not when I knew you, no."

His words were delivered without emotion, but Calley felt a warm shiver run up her spine as she remembered what she and Max Slade had meant to each other in those days.

He continued to stare out at the sunset. "Sometimes I'd think about being back here, but not often."

"Then you'd been here before the boys' parents were killed?"

He turned toward her, shadows shifting over his face. "What do you mean?"

"Well, so far, I've gathered that you and the boys have the same father, and their mother was his second wife and much younger than he. I don't know, I guess I've assumed your parents were divorced, and your father always dreamed of living in Wyoming and came out here after the divorce and remarried."

"For a financial type, Calley, you've got a vivid imagination."

"So I'm wrong?"

"Not entirely. My parents were divorced. My mother lives in San Francisco."

"Yes, I remember you mentioning that when we were

dating. That's where you grew up, right? San Francisco?"

He shook his head. "No. I grew up here."

"*Here?* You mean you're from the wilderness? I never had a clue. You never said—"

"My parents divorced when I was fifteen." He spoke matter-of-factly, without emotion. "My mother lived in Jackson until I graduated high school. Then she took off, and so did I."

Calley winced. She'd known nothing about this man when they were together. *Nothing.*

She still didn't. Four years ago, she'd fallen in love with a mirage. She'd fallen for the man she'd wanted Max Slade to be, not the man he was.

"Surprised?" he asked, amused.

"Well, I'd always figured—I guess I thought—"

"You assumed I was a city boy, born and raised."

"Yes, I suppose I did." She tried to keep her focus on the sunset that seemed to envelop them, rather than on the hardened man beside her. "I never would have said you'd grown up on a Wyoming ranch. I can't believe you never mentioned it when we were together."

He shrugged. "I guess it just never came up."

"Did you hate growing up here?"

"No, I didn't hate it. It wasn't easy, but it had its moments, good and bad. My parents weren't happy together for a long time, and the isolated life out here didn't help matters. It's not as bad as it used to be. The area's grown."

He paused a moment, and Calley thought she could see a glimpse of the boy he'd been, lonely, torn, driven. Then the mask dropped, and the hardness of the man he'd become closed in.

"Things change, I guess," he said.

"This was your father's ranch?" Calley asked.

"It's been in the Slade family almost a hundred years. We've always bred and boarded horses. My great-grandfather earned a lot of money in the silver mines, and this was what he wanted, a Wyoming ranch, land as far as the eye could see. My father loved it here."

"Did he approve of your moving to New York?"

"It didn't much matter whether he approved or not. I went."

"Max—"

"I mean to see that my brothers have a better life than I did. My father wasn't an easy man, but he was happier with Lissa, less driven and difficult, less controlling—more content inside his own skin, if that makes any sense. If he'd lived, I think he'd have been a good father to the boys."

Unfortunately, he hadn't lived. "What about their mother?"

"Lissa seemed happy with my father, despite the disparity in their ages. She wasn't that much older than me. We got along all right. She loved the ranch."

"She was from Wyoming?"

He smiled. "California."

A breeze stirred, carrying with it the smell of evergreen and wildflowers. Calley could hear the horses making noises, moving about. She was a long, long way from her life in New York. "So when she and your father were killed, you decided to come back here."

Max didn't answer at once. As he stared out at the same view she did, she wondered what he was seeing. The same beautiful sunset, or childhood memories charged with conflict, longing, disappointment?

Finally, he said, "I couldn't justify uprooting the boys. This was their home. They needed to be here, and so did I."

"I can see how Christopher might be confused about what happened to us." She turned around and leaned back against the fence, looking out across the rolling meadow toward the house. Dorothy beamed to Oz, all right. She'd never felt so out of place, so far from home. "I didn't go out of my way to impeach your character, but I've assured him the accident just gave you an excuse to hit the trail. You'd have found another way without it. Either that, or I'd have come to my senses and dumped you myself."

Max drew away from the fence, studying her through half-closed eyes. Calley was surprised at how unnerving she found his scrutiny. She made herself focus on the quiet sounds of the evening.

"You're still angry," he said finally.

"I am not." She snorted. "What an ego. I'm not some pitiful woman who's been nursing her resentment of some jerk ex-boyfriend. So you can forget that one. Seeing you again has just gotten me in touch with how I felt when it finally dawned on me that you'd picked up stakes and hit the road without so much as spitting in my eye." Though Calley knew she wasn't being completely honest, she needed to save face, and to shield her lingering pain from Max's probing gaze.

"Calley, I never wanted to hurt you."

"Water over the dam, Max. In hindsight, I'm glad you did what you did. I learned a lot about myself, men and you in particular. If we'd stayed together, who knows? I could have ended up trying to push you off the Empire State Building. We just weren't meant for each other."

He continued studying her, his expression suggesting she might as well have been talking to herself. "You were hurt, Calley. It's never been easy for you to admit your softer side. You like to think you can brazen your way through anything."

"Max, lest you forget, I *did* brazen my way through losing you."

"I should have called."

His tone remained quiet, serious, but something shone in his eyes that she couldn't identify—maybe didn't *want* to identify. Or she was just imagining it because of the hat. She would have to get herself a cowboy hat. Then Max could try to figure out things that came into *her* eyes.

He should have called. Right. Well, pal, she thought, you're four years late.

She started back toward the house. She didn't want to hear about what Max Slade should have done four years ago.

"I started several letters to you," he said behind her.

She stopped, but didn't turn around.

"I kept them. They're stuck in a trunk in a storage room. I think they're what led Christopher to you. I never finished them. I couldn't."

She inhaled, taking in the dry, clean air, trying not to read into Max's soft voice emotions that weren't there. He was setting the record straight. Nothing more.

"I was overwhelmed, Calley. My father was dead. Lissa was dead. My little brothers were orphans. In my own mind, I couldn't justify overwhelming you, too. I didn't want you to feel the same despair I was feeling. At the time, I thought I was sparing you, but now I realize I was just sparing myself. Deep down, I think I was hoping if you continued your life in New York without me, without knowing what had happened to me, a part of me would be untouched by the tragedy of Lissa's and my father's deaths."

Calley listened without interruption, but still made no response. What could she say? How could she compare the pain she'd felt when he'd abandoned her without a word to the pain he'd felt over two deaths? It wasn't a contest, she knew. But she still didn't know what to say.

"I was wrong, Calley."

"Max."

He didn't seem to hear her. "I know there's no excuse for what I did. But I couldn't put you into the position of having to choose between the life you wanted and deserved in New York and a life out here with me and three little kids."

She whipped around, not expecting him to be so close. She nearly barreled into his chest, stopping herself just in time. "So you let me hate you instead."

"Yes."

"Mission accomplished. I've gotten comfortable disliking you, Max Slade. I wouldn't forget that if I were you." Her voice was low and intense, the anger and hurt and loss—the horrible confusion—she'd felt four years ago fresh again. "You can trust me not to undermine your relationship with your brothers while I'm here. I'm not staying so they can end up disliking you. I just want them to realize they went to a lot of trouble to get me here for nothing."

"They're not your responsibility."

"I know that. But I'm responsible for the consequences of my own choices and actions. I fell for their story, and now I'm here."

"Whatever goes on between us, I won't have those boys hurt."

She swallowed. She could feel his intensity, his determination to protect his younger brothers and meet his responsibilities as their guardian. But his determination was more than a question of duty. She could also feel his love for Christopher, Timothy and Wynne Slade.

"I couldn't agree more," she said. "But nothing's going to go on between us. You waltzed out of my life four years ago, Max. You can rationalize now it was because of grief and shock and wanting to spare me a difficult choice. But I believe you'd have found another reason if you'd had to. We just weren't meant for each other. Your brothers will see that before too long."

She whipped back around, the sun setting fast now, darkness gathering around them.

After a moment, Max said behind her, "Will *you* see it?" he asked softly.

She pretended not to hear him. Arguing with his sizable male ego would get her absolutely nowhere. So what if the basic physical attraction she'd had for him four years ago was still intact? So what if he'd abandoned her for noble reasons? So what if he wasn't living the life she'd imagined him living, filled with fancy restaurants and fast cars and beautiful women?

So what? she thought, marching up toward the house.

They hadn't belonged together four years ago. They didn't belong together now. Max Slade could go ahead and think what he wanted to think. He would know she was long and well over him when she boarded her plane and headed home to New York.

Chapter 5

The woman had to go.

Max stumbled to the coffeepot at five in the morning. Jimmy Baxter was the only one up, doing his list for his weekly trip to town. He eyed Max from his post at the long, scarred counter. "Rough night?"

Max ran one hand over his morning beard and just glowered as he filled his mug. He'd awakened twice during the night thinking—dreaming—that Calley was in bed next to him. Not good. Scary as hell, in fact, considering she was a stubborn woman and no doubt meant to stay her full two weeks in Wyoming. Determined to prove there was nothing between the two of them, she was.

Just as well she hadn't been privy to his dreams.

But he wasn't about to explain his complicated feelings toward Calley Hastings to Jimmy. He didn't understand them himself. On the one hand, he wanted to put her on the next plane east. Hell, the next plane anywhere.

On the other hand, he couldn't stop thinking about them finishing what they'd started the other day in the guest room.

He took just one sip of coffee before he started for the back door. "I've got a lot of work to do," he said, knowing it sounded more like a growl. "Be down in the lower pasture most of the day. You and the boys can find me there if you need me. I won't be back for lunch."

Jimmy glanced up from his grocery list. "You're just making up work so you won't have to hang around here. Running isn't going to help, you know."

"I'm working, not running."

The old man shrugged his lean shoulders. Even with his bad leg, he wasn't to be underestimated. And Jimmy Baxter *always* spoke his mind. "You ain't got nothing going on down there somebody else can't do."

Max wrenched open the back door. He knew Jimmy was right. He liked to spend as much time as possible with the boys. They tried to have lunch together whenever possible, and they were always welcome to join him out on the ranch, provided conditions were safe for them.

But today, Max knew, he needed to be alone.

Before he could make good his escape, Calley materialized in the kitchen. Max hadn't heard her walking up the hall from the guest room, and her appearance took him by surprise. She had on jeans and her Knicks sweatshirt. No shoes. No socks. Her hair was tousled, and her eyes looked bleary behind the lenses of her glasses.

She yawned. "What was that noise?"

Max frowned. "What noise?"

"You didn't hear it? Sounded like all the beasts of hell coming after me."

Mystified, Max turned to Jimmy, who looked thoughtful a moment, then said, "Must be that barn owl. He usually isn't up and about this close to dawn. He's a real night fellow. Took up residence in the stable this spring. Don't often get barn owls this far north."

Calley was unimpressed. "Well, whatever it was gave me the willies. Look here." She pushed up one sleeve of her sweatshirt. "Goose bumps."

Jimmy shrugged. "Barn owls have a hell of a screech." He glanced at Max, his dark eyes clearly communicating a deep perplexity with city folk. An owl giving someone goose bumps? It was beyond the realm of Jimmy Baxter's considerable experience. He turned his attention back to his houseguest. "The fellow you heard'd swoop down and tear a mouse or even a cat to shreds, but he wouldn't hurt a big ol' gal like you."

Max suppressed a grin. Calley made a face and retreated down the hall, muttering about the damned woods, needing a little concrete underfoot and, no thanks, she didn't want to see a mouse ripped apart.

"I say something?" Jimmy asked.

Max laughed. "She's just not used to the country."

"Well, I don't think it was any barn owl scared the wits out of her."

"Don't hold supper for me," Max called, ignoring the last, knowing comment, and went through the door, out into the cool, dry morning air.

Around noontime, when he was sweating and exhausted and nowhere near to having worked Calley Hastings out of his system, Max spotted two horses coming over the rise. Christopher was on one, no surprise. But Calley was on the other, a big, gentle Appaloosa named Stubbs. She sat up high and stiff in the saddle. Anyone seeing her would have to guess she'd never been on a horse before.

Probably she hadn't, Max thought. However smart and experienced she was with money, Calley Hastings was neither with four-legged animals.

Christopher had been riding, if not alone, since before he could walk and was perfectly at ease on a horse, although Max had no illusions the eldest of Ernest and Lissa Slade's children would stay on the ranch or even in Wyoming as an adult. Max had vowed never to put that kind of pressure on any of his brothers. He would sell the ranch first.

"Jimmy had us bring you lunch," Christopher said, moving closer.

Calley frowned, hanging on tight to the reins. "Lunch? Who said anything about bringing Max lunch? I wasn't consulted. You drag me out into the wilds on some horse and practically give me a heart attack splashing through that stream—" She sputtered, Max noting, however, that she had managed her tirade without moving in the saddle. As rigid as she was, if she fell, she would hurt herself for sure. "I swear, I never want to hear you ranch types muttering about New York being unsafe."

Christopher had turned around in his saddle, staring at her in bewilderment. Max grinned, expecting his brother was getting his first real taste of just how unsuited the woman he'd lured from New York was to life in Wyoming. Without commenting, Christopher dismounted, agile and unselfconscious, and got out the pack Jimmy had put together, devious old man that he was. Max had done without lunch before. It was no big deal. Usually he would mooch something off one of the hands, enough to tide him over until he got back to the house. Jimmy had never before seen fit to make sure he was fed. Either he'd wanted to get Christopher out from underfoot, or Calley, or both.

She still hadn't moved a muscle.

Max walked over to her. She had on a dirty white felt hat that must have been one of Jimmy's because it wasn't his, and it wasn't one of the boys'. It served to keep the sun off her face, but did nothing for her appearance. Her glasses were about halfway down her nose, and she had a smudge of dirt on one porcelain cheek. Max saw that she hadn't loosened her grip on the reins.

"Scared?" he asked mildly, without arrogance.

It didn't matter. Calley wasn't about to admit to being scared. She scowled at him. He thought he saw her grit her teeth. "Annie Oakley I'm not. I don't know how to get off this thing."

Max suppressed a grin. The woman did hate to admit a weakness, but he'd always admired her determination. "Old Stubbs here will let you experiment if you want to figure it out for yourself. He'd never throw off a rider."

"Just tell me what to do. I'm very good at following instructions."

"Since when?"

Her blue eyes fell on him, as scathing as Calley Hastings got, which was saying a lot. "Entertained by my predicament, are you, Max Slade?"

He let loose his grin. "More by your reaction to your predicament than your predicament itself. You can't stand not knowing something I know."

"Christopher," she called, deliberately ignoring Max. "Christopher, come over here and tell me how to get off this beast."

But Christopher was already back on his. "Can't. I promised Jimmy I'd come straight back. He's taking me to town with him." He got his horse moving. "Don't worry. Max'll show you."

"I've been plotted against," Calley muttered as Christopher trotted off over the rise.

Max laughed. "We both have."

Barely turning in the saddle and certainly not loosening her grip on the reins, she looked longingly back in the direction of the house, well out of view. "I could go on back myself—"

"You remember the way?"

"I think so. How hard could it be?"

"Real hard if you take a wrong turn."

She sighed, looking back at him. "This stinks."

"Besides," Max said, trying not to sound as amused as he was, "your glasses would fall off before you got halfway home."

She scrunched up her nose as if to urge her glasses back up where they belonged. "Halfway home is Indiana."

"Calley." He gently touched her knee, not wanting to startle her; every muscle in her body had to be tensed. "Let me help you off this animal. It'll only take a second."

She made a face. "I never even liked the merry-go-round as a kid. Gave me the creeps. Probably someone like me invented the subway. You walk down the stairs, you pay your fare, you watch your purse. Easy. Civilized."

"Calley."

"Oh, all right. What do I do?"

"Ease your weight down onto your left foot, keeping it in the stirrup, and swing your right leg behind you. I'll hold the reins for you. You can hang on to the saddle horn with your left hand if you want, but try to keep your right hand free or you'll get all tangled up."

He took the reins, not that she had let go. He was trying to be considerate of her fears, even if she was reluctant to admit to them herself. But he wasn't worried. He had no intention of letting her fall, and Stubbs wouldn't throw her. Being out of control was what she hated.

"Stubbs here is a good horse," he said. "He won't throw you or take off with you just hanging on to the saddle."

Calley didn't look particularly encouraged. "Left foot in stirrup, right foot up over the back, left hand on saddle horn, right hand in thin air. Oh, sure. I might as well be five on the merry-go-round again. It was bad enough with a wooden horse."

"You want me to pull you off?"

"No!"

"Then you're going to have to get off on your own."

"All right. I'll do it. I've had my wisdom teeth out. I can get off a horse. But don't you dare do anything sudden."

She seemed to be muttering to herself more than to him, psyching herself to do the deed. She could be a very determined woman. Max suspected she was more afraid of embarrassing herself than of hurting herself. Calley Hastings definitely had her pride, something he'd known when he'd left her in New York, not giving her the chance to join him in Wyoming. Her pride might have compelled her to take on his grief, his new life. He hadn't wanted that.

He made a move toward her.

She shot him a glance. "Don't touch me unless I'm in danger of being trampled or cracking my head open."

"You want me to push up your glasses before you get started?"

"Do not touch me, Max."

It occurred to him she might not want anyone to touch her, to avoid being startled atop a horse. Then again, she just might not want *him* to touch her.

She took a deep breath, eased her weight down onto her left foot and leaned forward. For a brief moment, Max thought she might surprise him and actually pull this thing off on her first try. But as she started to swing her right leg up and back, the horse moved just a hair, nothing an experienced rider would even have noticed. Calley, however, wasn't an experienced rider. Lurching forward, overcompensating for the horse's movement, she grabbed hold of the saddle horn with both hands. It was a natural move for a beginner.

But she'd forgotten about her right leg. Its momentum had carried it partially over the saddle, but with her left foot still in the stirrup, there was nowhere for it to go.

She was all tangled up, in no real danger of harm, but in great danger of humiliation. "I hate horses," she muttered. "I really do."

"You want a hand?" Max asked laconically.

"Just tell me what to do."

He suspected she wasn't screaming bloody murder because she didn't want to spook the horse. Stubbs glanced behind him, as if wondering what all the fuss was about. "She's from the city," Max said in his soothing tone.

Calley scowled. "You're damned right I'm from the city. What do I do now?"

She'd slipped half off the saddle, left foot in the stirrup, right leg wandering, both hands hanging on to the horn as if she were in imminent danger of being trampled to death if she let go. If he didn't tell her what to do, Max had a feeling she would stay like that until she ran out of steam and slid off or Stubbs decided he'd had enough and bucked her off. Either way, she would be off the horse and on the ground.

Max still had hold of the reins. "Take your foot out of the stirrup and drop down to the ground. You're practically there already."

"Easy for you to say. You're not the one hanging off this damned horse." She shifted around, apparently struggling to remove her foot from the stirrup as she started sliding off the saddle. "I can't do it. I'm twisted around the wrong way or something."

"You're too low. You have to pull yourself up a little."

"The idea is to get *off* the horse, not back on it."

"Calley—"

"I wish your brothers were here. They'd see I belong in New York. I can't—how long is this horse going to stand here?"

"Long enough for you to get off his back, I reckon."

Her hat came off, dark hair shining in the noontime sun. Max had a marvelous view of her behind. He did not, however, comment on it. "If you let go of the saddle horn, you'll be fine. Your body will do the natural thing."

She snorted. "It's too late for my body to do the natural thing."

Max let that one go without a rejoinder, several options for which came to mind. She was mad enough as it was. She started to let go of the horn, but grabbed hold of it again, fast, before she could see that she wasn't in as bad a mess as she thought.

"I'm hungry," he said.

"Max, when I get off this horse, I swear I'm going to—"

He sighed. Enough was enough. Very deliberately, he tugged hard on the reins, sending Stubbs forward a full step.

Calley cursed both horse and man. Max seized the moment, grabbing her by the middle and hauling her down to the ground. Her left foot had wedged into the stirrup tightly enough that he had to yank on her to pull it free. Not a happy woman, she cursed him some more.

When her foot was free, he tossed her onto the grass and scooped up her hat.

She sat up spitting and sputtering, hair flying. "I thought you said Stubbs wouldn't throw me."

Max grinned, handing her the hat. "*He* didn't."

She was breathing hard, shoving the hat onto her head, unmindful of her hair hanging down her forehead. Her smart eyes narrowed on him as she figured out what he'd done. "It's your fault. You made him throw me."

"He didn't throw you. He just moved forward."

"Because you made him."

"Like I said, I'm hungry."

She was, too, from the looks of her, not that she would admit it. "Well, don't let me come between you and lunch."

He had before, in New York. Suddenly, without warning, he remembered making love to Calley Hasting with the noon sun spilling over them. It seemed forever ago. As if another man had made love to Calley Hastings, not him. The memory almost paralyzed him. She didn't seem to notice. She tore open the pack. Jimmy had thrown in some cold fried chicken, pimento cheese, crackers, cucumber wedges, purple plums and boxed chocolate-chip cookies. A veritable feast. What had the old cowboy been thinking?

Naturally, the meal wasn't to Calley's satisfaction. "Fried chicken? I didn't think anybody ate fried chicken anymore, and what's that red stuff in the cheese? Pimento? I stopped eating cheese spreads a couple years ago. They're loaded with fat. I don't suppose these are low-fat crackers?"

"Not if Jimmy packed them."

"You don't always eat like this, do you?"

"I didn't plan to eat lunch at all today, unless I scrounged a piece of fruit from one of the hands." He noted the small throw blanket Jimmy had stuck in the pack and pulled it out, spreading it on the ground beneath the endless sky. It wasn't like a summer picnic on Long Island, but northeast Wyoming's raw-edged beauty seemed to suit Calley's mood. "I guess Jimmy means for this to be a special occasion."

"My second time on a horse. Some special occasion."

"First time. Merry-go-rounds don't count."

She shook her head at him. "I was on a real, live horse once in college. A rich friend took me riding out at her family's place in Connecticut. It was a lot more civilized than this. No offense."

"None taken. No one would ever mistake Black Creek Ranch for Connecticut."

"That's for sure."

Max grinned. Now that she was on terra firma, her natural cockiness was returning. "You must have managed to get off your Connecticut horse."

"Yes. I don't recall it being any big deal. But I wasn't worried about rattlesnakes or running wild through the countryside, and I didn't have you there to distract me."

He settled back on the blanket, in the swirling shade of an oak. He could feel his morning's work and his bad night in his muscles. "So I still distract you?"

"Not still." She bit into a chicken leg, its high fat content not so great a deterrent she wasn't going to eat it. "You distracted me in a totally different way when we were together."

"How do I distract you now?"

"Well, I never know when you're going to kick a horse out from under me."

"For a brass-tacks financial type, Calley Hastings, you have a way with exaggeration. I didn't kick Stubbs out from under you. I just urged him forward. You needed a nudge."

"Did you or did you not deliberately dump me off that horse?"

"I did."

"Not sorry, are you?"

"Not in the least." How had he managed four years without Calley Hastings in his life? He leaned forward, feeling the cool shade on his face. "Let's say you still distract me, too."

"But in a different way."

He smiled. "No. Not in a different way at all."

She quickly dug into the pack, pretending she hadn't heard him. "I think I'll try some of Jimmy's pimento cheese."

"Go ahead. I'll just sit here a minute and be distracted."

Her eyes shot up to him. "You know, Max, it's not going to work. I'm not going to pack up and leave just because I distract you, in whatever way."

"Who says I want you to leave?"

"Jimmy Baxter."

Max gritted his teeth. That old cowboy needed to learn to mind his own business, not that he ever would. "I'm the one who gave you the choice of leaving or staying the whole two weeks."

"But you wish you hadn't. Jimmy says—"

"You should be listening to me, not Jimmy."

She ignored him, spreading pimento cheese on a cracker. "Jimmy says you're not sleeping well. You're not eating well. You're making up work to keep you out on the ranch. He says you want me out of here so you can get your life back to normal."

"Then why did I let you stay?"

"Because you didn't realize I'd have the kind of effect on you I'm having—according to Jimmy." She popped the pimento-cheese-covered cracker into her mouth. "This stuff's pretty good. I think I'll get the recipe. Anyway, I'm not saying Jimmy's right. I'd never accuse you of trying to run me off just because I kicked your male hormones into gear."

"Calley—"

"The idea is for us to show your brothers we're not suited for each other. I suppose that can happen if you kick me out. Jimmy says you'd never tell them the real reason—"

"I'm telling Jimmy to stay away from you."

She gave him a smug look. "Admit it, Max. *You're* the one who's not over *me*. You didn't kiss me the other day to prove I still felt some kind of lustful spark for you. You did it because you felt a spark for me. You *wanted* to kiss me, Max."

"I don't deny it."

"And you still do, and that's why you're hiding out here and trying to provoke me into leaving early. You don't want to look like the bad guy to your brothers, so you'll do what you can to drive me out."

Max stretched out his legs, eyeing her under the brim of his hat. "Let me get this straight. I want you out of here because I want to kiss you?"

"Possibly more than kiss me." Her tone was brisk, businesslike.. "It's just libido, of course. We both know that. Nothing will come of it, physically or emotionally."

"Calley."

"What?"

"Quit thinking and eat your lunch before you get yourself into trouble."

"I—"

But she looked at him and apparently thought better of arguing, and instead spread another cracker with pimento cheese. Max wondered if she realized she already was in trouble.

He knew he was.

Chapter 6

Calley was expounding on the virtues of New York bagels a couple of hours after Max had grabbed one of the hands, put her back on her horse and set the two of them on the trail back to the house. She'd gotten off old Stubbs just fine. She hadn't needed any help from a ranch hand who had a patch over one eye and reminded her of John Wayne in *True Grit*. He'd looked as if he would have no truck with some New Yorker who didn't know how to dismount a horse.

If nothing else, she was a quick learner.

Jimmy Baxter had returned from "town"—wherever that was—with groceries and odds and ends, and the boys had gathered in the kitchen for juice and frozen bagels. They thawed them in the microwave, tore them apart and browned them in the toaster. The two older boys put light cream cheese on theirs. Wynne had insisted on grape jelly.

It was all enough to make Calley gag.

At her urging, Jimmy had bought a tin of loose-leaf Earl Grey tea. He'd directed her to the pantry, where she'd unearthed a teapot that she now had steeping. Miraculously, he'd also produced a small, dented strainer that fitted over a cup. Wynne and Timothy, and even Christopher, showed an interest in the entire process, the Slade household apparently devoid of tea drinkers.

The three boys watching closely, Calley poured a little of the tea into her china cup, which she'd retrieved from the dining room. Jimmy had warned her to wash it out first. Neither the china nor the dining room was used often.

The tea was the perfect strength. The boys munched on their bagels as she poured the tea through the strainer. She eyed the bagels dubiously. Cardboard probably tasted as good.

"Sometimes in the morning on my way to work," she said, "I'll stop off at a deli where they bake their own bagels. I get them warm out of the oven."

"With jelly?" Wynne asked.

"No, not with jelly. A light layer of cream cheese."

"I hate cream cheese," he said.

She had already discovered Wynne was remarkably forthright about his likes and dislikes. She liked a kid who spoke his mind. The two other boys munched on their bagels as she added a dollop of milk to her tea.

"How come you don't use a tea bag?" Timothy asked.

"I prefer loose leaf when I can get it, and when I have time. Tea bags are fine in a pinch."

"I hate tea," Wynne said.

Christopher finished the last of his bagel. "I want to go to New York sometime."

Calley remembered "Jill Baxter's" believable, wrenching desire to experience life beyond Wyoming. How much of that longing had been Christopher Slade's own? She smiled at him. "I'm sure you will."

"Max used to live in New York," Wynne said, squirming onto her lap. After a day playing outside, he smelled like sweat and dirt, and had to be the filthiest child alive. But she found, to her surprise, she didn't even have to repress an impulse to dump him off her lap.

Timothy nodded thoughtfully. "Dad said Max never wanted to come back to Wyoming. He liked New York. He'd have lived there forever if—"

"You don't know that."

Max spoke as he walked into the kitchen through the back door, his deep voice catching Calley off guard. He looked tall and dusty and tired, and utterly male. His presence immediately changed the mood of the offhand conversation she had going with his brothers. They looked caught, as if they'd strayed into forbidden territory. But Calley noticed no fear in their expressions, only respect. They weren't intimidated by their big brother.

His tone softened. "I don't know it, either. It's something none of us can know."

Wynne scooted off Calley's lap. She immediately felt ten degrees cooler. The kid seemed to radiate heat and energy. He ran up to Max. "Did you eat New York bagels?"

"Sometimes. Why?"

"Calley says they're the best."

She sipped her tea as nonchalantly as she could manage with Max Slade in the room. She saw no reason to apologize for her opinions. "They're better than frozen grocery-store bagels, for sure."

Max didn't respond. He went to the sink to wash his hands, and Calley watched him soap them up. It was enough to make her squirm. She didn't know why. She only hoped the boys weren't old enough to notice her reaction or attribute any significance to it if they did.

"I'm not much on bagels," Max said.

"Yes," Calley said, "I remember."

Christopher glanced at her as if he'd finally confirmed that she and Max really had known each other in New York and it hadn't all been a figment of his active imagination. The kid, Calley thought, missed nothing.

"I want to see the Empire State Building," Timothy put in. "Are you ever going to take us to New York, Max?"

"Maybe."

The man was in a taciturn mood, Calley decided. Was it fatigue? Too much Wyoming sun? Her?

So far as she could see, his little brothers paid no attention to his mood, refusing to let it dampen their spirits. Christopher started yammering about the Statue of Liberty, Ellis Island and the Museum of Natural History, but Wynne was stuck on bagels and Timothy on the Empire State Building. Max just continued to wash his hands, letting the boys go on. They seemed to believe he was listening. Maybe he was. Mesmerized by the almost sensual motion of his hand-washing, Calley couldn't even guess what was on Max Slade's mind.

He turned from the sink, drying his hands with a

flour-sack towel. "We'll worry about New York another day."

Wynne draped his stuffed puppy over one shoulder. "Calley says—"

"Calley knows New York," Max said. "I'll give her that."

Christopher, looking thoughtfully at his older half brother, suggested his brothers join him in departing from the kitchen. He promptly made good his exit. Timothy retreated to the living room to practice his piano lessons. Wynne, however, wasn't going anywhere.

Max took a seat at the table where Calley had given up any notion of having a cup of tea in peace and quiet. She refilled her cup. Wynne crawled up on Max's lap. Max hardly seemed to notice the extra weight, the dirt, the sweat. He frowned at Calley. "What's this I hear about piano lessons?"

She shrugged. "Oh, I'm just introducing Timothy to the keyboard. It's no big deal. He's really very interested."

"Can't accomplish much in two weeks."

"I don't intend to."

Wynne swung around, looking eagerly up at Max. "Can I take lessons, too?"

"Actually," Calley said, "you should wait until you can read. It'll be easier. Right now, you can mess around on an electronic keyboard or maybe get a recorder."

"Cool. Can I get a recorder, Max?" As if he knew what one was.

Max looked ready to growl. "New York, bagels, piano lessons, recorders. Anything else you've got these boys wanting?"

Wynne, either sensing a shift in mood or more likely

just bored, wriggled off Max's lap and skipped off to join Timothy in the front room. Calley heard Jimmy barking at him to wash up before he touched anything. Wynne protested that his hands *were* clean.

Max had his searing slate eyes pinned on Calley. "It's not fair to let those boys get attached to you."

"What, I should be an ogre so they'll be glad to see me go?"

His expression didn't change. "The point is for them to see that we don't belong together. If they like you, they won't understand why I don't want to marry you."

Calley nearly spit out her tea. "*Marry* you? Who said anything about marriage? They just hauled me from New York so we could—I don't know—have some fun together. I never assumed they thought we'd end up *married*."

"Then you are naive."

"I never claimed to be an expert on kids. Your brothers hoodwinked me into coming here in the first place, so I have no confidence in my judgment where they're concerned. But marriage—" She scoffed. "They're little boys. What do they know about marriage? I'm sure that just because I'm nice to them they won't jump to the conclusion that I'm in love with you or that you ought to be in love with me. I mean, they can't possibly think like that."

"Of course they think like that. If they didn't, you wouldn't be here."

She set her cup on its matching saucer, her pleasure at having a nice afternoon tea vanishing under Max's scrutiny and dark mood. "So you want me to act like a jerk so they'll see why you dumped me four years ago. They won't blame you or themselves. It won't matter why you don't want me in your life now. They'll just be glad to see Calley the Jerk head back to New York."

He sighed with barely disguised impatience. "You don't have to act like a jerk. But you don't have to give piano lessons and talk about New York. Just keep to yourself and enjoy your stay."

"Pretend your brothers don't exist? Ignore them?"

"I didn't say that. Just don't let them become attached to you. Be distant. Pretend you're staying in a bed and breakfast on vacation and don't want to be bothered with kids." His eyes seemed to darken. "Which you don't."

"You don't know anything about what I do and don't want, Max Slade. And this isn't like any bed and breakfast I'd ever stay at."

"All right. Pretend it's a dude ranch."

"Me? At a dude ranch?"

"Calley—"

"Okay, okay. I can see I'm making you cranky."

Max said nothing, her light tone having no visible impact on his dark expression. She swallowed, suddenly aware of how damned sexy he looked all dressed up like a cowboy. He *was* a cowboy of sorts: born and raised on a Wyoming ranch and running it for the past four years. Who would have ever thought? Max Slade as Clint Eastwood? It would amuse his friends back in New York, if he had any left.

Then again, who would have ever thought she, Calley Hastings, would fall for a sob story by three preadolescent boys? People did have their surprises, she supposed.

Max leaned forward, his intensity not lessening

one iota. He said in a deep, low voice, "I wouldn't call 'cranky' what you make me, Calley."

"Then what would you call it?"

Something gleamed in his eyes, and she caught her breath, realizing what a stupid question *that* had been. A sudden image of them in bed together assaulted her mind and senses. She could almost feel his mouth on her.

She managed, just barely, to eke out her next words. "Never mind. I withdraw the question."

Max shot to his feet. She wondered if he'd had any images assault him, but decided she would be a fool to ask. She didn't want to know. What good would it do anyway? There had never been any problem between them in bed and probably still wouldn't be, not that she had any intention of finding out.

"Just keep your distance," he said, and retreated to the front room.

Calley judiciously chose not to follow him.

The unearthly screech of the barn owl jolted Max awake well after midnight. He couldn't go back to sleep. The owl, he knew, wasn't the problem. Finally, he pulled on a pair of jeans and a flannel shirt and headed downstairs, aware of the other people asleep in the house: three boys, Jimmy Baxter and one woman from New York City.

Had the owl awakened his houseguest, too?

He crept past the closed guest-room door and into the kitchen. Night-lights he'd installed for the boys provided the only illumination. There were no streetlights out on Black Creek Ranch. He wondered if Calley had noticed.

The night drew him outside. The air was clear and still, cooler than he'd expected. Again came the screeching, eerie cry of the barn owl. It seemed very close, ghostlike. Max had no romantic illusions about owls; they were top-of-the-food-chain animals, predators. He'd seen them rip apart tiny baby birds.

Down toward the stable, the silhouette of a female figure took him by surprise. It had to be Calley, of course—never mind that he wouldn't have expected her to venture out at night. She had her back to him. As he moved closer, he could see that her dark hair was tousled from sleep, or perhaps an attempt at sleep. She had on some kind of sweatshirt that was pulled down over a filmy ankle-length nightgown, its fabric drawn close to her legs. She was staring up at the sky. Max wasn't sure if she'd heard him. He approached carefully so as not to startle her.

She spoke as he came up behind her, apparently very aware of his presence. "What an incredible sky," she said.

Max wasn't sure if the night sky really had captivated her, or if she were using it as an excuse to explain why she was outside before dawn. Being caught looking at stars wouldn't sit well with her urban self.

"I've never seen so many stars," she went on, still without looking at him. "No city lights to wash them out, no buildings to distract. Just stars. Do you know any of the constellations?"

"Some."

Turning around, she looked at him, her eyes luminous in the darkness. He thought she smiled slightly. He couldn't be sure. "Point some out," she said.

He moved closer to her. He could smell her hair and

the baby powder on her skin. She must have bathed before bed. An image flashed of him applying powder to her stomach, her breasts. It must have been in another lifetime. How could he have left her otherwise? But he'd been a different person then, he reminded himself. Committed to his life in New York. Determined never to return to Wyoming to stay. Resolved to his father having started a new life and a new family, and to give all his love and attention to carry on the Slade ranching tradition. Then the phone call had come, and Max's life had changed. He had changed. There was no going back.

He pointed out the Big Dipper, which Calley claimed she knew, and Pegasus, Hercules, the Northern Cross. At first she didn't make out Cassiopeia, but applied her powers of concentration to the task, gazing up at the sky. Then she jumped, excited and pointed. "I see it!"

Max smiled. "It's fun when you start seeing the constellations. Makes the night sky come together a little."

"I can't remember ever seeing so many stars."

"One of the perks of living out here."

"Yes."

She seemed wide-awake. Max wondered if she'd slept at all. He and the boys had played cards before bed. Calley discreetly joined in only two games. Timothy and Christopher had caught her letting their little brother win, which they never did. She'd pointed out who was eleven and who was nine and who was just six, and maintained she'd only leveled the playing field. They hadn't bought it. Wynne, of course, had gloated, almost as obnoxious about winning as he was about losing. Calley had tried to give him tips on being a gracious winner, but he'd had none of it.

Max hadn't intervened. Calley Hastings and the boys would have to figure each other out for themselves. After she'd retreated to her room, Max had watched a movie with the boys, then shooed them off to bed while he sat up reading. Concentrating was no easy task when he knew Calley was in the same house. When he went to the kitchen for a drink, he'd seen the light under her door. The boys were asleep. Jimmy was out for the evening. Max had only to knock on her door. Maybe she would let him in. Maybe she would tell him to go to hell. How would he know if he didn't do it?

But he hadn't. He'd taken his book and gone up to bed, frustrated and annoyed with himself.

Calley drifted into silence beside him. Finally, she said, "I can leave in the morning."

"Calley—"

"No, don't. I've been thinking about it." She turned sideways, facing him. Her face was cast in shadows, impossible to read. "We both know it's for the best."

He nodded. He knew. She was a complication the Slade household just didn't need. Four years ago, he'd made up his mind to go on without her, no matter the cost. What was the point in undoing what had been done? Never mind that her presence had reminded him how much he'd once loved Calley Hastings, how alive he felt around her, how very much he'd lost the day he'd packed up and left New York without her. But there was no going back. She knew that as well as he did.

"I'm sorry, Calley. If I'd known what the boys were up to, I'd have put a stop to it. Now you've given up two weeks' vacation. It won't be easy making new plans at this late date, and the money—"

"It's okay, Max. Playing Frisbee with a turkey and

nearly getting bucked off some stinky horse have revived my appreciation for life and work in New York."

He managed a small smile. "Don't let Stubbs hear you say he stinks."

"*All* horses stink."

"Even Connecticut horses?"

She didn't smile, her mood pensive yet difficult to read. Was she glad to be going? Did she have any doubts? Was she acting for her own sake, the boys', even his?

"I've already made my reservation," she said. "There's a flight out in the morning, around ten. I caught Jimmy when he came in and asked him to drive me to the airport."

"He agreed?"

"More or less. He said I'd better have my mind made up because he wasn't going to put up with me changing it halfway to the airport. You know Jimmy. He's gruff and direct to a fault, but at least you know where you stand with him." Her eyes zeroed in on him. "Unlike you."

"I've tried to be straight with you, Calley."

She shrugged. "Maybe, but you've always been a hard man to figure. Not that I care to figure you out, you understand. Anyway, I assured Jimmy my mind was made up. He said he wouldn't hold me to my decision until we were off ranch property."

"If you changed your mind halfway to town, he'd put you on that plane anyway. You'd have to fly to New York and back again. He's like that. He's not the most spontaneous, flexible man around. I have the occasional go-round with him over the boys. But they understand him."

"I'm not changing my mind."

Max sighed. He wanted to look at the stars, feel Calley's shoulder brush against him. He didn't want to talk about what morning would bring. "Why are you leaving?"

"Because I don't belong here."

"That's a given."

"And because you have a point about the boys becoming attached to me," she added. "And me to them."

Her to them. Suddenly he could imagine it, where he'd never been able to before. Calley and kids in general—never mind three orphaned boys born and raised on a Wyoming ranch—were an incongruity—something that just didn't go together. Yet here he was, imagining her having an affinity for his younger brothers. Indeed, becoming attached to them.

It must be a lack of sleep, he told himself. Calley Hastings hadn't changed since he'd left her in New York four years ago. If anything, she was more urban, more suited to her fast-paced city life than before. When and if she became a mother, it wouldn't be to three orphaned boys on a Wyoming ranch. Max could let her leave because of them, but he couldn't let her stay because of them. If ever she chose to stay, it would have to be because of him, not his brothers.

He turned, abruptly starting back toward the house. Calley fell in beside him. He could hear her breathing. "I'm not going to ask you to stay," he said.

"I don't expect you to."

"But I'm not going to throw you out."

She nodded without comment.

All at once, without any warning, he stopped dead in his tracks. Calley nearly plowed into him. He touched her hair at her temple, sucking in his breath at the feel of her cool skin. She didn't pull back.

"I wish we could have ended things some other way," he said. "Some way that wouldn't have left either of us hurt, angry or wondering."

"So do I."

"I should have finished one of my letters to you, should have mailed it."

"Maybe I should have tried to find you, talked to your co-workers, trusted you enough to know something had to have happened for you to leave me high and dry. But what's done is done, Max. We both have to move on."

"I'll explain that to the boys. Obviously, they see more than I ever thought they did."

"I'm glad I came to Wyoming. Tell them that. I needed the answers I've gotten out here. A week ago, I'd have said I was well over you, Max Slade, but that's not true. Oh, it's not that I want to resume our relationship where we left off. I'm over you in that way. But you didn't exactly leave me open and trusting of men and new relationships. When I go back to New York—" She lifted her shoulders in an exaggerated shrug, then let them fall. "I don't know. Maybe things'll be better on that level."

Max forced himself to nod, but he couldn't imagine Calley Hastings with anyone but him. He didn't want to. "I hope so."

"You were in shock four years ago. I'm not excusing what you did. I don't like people making choices for me, 'sparing' me the burden. But I do understand a little better where you were coming from, and if it makes a difference, I do forgive you."

"It makes a difference."

"And I forgive myself," she added quietly.

"For what?"

"For hating you. For blaming myself. It was the easy way out. I can see that now. Life should be so simple as my view of what went wrong, you the bastard and me your unwitting victim. But life's not like that, is it?"

He shook his head. "No." He dropped his hand to his side, only some bizarre sense of nobility keeping him from kissing her. She'd made her decision. Let her get out of Wyoming cleanly, without him muddying up her thinking. "But I'm not sure you do understand what I was feeling four years ago."

"Max, you don't have to explain."

"I was afraid if I called you—if I'd left a message and you called me—I wouldn't have had the courage to do what I knew I had to do, which was to leave New York and come back here. I couldn't take that chance. I'm all these boys have. I *had* to be here. And I couldn't force you to make the same choice I had. It all seemed so logical at the time."

"Yes, I can see that now. Look, my anger with you hasn't been all bad. Part of me would like to hold on to it. It got me through some tough times. I could always say to myself you didn't abandon me because of me, but because you're a bastard. Who but a bastard wouldn't have left some kind of word? I envisioned you off in Chicago or L.A., off with other women—women I wouldn't like. Maybe I turned too distrusting, too leery of being hurt again, but I can see I needed to be more realistic about people and less naive. I've grown up a lot in the last four years."

She had, he realized. In many ways she *wasn't* the

same woman he'd loved and left so abruptly, so cruelly, out of his own fear and need and sense of responsibility. "I'm glad you came," he said simply.

"Me, too." She grinned at him, her mood suddenly lightening. "At least I know I really don't belong in Wyoming. I belong in New York with my friends, my work, pizza delivery, dirty subways, museums, all of it."

It was true. She did. Max smiled back at her, wishing he didn't feel so damned conflicted about the decision she'd made. She had to go. Sooner or later, she had to go. "I understand."

She was silent a moment. "Good."

He touched one finger to her lower lip, then kissed her lightly, gently. "Be happy, Calley Hastings."

And he went inside before she could respond, before he could carry her off to bed and convince himself he wasn't still in love with Calley Hastings of New York, New York.

Chapter 7

"I've changed my mind."

Jimmy Baxter shook his head as he steered his spotless old truck down a straight, narrow, beautiful Wyoming road. "Too late."

They were in the long, narrow valley of Jackson Hole, somewhere between Black Creek Ranch and the popular, picturesque village of Jackson. Mountains—*serious* mountains, Calley thought—loomed all around. A meadow of wildflowers spread out on the right side of the road, a stand of what she had learned were quaking aspen on the left. Gorgeous country, no question.

But Calley was preoccupied with the predicament she'd gotten herself into. Stay. Leave. Prove to the Slade boys she didn't belong with their big brother. Prove to *herself* she didn't belong with their big brother. She didn't know what to do.

"I'll rent a car if I have to."

"It's summer in Jackson Hole. You might not find a car to rent."

"Then I'll hitchhike."

The old cowboy glanced at her. "You know, you sounded just as determined last night, except it was about leaving."

"I *will* leave. Just not today."

He spit something out his window. The truck still rolled down the road at a speed well above the posted limit. Jimmy Baxter, she had discovered, lived life largely on his own terms. "Supposing I do turn around and you change your mind again?"

"I won't change my mind again."

He snorted, not believing her for even half a second. She'd squandered any credibility she had left with him by announcing she wanted to go back to Black Creek Ranch.

Calley raised her chin, insulted and a little embarrassed. "Normally, I'm very decisive."

"Yeah, I'll bet you're decisive as hell when it comes to money. Men, on the other hand—"

"My changing my mind has nothing to do with men."

He raised both bushy eyebrows, not saying a word. He didn't need to. His expression made his dubiousness quite plain.

She felt color rise in her cheeks. "It's true. Max and I— It's been four years. There's nothing between us. Nothing at all. That's why I've changed my mind. If there were something between us, I'd have to leave. But since there isn't, I can stay."

"That doesn't make sense."

"Sure it does. It's just a little convoluted. I've been

working it through in my own mind. You see, if either of us still harbored romantic feelings toward the other—not that he ever really did toward me, although there were certainly other feelings. Well, you know what I mean."

Jimmy grunted. "Yeah. I know."

"Anyway, if that were the case, I'd have to leave."

He still didn't get it. "I can see your point if one of you felt that way and the other didn't. Things could get ugly, especially you both being so stubborn and bad tempered about that kind of thing. But if you both felt the same way—"

"All the more reason to leave." She decided not to touch the remark about being stubborn and bad tempered. What did Jimmy Baxter know about her?

He shook his head in confusion. "Now that's downright crazy."

"You're not following my logic."

"Logic? There's logic here?"

"Of course there is. You see, if Max and I did fall for each other again, there's no way we could stay together without destroying each other, and we both know it. But it's too complicated for the boys to understand, and there's no reason to confuse or hurt them. So I'd leave."

"How come you'd destroy each other?"

"He's a Wyoming rancher with three little boys to raise. I'm a New Yorker with a New York career and a New York life. Enough said."

Jimmy was silent a moment, his mouth twisted in thought. Finally, he sighed. "Nope. Still doesn't make sense. You're saying you're staying because you're convinced Max and you don't have a chance together?"

"Exactly."

"If you did, you'd leave for sure?"

She smiled. "See. It does make sense."

"If you call that sense— Well, I won't get insulting. That the only reason you're changing your mind? Because you figure you and Max don't have any romantic feelings toward each other?"

"No. I have another reason."

"Is it just as logical as this one?"

She shook her head. "It has nothing to do with logic."

"Then I don't want to hear it."

She'd had no intention of explaining herself to him. Lying awake at dawn, she'd realized that what Christopher, Timothy and Wynne's manipulation had been about was, simply, their brother Max. They wanted him to be happy. They wanted him to stop sacrificing his happiness for theirs, to see that he *deserved* to be happy.

And they deserved to see him happy.

Just not with her, of course. But with someone. Before she left Wyoming, Calley wanted Max to see that.

Jimmy put on the brake and swerved to the side of the road, doing a U-turn with one hand on the wheel and way too much gas.

"You're taking me back to the ranch?" Calley asked.

"Yep. No need wasting money on renting a car, and I'm not going to have your hitchhiking on my head." He brought the truck quickly back up to speed, driving with one hand. "Well. Now I owe Max twenty bucks."

"Twenty bucks? What for?"

The old cowboy grinned over at her. "He bet you'd change your mind before you got to town."

"On what grounds?"

"Opposite the ones you just gave me. They were about as logical as yours."

She frowned, thinking that one over, wondering if she should be incensed or confused.

Then she got it, and she was instantly so mad she could have leaped from the truck at seventy miles per hour and flown herself back to New York.

"That bastard! That arrogant, miserable—he thinks *I* still harbor romantic feelings toward *him?*"

Jimmy remained calm. "I don't remember him using the word 'romantic.'"

"That's it. Stop the truck. Turn around. Take me to the airport. I'm going back to New York. I can't possibly stay if Max Slade has such a high opinion of himself that he thinks I would—that I want—that I—"

She couldn't say it, not to a near stranger. Forget romance. Forget happiness and emotion and what kind of life she wanted to live. Max Slade believed she would change her mind about staying in Wyoming because she still lusted after his body. Period. No other reason.

Of course, she did harbor a certain physical attraction to him. She was *human,* for heaven's sake. But that had nothing to do with her changing her mind.

Not for all the sagebrush in Wyoming, she thought, would she go to bed with that man.

"I mean it, Jimmy." She spoke through clenched teeth, not liking the idea of Jimmy Baxter and Max Slade placing bets on her state of mind. She had tossed and turned and agonized, and those two had wagered twenty bucks on what she would do. Of all the nerve! Obviously, Jimmy had his own ideas about what was between her and Max, ideas she doubted she would like any better than Max's. "I want to go back to New York *today.*"

The old cowboy shook his head, adamant. "Too

late, missy. We're going back to the ranch. One change of mind's all you're allowed."

Calley got to Max before he could collect his twenty dollars from Jimmy Baxter and crow a little about winning their bet. He was in the office down in the main stable. It was a double room that hadn't changed much since his grandfather's day, except for the addition of a computer and printer. But the atmosphere, complete with old filing cabinets, shelves and two big oak desks, remained the same. Max had added his own oak captain's chair, an heirloom from his mother's side of the family. Oil paintings his grandmother had done of the ranch and of a couple of the horses graced what wall space there was. A window looked out on the lower pasture and Black Creek. He couldn't ask for a better view.

He'd been talking to several of the hands, but when Calley stormed in, they cleared out, grinning, making the obvious assumptions. Max hadn't even tried to explain her. Not many women turned up on the ranch to see him, and none like Calley Hastings. They'd already figured out she was from New York. It hadn't taken much figuring.

She was dressed for the city, black pants, crisp white shirt, silver earrings and just the right amount of makeup for flying.

She waited until she and Max were alone before bursting. "Of all the egotistical, self-centered men I have ever encountered, you, Max Slade, take grand prize. I cannot believe you think I changed my mind about leaving because I'm—because I've thought—" She sputtered, so mad she couldn't talk. Or maybe it was just embarrassment because he'd called a spade a spade and had said what he knew was on her mind. But Calley was a woman seldom at a loss for words, and seldom embarrassed. "I'll have you know I am not lusting after you."

Max tilted back in his chair, crossing his ankles up on his desk. The color was high in her cheeks, and tendrils of hair had fallen into her face, despite the barrette struggling to hold the rest of it back. Her intensely blue eyes were fixed on him behind her glasses. It was entirely possible that Jimmy, having lost their bet, had exaggerated Max's reasoning on why she would change her mind and stay in Wyoming.

Then again, perhaps not.

He regarded her with frank amusement. "So the thought of going to bed with me hasn't crossed your mind since you arrived in Wyoming?"

She sniffed. "I don't have to answer that. You're not entitled to know my private thoughts."

"Is that a yes?"

"It's neither a yes or a no. It's a none-of-your-business. If I answer one personal question—even to save my skin—you'll think of another to ask, and there'll be no end to it. I need to protect my privacy. Obviously, you have no sense of boundaries."

"When's the last time you had an intimate relationship with a man?"

"I beg your pardon?"

He swung his legs back down to the floor and rose. "Sex, Calley. When's the last time you had sex?"

"I swear, I'll *walk* to New York if I have to."

He came around the desk. "It hasn't been four years, has it?"

"I'll bet I can get to Jackson before sundown. I'll sleep at the airport if necessary."

"We'll conduct a test. I'll kiss you as best I know how, and if you don't respond, I'll take your word for it that you haven't thought about going to bed with me."

She shot him a look. She couldn't keep ignoring him, and she knew it. "That's a challenge, isn't it?"

"Yep."

"You'll keep your word?"

"Sure."

"I don't trust you."

"Of course you don't. No reason for you to. But I'll keep my word."

"If I don't agree, I suppose you'll consider yourself right by default."

He grinned. "Either way, Calley, if I kiss you or don't kiss you, I'll still know I'm right."

"I swear, Slade—"

"I kiss you or I don't. It's your choice."

"All right, fine." She inhaled, that New York financial mind of hers thinking over all the pros and cons, all the potential consequences. She wouldn't just let herself go. She wouldn't just do what she knew deep down she wanted to do. Finally, she exhaled. "Go ahead, Max. Kiss me. I assure you, I won't respond the way you think I will."

"It's going to be a proper kiss."

"I can handle it."

As if it were gum surgery. Max smiled, moving closer. She didn't back up even an inch. Once committed, Calley Hastings had never been one to back off from a challenge, even when it was clearly in her best interest to do so. It was one reason she'd thrived in New

York's financial world. Smart, talented people without a backbone got eaten alive there. He'd seen it happen.

But Calley wasn't in New York. She was in Wyoming. She was on his turf, and she would be wise to remember it.

Max slipped his arms around her. She snuggled in close. In for a penny, in for a pound. That was Calley Hastings. But her body gave her away. He could feel her tension, her anticipation. She wasn't at all sure she'd made the right choice, and it had nothing, he thought, to do with him. It was herself she was afraid of.

"Change your mind?" he asked, his mouth close to hers.

"No."

"You want me to kiss you?"

"To prove a point, yes. It's sort of a clinical test."

A clinical test. He would give her clinical.

He covered her mouth with his, drawing her against him. The taste of her took his breath away, but he didn't want to concentrate on his own reaction. He wanted to focus on hers. He wanted her to feel what he felt when he looked at her, touched her, thought about her, dreamed about her. He wanted her to acknowledge that being near him drove her nearly as mad as it did him. He wanted to *know* it did.

Not that they had a future together. They didn't. But what they'd had together four years ago wasn't dead, buried and forgotten. Maybe it had to get that way. But it wasn't there yet.

He deepened his kiss—and it *was* his kiss, not hers. She was letting him take the lead. Insisting. Her response, so far, was tentative. Polite, even. He drew her tight against him, so that every inch of her body was in contact with his.

He'd changed, he thought. He was harder than he had been four years ago, his muscles toughened by his work on the ranch. He had more scars, more calluses. Let her feel the changes in him. Let her know that he wasn't the same man he'd been in New York.

Except in one way. He had the same driving hunger for her he'd had then. But let her feel that, too, he thought.

Finally, when he was on the verge of finding some hayloft and making love to her until dawn, he ended the kiss and stood back, studying her reaction.

She was trying hard not to give him one. Her glasses were crooked, her eyes sultry, her breathing not too steady. Swallowing visibly, she adjusted her shirt and straightened her glasses and, finally, cleared her throat.

"There. You see? No effect."

Max smiled. "Right."

She glared at him. "Don't give me that knowing look. You don't know anything. You tried a toe-curling kiss on me, and my toes didn't curl." Her hoarse voice forced a pause; she had to clear her throat again. "End of story. You failed, Max."

"Uh-huh."

"Admit it."

"Admit what?"

"That you failed. Your toes curled, but mine didn't."

He moved back around his desk, shaking his head. "I'm not the one who has to admit anything. You are, Calley. Don't tell me anything if you don't want, but at least don't lie to yourself. You know damned well that kiss got to you."

She started toward the door, in no mood to admit anything to him. If he told her she wore glasses, she would deny it. She tossed him a parting look. "I'm going to tell Jimmy he should get twenty dollars off you because he didn't lose any bet. I didn't change my mind because I was lusting after you."

"Then why did you?"

"As if there could be no other rational reason!" She snorted, but Max was betting it was just a cover for her curled toes. "As I explained to Jimmy, I'm staying precisely because I don't have any romantic feelings toward you."

Max dropped into his chair, unable to resist a grin. "Who said anything about romantic feelings?"

She slammed the door on her way out.

Chapter 8

Wynne pounded on Calley's door, yelling as loud as any six-year-old could. "Come on out! Come on out!"

She groaned, shutting the book she'd been pretending to read. Wynne Slade was not a child to be ignored. What Slade was?

After Max's challenge kiss, she had retreated to her room, the only place she could be sure of her privacy. She needed to sort out what had gone awry in her mental state that she'd actually insisted on turning back when she was well clear of Black Creek Ranch. She should have pressed on to New York.

Instead, she'd come back, and she'd risen to Max's bait and let him kiss her.

It could be argued, she supposed, that she'd kissed him back. Well, what of it? For four years, she'd been haunted by dreams of kissing Max Slade again. Why not make the most of the opportunity? Why not kiss him back and prove to herself her dreams were just that. Dreams. Not reality.

Except reality had been even more alluring, even more unsettling than her dreams. The Max Slade of elusive memory didn't compare to the Max Slade of stark reality.

In short, he had not disappointed. She wanted him no less after their kiss than before.

But of course, *that* had nothing to do with romantic feelings. He had not engaged her heart. She had not engaged his.

Or so she kept telling herself as she'd given up on sorting anything out and had, in desperation, grabbed a book.

She was committed to staying. Whatever manner of insanity had gripped her, she wasn't going to give Max the satisfaction of seeing her leave. He would say it was because she still wanted him and was afraid to admit it. He would say it was because of the kiss. He would say it was because she was a coward.

"Calley," Wynne whined. "Come on out."

"Maybe I'm taking a nap."

"You're too old."

"Never try to win an argument with a Slade," she muttered, swinging out of bed.

Hiding in her room wasn't going to accomplish a thing. Max would put his spin on that, too. He would say she was just avoiding temptation or some such nonsense. He had his own way of looking at things.

She sighed at herself in the mirror. She still looked as if she'd just had her toes curled by a kiss, never mind that it had happened three hours ago. Max had not gone unaffected, either. She had eyes. She'd seen what their kiss had done to him.

That knowledge, however, was of no consolation whatsoever.

Wynne pounded on her door again.

"You keep that up," she called to him, "and you're going to knock it off its hinges."

"Lucky wants to play Frisbee. And Fred wants to meet you."

She paused, her sweatshirt half-on. She had yet to meet Fred. She had yet to learn who—or what—Fred was. In her current state of mind, she had no reason to trust that Fred was anything she wanted to encounter.

"Who says I want to meet Fred?"

"You'll like him. He doesn't bite."

"Does he slither?"

"Huh?"

"Never mind."

Kids, she thought. Not realizing she'd tried to make good her escape from Black Creek Ranch that morning, Wynne didn't hold a grudge. Christopher and Timothy, however, seemed to view her near-departure as some kind of betrayal, never mind their antics in getting her to Wyoming. They'd given her dirty looks when she'd fetched a pitcher of water to take to her room. She knew enough about preadolescents to recognize a dirty look when she saw one.

Max was their big brother and guardian, she thought. Let *him* explain.

Except she was the one who'd run out on them, leaving only a promise via Jimmy Baxter that she would send postcards of various Manhattan sights. Well, she thought defensively, what was she supposed to have done? She was used to being responsible for herself, period. She wasn't used to dealing with kids.

"Calley!"

"Don't whine," she said, tearing open the door. "I hate whining."

Wynne blinked at her. "What's whining?"

"You could get a Ph.D. in it, kiddo."

"What's a p-d-h?"

She sighed. "Never mind. Now, what about playing Frisbee with Lucky and meeting this Fred character can't wait?"

He lifted his shoulders and spread out his hands in a manner that was deliberately cute, no doubt designed to keep her from extracting answers he didn't have. He'd wanted her out of her room and in his presence, and he'd succeeded in his mission. Tactics were inconsequential.

"You do know how to get your way, Wynne, my friend." She patted him on his sweaty, dirty head. "But I guess if you can't have the world spin for you when you're six, you never can. We'll do Lucky first. I'm not meeting Fred until I have a better idea of what he is."

"Oh. Fred's a snake."

She'd feared as much. "I hate snakes."

Wynne giggled. "You hate *everything*."

She smiled back at him. "That's why I live in New York."

Calley didn't know what had brought the older two Slade boys around. Either it was her rusty, pathetic Frisbee playing—the turkey caught better than she did—or it was her reaction to Fred.

Fred was a big snake, the biggest she'd seen outside of the Bronx Zoo.

"He's not poisonous," Timothy said, as if that fact should make more of a difference to her than it did.

Apparently, Fred lived in the area just behind the stables, in a hole in its old root foundation. The boys showed her the rock where he liked to sun himself. Calley duly noted its precise location. She would not sun herself on the same rock. Although they'd named him, Fred was—mercifully—not a pet.

"Max said we can't bring him in the house," Christopher explained as they all gathered around the foundation, where Fred, having been disturbed by three Slade boys and one non-Slade New Yorker, had retreated into his hole. The boys were disappointed. Calley was not.

She shuddered at the thought of a snake in the house. Give her a sink full of New York cockroaches any day over a snake. "I'm with Max on that one."

"Yeah," Wynne put in, "Jimmy says he'll cook Fred for supper if we bring him inside."

Timothy nodded. "He would, too. Jimmy likes snake."

Calley could feel her brow furrow as she considered the implications of Timothy's statement. "Are you saying Jimmy— He wouldn't—he doesn't—"

"Oh," Timothy said, "Jimmy loves snake. He says it's got to be the right kind of snake, or the meat's tough."

They were teasing her. They had to be. Then again, this was Wyoming. Who knew what old cowboys would eat? Calley tried not to overreact. "He hasn't cooked up a snake while I've been here, has he?"

"I don't know." Timothy looked at his older brother for help. "Has he, Christopher?"

"Hmm." He thought a moment. Calley forced herself to remember he was a child with a vivid imagination he was all too willing to put to ill use. "I don't know, that stuff he said was chicken the other night could've been snake."

Timothy shook his head. "Didn't taste like it."

"I know it. Have you ever had snake, Calley?"

"No. I have not."

"Some folks say it tastes like chicken, but I don't think so."

Calley's stomach lurched. "What does it taste like?"

Timothy and Christopher looked at each other, considering how to explain such basics to a New Yorker. Finally, Christopher shrugged. "Snake tastes like snake."

"How encouraging," she said.

"You'd like barbecued snake," Timothy put in. "Jimmy does the best barbecue sauce in the whole world, and it's really yummy on snake."

"I *love* barbecue," Wynne, not to be left out, interjected.

Calley made a face. "You boys see why I like New York?"

Christopher didn't answer. He turned to his brothers. "Come on, you two. Jimmy said we had to get back and help him."

"With anything in particular?" Calley asked. "I'd be happy to lend a hand, if I can."

The oldest of Max's three orphaned half brothers glanced around at her as he started back around the stable, grinning in a manner that would give women fits in the not-too-distant future. "We're having a picnic tonight."

"Yep," Timothy said. "Jimmy's fixing his barbecue sauce."

Wynne skipped up the path. "Yeah! Yippee! We're having snake for supper!"

If she'd been anywhere but the wilds of Wyoming, with anyone but Slade males, Calley would have assumed they were just pulling her leg. But she'd been on Black Creek Ranch long enough to know to assume nothing.

Barbecued snake for supper was not beyond the realm of possibility.

"What're you looking at?" Max asked as Calley peered around him to get a good look at the platter of marinated meat Jimmy had just brought out to the grill.

She didn't spare Max so much as a glance. "This is chicken, right?"

"I think so."

"You could tell if it wasn't, couldn't you?"

"If it wasn't chicken?"

She nodded.

Max laid several pieces on the hot charcoal grill. He hadn't seen her since their kiss in his office. Jimmy had said she went out with the boys, who weren't too happy with her for trying to sneak out on them. Max had not risen to her defense, but was sticking to his original plan. However long she stayed in Wyoming, Calley's relationship with Christopher, Timothy and Wynne was for them to sort out.

"Calley, why wouldn't it be chicken? What else could it be? It's obviously not beef—"

"It could be turkey," she said.

He grinned. "Not with Lucky around."

"Well, it could be anything, really. It's boneless, and the meat's pale." She chewed on one corner of her mouth, clearly dubious about dinner. "If Jimmy had a mind to, I suppose he could slip us snake meat and we'd never know it."

"I'd know it."

"How?"

"I've had snake."

She winced, moving away from the platter. "You mountain men."

"I didn't say I liked it."

"Do you?"

He shrugged. "It's okay if you're really hungry and that's all there is."

"What about Jimmy?"

"Oh, he's had snake lots of times, or claims he has. You never know when he gets going with his tales. I still sometimes can't tell truth from exaggeration, even outright fiction."

"Would he try to slip snake onto the barbecue?"

Max set down his barbecue fork and eyed her. For all the upheaval she'd endured that day—leaving, coming back, responding to his kiss challenge—she looked none too worse for wear. In fact, she looked ready to take on whatever Wyoming threw at her. She had her hair pulled back and her dirty borrowed white hat on, and she wore a blue chambray shirt with the sleeves rolled up, jean shorts and running shoes. He could have swept her up into his arms then and there, something he chose not to mention when she had snakes on her mind.

"Why would Jimmy slip snake onto the barbecue?" he asked, fearing he already knew the answer.

"Because he's a former cowboy and probably thinks

snake's good eating. How would I know? And I'm not accusing him of anything. I'm just asking."

Before Max could devise an approach to get the truth out of her, Jimmy Baxter himself graced the scene, limping in from the kitchen with another platter. "Thought we'd throw some squash on the grill. I like it fried myself, but I guess it's better if we cut down on the fat. I brushed a little olive oil on it and sprinkled on some oregano, like you suggested, Calley. Guess it'll taste all right. I don't know."

She was eyeing the squash, cut in lengthwise strips, as if it, too, might be snake. She was, Max thought, a woman spooked. He picked up his barbecue fork and flipped the chicken, already nicely browned on one side. "Jimmy, Calley here thinks you might try and hoodwink us into eating snake and making us think it was chicken."

Jimmy set the squash next to the platter of meat. "Why would I do that? If I cook up some good snake, I'm not going to pass it off as chicken."

"You'd tell us," she asked, looking somewhat encouraged.

"Sure. Max, you know I would. I've got no reason to slip anything past anybody. I cook up snake, you all'd know it, and you all'd eat it, too. Right, Max?"

"Yep, Jimmy, that's what you'd do. I remember the time you fed us fried grasshoppers. You didn't try to pass them off as anything else."

"Well, it'd be hard, you know, with those little legs of theirs—"

"That's it," Calley muttered, "I'm sticking to cold cereal and toast. You ranch types aren't to be trusted with meals."

Jimmy sniffed. "That's what's wrong with you New Yorkers. You don't know good food when you see it. You're spoiled. You get out on the range with not even a grocery store within a hundred miles, never mind a restaurant, and you work hard and get hungry, you won't be turning your nose up at fried grasshoppers or snake or anything else."

Calley was not in the least intimidated by the old cowboy. "I have no intention of *ever* being hundreds of miles from the nearest restaurant."

"City folk," Jimmy grumbled, stalking back to his kitchen.

"Fried grasshoppers." Calley gave an exaggerated shudder. "That's even worse than barbecued snake."

Max laid some of the squash on the grill. "Seems to me the boys have had their revenge on you."

"On me? What'd I do?"

"You snuck out on them."

She sighed, quickly glancing in their direction. "I know I did. But Max, they can't think I'm staying forever."

"You promised you'd stay the full two weeks—unless I kicked you out first, of course. You didn't. *And* you added insult to injury by not saying goodbye. Their sob story to get you here notwithstanding, they have a heightened sense of fair play."

"We're not supposed to get attached to each other, remember? If this were a bed and breakfast and I were a paying guest, I wouldn't feel obligated to say goodbye to the owners' children." She was squinting in the pale early-evening light at Timothy and Wynne on the swing set, Christopher tossing his baseball high up into the air and catching it. "Of course, this isn't a bed and breakfast, and I'm not a paying guest."

Her tone was almost whimsical, as if she didn't quite know where she was, or who. Max suspected their kiss had confused her. But to suggest as much to her, he knew, would only annoy her. She would lash out at him because she herself was confused. He knew the feeling. But he would let Calley Hastings figure out for herself what impact coming to Wyoming, staying on Black Creek Ranch, would have on her...*if* she had any choice.

She turned to him abruptly, eyes narrowed. For a raw instant, Max had a feeling she'd read his mind. "Don't you go getting any weird ideas, Max Slade. I *will* leave at the end of my two weeks."

He smiled. "Of course. You belong in New York."

"That's right." One of the dogs came up to her, looking for a handout, sniffing her fingers. She patted him on the head. "Bet you don't like snake, either, do you, sport? You'd like Central Park, yes, you would. You could chase pigeons to your heart's content, wouldn't have to worry about wolves and coyotes, no elk to tempt you. Yeah, city life."

Max made a face. She was the stubbornest woman alive. Had to be. "What if you change your mind and decide to stay in Wyoming?"

She shot him a dubious look. "Then I appeal to your sense of honor and decency, Max."

He arched a brow, implying the question.

She gave him a not-so-innocent smile. "I'm talking about the honor and decency that brought you back to Wyoming from New York to raise your brothers, not the weasel in you that had you issuing that challenge in your office."

"Ah. You didn't react as if a weasel had kissed you."

"I will next time. Trust me."

He grinned at her, unable to resist. "There'll be a next time, Calley?"

"Not on your terms, I assure you. But one challenge begets another. When you least expect it, Max Slade, I'm going to nail your hide to the hardest oak tree out here." She cleared her throat, gently shoving the dog on his way. Thoughts of kissing him and nailing his hide to anything had clearly distracted and unsettled her, not that she would ever admit it. "I'm counting on you to put me on a plane regardless of what I say I want to do. Who knows what's in the air around here? I might lose my mind and decide to stay. Don't believe it. Put me on a plane and tell me to call when I've come to my senses."

He flipped the chicken and checked the squash, digesting her words. Finally, he gave her a sideways glance. "Don't trust yourself around us Slades, do you, Calley?"

"Nope. I don't trust you Slades around me."

Calley immersed herself in life on Black Creek Ranch.

The Slade boys, having had their revenge, forgave her for sneaking out on them and encouraged her to join them on their chores as a way of learning about ranch life. She had a feeling it was more a way of getting her to do their work for them. They were devious rascals, but she was on to them.

Each was assigned indoor and outdoor jobs appropriate to his age. Christopher, being eleven, did more with the horses. Timothy was in charge of the dogs.

Wynne fed Lucky. They all took turns—and generally argued about whose it was—cleaning up after him, a free-roaming turkey not the neatest of animals. Since she was determined to do ranch life, Calley acquiesced to taking a turn at the nasty task herself, just to prove she was no squeamish New Yorker.

It was no treat. Lucky was big even for a turkey.

The boys also took turns at caring for the other small animals, and Jimmy kept them well-informed on what they were to do regarding housework, meal preparation and cleaning up after themselves. None, however, was overworked, despite complaints to the contrary.

Calley got along with Jimmy, provided she didn't "girlie" up his kitchen. She took that to mean he had low tolerance for her filling little china cream pitchers with wildflowers, her afternoon teas with the boys, her request for dried currants and cranberries to make her own scones.

She would soften him up by getting him to talk to her about horses and his days as a cowboy. From what he said and her own observations, she'd deduced that Black Creek was no struggling ranch and Max Slade no pauper. In fact, quite to the contrary. Jimmy Baxter himself had never ventured east of the Mississippi River. His opinion of New York was forged by tourists, the news and reruns of "Barney Miller." Calley had the feeling her ignorance of ranch life only confirmed his prejudices.

Not that she didn't have *her* ideas about the Wild West.

Max, of course, continued to be a problem.

He was polite and deliberately nonthreatening, which was all the more unsettling *because* it was so deliberate. It said he could change at a moment's notice. It said he might challenge her to another kiss. It said he knew she was watching his every move, reacting to him, *aware* of him.

It said he knew too damned much about her.

Friends of Max's from Jackson and a couple from California who boarded several horses at the ranch came on the weekend. Jimmy packed a lunch for the couple, and they set off for the day. The friends—John and Maura Parker—brought their two kids with them, a girl, ten, and a boy, eight. Maura was an architect, John a chef at one of Jackson's trendy restaurants. They gathered on the front porch for ice tea and lemonade while Jimmy, at his insistence, made dinner. Max, meanwhile, was down at the stables dealing with some horse matter. Calley didn't ask what. Her knowledge of horses remained blissfully limited.

With thunderclouds gathering on the horizon, the kids joined in a loud game of cards off to one end of the huge porch. The Parkers, obviously trying to figure out who Calley was and how she'd ended up on Black Creek Ranch, offered to show her around Jackson one day. Through a series of polite, if transparent, questions, they elicited basic background information about her, intrigued when they learned she was a financial adviser from New York. They suggested they knew people in the area, themselves included, who could use her skills. With the growth in Jackson Hole and Wyoming in general, such local talent wouldn't go underworked.

Calley said that was nice, but she was only in Wyoming for two weeks and intended to go back to New York and her Wall Street office.

An attractive woman in her late thirties, Maura

Parker raised an eyebrow in interest. "Do you live in Manhattan?"

"The Upper West Side." Calley envisioned her apartment, its view of the street, its charm, its shortcomings, and smiled, nostalgic. "I have a neat little apartment. I love it."

John shuddered. "I could never live in the city again."

"You're from New York?"

"Oh, no. St. Louis. We moved out here after the kids were born."

"We just love it," his wife said.

"That's nice," Calley smiled, not defensively. "But I don't hate the city. I'm not saying I hate the woods, either, but— Well, folks in Wyoming should be glad some of us still like city life or they'd be overrun."

As their conversation continued, Calley still got the distinct impression the Parkers couldn't quite figure out who she was or what she was doing with Max Slade out on Black Creek Ranch.

So the Slade boys, having big ears and even bigger mouths, provided an explanation.

"She's Max's old girlfriend," Timothy blurted.

"Yeah," Wynne said, giggling.

John and Maura both glanced at Calley, not bothering to conceal their curiosity. Calley smiled, noncommittal. She had no intention of explaining her relationship with Max. She didn't understand it herself anymore. She shot the boys a warning look, but they were oblivious.

His two younger brothers pressed Christopher into telling the entire gory tale. About how he'd tracked her down and pretended to be a lonely widow with five kids, a dying grandmother and a ranch. Once he'd figured out Calley had no idea her ex-boyfriend was living out west or even what had happened to him since he'd vanished from New York—or why he'd left—he'd persuaded her to come to Wyoming.

Maura Parker clapped her hands together, delighted. "What clever matchmakers you boys are." She turned to Calley, apparently oblivious to any embarrassment she might be experiencing. "You must have been *mortified* when you saw Max."

Max, fortunately, was still nowhere in sight and not able to witness Calley's expression, which was not nearly as delighted as Maura Parker's. In spite of her discomfort, Calley liked the other woman immensely. She would take frankness any day over phony politeness. "I wouldn't say mortified. I'd say—" Well, what she'd been was enraged, outraged, suspicious and not happy at all, which the Parkers could figure out for themselves. "I'd say I was surprised to see him."

John Parker was grinning. "I'll bet. You don't look the type to fall for such an obvious sob story."

"It wasn't so obvious at the time." She kept her tone matter-of-fact, as if they were discussing an error in judgment of no consequence, not one that had put her on a ranch in the middle of nowhere with an ex-lover she hadn't seen or heard from in four years. The boys were watching her intently. She could have strung them up on the spot for blabbing. But she went on calmly, "Christopher's quite the writer. He's imaginative and clever. He was very convincing."

"Yes, but you must have had *some* idea it was a hoax—"

His wife laid a hand on her husband's knee. "Perhaps not. We weren't there."

He got the message. "No, of course not. Well. Max must've—hell, if one of *my* old girlfriends turned up out of the blue—"

"Darling," Maura Parker said, "you'd better stop while your head's still above water. If Calley doesn't drown you, I will."

At that moment, Max climbed up the steps to the front porch. He had on a denim shirt with the sleeves rolled up, and there was a hard look about him that seemed to have become a part of him. His eyes caught hers, just for an instant. He seemed to understand that she was on the hot seat regarding her presence in Wyoming, although his expression was remarkably without sympathy.

"The boys here were just telling us how they hoodwinked Calley into coming west," John Parker said.

"Were they? Well, Calley and I hadn't seen each other in a while." He poured himself a glass of ice tea, remaining on his feet. He drank. Then he glanced at his friends. "Looks like the storm's pushing south. You all up for a game of volleyball before dinner?"

All five kids leaped to their feet before the adults could respond. They started yelling about who would be on whose team.

Max grinned. "Guess you'd better be."

The kids decided there would be two games. First, the Parkers against the Slades. Calley would have to play on the Slade team, they'd reasoned, since Max was the only adult and Wynne would get mad and quit before they could get a game in, a comment designed to get him to do just that, something Max darkly pointed out to Christopher and Timothy. The second game would be the adults against the kids. Timothy started to say the adults could have Wynne, but retreated when Max shot him a silencing look, and instead, he slung one arm over his little brother's shoulder and promised to show him a few volleyball tips.

"I don't need any tips," Wynne said, Slade stubborn to the bitter end. "I already know how to play."

Max glanced at Calley as the Parkers and kids pounded off the front porch. "You mind being a Slade for a while?"

She swallowed, then shrugged. "It's just a game."

"That's what I keep telling my brothers." He started down the steps, looking less tired than he had when he'd come up them a few minutes earlier. "It hasn't sunk in yet. They're Slades, too."

"Meaning they hate to lose."

He grinned over his shoulder at her. "But they do love to win."

Chapter 9

Max charged from the kitchen out into the rain. It was a warm, gentle rain, unlike the storm raging in him. What in hell was wrong with him? Why hadn't he let Calley Hastings spend that first night in the airport and catch the first plane out in the morning instead of taking her back to the ranch with him?

He remembered seeing her, standing amid her luggage, radiating her energetic charm, her impatience, her uneasiness with her Western surroundings. She'd fallen for a crazy sob story. She'd come to Wyoming. She was *there,* and he'd been unable to force himself to let her go. It was that simple. He could have taken her to the Parkers'. He could have left her to her own considerable devices.

But he'd taken her home to Black Creek Ranch, and now she had two days left before she returned to New York where she belonged.

He kept moving, unable to do anything else, even to think. Through an open window, he could hear Timothy practicing the piano in the living room. Calley had given him a couple more lessons, and he'd badgered Max to find him a regular teacher.

"But if Calley stays, she can teach me."

If Calley stayed…

Max squashed the thought before it could fully form. She couldn't stay. There was no point thinking about what would happen—what *could* happen—if she did.

Wynne had taken over the kitchen table to play a game of solitaire Calley had taught him. It was simple enough for a six-year-old to comprehend, and easy to win, which he liked. He would hoot and holler every time he did.

At the first sign of rain, Christopher had retreated to his bedroom to write poetry in a blank book Calley had bought him in Jackson. It had pictures of the solar system on the front. Max hadn't even realized Christopher liked to write poetry. He'd asked to read some of it, but Calley had glared at him as if he'd just embarrassed the kid. Max didn't get it. Later, Calley explained that an eleven-year-old boy needed privacy and space to explore his artistic inclinations without having his sensitivities trounced on by a hardcase older brother with no poetry in his soul.

Max hadn't been entirely sure what she was talking about. He figured the kid just had a crush on his sixth-grade history teacher and was getting it off his chest. Calley had groaned at his comment, saying she rested her case.

"You respect Christopher's imaginative nature," she'd said, "but you don't understand it."

His mind back on the present, Max noticed that the rain had soaked his hair, had nearly soaked through his denim shirt. He didn't care. Piano lessons, solitaire, poetry. Calley's impact on Black Creek Ranch would be felt for a long time. Even the damned turkey would feel her absence. He'd taken up waiting outside the kitchen door until she came outside and threw him the Frisbee.

Madness, Max thought.

He'd taken Calley to Jackson himself and showed her around, let her play tourist for a day. She'd poked in the trendy boutiques and galleries, bought herself her own cowboy hat, sat in the shade of the central town square. They'd eaten lunch at John Parker's restaurant and talked about things she wouldn't mind doing if she had more time in Wyoming, like river rafting and kayaking and hiking in the Grand Tetons, maybe even going for a long bike ride.

It had been an amiable day, as if they were a pair of old friends.

Which they weren't and never could be.

Max exploded into the main stable. He was tense and distracted, in a dangerous mood.

She had two days left in Wyoming. Just two days. He felt no relief. He couldn't begin to define what he did feel. In Jackson, he'd imagined Calley staying longer, staying forever. He'd imagined a future with her. It was as if he'd been sucked back four years, to the days before his father and Lissa had died, when he'd wanted nothing more than to spend his life with Calley Hastings.

But it wasn't to be.

He intended to keep his promise to her. If she took leave of her senses and tried to tell him she wanted to stay, he would put her on a plane back to New York. That was where she belonged. He knew it, and so did she.

She was in the kitchen now, arguing with Jimmy over what color to paint the kitchen that fall. As if it made any difference to her.

Max brushed dripping water from his face and took a deep breath, knowing nothing had changed in four years. Nothing.

He'd loved Calley Hastings then, and he did now. But she still didn't belong in Wyoming.

And he couldn't leave.

Calley saw the blood dripping from Max's arm even before the screen door banged shut behind him. He burst into the kitchen, his jaw clamped shut, his face contorted more in anger, it seemed to her, than pain. Blood soaked the upper left arm of his shirt along a tear in the sleeve.

Calley abandoned her paint chips and rushed to him, never mind that she well knew Max Slade could manage without her help. "What happened?"

"Snagged a nail." He snarled at her through clenched teeth, ripping off his shirt as he started for the sink. It was after dinner, a cool, dark evening. "I'm fine."

"You're bleeding all over the place."

"It'll mop up."

"Max—"

He eyed her darkly. "Jimmy and the boys left yet?"

She nodded. "Twenty minutes ago. They looked for you to say goodbye, but they couldn't find you—"

He didn't let her finish, instead slamming his right fist onto the counter and cursing a very blue streak.

With the boys safely out of earshot, he could indulge himself. And he did.

"Feel better?" Calley asked mildly.

He glared at her. "Not particularly."

"Seems to me you're more annoyed than hurt. Must have cut yourself doing something stupid. Want me to have a look?"

"No."

He cast his shirt onto the floor. Blood dribbled down his arm all the way to his wrist bone, mingling with the dark hairs on his arm. The wound itself was jagged, about three inches long, deeper as it wound down toward his elbow. Calley grabbed a flour-sack towel from a drawer. In spite of Jimmy Baxter's territorial nature, she'd learned her way around the Slade kitchen.

"It looks worse than it is," Max said.

Her hands were shaking. "One would hope."

"Damned nail was sticking out where it shouldn't have been. Hurt like hell." His dark eyes focused on her. "What're you doing with that towel?"

"Wetting it."

She'd turned on the faucet, dampening the towel with cool water, trying to ignore how close he was standing to her. He smelled wet, earthy. She swallowed, squeezing the excess water from the towel.

"I can sponge off some of the blood and clean out the wound. Your tetanus shots are up-to-date, aren't they?"

"Calley—"

"No communicable diseases?"

He sighed. "None. I was tested last month for insurance purposes."

"Insurance, huh?"

He managed a grim smile. "I knew that'd get a gleam in your eye."

"More so than the sight of blood, I assure you."

She turned to him with the towel. The expanse of tanned, muscular chest took her breath away. Scars that hadn't been there four years ago marked his abdomen, his shoulders, as if to remind her his life had changed since New York. He'd changed. She had, too. She wasn't as trusting, not just of men and romance, but of herself.

"I'll be careful," she said.

"I'm not worried."

"Are you like a wounded bear when you're hurt?"

"Just do the deed, Calley."

Her hands steadier, she dabbed at the wound, which appeared to be free of debris. If everything else had changed in four years, she thought, her physical attraction to Max Slade hadn't. Coming to Wyoming had proved that much to her. If they saw each other when they were eighty, she would feel that same potent, irresistible pull to him. It was just one of the givens in her life. It didn't mean anything. It certainly wasn't something she had to *act* upon.

Never mind how much she wanted to.

She shook off the thought, trying to concentrate on the task at hand.

What made matters worse, she knew, was that in the past two weeks she'd also discovered a new, utterly unfathomable emotional attraction to him. It was different than what she'd felt for him in the past. He'd been cocky, optimistic, determined, driven. It wasn't that he'd mellowed in the intervening years. Max Slade would never mellow. In many ways, he was harder, more uncompromising, not as driven, not as optimistic. He had sacrificed his dream of a life in New York for the sake of the brothers who needed him and had no one else. The harsh realities of his life on a sprawling Wyoming ranch and his responsibility as guardian to three young boys had given him a depth he hadn't had four years ago.

To her distress, Calley found herself wanting to explore this complex man. Max was compelling, interesting, and she liked his company. She liked *him*.

She just wasn't so naive as to think she could ever be friends with him. There was, after all, that physical attraction, not to mention her impending departure.

"Would Jimmy be doing this if he were here?" she said.

"No. I'd just turn on the faucet and stick my arm under it."

"You tough cowboys."

He shrugged. "Works."

"Is that what you do when one of the boys gets hurt? Just stick the wounded body part under the faucet?"

"Depends."

"On what?"

"On how loud they're screaming."

She eyed him. "You're being sarcastic."

"Calley, I would never deliberately hurt one of those boys."

"I know. But you're an example to them. They watch everything you do, and they learn from it. If you stick your bloody arm under the faucet, they're going to think that's what they should do. Max—" She inhaled, the proximity of his bare chest in no way helping her powers of concentration. "Max, they deserve to see you happy."

He furrowed his brow. "What?"

"You know what I mean. They lured me out here not so we could be together, but so you could be happy. They didn't know me from a hole in the wall. But they know you. They want you to be happy. When I head to New York—" She hesitated, not sure she wasn't stepping into something she didn't want to be stepping in, something that was plainly none of her business. "I think you should try to have a romantic life after I've left."

"Who says I didn't have one before you got here?"

"Christopher and Timothy have said as much. So has Jimmy. Wynne, too, if not in as many words."

"Lucky been squealing, too?"

She grinned at him. "I haven't learned to talk turkey yet."

"Ha."

"Max, don't make this any more difficult than it is. You know damned well what I'm trying to tell you."

"Suppose I've been having a romantic life while you're here?"

"That's not funny."

He seemed to smile and grimace at the same time. "Who says I'm trying to be funny?"

She ignored him. He was amusing himself at her expense, probably trying to keep his mind occupied on something besides his injury, maybe even besides their physical closeness. "I should bandage this thing. It'll need gauze and tape to hold the wound closed, but I don't think it needs stitches."

"Jimmy keeps the first-aid kit on top of the refrigerator."

While she got it down, Max moved to the kitchen

table, seemingly oblivious to his wound. He sat still, staring out at the raw, beautiful landscape that belonged to him and his brothers. In the past two weeks, Calley had never sensed that he'd regretted his decision to return home after his father's and Lissa Slade's deaths. It had meant losing her, but he'd made his peace with that loss.

In her own way, maybe so had she.

So why didn't she feel at peace?

She set the first-aid kit down on the table and opened it up. With no ambulance readily available to Black Creek Ranch at a moment's notice, it was fair sized and well stocked. After a few seconds' rummaging around, she found antibiotic ointment, a ball of gauze, adhesive tape and ancient scissors.

Max looked up at her. "Never figured you for a nurse, Calley."

"We New Yorkers are a resourceful bunch."

"You always were one to rise to the occasion."

She gave him an irreverent grin. "So were you." Before he could reply, she snipped off a length of gauze. "Now, hold out your arm, and let me know if I'm pulling too tight. I wouldn't want to make things worse."

The bleeding had subsided, but Calley was careful as she dabbed on a little of the antibiotic ointment and wound the gauze around his rock-hard upper arm, securing it as best she could with the adhesive tape. She had to hack off a couple of lengths before she got one that didn't curl back up on itself, proof she was no nurse. Max remained patient, watching her in silence, no evidence he was in any pain. She could feel his slate eyes on her as she worked. They seemed softer than they had that first night at the airport. Or maybe that was what she wanted to see, hoped to see. A softer Max Slade. A Max Slade who was less remote, less hard to read.

What she ought to see, she thought, was what was there. The real Max Slade. Not the one of memory, not the one of hope.

His arm bandaged, he got to his feet. "Thanks."

She nodded. "It'll probably throb awhile. Watch out for nails next time."

"I guess I should be glad it was only a nail I ran into, the mood I was in." He headed back to the sink, scooping his shirt up off the floor. "Jimmy's out for the night, too, you know."

"He told me he has to get off the ranch once a year or he goes nuts."

Max grinned. "You believe him?"

"I smell a conspiracy."

"So do I." He slung his shirt over one shoulder, and she couldn't help but notice the movement of muscles in his shoulders and chest. "The Parkers offer to take all three boys for the night, and Jimmy suddenly needs to visit his daughter up in Cody."

"Daughter? I didn't hear that part."

"He was married once, aeons ago. Had a daughter. She's as stubborn and miserable as he is. Jimmy likes to see her when he can. Sometimes she comes down here. They can usually stand each other about twenty-four hours."

Calley laughed. "Jimmy does defy stereotyping."

"Most people do. Well, conspiracy or not, it's going to be a quiet night. I plan to stay up for a while, wait until this thing stops throbbing." He glanced at her as he started out of the kitchen, his taciturn mood seeming to subside. "You?"

She shrugged, suddenly aware of how quiet the place was without Jimmy grumbling and the boys racing around. "I guess I'll turn in early and read. Hope your arm feels better. If you need me for anything—" She swallowed, unable to imagine Max Slade needing anyone for anything. Or admitting to it if he did. "You know where to find me."

"For the next two days, anyway."

After an hour alone in her room reading a lurid horror novel, Calley would have welcomed the ungodly screech of the barn owl to break the silence. The rain had stopped. The dogs and turkey and other critters had settled down for the night. There was no wind. Of course, there were no cars, horns, taxis, sirens—none of the sounds she'd come to regard as background noise in New York and as a part of her life. Just silence. And darkness.

And thoughts of Max Slade in the living room, her only company for miles.

She turned a page in her book. Really, she could have picked something more conducive to calm and relaxation.

A knock on her door sent the book flying, but she swallowed a scream just in time.

"Calley?" Max called through the door. "Are you awake?"

"Yes, I'm awake," she said irritably. "It's too damned quiet around here to sleep. Something wrong?"

"I need a hand."

A hand. Great. As if *she* needed another distraction. She sighed, throwing off her quilted covers. "I'll be right there—"

"No, don't get up. If you're decent, I can just come in. I'll only be a minute."

She was in her Mets nightshirt. She was *in bed,* for heaven's sake. By definition, she wasn't decent, not to entertain Max Slade, injured or not. But if she went out to him, she would still be in her nightshirt, which came just to midthigh, and it was a chilly evening, the fabric of her nightshirt thin.

Maybe it was best he come in to her.

"Okay," she said without enthusiasm.

The door opened. Max walked in wearing nothing but jeans. He dropped a roll of gauze and adhesive tape and a pair of scissors onto the edge of the bed. Nothing in his demeanor suggested he even noticed she was sitting up in bed in her Mets nightshirt. The man had ripped open his arm on a nail, she reminded herself. He probably wasn't up to noticing her or anything else. Just because she noticed everything about him didn't mean he was as prone to such insanity.

"I need you to change my bandage," he said, his voice clipped, his expression grim. His eyes fell on her. She felt her mouth go dry at their intensity, no matter what they saw or didn't see. "If you don't mind."

Blood had oozed through the current bandage, which also had loosened considerably, probably because it was the creation of an amateur. Given the logistics, it would be difficult for him to rebandage the wound himself.

Calley met his probing gaze. "Not just going to stick your arm under the faucet?"

He managed a curt smile. "Not with Florence Nightingale in the house."

"You shouldn't be sarcastic with someone who can inflict pain on you. All right, I'll do the best I can. No point in having you get lockjaw on me."

"I said my tetanus shots are up-to-date—"

She eyed him. "Don't push me, Max. It won't take much to get me to change my mind and make you wrap a towel around that arm and be satisfied with it."

He laughed, offering no evidence he was in any pain whatsoever. "Infection, then. No point in having my arm get infected on you."

"There. I knew a good rationalization was lurking somewhere. Here, sit down."

She scooted over, making room for him. She silently thanked whatever force in her life was responsible for her dislike of slinky nightgowns. She was conscious enough of her state of dress as it was.

Max, she recalled, had never been a Mets fan.

"I'll cut off the old bandage first," she said, keeping her tone perfunctory and her mind on the matter at hand. She grabbed up the scissors and unceremoniously stuck one blade under the bandage and snipped it in two.

Max watched her dubiously. "I can see why you mind other people's money. Your bedside manner leaves a lot to be desired."

"I didn't cut you, did I?"

"You could have checked to make sure the bandage wasn't stuck to the wound."

"Was it?"

"No."

She grinned. "Lucky for you, huh?"

"I'd say it was lucky for you."

She dropped the bloody bandage onto the floor, to

be disposed of later. "Your threats don't scare me, Max Slade. In any pain?"

"Not at the moment."

"That's what I figured. Looks as if the bleeding's stopped again. Want any antibiotic ointment?"

He shook his head, his slate eyes narrowed on her as she continued, rather inefficiently, with her work. Her hands were shaking. This time, it wasn't because of nervousness. It was, quite simply, because Max Slade was on her bed.

But not *in* it. There was a difference, she reminded herself.

"Hold still," she ordered. "Let me get a good look at this thing before I cover it up again." She peered at the jagged wound, but saw nothing that struck her as out of the ordinary, except for the well-developed muscle. "Did you hit your arm on something and open it up?"

"Must have. I don't really remember. I've been distracted today."

"A lot on your mind?"

"Mmm." His eyes stayed on her, darkening.

"I guess the ranch is a big responsibility." She kept her tone light as she tended his wound, her mouth still dry, awareness—of him, of herself, of the dark, quiet night—swirling through her. "There's more involved in raising and minding a bunch of horses than I ever thought."

"It's not the ranch," he said.

She swallowed. "Hold your arm out some so I can get the gauze around it."

Without comment, he did as she asked. She slipped the length of gauze under his arm, her fingers brushing against his chest. It had been distracting before, in

the kitchen. Now, with nightfall and their intimate surroundings, it was downright unnerving. She lost her
grip on the bandage, but caught it up again.

Max noticed. "Nervous?" he asked.

She licked her lips, aware of him watching her. "I
just don't want to hurt you."

"You won't." His smile almost reached his eyes. "I'm
tough."

"Not as tough as that nail you snagged." She had
him hold the bandage in place while she cut a piece of
adhesive tape, having less trouble with it folding back
on itself than she had earlier. "If I ever live out in the
wilderness, I'd make sure I took a class in advanced
first aid. Of course, Jimmy says this really isn't the
wilderness."

"By his standards, it's not."

"Well, he's never been to New York."

"True. That's more his idea of the wilderness."

In another few seconds, she had the bandage se-
cured. "There," she said, proudly, her relief palpable
as she sat back away from him. "Done."

"Thanks."

She looked at him. "I didn't hurt you, did I?"

"No. Calley—" He raised a hand, brushing his
knuckles across her cheek. "You didn't hurt me."

"Max—"

"I was the one who hurt you. I wish I never had. I
wish I could have that day back four years ago when I
didn't finish my letter to you, didn't call, didn't come
see you."

"Me, too. Not so you could have called me, but so
I could have tracked you down. It wouldn't have been
difficult. Look how fast your brothers found me. I could

have found you. If you'd been the heel I thought you were, I could have had my revenge and gone on with my life." She twisted her hands together, wishing they would stop trembling. "But what's done is done."

"I'm glad you came to Wyoming, Calley."

She nodded. "Me, too." Awareness and arousal shimmered through her, startlingly powerful, impossible to ignore. "My friends are all tired of hearing me curse you to the rafters."

He smiled, touching one finger to the corner of her mouth. This time, she was telling him the truth, admitting in her own way she'd been hurt. "You must have missed me to keep cursing me after four years."

"You're such a cocky bastard, Slade."

His smile broadened, and he leaned in closer, his mouth almost on hers. "Tell me you didn't miss me."

Arousal washed through her, sensitizing every inch of her body. She could have kicked him out. He would have gone. She trusted him to leave if she asked him to.

But she didn't want to ask him to leave.

And there it was, she thought. The undeniable, simple truth of the matter. She wanted Max to stay with her, to make love to her. There was no doubt in her mind.

"Did *you* miss *me?*" she asked softly.

His hand dropped from her face, down her neck, then skimmed her breasts. She gasped at the sensations pulsing through her. His eyes locked with hers. "Every day," he whispered, and his mouth closed over hers. He explored, tasted, teased until her breath came in short, shallow gasps. They fell back together against the pillows. Somehow, he caught the hem of her nightshirt and raised it up, gazing all the while at the skin he exposed, as if drinking in the very sight of her. She'd never experienced anything so erotic.

"I've dreamed about this moment," he murmured, sliding both hands, his wound not interfering, up her abdomen, until he cupped her breasts with his palms. His mouth followed. She could feel herself losing control. Then he slipped one hand between her thighs, and she cried out.

He raised his eyes to her. "Did you miss me, Calley?"

"Yes. I tried to make myself stop, but I couldn't."

"I know. There were times I thought I'd die if I didn't see you."

She shut her eyes at his admission and tried to tell herself he was just speaking out of the passion of the moment, that she couldn't take his words to heart. But she found that she wanted to believe him. Needed to.

He pulled the nightshirt over her head, and she opened her eyes as he cast it aside, gazing at her as if for the first time. To her surprise, she felt no embarrassment, no awkwardness, just the overwhelming sensation that this was right. He was different. She was different. Yet what they'd been together four years ago was a part of them.

"Calley..."

"It's okay. I'm not changing my mind."

His eyes reached hers, but he said nothing, swiftly removing his jeans and discarding them in a heap. When he came back to her, his body was sleek and hard and even sexier than she remembered. She wanted to touch him, feel him, stroke him everywhere. She would never get enough of him, she realized. She would never stop wanting him. It wasn't just physical desire at work; it was the longings of her heart, her very soul.

But he had broken her heart. Four years later, she finally knew why. Four years later, she finally understood. There was, however, no going back and picking up where they'd left off. If loving Max Slade was a part of her, so was being angry with him, knowing how deeply he'd hurt her, then accepting it and moving on.

All she could do was open herself to him, to herself and her own need and longings. She wanted to feel him pulsing inside her again. She wanted to ease the unspeakable ache that had her quivering and quaking all over.

"Max…there's something…I need to tell you…." She caught her breath, willed herself to be coherent. "There's been no one else since you."

He got her meaning immediately, inhaled deeply, his control shredded. "Calley…"

"Don't. Don't say anything else. It doesn't affect anything. I just wanted you to know."

"But you sacrificed—"

"I didn't sacrifice a thing, Max." She ran one palm up his smooth, hard back and smiled to herself. "Not a thing. New York's social life isn't all it's cracked up to be, I guess."

"I never would have expected you not to have anyone else."

She gave him a wry smile. "I didn't expect it of myself."

"It wouldn't have mattered—"

"It *doesn't* matter."

He kissed her then, a long, deep kiss that made her glad she'd spoken up when she had, because now she couldn't speak, couldn't even begin to articulate any of what she thought or felt with any coherency. She couldn't remember wanting him as much as she did now. In every way she could manage, she communicated that want to him, until finally, slick and hard with need himself, he slipped inside her, and all she'd felt for him four long, long years ago was fresh again.

Later, when the night was again quiet and they lay together in the darkness, she could feel him breathing, and she knew she never wanted to be without him in her life.

But out of nowhere, he said, "I mean to keep my promise to you."

"What promise?"

He turned onto his side, his eyes lost in the dark night. "To put you on your plane back to New York."

"Then tonight doesn't matter?"

"It matters. It just doesn't change anything. You belong in New York," he said, "and I belong here."

Long after Max had fallen asleep, Calley lay with her eyes wide open. Max Slade was a stubborn man, determined to do the right thing by her, especially after their last, disastrous parting. And she'd forced him to make that blasted promise. He *would* put her on a plane to New York. In his mind, it would be fhe right thing to do.

Well, she thought, snuggling closer to him, she would just have to outwit him. As she drifted off to sleep, a plan started to form.

Chapter 10

Saying goodbye to Timothy and Wynne was painful, but saying goodbye to Christopher was worst of all. Calley found him out back behind the stable waiting for Fred to slither out of his hole.

"I think I'm going to write a poem about snakes," he said without looking up at her.

"What kind of snakes?"

"All kinds."

"You've seen your share, I suppose."

He squinted up at her, too much knowledge, too much disappointment, in those young Slade eyes. "I have."

It wasn't even nine o'clock, a bright, sunny, startlingly clear morning. Calley had on a functional travel outfit of black chinos, white shirt and sneakers. Max was insisting on driving her to the airport. She hadn't bothered trying to argue him out of making her go back to New York. She had extracted a promise from him to make her go. He needed to keep that promise. She needed him to keep it.

But she didn't want to go.

She cleared her throat, reminding herself that Christopher Slade had endured far worse pain than having a woman he'd known for all of two weeks head back home. But there had been all those weeks on the computer, too. "You still have my email address. You can write to me."

He shrugged his bony shoulders. "I might."

"Christopher—"

"You'd better go. You don't want to miss your plane."

"Christopher, I want you to know I don't regret coming to Wyoming. I've had a wonderful time. I'm not sorry you weren't Jill Baxter." She smiled, but he'd turned back to his snake hole. She sighed. "I'm glad you're you."

He ignored her.

It had been a lame statement anyway. She was glad he was Christopher Slade instead of Jill Baxter. At least the kid had known all along who *he* was. The problem was who Calley was. Who she was, what she wanted, where she wanted to be. When she'd come to Wyoming, she thought she knew. She was Calley Hastings of New York, New York, financial planner, a woman who loathed Max Slade.

Well, she was still a financial planner, still Calley Hastings.

"I've got to go," she said, her voice cracking. Not since she'd been a kid herself had a kid seen her cry. What good would tears do Christopher Slade?

He didn't look back at her. "So go ahead. Go."

She touched his shoulder. He had on a ragged T-shirt, ragged shorts. He had plenty of nonragged clothes. She figured it was his penniless-poet look. He was eleven, after all. Still trying on new identities. In a way, so was she.

"Christopher, if you'll promise…"

But she stopped herself. She couldn't make him promise not to tell Max something. Max was his older brother, his guardian and as much as he would ever have in the way of a father. It would be irresponsible to undermine their trust in each other. She bit down on one corner of her mouth. Such complications. Of course, she'd never been one to think parenting would be easy.

Christopher turned to her, expectant.

She sighed. "There's no reason we can't still be friends."

He looked back at his snake hole, disgusted.

There was no patronizing the kid, Calley thought. He saw through everything. She inhaled, hating to see him so obviously disappointed that her two weeks on Black Creek Ranch had come to naught. But her relationship with his big brother was complicated, and there were things about her and Max an eleven-year-old just didn't need to know.

"Okay. I'll be as straight with you as I can."

He refused to meet her eyes one more time. Jimmy would have climbed all over him for being rude, but Calley understood. Somewhere, deep in that cowboy poet's soul of his, Christopher Slade knew that she and Max were in love with each other.

"Just remember," she said to his back. "I have a plan."

He shot her a quick, sideways look, then gave her a grin that was pure, conniving, unadulterated Slade.

Max, his three younger brothers and Jimmy Baxter arrived in New York on a warm, clear summer day ten days after Max had put Calley Hastings on her plane east. She hadn't kicked and screamed. She hadn't begged to stay in Wyoming. She had simply said, "I'm glad I came, Max. I enjoyed meeting your brothers and Jimmy and seeing the ranch. It was a good vacation. I guess I needed the break more than I realized. New York will probably never be the same to me again."

She had intended, Max was quite certain, to sound as if she were being perfectly sensible and meant to get on with her life and stay in New York where she belonged. She wouldn't kick and scream and pitch a fit and pretend she wanted to live with him and Jimmy and his three brothers on a ranch in Wyoming.

But Max had detected a gleam in her eye, a kick in her step, that suggested Calley Hastings was devising herself a big plot.

In the past, her plots had usually involved money. Now that she'd seen Wyoming, Max just didn't know. He'd let her go, expecting he would find out his answer soon enough.

Then, a day or two after her departure, Jimmy had let it slip about the carpenters.

"What carpenters?" Max had said.

"Uh—uh—" Jimmy had said.

"Jimmy, what's going on?"

"Calley—well—she—" But Jimmy was no good at dissembling, and he'd finally spit it out in his own way. "That woman of yours wants to turn my storage room into an office. She lined up carpenters to come take a look."

"Whose office?"

"Nope. Uh-uh. I said I'd keep my mouth shut."

Then, after that, the delivery man had arrived with the mountain bikes and the tent.

"What mountain bikes?" Max had asked. "What tent?"

Christopher had bit back a grin as if he knew exactly what mountain bikes, what tent. He and his two younger brothers tore open the boxes. Wynne produced a card and immediately recognized Calley's name on it, jumping up and down with unseemly delight. Timothy had grabbed the card out of his hand and read it. "Calley—um—she says this is a thank-you present."

"A thank-you for what?" Max had growled.

"For her vacation. 'If it weren't for you boys, I might never have seen Wyoming. I hope you like my surprise.'"

It had been one hell of a surprise. With five mountain bikes and a tent big enough for a platoon on his front porch, Max knew what the gleam in Calley's eye had been all about. A graceful exit from Black Creek Ranch just wasn't in her.

"I think she's coming back," Wynne had blurted.

Christopher couldn't stop grinning. The rascal *knew* she was coming back. Max just couldn't be sure if it was that damned poet's soul of his talking, or if Calley had taken him into her confidence. He wasn't going to put the kid on the spot by demanding to know which it was.

Instead, he'd booked five round-trip tickets to New York, New York.

He was relieved the weather wasn't hazy, hot and

humid. The boys might not have minded, but swelter-
ing heat would have sent Jimmy right back to Wyoming.
It was all the old cowboy could do to endure traffic,
noise, tall buildings and millions of people crammed
together. He had only agreed to come because Max
needed him to watch the boys while he got to the bottom of Calley Hastings—and her carpenters, tents and
mountain bikes.

They took a cab to their small, boutique-style hotel
on the Upper East Side. It was built at the turn of the
century, located in the midst of some of New York's
finest museums, which thrilled Christopher. Timothy
was more intrigued by the bagelry down on the corner.
He couldn't wait to try New York bagels. Wynne was
happy just riding the ornate elevator. Jimmy tolerated
his surroundings as he would a desert dust storm. He
muttered incessantly about smog, claustrophobia and
the hotel's decor, which apparently reminded him of
a "house of ill repute" he'd "heard of" back in his old
cowboy days.

Max had promised the boys a ball game and visits to
the Empire State Building, the Statue of Liberty and the
dinosaur skeletons in the Museum of Natural History.

They just had to give him time to deal with Calley.

"You don't know where she lives?" Timothy asked.

"Oh, I know where she lives. She hates to move.
She has an apartment on the Upper West Side, across
Central Park from us. We're on the Upper East Side."

"East side of what?" Christopher asked.

"Manhattan's an island. The numbered streets go
across it, east to west. The further north, the higher the
number. The avenues run lengthwise, north to south.

Fifth Avenue's the dividing line between east and west. Check out your map. There's a logic to it."

"Wow," Wynne said, as if he understood everything Max had said.

Christopher was gazing out one of the windows in the suite Max had reserved. "I can't believe you used to live here."

"For seven years," Max said, trying to remember the man he'd been then. Seven years in New York, four years in Wyoming. A lot had changed.

Wynne emerged from the bathroom with a little basket of complimentary toiletries, which he promptly dumped on the bed. Max smiled. His brothers would have a grand time during their week in New York. It wouldn't take much to keep them happy. An elevator, a view of the street, little bars of soap.

Jimmy was another matter. He was pacing back and forth with his bad leg, muttering about city folk.

"The hotel offers a complimentary afternoon tea," Max told him. "Maybe you can take the boys down while I'm gone. They have a live harpist."

Jimmy grunted. "Better'n a dead one."

Max laughed, and headed out into the streets of Manhattan. He knew he didn't belong here, not anymore. There was no question of that. The only question, he thought, was where Calley Hastings thought she belonged.

Calley walked up West End Avenue, barely aware of the crush of rush-hour traffic as she enjoyed the beautiful late-summer afternoon. No matter what her future held, she knew she would always love New York. It was her city. It was where she had established her career and made so many friends, and it was where she had first fallen in love with Max Slade.

She had fallen in love with him a second time on Black Creek Ranch, Wyoming.

Of all places, she thought. Who would have ever guessed it? She glanced up at the residential buildings of the Upper West Side. In many ways, Wyoming might have been on another planet. Yet she could almost smell the wildflowers in the meadow beyond the stables, hear the horses in the pasture. Her friends thought she was coming unglued. Why *Wyoming?* they would say. Because Max Slade was there. Ah, they would counter, wasn't he the one who'd turned her off romance? Hadn't she found a dried rose he'd given her for Valentine's Day and burned it and thrown the ashes off her roof?

Yes. That was her Max. He was pig-headed and stupidly honorable and utterly reliable, if only he could trust her to make up her own mind about things.

By the time she reached the lobby of her building, she'd worked up a good head of steam.

And there was Max Slade, chatting with the doorman. He might have just climbed off a horse. Nothing about him suggested he'd ever lived in New York or ever would.

Calley stood rock still. Maybe she'd just conjured him up. After a week, she was allowed.

Then his slate eyes fell on her. He was real.

She inhaled. "Max."

"Afternoon, Calley."

"What are you doing here?"

"Rumor has it someone in this building's been fantasizing about a tall, dark rancher sweeping her off to Wyoming."

She felt blood rush to her cheeks as the doorman looked at her in surprised amusement. She cleared her throat. Max Slade certainly could play havoc with her reputation. "You're not supposed to be here—"

He smiled, confident. "I know."

"You—" She frowned, growing wary. "What do you know?"

"Maybe we should talk up in your apartment."

She glanced at the doorman, who was watching with interest, never having seen Calley Hastings with a man so obviously not from the East. She didn't remember Max sticking out four years ago. But, of course, that was one of the reasons he'd gone back to Wyoming. Because deep down, he'd known he was trying to be something he wasn't in New York, trying to fit into a life in which he didn't belong. She understood that now.

But first she had to get him out of her lobby.

"I'm on the tenth floor," she said, briskly leading the way to the elevator.

"I remember."

His voice, deep and deliberately languid, curled up her spine. She banged the Up button. Fortunately, the elevator was right there. Unfortunately, it was small and without air-conditioning. Standing next to him, she found herself assaulted with memories of the second time they'd made love that night in Wyoming, their bodies hot and wanting.

He smiled. "You're squirming, Calley."

"I can't believe you're here."

"The element of surprise," he said.

"Are you alone?"

"Jimmy's with the boys back at the hotel."

New Yorker that she was, she couldn't resist asking

him which hotel. His choice met her approval, especially if he planned to take the boys to the major museums. She started to suggest restaurants, but Max stopped her.

"Calley, I'm not here just to show the boys around New York."

She licked her lips. "Max—I'm not—I can't—" She sighed. "Dammit, I'm not *ready* for you."

He leaned back against the elevator, one leg bent. Cocky, sexy. Amused. "You never will be."

That brought her up straight. "You're such a smug bastard, Slade."

"And you're so much fun to catch in the act. Spoiled your plans, didn't I?"

She tossed her head back. "Maybe not. Maybe it's better this way."

The elevator stopped, and the doors opened. Calley went ahead of him. She could feel his presence close behind her. He made no smart remarks about life in New York as she unlocked the series of locks on her door and pushed it open.

"After you," she said, motioning broadly.

Her one-bedroom apartment was small and charming, bathed in the strong late-afternoon sunlight. In the four years since Max had exited from her life, she'd added personal touches, making the place feminine, sophisticated, very much a reflection of her own personality. She'd painted the walls in shades of cranberry, had the love seat and high-backed chair covered in a flowered print, put up chintz drapes, as if thumbing her nose at the idea of ever sharing her space with a man.

Max seemed as out of place standing in front of her butler's table in her living room as she must have seemed caught in a staring match with his Frisbee-playing turkey out on Black Creek Ranch. Yet he didn't seem to mind. He didn't seem any less masculine, any less confident of himself and his mission.

"Something to drink?" Calley asked briskly.

"Ice tea would be nice."

On Black Creek Ranch, Jimmy Baxter would put out a huge jar and make "sun tea." Calley used a mix, sometimes cans. When the mood struck and she had the time, she would make up a pot of loose-leaf tea and pour it over ice. But she offered no apologies when she returned to the living room with two tall glasses of ice tea from a mix. She'd made sure there was no powder on the edge of Max's glass. Hers she didn't care about. She was so taken aback by his presence she could have been drinking straight powder.

Max sipped his ice tea without comment. Calley followed his gaze to the fabric swatches spread out on the butler's table and the stack of wallpaper books underneath it. She winced. Caught in the act indeed.

"Redoing your apartment?" he asked. His tone was deceptively mild. He was daring her to lie to him.

He knew everything, Calley decided. She took a huge gulp of her ice tea. "Jimmy ratted me out?"

"You ratted yourself out. You went behind my back. You tried to manipulate me."

"Manipulate *you?*" she scoffed. "That I'd like to see."

"You know what you did."

She shrugged, drinking more of her tea, trying to ignore the shaking in her knees. "A tactical decision."

"Calley."

"That's the truth."

"You made me look like a bad guy to my whole family."

"How?"

"One, it seems I don't know what's going on in my own house. Carpenters, tents, mountain bikes. Two—"

"You forgot the air mattresses," Calley said, dropping onto the love seat before her knees gave out. This wasn't going according to plan. Max had messed up everything.

He glared at her. He wasn't about to sit down. "What air mattresses?"

"They must be on back order. Well, that surprise is out of the bag."

"Calley."

She blinked at him. "You don't think I'd go camping without an air mattress, do you?"

"Who said anything about you going camping?"

"Yes. Well. Never mind about that, then. Go on. What's the second way I made you look like a villain?"

He bit off a sigh. He wasn't finished with her camping plans, she could see. "All right. I'll move on. My family thinks I'm the villain because I'm the one who put you on the plane back to New York."

"You didn't force me onto the plane at gunpoint."

"But I didn't ask you to stay."

She waved a hand in dismissal. "It wouldn't have made any difference. You were honor bound to make sure I got back home, even if I'd said I wanted to stay."

"Which you didn't," he argued.

"True."

He moved toward her, his expression unreadable. "Calley, what are you trying to accomplish?"

She leaned back and crossed her legs, swinging her ankle, trying to look more casual than she felt. "I am trying to get you to let me decide for myself what I want and where I belong. I am trying to get you to *trust* me."

"Let you?" He tightened both hands into fists as he obviously reined in his self-control. "I'd like to know who the hell could keep you from doing something you set your mind to."

"You did four years ago when you left New York. You didn't give me the chance to make up my own mind about what I wanted." She spoke quietly, without anger, because she felt none. She'd come a long way in her opinion of Max Slade since departing for Wyoming several weeks ago. "I understand why you did what you did. But I'm not going to allow your sense of duty and honor to determine my course of action. I had to find a way to convince you that I—to show you that I—" She broke off, floundering, annoyed with herself.

"That you what, Calley?"

His eyes, his voice, his stance—everything about Max was intense, on alert. She shifted restlessly on the love seat, then exhaled at the ceiling. "That I deserve to make up my own mind."

"Ah." His tone was disbelieving, as if he knew she would back away from telling him the whole truth. "Am I to conclude by your conduct you want to move to Wyoming?"

"That would be one conclusion."

"What would be another?"

"I want to go camping."

He gave her a hard, dark look. "Calley."

She shot to her feet, agitated, suddenly very warm. "Max, maybe you did me a favor four years ago. You made it easy for me to stay here. If you'd asked me to go with you to Wyoming with your father and Lissa dead and three confused, grieving little boys to raise, I don't know what I would have done. I might have gone with you, I might have stayed in New York. It doesn't matter. It's a moot point. But I've had four additional years here. I've had a great life." She gave him a small smile. "Even loathing you became sort of fun. My combat wounds, so to speak."

He didn't smile back. "I wish I could have found a way not to hurt you."

"No. No, don't, Max. Don't beat yourself up over what you did. You tried to spare me. You tried to do the right thing by your brothers, your father, the people who make their living off the ranch. You *did* do the right thing. And that's not my point. Yes, I love New York. It has its problems, but I love its energy, the people, my work."

"I wouldn't ask you to give up your life here."

She held up a hand, stopping him, trying not to relent before she'd finished. "But I fell for a sob story about a widow in Wyoming not just because Christopher, Timothy and Wynne were good, but because I was a prime candidate for swallowing such a story. Something was missing in my own life. I think I went to Wyoming to see if I could figure out what it was."

"Did you?" Max asked softly, not moving toward her.

"Yes. It was missing you, the boys, Jimmy, the ranch."

"Calley—"

"The carpenters, the tent, the mountain bikes, the air mattresses—they were just an attempt to find a way to get you to believe that I've changed. I'm not the same woman who needed to stay in New York four years ago."

"Calley." His voice was more insistent, and she stopped, giving him his chance to speak. He moved close to her, then ran his thumb along her lower lip. Just that feathery touch sent shivers of awareness through her. Finally, he said, "Tell me where you belong."

"You won't believe me."

"Tell me, Calley."

She swallowed, meeting his dark eyes. "I belong with you."

For a long moment, he didn't speak, and neither did she. Then he withdrew something from the pocket of his tan canvas pants and handed it to her.

It was a ticket from Jackson, Wyoming, to New York, New York. Calley glanced at it, confused. He was here. Obviously, he'd flown.

"Look at the purchase date," he said.

She did so. The ticket had been purchased the same day she'd left Wyoming for New York over a week ago. She frowned at him. "I don't understand."

He smiled. "I bought this ticket the minute you took off. I knew I had to find a way to keep you in my life. If it came to it, I was willing to divide my time between New York and Wyoming, anything if it meant not losing you. Then Jimmy spilled the news about your devious ways, then that stuff landed on my porch and I figured I had to fight fire with fire. So here we are."

"Max—"

"I love you, Calley Hastings. I have for a long, long time." He kissed her deeply, gently, and whispered into her mouth, "And I believe you."

Epilogue

Christopher tacked up pictures of Max and Calley's wedding on the bulletin board in his room, next to the pictures of his trip to New York City. They'd gotten married right away in a simple service held at the ranch. They figured they'd waited long enough. Jimmy and John Parker had cooked, and friends from New York and Wyoming had come. Even Max's mother had flown in from San Francisco. Wynne had served as ring bearer. Timothy as usher. Christopher had served as his brother's best man.

There was one picture of the five of them, with the dogs lying at their feet and Lucky holding in his beak the new, shocking pink Frisbee Calley had bought him. Max had vetoed Timothy fetching Fred.

But Christopher's eyes kept drifting to his pictures of New York. What a trip. He would never forget it.

He'd particularly loved the Statue of Liberty and the view of the New York skyline at night. He'd told Max he wanted to live in New York someday. Max had said that would be fine, if it was what Christopher wanted. He knew their father hadn't been so agreeable when Max had expressed the same desire. But Christopher also knew that Max would never hold his brothers to the ranch.

Timothy was downstairs playing the piano. Calley had had it tuned. She played in the evening sometimes. Christopher tolerated ragtime, but he wasn't much on most of the other stuff she played.

Wynne was "helping" Calley and Max wallpaper her new office. The carpenters had left yesterday, after expanding Jimmy's old storage room to her liking. She had lots of windows with views of the mountains and the river. Her equipment would be arriving in a few days. She already had a half-dozen clients.

His last wedding picture tacked up, Christopher grabbed his blank book and ventured downstairs. He had no desire to be put to work. He particularly hated wallpapering. He slipped past Timothy at the piano out to the front porch, then ran around back to the stable. It was a coolish, late-summer evening, perfect for his purposes.

He ducked into the storage room and pulled on the lightbulb overhead. Max's old trunk was gone. Calley had appropriated it for her office, and they'd all gone through the photo albums together, her and Max and Timothy and Wynne and Christopher. Even Jimmy had checked out a few of the pictures, commenting on how full of himself Max was back in those days. Christopher had snuck out the one of his brother and Calley on the steps of what he now knew was the New York Metropolitan Museum of Fine Arts. He'd had it blown up and framed for their wedding present.

But now he sat on the floor of the storage room and leaned back against the old desk, and opened his blank book. He closed his eyes and thought of his mother and his father, and then of Max just that morning at breakfast, smiling the way he had in that picture on the museum steps four years ago. And he thought of a poem, and he wrote.

* * * * *

THE TEXAS RANCHER'S
MARRIAGE

Cathy Gillen Thacker

Chapter 1

"Breathe."

Merri Duncan turned to her best friend, Emily Mc-Cabe Reeves, aware she had never been so nervous in her life.

"That obvious, hmm?" Merri drawled, glad she had thought to get a babysitter for the twins. Right now, as they all waited for their beloved guest of honor to show, she could barely contain herself, never mind two rowdy preschoolers.

Over two hundred other local residents and family friends had gathered on the Armstrong ranch. Texas barbecue scented the air. A country and western band warmed up next to the dance floors set up on the lawn.

"I know the last time Chase was home was pretty awful," Emily commiserated.

"An understatement," Merri murmured back. Together, she and Chase had weathered the aftermath of a horrific helicopter crash, and buried her sister and his brother. Then Merri had taken custody of Sasha and Scott's eight-week-old infants, and Chase had headed back to the army field hospital in the Middle East.

Four and a half years had passed.

Chase hadn't been back to the States since.

Although Merri and the twins had heard from him sporadically—mostly at Christmas, and on birthdays— the big, strapping Texan never disclosed what he intended to do, long-term.

If anything… All Merri knew for sure was that he had finally completed his tour of duty and had accepted a job at the Laramie Community Hospital.

She and the twins were now settled comfortably on the once-luxurious ranch where Chase and his brother had grown up, and where her business, though still small, was thriving. In addition to the excitement and upheaval of Chase's homecoming, the Christmas holidays were approaching and Thanksgiving was just a few days away.

Merri released a tremulous sigh. Life sure had a way of taking unexpected turns.

And she had the nagging feeling that as soon as she and Chase talked about the information she had accidentally discovered, her already complicated life would take another unscripted detour. Merri knew from firsthand experience that the circumstances of the twins' origins would not be dealt with as simply as she had initially hoped. And soon, like it or not, Chase would realize that, too.

Misreading the reason behind Merri's obvious apprehension, Emily gave her friend an encouraging hug.

"Stop worrying! It's going to be a great welcome home party for Chase."

Merri sure hoped so. The returning trauma surgeon deserved to be celebrated for the true hero he was.

And she…she needed to stop agonizing.

Chase was a decent guy, and he would do the right thing, just as he always had. In fact, that was likely the reason he was back—to lend a hand in the way only he could.

Although what he would want to tell people about the truth of their situation was as much a mystery as it ever had been.

Emily smiled and lifted her arm in an excited wave as her husband's pickup truck turned into the long, tree-lined drive. "Here they come now!"

Merri slipped into the ranch house and emerged with the twins in hand.

Curly blond heads tilted upward and their big brown eyes gleamed excitedly as they watched the truck come to a halt. A tall man emerged from the passenger seat, and when Merri got a look at Chase Armstrong, her heart took a little leap.

She hadn't realized until this very moment how scared she had been. That something would happen over there and the sexy physician wouldn't come back. At least not alive.

But there was no question the ruggedly handsome, sandy-haired man was very *much* alive.

His skin was tanned, his shoulders every bit as wide and inviting as she recalled, his body lean and hard and solidly muscled enough to make her insides quiver. He should have looked tired and unkempt after the long flight, but his face was cleanly shaved, his short, clipped hair as neat and clean as the army fatigues he wore.

Dark sunglasses shaded his beautiful amber eyes, and a slow grin tugged at the corners of his sensual lips as, with an unhurried stride, he moved toward the crowd waiting to greet him.

A cheer went up.

Caught in the raw emotion of the moment, Merri found herself cheering, too.

The crowd parted. Chase continued on his mission, coming closer still. Then he was standing directly before her and the kids, lazily taking off his sunglasses and slipping them into the pocket of his shirt.

At six foot four, he had always dwarfed her five-foot-seven frame. Today was no exception; she had to tilt her head back to look up at him.

And as their eyes met and held, there was absolutely no clue in his about what he intended to do about this fix they were in. Or when he planned to talk to her about the biggest conundrum of all.

Chase knew coming back to the only real home he had ever known was going to be difficult.

Just being on the ranch reminded him of the family he'd lost and the nonstop disappointment life had brought his way.

Seeing the crowd gathered on the property he could no longer call home made it even harder.

It reminded him of the aftermath of the dual funerals, when everyone who had ever cared about Scott and Sasha had stopped by to pay their respects. And the burials of his parents, in the half-dozen years before that.

There had been a lot of loss on the Broken Arrow Ranch. Now the future of it was embodied in the two impossibly cute preschoolers holding on to Merri Duncan's hands.

Their sweet, cherubic appearance was no surprise. He had seen dozens of photos and the occasional video of the kids during the years he had been overseas, so was well-versed in the milestone events of Jeffrey and Jessalyn's infant and toddler days.

But Merri had always managed to keep herself out of the photos.

And now Chase could not help but be stunned by the changes he saw. Her shoulder-length, golden-blond hair was still thick and silky, her face just as elegantly beautiful, her wide, friendly smile as arresting as ever. But there was a soft, maternal air about her now. A tenderness in the way she gently clasped the twins' hands, and held them even closer to her sides. A new maturity—as well as a lingering question—in her pretty, glacier-green eyes. And a lithe, sexy body that made him all too aware just how long it had been since he'd been physically close to any woman.

Too long.

Their eyes locked and his heartbeat kicked up.

Warning himself to play it cool, he leaned over to give her a casual one-armed hug and a light kiss on the brow.

"Welcome home," she said in a husky voice.

Her emotion was contagious. Chase cleared his throat to get rid of the catch in his own voice. "Thanks." He released Merri as quickly and efficiently as he had hugged her, and then knelt before the kids.

Jeffrey and Jessalyn regarded him shyly.

"Say hello to Chase," Merri prodded.

An awkward silence fell. The twins stared at him mutely, probably still deciding if he was friend or foe. To his disappointment, they seemed inclined to put him in the latter category.

Deciding it would be best not to push them, Chase looked into their eyes. He smiled at them reassuringly once again, letting them know they could trust him, then stood. "It's okay," he told a concerned Merri under his breath. "We'll have a chance to get acquainted later."

Eyes glistening, she nodded, as if suddenly not trusting herself to speak.

Chase knew exactly how she felt. Confronted with the only real family he had left, he had a lump in his throat, too.

He had never expected to feel so alone and adrift at this point in his life. But maybe that would change now that he was back in Laramie. Back where he'd grown up, Chase thought, as familiar figures came forward to shake his hand and give him a hug.

"Hey, Chase!" His old high school classmate, Travis Anderson, stepped up to shake his hand. "Didn't think we'd ever see you again!"

"Great to have you back in Texas!" His former high school English teacher beamed. "Don't leave us again, you understand? We missed you!"

"I was beginning to think you'd left us for good," the owner of Sonny's Barbecue teased, giving him a slap on the back...and a hug. "Come by and see me when you get a little time."

And so it went. Everyone complaining good-naturedly about how long he'd been gone, worrying

he'd up and leave Laramie County again, warning him
that if he did take off again their hearts would be broken beyond repair. The twins' eyes got even wider as
they soaked it all in.

"I think you'd all survive," Chase joshed back when
the rush of sentiment got a little much. Any more of this
and they'd have him getting all weepy, too.

He looked around for help. Merri seemed to have
faded into the background, but members of the band—
also old pals of his—got the hint. They immediately
started playing a rowdy rendition of the perennial Texas
party favorite, "Friends in Low Places."

An appreciative roar went up. Everyone joined in the
raucous singing and swaying. Dancing soon followed.
And, to Chase's joy, the real homecoming began.

Hours later, Chase and Merri stood side by side as
the last of the taillights disappeared down the drive. It
was the first time they'd been alone since he arrived,
and Chase was more than a little aware of her. Not that
this was a surprise. The first time he had seen her, at
his brother's engagement party, he'd wanted her. But
Merri had been living with another guy and practically engaged, so he'd done the honorable thing and
walked away.

She turned to him now with heartfelt apology. "I'm
sorry about the cool reception you received from the
twins."

Cognizant that he probably should have expected
as much, given how little contact they'd had, Chase
shrugged. "Don't worry about it."

"I tried to prepare them for actually meeting you,

instead of just seeing your face on the screen in a video chat, or hearing your voice on the phone."

Which, Chase reflected, given some of the rough-and-tumble sites where he had been stationed, hadn't happened all that frequently. He tore his eyes from the curves beneath Merri's snug-fitting T-shirt, cropped denim jacket and jeans. Her burgundy western boots were nice, too. Obviously custom, from Monroe's. He recognized the signature Texas rose hidden in the fancy feminine embroidery adorning the sides.

"But I'm not sure they believed it was really going to happen," Merri continued, oblivious of the impact she was having on him. "Or understood what your coming here would mean to them." She released a sigh. "Because at the time I told them, I wasn't sure if you were just coming for a visit or staying long-term."

Had she always smelled this good? Like lavender... and woman? Wishing he could make a move on her, without complicating things unnecessarily, Chase shrugged. "I'm sorry about that." Because the kids were already inside, fast asleep, he remained on the porch, speaking quietly with Merri. His gaze roved her upturned face. Although she'd been gorgeous in daylight, she looked even more radiant in the soft glow of the porch light.

Gruffly, he confessed, "I didn't know what I was going to do myself till a few days ago." It had been a tough decision to make. Complicated by the fact that if he came back to stay, Merri was going to expect him to be an uncle to the kids, and behave in a brotherly fashion to her. And his feelings for her were anything but fraternal. Although, thankfully for both of them, she didn't know that.

Merri studied him, a new realism shining in her lovely green eyes. As if the fairy-tale wishes she had once harbored had faded, and she knew now what life was—and what it wasn't. She stepped a little closer, further inundating him in her deliciously feminine scent. "You were really thinking of reenlisting?"

Chase ignored the mounting desire generated by her closeness; and the sight of her running a delicate hand through the soft, thick layers of her honey-blond hair. "It's important work. I made a lot of good friends over there. But…there's important work to be done here, too, and I also have a lot of friends here, so…I finally decided to come home."

Chase saw her shiver a little in the cooling night air. She pulled the edges of her jacket together, but not before he noted her physical reaction to the declining temperature.

"I'm glad you did." Flushing self-consciously, she said, "I know the kids are, too. They just don't know how to express it yet. In any case, I prepared the guest room for you."

"You don't have to put me up tonight," Chase said. "I can sleep in an on-call room at the hospital, till I have time to find a place." Thanks to the local auto dealer's cooperation in making an advance sale, he even had a brand-new pickup truck to drive, waiting in the parking area next to the ranch house.

A mixture of disappointment and guilt colored her expression. "This is your home."

"It was once," Chase agreed, his tone flat, as old decisions neither of them had anything to do with came back to haunt them once again. He brushed aside the hurt he'd felt for years now. The hurt that had helped keep him away, and made him wonder if he should return to Laramie County at all. "But not anymore."

Merri wondered if this was the reason behind the rift that had existed between Chase and his younger brother. One that had seemed to only get bigger as time passed, reaching a point of no return shortly before Chase went off to war. Which, of course, made his eventual generosity regarding the birth of the twins even more difficult for her to understand.

Now that he was back, however, and going to be part of the twins' lives, it was time she rectified that.

"I never understood why your mother willed the entire property to Scott." The one-sided terms of the late Lydia Armstrong's estate had shocked everyone when the will had been read. Especially Chase, Merri remembered, because he hadn't known the disinheritance was coming.

He glanced up at the half-moon overhead, then restlessly walked the length of the porch that lined the large stone-and-cedar ranch house. His gaze traveled over the manicured lawn and the lush shrubbery, to the now-empty pastures. He didn't seem to find fault with anything he saw in the pastoral scene. Which was no surprise to Merri. She had done a good job as conservator of the property, on behalf of the twins, who had inherited it all upon their father's death.

Chase ignored the chain-hung swing at the end of the porch and ambled back to her side. "She figured I was a doctor. I'd make plenty of money and never have time to ranch. Whereas Scott needed a job and a place to live."

Merri knew enough about Scott and Sasha's self-ishness now to realize undue pressure had been ap-

plied to the elder, ailing Armstrong, her emotions likely
played upon. Because, hard as it was to admit, at the
end of the day, all Merri's sister and Chase's brother
had ever thought about was themselves. Their desires.
Their needs.

And Chase knew it, too.

Aware it was a little too intimate to be standing
there together in the semidarkness, Merri pivoted and
led him inside. "Your mom could have left you half
the land anyway," she said over her shoulder. "I mean,
we're talking about over five thousand acres! Or Scott
and Sasha could have willed the property back to you,
instead of putting it in trust for their children." *And
naming me as executor and guardian of that trust.*

In the living room, Chase watched her remove the
screen on the fireplace. He seemed as oblivious to the
chill in the air as she was sensitive to it.

"It's okay. I got over what happened a long time
ago."

Had he? Truth was, Merri couldn't see how. She
knelt before the hearth, and admitted with total frankness, "I still feel funny about us living here and you
not. It doesn't seem right."

Chase continued to watch as she arranged the firewood. "Life's not fair. We all know that."

He was right. Merri wadded up some newspa-
per and stuffed it in the gaps between the oak logs.
If it had been, her sister would have had functioning
ovaries. She would not have required donated eggs—
from Merri—to become pregnant. Had life been fair,
Scott wouldn't have needed to go to Chase for his assistance, too.

Still surprised that Chase had helped Sasha and Scott

out in the end, even after initially turning the couple down, Merri decided it was past time to ask the question that had been burning in her gut for several years now. Nervously, she blurted out, "What about the twins?"

Chase gave her a mystified look. "What about them?" he asked carefully.

She struck a match and lit the fire. "What are your intentions there?" she prodded.

Chase watched the paper take the flame, before turning his gaze to Merri again. "You're their biological mother. You should be telling me how you want this to work."

Her anxiety rose. Chase was decisive in all other areas of his life. His apathy and indifference here were daunting, to say the least. "But like it or not, you're involved, too," she persisted, trying to squeeze some emotion out of him, to get him to tell her where this predicament was likely headed. "Biologically speaking, anyway."

A tense silence fell. Chase stared at her as if she had either lost her mind or was a disaster waiting to happen. "What are you talking about?" He slowly enunciated every word.

Weary of maintaining the public ruse her late brother-in-law and sister had insisted upon, Merri looked Chase square in the eye and admitted, "A few months after Scott and Sasha died, I found the paperwork from the fertility clinic, indicating that Scott received help there, too."

Chase shrugged. "Although it wasn't common knowledge, you and I both know my brother had problems in that regard, too. That he was, for all intents and purposes, as sterile as Sasha."

"Which was why you jumped in to help, just as I did."

"And," Chase continued matter-of-factly, "set him up with the top infertility specialists at the medical school I attended."

His involvement hadn't ended there and Merri knew it. Frustration mounting, she rose and walked toward him. "Look, I don't know what kind of deal you and your brother made…probably something similar to the one I made with Sasha and him. But you don't have to hide anything from me, Chase. Not anymore. I know that you 'helped out' a heck of a lot more than just setting them up with the right professionals."

Chase studied her. "I don't know what Scott told you—or Sasha, for that matter. My brother had a way of bending the truth to suit his needs, never more so than when his back was against a wall. But I did not do what you did, Merri. I didn't offer up my genetic material to help them out." He exhaled sharply. "They asked me—before I went overseas…as you well know—but I told them I couldn't handle having a child raised by someone else, not even my own kin. It's not in me to be a spectator in my own child's life."

Merri knotted her hands in frustration. She remembered the chaos his refusal had caused among the four of them. The rift that had left Chase and his brother barely speaking. "Then why did you sign those papers, allowing Scott to use sperm you had already donated to the university for medical research, for Sasha's in vitro fertilization procedure?"

Chase's mouth dropped open in dismay. "I never signed anything."

"But you did!" Merri went to the desk, unlocked the drawer and pulled out a slender file of papers. She handed it over.

Chase studied the medical forms and legal documents. A muscle worked convulsively in his jaw. "Scott must have forged this. Damn him!"

Merri's heart sank as shock turned to comprehension. *Oh, my heaven.* "You mean…?" she croaked.

"I never gave my permission." Chase rifled through the papers, scanning them again and again, as if unable to believe what he was seeing. With anger flashing in his amber eyes, he let out a string of swear words that would have burned the ears off a nun.

Merri placed a hand over her heart, trembling, she was so upset. "So all this time… You never had a clue that you were the real father of the twins or were in any way biologically connected with them?" That certainly explained his lack of input or involvement. He hadn't thought Jessalyn and Jeffrey were family at all!

Chase sat down, scrubbed a hand over his face and dropped his head in his hands. "None whatsoever," he said miserably.

A silence fraught with heartache fell.

"So what now?" Merri asked eventually, afraid she already knew.

Chase lifted his head, already taking charge, like the kick-butt Texan he was. "We do everything and anything we have to do to make things right."

Making things right, according to Chase's world, meant verifying facts. So as soon as the hospital lab opened the next morning, Merri and Chase and the twins were there.

Unfortunately, no sooner had they all submitted to a simple and painless DNA test than Chase was summoned to the E.R., to help out with an incoming trauma.

Subsequent surgeries had him staying in the hospital on-call room overnight. And by the time Merri and Chase got to attorney Liz Cartwright Anderson's office the following afternoon, they already had the results they had expected.

Quickly, the two of them brought Liz up to speed on everything that had happened thus far. Chase concluded with, "—I never would have given my brother permission to use my sperm."

"But you were okay with the egg donation from the beginning?" Liz asked Merri.

She nodded, still at peace with what she'd done. "I knew how important it was to my sister to have a baby. Her eggs weren't viable. So for her, to have a baby with the Duncan family genetics, harvesting my eggs and implanting them in her was the only way."

"It was still a lot to ask," Chase said fiercely.

"I understood where she was coming from." Merri turned to him. "Sasha and I never knew our father. We had lost our mother. I wanted my sister to have the baby she had always dreamed about."

And, Merri added silently, *at the time I was still living with Pierce, and thought marriage and a family for me were just around the corner, too. I thought that Sasha and I would be rearing our children together.*

"My sister had promised me I would be an integral part of the twins' lives. And for those first two months, I was there so much, helping out, I practically was a second mother." Which had made taking over, in the wake of their parents' sudden, unexpected death, a lot easier than it would have been otherwise.

"What about the secrecy?" Liz continued to make notes on the legal pad in front of her. "Were you okay with that?"

"I knew the whole thing might seem weird to some people—" Merri shot a telling look at Chase "—who would probably fixate on the fact that it was my eggs and my brother-in-law's sperm making the babies."

"Except it wasn't Scott's genetic material," Chase interrupted brusquely, all domineering Texas male. "It was mine."

Merri wished he wasn't so big, strong, sexy and by the book! "Yes, well…" Merri eyed him testily, aware his take-charge attitude was really beginning to get under her skin. Almost as much as the thought that they'd unknowingly made two babies together. "I didn't realize that at the time." So it wasn't as if she'd done something dishonorable!

"And now that you are aware?" Liz interjected, with her usual lawyerly calm.

Merri sighed, pushing away the emotion welling inside her. "It actually makes it less—" she paused, searching for the right word, as she once again met Chase's angst-filled gaze "—*controversial* to think the babies are Chase's." She gulped at the heat of awareness flaring up inside her, then turned back to Liz. "Because Chase was never married to my sister."

Chase and Liz acknowledged her sentiment with slight nods.

"But back to my willingness to stay silent…" Merri forced herself to go on. "I agreed with Sasha and Scott that it really wasn't anyone else's business how the twins were conceived. Nor would it ever have been, if they had lived to raise the twins."

But sadly, that hadn't happened.

Merri shrugged, forcing herself to continue her recollection of the heart-wrenching events that followed. "And then when Scott and Sasha died, I was named guardian of the children, as well as guardian of their estate, so…"

Nodding, Liz jumped to the logical conclusion. "You saw no reason to set the record straight."

Merri lifted her hands. "We were grieving. It didn't seem like the right time to disclose all that, in court, since I was already technically their mother…because of the guardianship. And then, a few months later, when I finally went through their things and found the paperwork identifying Chase as the biological father, I erroneously assumed that he wanted that to be kept private, too—"

Merri stopped abruptly, reeling from the memories of that tumultuous time. Of how things might have been different if she and Chase had known about his involvement. That he, too, was a parent to the children—at least biologically.

Merri swallowed hard. Aware Chase and Liz were both waiting for her to continue, she stammered. "So there was just no way I could c-come forward without making things more difficult than they already were."

"So rather than stir up a hornet's nest, you just let things be," Liz said.

"Yes. Because I thought Chase didn't want to be involved. That he didn't want to discuss it. Otherwise…

I was sure he would have laid claim to the children at the time of Scott and Sasha's death."

"So you went on. Alone," Liz surmised.

"Yes," Merri admitted in a choked voice. Though she had always known, in the deepest recesses of her heart, that a day of reckoning might come.

As it finally had…

Liz looked at Chase. "What would you like to do here?"

"These kids are mine. I want to be their dad and help Merri raise them. But I also want to do everything we can to protect the twins from scandal."

"Meaning, keep this quiet," Liz asserted.

The two nodded in unison, and then Merri added, "I'm no more comfortable with the lies that started all this than Chase is. But we agree—the twins are far too young to understand."

"If they don't ever have to know, we'd rather they didn't," he added.

"So," Merri said, "if there was a way this could be handled privately…the court records sealed to ensure word never gets out…"

Liz tapped her fingers on her desk. Looked from Chase to Merri and back again. "I understand what you're asking me to do. Unfortunately, there are a couple of pretty big problems with all this," she said. "The twins turned four…"

"Last March," Merri qualified.

"Hence, in Texas, you can no longer challenge paternity based on DNA. That option ends when a child turns four, no matter what the circumstances. You can *terminate* the parental rights of Scott and Sasha, and *adopt* the children, but a judge would first have to determine if that is in their best interest. And I'll be honest." Liz sighed. "I don't see that happening. At least not in the immediate time frame you want."

Chase lifted a hand. "Wait a minute. Why would we have to adopt them when the DNA tests prove they are ours, biologically?"

"Because in Texas, in the eyes of the law, they are *not* your children," Liz explained calmly. "You terminated those legal rights when you donated the sperm and the eggs."

"Except Scott lied." Chase grimaced. "He forged my signature. I never agreed to give him that sperm to make a baby."

Liz gestured matter-of-factly. "But you *did* give sperm to the research facility. And that permission trumps any legal rights you had prior to that."

"What happened was still fraudulent," Chase insisted.

Liz nodded in solemn agreement. "You could sue. There would be a lot of ugly publicity. It would take years. Which is not what you want."

No, Merri thought miserably, it wasn't. The kids had been through enough already, being orphaned as babies and spending the past four-plus years without a father figure or steady male influence.

"Then what would be the best course?" Chase countered, obviously still determined to be a part of the twins' lives.

The attorney leaned back in her chair. "I suggest you look at the matter the way the family court will. The twins have a guardian, and they are doing well. The court is going to want to continue the status quo. So if you want to have access to the children, your best bet is to petition to be a co-guardian with Merri."

How often would Chase be around, anyway? she wondered. Given the fact that he was a surgeon, he'd probably be at the hospital all the time. When he wasn't, well, they would figure out how to coparent. It might even be good for the kids to have a man around all the time. Something she and Sasha had never had when they were young. It would give the twins a male role model, fill the void.

"I could handle that," Merri murmured.

Chase nodded in relief. "Me, too."

Liz continued to frown. "That's a very generous attitude," she acknowledged. "Unfortunately, for both of you, it's not quite that simple."

Chase and Merri groaned in unison as they waited for the ax to fall.

"You see...I know Judge Roy," Liz continued bluntly. "She is not going to grant this, even on a temporary basis, unless you are married."

Well, *that* was out of the question, Merri thought. When she married, it would be for love. Period. To her relief, Chase appeared to feel the same way.

"Isn't there another judge?" he asked Liz.

The attorney rocked back in her chair. "No. Priscilla Roy is it for Laramie County, in family court."

"Well, we can still ask," Chase insisted, as determined as ever to do the right thing. "Explain the situation to her. All Judge Roy can do is say no."

"That's true." Liz pressed her fingertips together in front of her. "But if you lose, you would then have to go to appeal, which would halt the whole process for at least a year."

Silence fell as they all thought about that.

The last thing Merri wanted was more time in limbo.

Liz leaned forward and concluded kindly, "What I suggest you do is go home, think about all this, spend some time with the kids…and figure out if there isn't some way the two of you can handle this unofficially, at least for now. Because once you start this process," she warned, "believe me, there will be no turning back."

Chapter 2

Chase settled next to Merri on the porch swing. It was a beautiful fall day, sunny and clear, with the temperature hovering around sixty degrees. Broken Arrow land stretched out as far as the eye could see. But as good as it felt to be home again—and the ranch *was* home to him, and always would be—Chase was focused on the beautiful woman seated beside him. In tailored brown slacks, ivory sweater, and trendy tweed jacket, she was the epitome of a capable thirty-something woman.

The fact that she was so used to being on her own only made the job of convincing her all the harder. "It doesn't have to be a real marriage," Chase continued persuasively, determined to have his way on this whether she liked it or not. "At least not in the conventional sense."

"Well, that's a relief." Merri looked at him with

a mix of exasperation and cynicism in her vivid green eyes.

He regarded her seriously, aware he had a responsibility here. "Its only purpose will be to help us meet the objective."

She exhaled softly. "You becoming a father to your children."

Chase watched as she crossed her legs and clasped her delicate hands around her knee. When had she gotten so all-out beautiful? "While keeping you as the mother they know and love."

Her forehead creased. "People will talk." She pushed herself out of the swing, hips swaying provocatively as she began to pace.

Chase stayed where he was, admiring the view. "A lot less if we're married," he predicted.

Merri looked at him as if she knew that was true.

"You already asked me if I wanted to stay at the ranch with you and the kids." He stood and ambled over to join her.

Her hand encircled a post. "Temporarily. And your first instinct was to refuse."

She smelled like lavender again. Lavender and woman. "Things are different now. We have a lot more on our agenda."

"No kidding. Look, Chase, I get that we could handle this unofficially, and not get married, but…I don't want to live with someone again, without being married."

I don't want to feel used, unappreciated, not good enough.

Aware that he was scrutinizing her closely, she continued, "The problem with just living together is that it gets too complicated."

"I agree if I'm to take on the dad role—us getting hitched and becoming a 'traditional family' is the best solution."

On the surface, from a strictly practical point of view, his suggestion was workable. The ranch house had four bedrooms, only two of which were currently occupied, and comprised four thousand square feet. It was more than big enough for the two of them.

The problem was the enforced intimacy of sharing space. The fact that she was already terribly attracted to Chase and would have to be in his presence at all hours of the night and day. With vows exchanged and wedding rings on their fingers, and the whole world thinking they were husband and wife in a very conventional sense, it would be easy to believe their union was more than a means to an end.

Once before, Merri had deluded herself into thinking that proximity plus friendship and desire would grow into something wonderful. She had ended up feeling terribly disillusioned and disappointed, when Pierce finally admitted he *didn't* really love her and didn't want to marry her. She didn't want to put her heart on the line that way again, only to be rejected in the end.

Trying not to think what Chase's steady appraisal and deep voice did to her, Merri said, "When I made the offer for you to move in, I was doing so as one extended family member to another."

He lounged against the side of the house, opposite her, his hands folded against his chest. "You're worried our relationship wouldn't stay platonic."

Well, duh. Merri stared at him, knowing a guy so

virile and sexy had to have needs, too. Stubbornly, she kept her eyes locked with his even as her heart raced like a wild thing in her chest. "Aren't you?"

He shrugged, considering. "I think we're both adults and could handle whatever happens. Or doesn't."

Could they? Was she older and wiser now? More adept at limiting her emotional vulnerability? Certainly, she had lost the naivete that had made her believe in fairy-tale romance and happy endings for everyone. Merri gripped the porch railing. "So if I wanted to avoid physical intimacy..."

He squared his shoulders, suddenly looking like a knight charged with protecting his queen. "We would."

Now who was kidding whom? She hadn't had a man in heaven knew how long. The way Chase was looking at her...the place he had come from...indicated he was feeling equally deprived. Still, from a purely technical standpoint, it was a win-win solution for both of them. Especially Chase.

Up to now, he had been dealt a very bad hand in all this. Merri felt for him, and wanted to make it up to him, in whatever way she could.

"How long are we talking about?" she asked cautiously. She had lived with Pierce five years. And in the end, lost a big chunk of her prime child-bearing years to a relationship that culminated in pure heartache. Had it not been for having guardianship of the twins, she wasn't sure what she would have done.

Chase's big body began to relax. "A year? Maybe less. It all depends on how fast the twins acclimate to the idea of me being their dad."

Although the pair had been wary when they'd first greeted him, Merri knew they'd warm up to him a lot more quickly than he probably thought. "And once they do," she prodded, taking a deep breath as she searched for other pitfalls, "then what?"

He frowned, all protective male again. "If we're happy—and I have every faith we will be once we all adjust—then we stay a family."

Merri cautioned herself not to be overly optimistic about that. "And if one of us…wants more than a mere arrangement?" Such as enduring love, which had always eluded her in the past. "Then what?" she prodded.

"We can always divorce," he said simply.

Merri groaned in dismay.

He shrugged, looking ready for whatever came. "People do it all the time. The kids would adapt to that, too."

Merri drew another breath as her pulse picked up a notch. "Is that what you want?" She studied him. "A hasty marriage followed by a broken family?"

"What I want," Chase groaned, "is for this not to have happened. For Sasha and Scott not to have betrayed me. Or put either of us in this impossible situation." He grimaced. "Since I can't undo their mistakes, I guess I want what I've always wanted. A wife who will stand by my side, and a family to come home to every night."

He paused as they both reflected on that. Merri realized they were closer in outlook than she'd thought.

"But—" Chase sighed "—that hasn't happened." He shrugged his broad shoulders. "It may never happen. Let's face it, Merri. I'm thirty-six…"

Achingly aware she needed to be realistic, too, she murmured, "I'm thirty-four." And her own fertility was waning by the day.

Their gazes met.

"Maybe it's past time to quit waiting for everything to be perfect," he said simply.

Merri thought about what he was proposing. She struggled to contain her shock. "Together," she affirmed softly.

He rubbed a hand across his jaw. "Arranged marriages have succeeded on a whole lot less."

With a beleaguered sigh of her own, Merri said, "I think this is more a marriage of convenience."

"Whatever." Briefly, irritation creased his handsome features. "You get my drift."

She did. And the most startling thing was that his suggestion didn't feel nearly as outrageous as it should. Maybe because she was disappointed in the hand fate had dealt her thus far, too. She was tired of waiting for the once-in-a-lifetime love that might never happen for her. And depriving herself of all the things she wanted in the meantime.

A contentious silence fell between them.

Merri figured as long as they were discussing this, she might as well put it all out there. She folded her arms. "Okay, let's pretend for a moment that the family part works out great. What are we going to do about sex?"

Because if she was honest, she could easily see herself succumbing to his considerable charm. Whenever she was close to him, she felt a zing of chemistry between them.

Chase narrowed his eyes. "If it happens, it's consensual. And only with each other, as long as we're married."

"I agree anything extramarital would be a very bad idea."

He cleared his throat and folded his own arms, the motion drawing her eyes to the muscular contours of his chest. "The point is, we can't do anything about the time I've already lost with the twins. I want to be part of my kids' lives and I want to do it in such a way that doesn't rob you of any time with them." He paused and leaned toward her, further invading her personal space.

He lowered his voice. "I respect and appreciate all you have done for them thus far. I just want to be part of the process, part of the family unit. And if marriage is the only way that Judge Roy will allow me to become their co-guardian—" he paused again, and she looked straight into his mesmerizing eyes "—then I don't see any other way for me to start making up for lost time."

"We could do it unofficially."

He flashed a crooked smile. "The kids deserve better than that. They deserve a real family. And if there's even a chance that we can give them that…"

He was right. Merri released a shaky breath. "Okay. I'll do it. On one condition…."

Lines of concern bracketed his sensual lips. "And that is…?"

Merri forged ahead. "That I get something I really want out of all this, too."

"And what would that be?" He lifted a brow.

Overwhelmed by the restlessness stirring inside her, Merri angled a thumb at her chest. "What I've never had and always wanted. To carry a child inside me."

"You want to have my baby?"

Her daring surprising her, too, Merri gestured

weakly. "We've already had two via medical procedure…"

Chase went still. His gaze roamed her, head to toe, then lingered on her lips. "You're asking me to impregnate you?"

He didn't have to sound so dumbfounded! "Donate sperm," Merri clarified.

Slowly, she saw her idea sink in. A corner of his mouth quirked. "I think if we decide to do this, I'd want to do it the old-fashioned way."

Me, too, if I was being completely honest. Merri suppressed a sigh. As their gazes continued to mesh, she wondered if she could really do that. Did she have it in her to love strictly as a means to an end? Amazingly enough, if the oh-so-sexy Chase Armstrong was the baby's daddy, and her lifelong dream was at stake, she imagined she could. Especially if it meant a more romantic conception for the only baby she was ever likely to have.

"All right," she allowed. "We'll…" She gulped and forced herself to go on courageously. "We'll try it the old-fashioned way." She lifted a cautioning hand. "But only when the time is right."

Chase nodded, suddenly acting more like a duty-bound medical professional than a sexually accommodating husband-to-be. "I trust you'll let me know when you're ovulating."

Merri nodded, pretending she was as relaxed about the idea of them making love as he seemed. "Sure," she said, in the most casual tone she could manage.

Another silence fell, this one more companionable. Suddenly the air was charged with hope. "In the meantime," Chase said in his typical take-charge way, "if we're really going to get hitched…how about we start taking care of the legalities?"

"You and that man—" Jessalyn pointed to Chase, still trying to comprehend what she and her twin brother had been told "—are getting married?"

Merri was still amazed at how quickly Chase had set everything up. But clearly he was a man on a mission—and the whole town seemed to have rallied around the returning local hero. "Yes." She slipped the blue velvet dress over the little girl's head, and buttoned up the back. "Chase and I are getting married."

Jessalyn sat down to shove her leotard-clad feet into her Mary Janes. "Well, then how come you're not wearing a white dress—like my Wedding Barbie doll?"

Merri turned to help Jeffrey button his shirt and slip on his tie. Quelling her own nerves, she explained gently, "Because it's not that kind of wedding. It's a small, private ceremony in the hospital chapel."

Jessalyn rose and flounced closer. "But weddings are s'posed to be in a church, not a hospital."

Merri smiled indulgently as her husband-to-be joined them. "Not always."

Looking resplendent in a dark suit, pale blue shirt and tie, Chase said, "Weddings can be anywhere you want."

Merri rose and checked her own appearance in the mirror. She had covered her navy tea-length dress with a delicate white cardigan. After much deliberation, she'd left her hair down and added pearl earrings and a necklace. The overall affect was one of understated elegance.

Aware that Chase was checking her out, too, Merri

turned away from the mirror. "And the hospital chapel is kind of a church, honey—it's just a small, cozy one." *And,* she added silently, *the most logical place for the ceremony to occur on such short notice.*

Merri bent to help Jeffrey put on his jacket.

"Can we go milk the cows?" he asked, obediently sliding his hands into the navy sport coat.

"Yeah, I want to see Bessie and Blackie and Benjamen," Jessalyn declared, twirling around, her arms outstretched.

Chase sent Merri a baffled look. Knowing now was not the time to get into *that,* she focused on the twins. "We'll do that another time," she promised vaguely. Turning to Chase, she asked, "Ready?"

He nodded. Together, the four of them left the ranch house and headed for town. The hospital chaplain was waiting for them, as promised. As were their witnesses—pediatric surgeon Paige Chamberlain-McCabe and her husband, Kurt.

Paige, who'd gone to medical school with Chase, hugged him hard. "You're just full of surprises, aren't you, soldier?" she murmured.

He grinned. And keeping to the arrangement Merri and he had decided upon, which was to keep their reasons private to protect the twins from scandal, he gestured expansively. "What can I say? The heart wants what the heart wants."

Wasn't that the truth, Merri thought, as she and Chase stood before the chaplain.

The ceremony began, the words familiar, but the man beside her little more than a distant, casual friend. More than once Merri wondered if they were making a mistake. But all she had to do was look at the children, standing trustingly beside them, and know that she and Chase were doing what was best for Jeffrey and Jessalyn. And in the end, wasn't that all that really mattered? Seeing that the kids didn't suffer for mistakes made by others years ago?

Finally, with vows exchanged and rings on their fingers, the ceremony was complete. "Chase, you may kiss your bride," the chaplain said.

And he did.

Chase hadn't meant to give Merri more than a peck on the lips, but with everyone standing there, watching, the adults with more than a little skepticism, he decided to take the plunge and give it his all.

Wrapping one arm around her shoulders, his other her waist, he drew her against him. She lifted her face and he lowered his. As contact was made, potent desire roared through him. She caught her breath and gave a little sound that was half murmur, half moan. Her unbidden response compelled him to draw her closer still, allowing the passion zinging through him to dictate the pressure and the pace. Only the fact that they had an audience made him put on the brakes.

Slowly, he released her. Merri stared up at him, dazed. He felt the same shock and amazement.

Kurt cleared his throat. "Wow," Chase's old pal murmured. "This is for real."

It certainly felt that way, Chase realized. He just wasn't sure if the chemistry between Merri and him was going to make things easier or harder in the days and months ahead.

A hospital volunteer appeared in the doorway of the chapel. "There you are, Dr. Armstrong! I heard you were here. These came for you!" The pink-coated woman rushed forward, a big autumn floral arrangement clasped in her arms. In the center was a large envelope with Chase's name written on it.

Jeffrey tugged on Chase's jacket. "Is that a present?"

"Open it!" Jessalyn demanded, crowding in, too.

Chase broke the seal, and pulled out a card.

It featured an eight-by-ten glossy photograph, not the kind that any groom should be receiving on his wedding day. As his "wife" looked over his shoulder, she seemed to agree.

"Wow," Merri murmured in shock.

Half a dozen young women were gathered in what looked to be a field hospital. All were clad in desert fatigues, boots and T-shirts. All were holding signs.

"What does it say?" Jessalyn demanded.

"Yeah, Mommy, read it," Jeffrey chimed in.

"Well, it says 'We love you, Chase. Miss you already! Can't believe you actually left us! Holidays are meant to be shared! Texas equals home and home is where the heart is.' And last but not least…" Merri read the sign held up by a particularly beautiful brunette. "'We hate that you left us, but…see you soon!'"

She turned to Chase. "Got quite a cast of admirers there," she drawled.

He grinned good-naturedly. "They like to tease me, that's for sure."

As long as teasing was all they were doing, Merri thought irritably.

"Where should I put them?" the volunteer asked. "Your office…?"

"Sure you don't want to take them home with us?" Merri asked tartly.

"Actually," Chase said, keeping the photo, and giving back the floral arrangement, "why don't you set this in the lobby? That way, everyone can enjoy it."

"Good idea." Smiling, the volunteer walked out, vase in hand.

Kate Marten-McCabe came in with a young nursing student at her side. Head of the hospital grief counseling services for the last thirty years, Kate was beautiful, kind and direct to a fault. "Chase, Merri, good to see you." She knelt by the twins with a charismatic smile. "I need to talk to the bride and groom. And it's grown-up talk." Kate made a face. The kids giggled and wrinkled their noses back at her. "How would you two like to go down to the playroom in pediatrics for a few minutes? We have a lot of fun toys, and Sally here—" Kate pointed to the nursing student "—would love to show them to you."

When Jessalyn and Jeffrey nodded, Kate looked at the newlyweds. "Is this okay with you?"

Aware that whatever this entailed was definitely not for children's ears, they assented. After the kids took off with Sally, Chase and Merri followed Kate into her office.

The grief counselor sat down behind her desk. "Luke Carrigan, the chief of staff, asked me to speak with you. There's no easy way to say this, so I'll be blunt. He heard about the marriage and he's concerned."

Chase frowned, clearly taken aback. "Because…?"

Compassion lit Kate's kind eyes. "You've just returned from a very stressful situation. And he wants to make sure you're not suffering from any kind of post-traumatic stress disorder."

Chase blinked, a little stunned by the assertion. He reached over and took Merri's hand, letting her know he was more than capable of handling this concern on their behalf. "I was never wounded. Or captured."

With a cajoling smile, Kate continued, "But you dealt with people who were.... And there are family deaths you never really had a chance to deal with, all of which could combine to make you do things that you wouldn't normally."

"I didn't marry Merri out of any reaction to that," Chase said, confident as ever.

The grief counselor relaxed. "I'm glad to hear it."

And yet, Merri thought, Kate obviously continued to sense something was up.

Eager to end this line of questioning, Merri slid her hand into Chase's and sent him a warning glance. "I think she's concerned because no one knew you and I were thinking along these lines, Chase."

Kate nodded soberly, picking up where Merri left off. "You have to admit it's a shock to the community at large."

Aggravation twisted the corners of his lips. "It's also no one else's business," he stated in a flat, implacable tone.

Suddenly feeling as if she were dealing with a bull in a china shop, Merri continued to play peacemaker. She stood, dragging Chase along with her. "I—we—understand where you and Dr. Carrigan are coming from, Kate, and believe me, we appreciate your concern."

Merri flashed a reassuring smile, while Chase played along, wrapping an arm about her waist. "But there's really no need to worry." Drawing strength from his warmth, she took another bolstering breath. "Chase and I know we did the right thing in getting married. Not just for the two of us and our future, but for the twins." She paused, letting her words sink in. "The kids need a daddy. And Chase and I are going to see that they get the complete family they deserve."

Chase's expression was maddeningly inscrutable as they left the hospital counseling center. "You didn't have to defend us," he stated.

Merri flushed self-consciously. "Uh, yeah, I did."

"How come?" he asked.

Aware this was a conversation that should not be overheard, she ducked into a small alcove in the painted, cement-block corridor. Defiantly, she lifted her chin. "Laramie County is a small, close-knit community, remember?"

He folded his arms across his chest and shot her a laser-sharp look.

With her back against the cool hospital wall, she ignored the sexual heat radiating from him, and lowered her voice to a whisper. "Everyone watches out for everyone else here."

He shrugged and leaned in closer yet, dropping his voice, too. "So?" he prodded in a sexy murmur.

Merri drank in the crisp, masculine fragrance emanating from him. "So people are understandably concerned and confused…given how fast this has all come about." She drew a breath, reassuring herself that despite the impact of their post-nuptial kiss, they were in no real danger of hooking up in the near future. Both of them were much too sensible. "You don't agree?"

He braced his hands on his hips, his expression becoming even more guarded. "I think they should mind their own business. We're adults, after all."

She forced herself to glance away. "Who, you have to admit, are now acting very mysteriously."

He bent down, caging her with his arms and lowered his face until their mouths were an inch apart. He lifted a strand of hair from her cheek and tucked it behind her ear. Came even nearer, so their bodies were touching and she could feel the heat emanating from his. "So what you're saying is we've got some convincing to do if people are going to believe this marriage is for real," he proposed silkily.

Out of the corner of her eye, Merri saw people lingering at the far end of the corridor, near the elevators.

"No." She swallowed as he cupped her face in his hands. "That's not what I said at all."

"Too bad," Chase murmured, the amorous glint in his eyes letting her know he planned to make their union as realistic and convincing as possible, for all the doubting Thomases in the vicinity. After all, he knew as well as she did that word of the incident would quickly spread, through the hospital grapevine, then the community at large.

His lips touched hers in a sweet, chaste kiss. "Because it's what *I* say," he vowed, planting a hotly possessive kiss on her mouth.

Merri knew it was all for show. As his lips moved slowly and sensually over hers, she swore that she wasn't going to kiss him back, but instead would let him do all the work.

It was a good plan. A very safe, intelligent way of resisting him. Unfortunately it backfired big-time. Before even a millisecond went by, her lips parted beneath the persuasive pressure of his. Her knees weakened and her heart rate skyrocketed. Succumbing, she wreathed her arms around his neck and kissed him back, melting against him.

And that was when the polite throat-clearing sounded, followed by rapid footsteps. Breathlessly, Chase and Merri moved apart, only to see Jessalyn and Jeffrey skid to a halt on the shiny linoleum floor.

Then came the confused, indignant demand, "Mommy! Why are you kissing that man!"

Reminded that although Chase might secretly be the kids' biological father, they barely knew who he was—a fact that would quickly have to be rectified—Merri flushed. "We'll talk about it at home." She took the children's hands and told Sally, "Thank you for watching over them."

"No problem," the nursing student replied cheerfully. "And congratulations, you two! Everyone is saying this came out of left field, but the way the doc was kissing you just now? No way!" she proclaimed. She pointed to Merri and Chase before heading off to resume her duties. "That's definitely the real deal."

"Mommy! You didn't answer my question! Why were you kissing him? Again!" Jessalyn said in annoyance.

"Because we're married and married people kiss sometimes. Especially—" Merri elbowed Chase "—when they are trying to make a point."

He leaned down to whisper in her ear, "Hey, it worked, didn't it?"

To rev her up, maybe. And start more gossip.

Jeffrey and Jessalyn looked at each other, perplexed. Clearly, they didn't know what to make of this. "So what now?" Chase asked as he and Merri left the hospital, kids in tow.

"I still want to go milk the cows," Jessalyn insisted.

"Me, too," Jeffrey chimed in.

Chase waited for Merri to decide. "Actually, we do have to get back to the ranch," she said eventually.

"Hurrah!" Jeffrey and Jessalyn cried in unison.

"I thought you got rid of the beef cattle years ago." Chase held open the car door for the kids.

"I had to. Scott and Sasha went deep into debt to pay for their fertility treatments, and it was the only way to settle the estate so it could get through probate."

Chase didn't look surprised to learn his brother and sister-in-law had gravely mismanaged the ranch. "And you've just leased the land since, for crops and grazing?"

Nodding, Merri leaned in to help Jessalyn fasten her safety harness. "Initially, all I did was allow others to plant alfalfa, hay and corn on the farmable land, and rotate the cattle on other parts, for grazing."

Chase did the same for Jeffrey. "And that brought in more than enough to pay the mortgage and the taxes and the upkeep on the property?"

"As well as a small salary for me."

"But...?" he prodded, sensing there was more.

Merri climbed into the passenger seat. "Eventually, I realized I needed to build something of my own for me and the kids, and take a more active part in the running of the ranch." She tugged her dress down over her knees. "Which is when I converted the barn on the south part of the property to a milking operation, hired one full-time hand to help me manage it and bought a dozen Jersey cows and a dozen Guernseys."

Chase did a double take. "You're turning the Broken Arrow Ranch into a dairy farm?"

"Uh, yeah....I am."

His jaw tautened. "You never mentioned it in any of your letters."

That's because I knew you wouldn't approve. "Hmm. Didn't I?"

He made a face.

"The cows are really cute," Jessalyn interjected from her booster seat. "Some are brown and white and some are black and white...."

"I like it when they moo," Jeffrey declared.

Chase continued gaping at Merri as if she were a complete and utter fool. She refused to let his skepticism get her down. "It's a good thing," she promised, sure about this decision even if she wasn't so certain about others. Cheerfully, she predicted, "And it will be even better in a few years, when we get the dairy operation expanded to quadruple the size."

Merri hadn't been kidding, Chase noted thirty minutes later when all four of them had changed into "ranch clothes," hopped in the pickup truck and headed for the south side of the Broken Arrow Ranch. Just as she had claimed, there were twenty-four cows pastured outside the big barn. All were big, robust, surprisingly handsome animals. Most were heading slowly for the barn door as the truck approached.

"The cows like to come in all on their own!" Jessalyn announced.

"But if they don't, Mutt—the doggie—will help Slim

get the cows inside the barn, so they can get hooked up," Jeffrey added helpfully.

"The cows know when it's time to be milked, so they head for the barn," Merri explained.

Chase parked in the gravel area and everyone got out.

A tall, thin cowboy in his mid-fifties came out of the barn, with a border collie at his heels. The gray-haired hired hand tipped his hat at Merri before glancing at Chase. "I expect you want to have a look around," he drawled, with the respect due one of the original Armstrongs.

Did he? Chase wondered.

Finding out what Merri had been doing to the place was his worst nightmare. He was stunned no one had mentioned it. But maybe they'd figured—rightly so—that it was going to be a sore subject with him.

Chase tipped his hat back to Slim, a cowboy he recalled meeting at the barbecue in his honor. "May as well," he grumbled.

Clasping the children's hands, Merri led the way inside the sparkling, clean barn.

Chase was stunned to see twenty-four stalls, and plenty of stainless-steel, state-of-the-art milking equipment with hoses running to a big steel vat.

Merri murmured with pride, "I joined a co-op dairy that supplies organic milk to a big grocery store chain. Every day a truck comes in and takes it to the processing plant, for ultrahigh-temperature processing and packaging."

"I don't like the truck," Jessalyn complained, covering her ears. "It's too noisy."

"But we like watching the cows get milked," Jeffrey said.

As the bovines were ushered into the stalls, they were hooked up to the milking machines. For all the activity, the barn was surprisingly quiet and peaceful.

Chase's cell phone rang.

He stepped outside to take the call, then walked back in to let Merri know the latest. "That was Liz Cartwright Anderson. She got us on Judge Roy's docket for tomorrow afternoon at four. We're the last case the judge is going to hear before the Thanksgiving break."

A fact, Chase thought happily, that put them one step closer to his ultimate goal: to have this family officially his.

Chapter 3

"You know what I think?" Judge Priscilla Roy said after listening to Chase and Merri's joint request for guardianship. In her black robe, glasses perched on the edge of her nose, the dark-haired justice cut an imposing figure as she glared at Chase. "None of what is going on here today, or what happened yesterday in the hospital chapel, has anything to do with the kind of unconditional love and commitment needed for a successful marriage, never mind a stable family unit."

She was right about that, Merri thought. Their union wasn't about the feelings she and Chase had for each other.

"I think you're just doing this to provide access to the children slash heirs and get back control of the family ranch."

Merri blinked. *What?*

"Your Honor. There has been no request from Mr. Armstrong for control of the children's estate," Liz interjected with lawyerly calm.

Judge Roy waved her hand, then drew her glasses farther down the bridge of her nose and peered at Chase. "Don't tell me you're happy about what happened to the ranch you grew up on. Armstrongs and the Broken Arrow have always raised beef cattle. Not dairy cows."

"That's true," Chase admitted with admirable candor. "What's happened there would not have been my choice. But I do understand." He turned to glance at Merri. "My wife had to raise these kids on her own and take care of the property. She's done the best she could under the circumstances."

Unmoved, Judge Roy continued, "But you could do better?"

Chase lifted his hands. "I'm a surgeon."

Sternly, the judge commanded, "Answer the question, please."

He released an exasperated breath and looked at her, squaring his shoulders deliberately. "Yes. I think I could do better. But that's not the point, Your Honor."

"Actually, Mr. and Mrs. Armstrong, I think that is exactly the point. Mr. Armstrong is back in town and wants what was previously denied him by his mother's estate—control of the ranch and its assets, which are currently held in trust for the children. To get that, he would have to be co-guardian of the kids." Priscilla Roy paused meaningfully. "And to achieve that, at least in my courtroom, he has to be married to Merri Duncan. Which he has managed in very short order, with no prior courtship, at least that anyone in the county seems to know about."

Merri didn't know what they could say to that, without breaking the promise she and Chase had made to each other to keep the twins' biological origins private and hence protect the children from scandal. It was bad enough that they'd been orphaned at eight weeks of age, without making Scott and Sasha out to be conniving liars.

Thank heavens the twins didn't understand any of this. At four and a half, they simply wanted Merri to be their mommy, and hopefully soon, for Chase to be their daddy.

"Judge," Liz interrupted, "if I may… I have spoken at length with my clients. They both want what is best for these children. Jeffrey and Jessalyn need a father and a mother, and my clients are willing to make the necessary sacrifices and work together to provide that."

Judge Roy looked at Merri. "An early Christmas gift?"

Wary of making a mistake that would put them in even deeper trouble, she admitted cautiously, "Something like that."

"Correct me if I'm wrong. You worked as a wedding planner before settling back in Laramie County?"

Merri nodded. "That's true."

Judge Roy rocked back in her chair. "And isn't that a romantic profession?"

Merri winced. "It's a profession that provides romance. I don't know how romantic it is for the planner at the end of the day." She sighed. "Weddings can be very stressful. And a lot of time, the days leading up to the ceremony are anything but romantic."

The justice pushed her glasses back into place. "So in other words, your work left you jaded."

Merri shrugged and risked a tiny glance at Chase, who stood beside her, sober and strong. "Maybe. A little." As had her personal experiences with relationships. "But also exceedingly practical." She paused, searching for the right words. "I do want what is best for the children. And I think having Chase in their lives, as their dad, will provide that." It was certainly better than splitting the children up, one night at her place, one night at his…. Which was the only other fair alternative.

"Okay." Judge Roy sat back, folded her hands on the desk. "You've convinced me to give you a chance. But that is all it is. An opportunity to prove that your marriage is a real one, not a sham, and what you are proposing is in the best interest of the twins. If I find out you're misleading this court in any way, if this marriage is simply a means to an end, I'll remove you both as guardians."

Remove? Merri blinked in shock.

Judge Roy turned to her clerk. "Schedule another hearing, for January 3." She banged her gavel, signaling their hearing had come to an end.

Stunned, Merri left the courtroom with Chase and Liz, as the next case was called. Their lawyer guided them down the hall to a spot where they could talk privately.

"Would the judge really do that?" Merri asked, her voice wobbling as badly as her knees. Clapping a hand over heart, she sank down on the closest wooden bench. "Take the kids away from us?"

"It's within Judge Roy's power. But she's not going

to do that, as long as this is a genuine attempt to build a loving, supportive family that will benefit all of you in the long run."

"It is," Chase said firmly, with laudable assurance. "Merri and I will make this work."

Merri only wished she felt as confident.

"So much for our plans to divorce if things don't work out," she murmured as the two of them walked to the parking lot. She still felt shaky and at a loss. Chase, on the other hand, looked more confident than ever.

"Judge Roy had a point. Nothing good was ever accomplished with one foot out the door."

Merri knew the words were truer than she wished. Still… "I'm scared."

He caught her to him as they reached the car. "Don't be," he murmured with both hands on her shoulders. He looked deep into her eyes. "We're two very strong people, who want only the best for the kids. We'll find a way to make it work."

Chase was as good as his word. He was there to help, with dinner and baths and story time. Jeffrey and Jessalyn still regarded him with wariness, but they were slowly warming to him, Merri could tell. As was evidenced by the last question of the day, as they were being tucked in for the night.

"Is Chase going to be our daddy…now that you two are married?" Jessalyn asked.

Merri looked at Chase. He waited, leaving the answer up to her. They hadn't broached the subject yet, because they hadn't wanted to rush the kids. "Yes, this makes him your daddy," Merri said, with as much ease as she could muster.

"Is that okay with you?" Chase asked.

Jessalyn and Jeffrey exchanged looks. Two lower lips slid out truculently. "No," Jeffrey said.

"We don't want a daddy right now," Jessalyn added.

Chase's expression was inscrutable, but Merri could tell from the faint sheen in his eyes that he was crushed. As was she. "Why not?" she asked the kids, when she found her voice.

"Because we already got a mommy, so we don't need a daddy," Jessalyn explained.

"It's okay," Chase assured them, seeming to understand that he had upset the equanimity of the household.

"You can change your minds anytime," Merri felt compelled to add.

Jeffrey sighed and hugged his teddy bear tightly. "We're not going to."

Jessalyn nodded in agreement. And that, it seemed, was that.

"Sorry they weren't more cooperative," Merri said as she and Chase went down the stairs together.

"They'll warm up," he predicted.

Merri hoped so. Thanks to Judge Roy's ultimatum, they didn't have a lot of time to make this work.

Unfortunately, Chase had an early call at the hospital. So the twins didn't see him at all the next morning before preschool.

"Try a lot of short visits," Merri's friend Paige said, when she talked to her later that morning. Paige was not only a dedicated pediatrician, but also an experienced mother of demanding triplets. "It will help the kids get used to Chase and vice versa, and put a lot less pressure on all of them."

Deciding it was good advice, Merri stopped by the hospital complex, after picking up the kids from school.

"How come we're going to the hospital?" Jessalyn asked.

"I don't want another shot," Jeffrey whimpered, holding his hand over his thigh.

Paige held open the door to the hospital annex, where all the physician offices were located. "You're not going to get one today. You already had your flu shots last month, remember?"

Jeffrey rubbed his thigh in memory. "That's why I don't want another one."

"So how come we're here, if we're not going to the doctor?" Jessalyn persisted, pausing to study the festive turkey and cornucopia display taped outside the pediatric services suite.

Merri took the children's hands and pressed on. "I thought we'd surprise Chase and see if he'd like to have lunch with us in the cafeteria."

More frowns. "I'd rather go to the Dairy Barn," Jessalyn said with a pout.

Merri paused outside the general surgery suite. "Another time," she promised.

She ushered the children in, only to be told by the receptionist, "You just missed him. He went down to the cafeteria to grab a bite to eat."

"Perfect!" Merri smiled and ushered the children back out into the hall. Not surprisingly, they grumbled and dragged their heels all the way to the cafeteria.

Chase had already gone through the line. Tray in hand, he was searching for a seat when he saw them. He flashed a devastating smile, set his tray on a table for four and strode toward them.

He was looking more handsome than ever in blue surgical scrubs and a white doctor's coat, and Merri felt her heart quiver in response. She knew this wasn't a real marriage in the traditional sense, but at the moment, it felt as if it were.

Aware that all eyes were on them, she beamed at him. "Hey."

Still smiling, Chase pressed a quick, casual kiss to her temple, then leaned down to do the same to the kids.

Instead of welcoming the gesture, they both shrank back, out of reach. The twins clung to Merri, hiding their faces in the fabric of her wool trousers.

"Can we go home now?" Jeffrey's voice was muffled against her leg.

Merri patted his shoulder reassuringly. "Let's have some lunch first, okay?"

The little boy was about to protest when a loud cheer went up behind them. Squeals of delight were followed by a chorus of "There he is!" "What a sight for sore eyes!" "Handsome as always, Dr. Heartbreaker!"

Dr. Heartbreaker?

Merri turned, coming face-to-face with the half-dozen young women from Chase's photo. They were clad in desert-hued camouflage pants, jackets and form-fitting beige T-shirts, and were all incredibly glad to see Chase. From the welcoming expression on her now husband's face, he was equally thrilled to see them.

En masse, the women streamed toward him. And one after another, with everyone in the hospital cafeteria looking on, they greeted Chase with more whoops and hollers and heartfelt hugs.

"What are you-all doing here?" he asked, beaming as if he had just won the lottery.

And maybe he had.

One of the ladies flashed a megawatt smile. "You said we could visit anytime and you'd put us up!"

"So when we all unexpectedly got a month's leave and decided to go on a road trip, we figured we'd take you up on it," a striking brunette added, going on tiptoe to give Chase another long, lingering hug. She drew back, the name-necklace at her throat glittering, and with an air of feminine possessiveness punched on his broad shoulder playfully. "Besides, what's a holiday without our favorite guy?"

Okay. Enough was enough, especially with a big chunk of the hospital visitors and staff looking on, absorbing every word.

"Or his family," Merri interjected sweetly, asserting herself once again.

The women all turned to look at her and the children.

Abruptly recalling his manners, Chase stepped back. Drawing Merri and the kids around him, he said, "Ladies, I'd like you to meet my wife, Merri, and our kids, Jeffrey and Jessalyn."

Our kids. Merri liked the sound of that almost as much as the sound of *my wife*.

"Wife?" the women echoed in shock.

The brunette with the name necklace—Starr— stepped forward. "Kids?" she demanded. "Since when?"

"Don't tell us you were married all along, you heartbreaker!" the freckled redhead said.

"Actually, we just got married yesterday," Merri told them.

Six brows furrowed in confusion.

Chase lifted a palm, not about to go into it there with

the entire hospital cafeteria crowd still watching. "It's a long story," he said mildly.

"Fortunately," the striking brunette, Starr, said with a playful moue, "we've got all the time in the world to hear it." She insinuated herself between Chase and Merri, snuggled up to his side and gazed up at him adoringly. "That is, if you're still as good as your word, Chase Armstrong, and intend to put us all up for the Thanksgiving holiday, Texas-style."

Chapter 4

"It's too much to ask."

Maybe for a casual friend, but for a presumably loving wife? Merri wondered.

"You don't have to do this," Chase told her, after his army buddies had promised to meet up with him when he got off work at five-thirty.

To Merri's relief, the bevy of attractive women had gone, en masse, to the shops on Main Street, to purchase some genuine "Texas" duds for their three-day stay. The twins were seated at a table by the window, happily chowing down on some ice cream, while Merri and Chase talked quietly, just out of earshot.

"I'll figure something else out," he promised, sipping his coffee.

Merri leaned her back against the cafeteria wall, glad most of the lunch crowd and staff had dispersed.

She turned to Chase, feeling the heat of his gaze like a physical caress. "Really?"

He didn't take his eyes off her. "Really."

She ran a hand through her hair, suddenly feeling a little too aware of her hunky new husband. "Where are your friends going to go? It's the Wednesday before Thanksgiving. Every hotel room in a hundred-mile radius has been booked for months."

A conflicted glimmer appeared in Chase's eyes. Obviously, he hadn't thought about the impact the holiday would have on hotel room availability in rural west Texas. He did, however, seem to realize that Merri was suddenly feeling as if she had been relegated to seventh-wheel status, in the pecking order of go-getting females who'd traveled thousands of miles to be with him.

His handsome features tightened in resignation. "I'm sorry, Merri. You and I should be focused on the kids now, getting them adjusted to the changes in our lives. Instead…" He paused, shook his head then sent her a beseeching glance.

They had houseguests.

Lots of very attractive, very smitten female house-guests.

Chase continued, "When I issued the standing invitation to everyone in my unit, I wasn't married."

Merri knew the appearance of his army buddies was unexpected—although maybe she and Chase should have gotten a clue from the holiday gift basket and card, and all the signs the women were holding up in the photo.

But that only made it a tiny bit better. Because Chase was right…it would be best if they could focus on the kids—and being married—without an audience of half a dozen very interested admirers.

Still, it was the holiday season, a time of thanks and giving. And these were friends and colleagues who had served in the military field hospital alongside Chase. Merri put her emotions aside, dug deep and called up the generosity the situation required.

She reached out and touched his arm gently. "It's okay, Chase. Really." She looked into his eyes, so he would know she meant what she said from the bottom of her heart. "It's only for a couple of nights, and we have room at the ranch—if everyone doubles up and two people volunteer to sleep on sofas."

Chase's brow furrowed as he calculated, same as Merri. There were two guest rooms, two sofas, one master suite…and eight adults.

"Obviously, you'll have to sleep in my room temporarily." Merri stepped back slightly. Thinking about what it would be like to share the sheets with him, she struggled to control a self-conscious flush.

Chuckling, he took her hand. Warmth spread throughout her body as his fingers engulfed hers. "There's always the barn…."

Merri's throat went dry as she gazed up into his mischievous eyes. "Hilarious," she muttered, then returned to the matter at hand. "But like it or not, we'll have to sleep together as long as we have company. Otherwise people will speculate more than they already are."

"How do you know they're speculating?" he asked in surprise.

Seriously? Merri rolled her eyes in exasperation. A hot development like the marriage was probably all over the hospital and town grapevines. "Did you not see the looks we were getting in the cafeteria when your lady friends arrived?"

"Uh…" Chase shrugged his broad shoulders, looking every bit the clueless male. "Not really…"

"What about before that?" Merri pressed. "When we said hello and the kids were anything but happy to see their new dad?"

A look of hurt flashed in Chase's eyes, then disappeared. That he apparently did recall, all too acutely, and Merri's heart went out to him. He had already missed so much. First steps, first words. All those Christmases and birthdays. The first day of preschool. Through no fault of his own.

His expression sobered, becoming all the more sincere. "I think you're being too sensitive," he countered softly. "People understand we just got married and are in an adjustment period here."

She studied his big, scrub-clad frame, deciding he was way too sexy in whatever he wore. Way too masculine and capable and kind. Aware that she could fall hard for Chase if she wasn't careful—and she intended to be careful, particularly with a bevy of female admirers suddenly in the picture. Merri folded her arms in front of her. "Maybe people also understand a lot more than we'd like them to—which is why everyone is so skeptical when they look at us."

What if they couldn't fool his friends? Merri worried nervously.

Or anyone else, for that matter. What would Judge Roy do if she concluded that Merri and Chase were just scamming the court, as a means to an end? Laramie County was a close-knit community. Sooner or later, everyone knew everyone else's business. Or at least most of it.

People certainly knew who loved whom, and who only pretended to care....

Zeroing in on her nervousness, Chase cupped her arms reassuringly and leaned closer. "We're going to make this work, Merri."

His hands felt as warm and strong as the rest of him looked. Shivering at his touch, she murmured distractedly, "You keep saying that." How could he have so much faith?

His smile was slow and sure. "I keep meaning it, too."

Inhaling the mixture of hospital antiseptic and his favorite bath soap rising from his skin, Merri edged back. "I'm beginning to see that," she returned softly. And although she didn't share his hope and faith—her past experiences had drained them out of her—she couldn't help but admire his bravura.

A tenuous silence fell.

Abruptly, Merri noticed that people were staring. Again. Including the twins, who had just about finished their ice cream.

Reluctantly, Chase relinquished his hold on her and dropped his hands to his sides. "So where are you and the kids off to next?" he inquired.

She shrugged, her emotions in turmoil once again. "Depends. What do you want to do about dinner? With—" she cleared her throat "—all our *guests?*"

Chase scrubbed his hand across his jaw, considering. "I could pick up Sonny's Barbecue on the way home."

Now, that was helpful! "Sounds perfect, thank you." Merri smiled. "Meanwhile, the kids and I will head to the grocery store to stock up on essentials for our guests, plus all the ingredients for the cooking I have to do tonight."

He studied her face, clearly puzzled, and Merri realized she should have warned him about that. "The community center Thanksgiving dinner is early tomorrow afternoon. It's a potluck. The kids and I attend every year. And this year I'm tasked with bringing ten crowd-size sweet potato casseroles."

"So it really isn't a good time to have all that company," Chase concluded with a frown.

Merri appreciated his consideration and clasped his biceps gently. "It's really nice that your army buddies got to come back to the States for the holidays. Even better that you all have a chance to be together for a few days." She released her hold, stepped back and tossed him the confident smile that had gotten her through many a challenging situation. "I'll do my best to make sure they feel welcome."

Merri made good on her promise to Chase. And as she got to know the women, found she had more in common with them than she first thought. Addie had grown up on a farm. Nissa had twin brothers. Davita's sister was a wedding planner. Harmony had never known her dad. Polly had entrepreneurial dreams. And Starr had the biggest crush of all on Chase.

A fact that seemed to go unnoticed by Merri's dashing new husband. Which made the queries that came up, as soon as the twins were sound asleep in bed, expected, if not exactly welcome.

"So," Starr said, sauntering over to stand next to Chase. "Tell us how the two of you met and fell in love."

All eyes turned to Chase, who finished building the fire in the hearth, then straightened casually. "I don't recall an exact moment. It was more an awareness that we had a connection—"

That is, Jessalyn and Jeffrey, Merri thought.

"—and that this was what we wanted to do," Chase finished calmly.

Faces fell in disappointment. It hadn't been a very romantic rendition, Merri acknowledged, although what he'd revealed *had* been completely truthful.

Smiling brightly as Chase came toward her, she added a few facts of her own. "Chase and I both grew up in Laramie County, so we've always known each other. Although not that well when we were growing up, since he was four years ahead of me in school."

"When did that change?" Davita asked curiously.

Chase sat on the arm of Merri's chair, took her hand in his. He turned her palm up and traced the lifeline. "When my brother and her sister became engaged. We were thrown together a lot in the months leading up to their marriage."

"But you never mentioned her," Starr protested.

Addie gave the striking brunette a reproving look, then turned back with a smile. "I think we all know that Chase is a guy who plays his cards close to his chest. Especially in the romantic arena."

He stood and, all protective male, pulled Merri to her feet beside him. "You-all must be exhausted," he said to their houseguests. "What do you say we turn in? Tomorrow morning will be here before we know it."

Ten minutes later, Merri and Chase were in the master bedroom, hearing just a few low voices as doors opened and closed. Merri slipped into the adjacent bath.

She emerged five minutes later in blue-and-white polka dot pajama pants and a gray henley.

To her surprise, Chase was already undressed, down to a pair of boxers and a T-shirt. His legs and arms were as sinewy and masculine as she had imagined. "That's all you're wearing?" she asked.

Laugh lines crinkled at the corners of his eyes. "Be thankful," he teased, pulling at the neck of his T-shirt. "It's more than I usually do. But you're right… With the kids and company around, I'm probably going to have to invest in pajamas."

Merri wasn't sure the image of him in cotton pajama pants would be any less sexy. Especially if he purchased the kind that would ride low on his lean hips.

Oblivious to the sensual nature of her thoughts, he sauntered into the bathroom, toothbrush in hand. Merri watched his retreating backside wistfully.

He was so darn buff, so hotly male. And she should not be objectifying him this way.…

To distract herself, Merri climbed into bed and started to make a list in her head. She had so much to do with Christmas less than a month away!

By the time Chase returned, she had switched off the light. The to-do list had grown to a daunting length.

Luckily for him, the combination of a night-light and the moonlight streaming in through cracks in the blinds gave him enough illumination to maneuver without bumping into anything.

As he neared, she decided lying on her back did not seem like the wisest choice. So Merri shifted to a less vulnerable position and propped her head on her upraised palm. "What are we going to do?" she whispered, when he finally settled beside her.

Chase turned onto his side, so they were lying there face-to-face. He surveyed her with a guileless grin. "Now?"

Merri tugged her attention away from the powerful muscles of his shoulders. She shouldn't be noticing, but hallelujah, he had a nice chest. Nice butt. Nice legs. And arms... She licked her suddenly dry lips, glad those boxers of his were loose fitting and an opaque army-green. "About all the questions," she said, trying in vain to get her thoughts—and her libido—back on track.

He continued to regard her nonchalantly, lying there in her bed, looking as relaxed as could be. "We'll do what we've already been doing," he murmured. "Distract. Divert. And not really answer. At least not all the way." He rolled over onto his back and folded his hands behind his head. Unfortunately, the action only served to show her how flat his stomach, and how well-endowed the rest of him, was.

"I don't think that's going to work." She snuggled more deeply into the sheets, wishing it didn't feel so cozy, lying here with him. "Not if they're as curious and probing as they have been."

"Sure it will." He turned his head and flashed her another sexy grin. "It will if we keep stonewalling."

Merri rolled onto her back, too. For several minutes they lay there in the semidarkness, side by side. Yet Merri could tell by the set of his shoulders and the sound of his breathing that he was no more inclined to go to sleep than she was.

Finally, Chase reached over and ran a hand along her forearm. "Is that the only thing bothering you?"

Her skin tingling from the compassionate touch, Merri turned her glance away from the shadows on the ceiling. If she was going to be one hundred percent honest, she'd have to admit she was a tiny bit jealous, having all those adoring females there with them. Not sure what that said about her, and certainly not about to admit she was already feeling so wifely and possessive, she rolled away from him, and retorted in a muffled voice, "I don't like being put on the spot."

He hooked an arm around her waist and pulled her back until her shoulders were pressed against the hard, unyielding muscles of his chest, and her bottom was nestled against his abdomen and thighs. The action was meant to comfort; she could feel it in the platonic nature of his grasp. Yet it was a very sexy, provocative embrace just the same.

"Neither do I," he whispered in her ear, with a lot more kindness and understanding than she would have expected. Was this the type of husband he was going to be? Gentle and affectionate? Up till now, she had put him firmly in the friends category, knowing that one day soon, when they were ready to make a baby, she'd have to move him into the friends-with-benefits group.

But this suddenly felt a lot more emotionally seductive. And hence, dangerous in the lose-your-heart-to-a-man-you-know-will-really-love-you kind of way.

Pushing aside her senseless fairy-tale wishes, Merri listened to the rest of what Chase had on his mind.

"But as you said earlier," he reminded her casually, "my friends are only going to be here for a couple more days."

Merri shut her eyes and told herself that this was not desire she was feeling. Though their thighs were pressed together, his hips were a safe distance away.

Pressing his warm chest against her back, he was

comforting her, in a husbandly sort of way, not se-
ducing. She closed her eyes, wondering if he was as
aroused as she was beginning to be.

Merri shifted her free arm across her breasts. A few
more days? "That's still long enough for your gal pals
to continue the inquisition." Which could put them in
an even more awkward position than they were now,
sharing her way-too-small bed, pretending it was a normal, expected event.

Grasping her shoulder, Chase turned her so she was
lying flat on her back once again. He positioned himself a safe distance away, propped his head on his hand
and stared down into her face, looking as if he wanted
nothing more than to kiss her again. This time, strictly
for them and no one else.

There was only one thing she could think of doing,
when he looked at her that way. The problem was that if
she gave in to the surge of recklessness she felt, all her
carefully constructed barriers would fall away. At this
moment, theirs was a marriage in name only. For both
their sakes, she needed to remember that, as did he.

Chase shrugged, his own desire under a lot better
control than hers. "Well, then, guess we'll all just have
to stay busy, won't we?"

"Speaking of that..." She swallowed, noting the sudden parched feeling in her throat, and struggled not
to think of how "being busy" making love with him
might feel.

Because that just wasn't going to happen.

At least not in the next couple of days—since a pack
of way-too-observant females had systematically taken
over the house.

No. When it finally happened, it would just be the

two of them. Alone in this house. No distractions. No time limits. No having to be careful or quiet....

Aware how all this trying-to-not-be-turned-on was actually arousing her even more, Merri jerked in an uneven breath. "Did I tell you I'm on duty for the milking tomorrow?"

Obviously enjoying how flustered she'd become, he tilted his head and gave her a cocky grin. "No."

Glad to talk about work, Merri replied, "Traditionally, Slim has Thanksgiving Day and Friday off, and then he does Saturday and Sunday for me."

"Want me to help?" Chase asked, gallant as ever.

Oh, Lord, if ever there was a knight in shining armor...

"No." Nor did she want him to forget everything they had previously agreed to, and make hot, wild, unrestrained love to her. Here and now, company be damned.

Shaking off the image of her stretched intimately beneath him, drenched in moonlight and asking for pleasure, Merri reached over to set her bedside alarm. Her thigh accidentally bumped his in the process and frissons of heat coursed through her. "I can handle it." She shifted farther away, toward her side of the mattress, warning herself to keep all physical contact to an absolute minimum.

Ignoring the quickening of her pulse, Merri added as calmly as possible, "But what I would like is for you to take care of the kids, so I don't have to wake them and take them down to the barn with me."

Ready to assist her in whatever way he could, Chase nodded. "No problem."

Mind on the list. Mind on the list! Merri swallowed

again. "Also, if your friends are up, maybe you could rustle up some coffee or juice or whatever till I get back to the house?"

He caught a strand of Merri's hair and tucked it behind her ear. "We can handle that," he promised, even more softly.

With her insides fluttering at the tenderness of his touch, she sucked in a breath. "And then, after that, I have to make those ten, crowd-size sweet potato casseroles."

He gave her a slow smile that suggested he would be a very patient, very thorough lover. The implication caused her to shiver all over.

His fingers stroked the inside of her wrist as she struggled to stabilize her soaring-out-of-control emotions. "I saw the recipe you laid out on the kitchen counter," he admitted.

Merri nodded, her breathing not nearly as deep or as even as she would have liked. "It was my mom's. She was famous for it. People asked for it every year." The only problem was, Merri thought worriedly, her rendition of the dish had never quite measured up to her mother's. No one said so, but she knew it. And after tomorrow, Chase would know it, too.

Misreading the reason behind her apprehension—the pressure of cooking for a very competitive, though appreciative, small-town crowd, Chase squeezed her hand again. "It's going to be all right."

Trying hard not to think about what it would feel like to kiss him again, privately this time, Merri nodded. She really had to stop wanting Chase like this. "I hope so."

Conversation lagged after that. Fatigue set in. Before

Merri knew it, she had fallen asleep, only to wake five minutes before the alarm went off. Acutely aware of the big, warm man lying beside her, Merri turned her head slightly and opened her eyes. Damn, but Chase was gorgeous, even in his sleep. His profile was strong and even and so very male, given his high cheekbones, chiseled jaw and sensual lips.

He was lying on his back, as he had most of the night, head squarely on the pillow, with his arms folded behind it. Which gave her a great view of his muscular chest, nicely formed pecs and six-pack abs.

His forearms were covered with crisp hairs a shade darker than the short sandy locks on his head. Ditto his long, lean legs.

He hadn't touched her once through the night. Which was a shame, Merri decided, since she had very much wanted to touch him.

But he was right to stay on his side of the queen-size sleigh bed.

Although they'd agreed to make a baby together—when the time was right—it wasn't right yet. And wouldn't be until they got through the guardianship process. Until then, Merri thought, throwing back the covers, they had best err on the side of the caution.

So no more kissing Chase. No more tempting fate. No more anything except walking the straight and narrow.

Through barely opened eyes, Chase watched Merri gather up her milking clothes—flannel shirt, down vest, jeans and boots. She slipped into the bathroom, and then a couple minutes later came out again.

Damn, but she was sexy, with her face scrubbed

bare and her honey-blond hair swept up into an untidy knot on the back of her head. As sexy as she had been in those pajamas. He'd had an ache that wouldn't quit the entire night, which had made moving closer to her distinctly unwise.

His body might be telling him all systems were ready, but his head knew different. Merri wasn't the kind of woman who could handle sex with no strings, even for the purpose of making a baby they both yearned to have. She was the kind of woman who needed tenderness as well as passion. Love. Commitment.

And though he could easily give her three out of the four, his gut told him that she would never be happy unless she had the Real Deal feelings included in any bedroom alliance: love. Even if it was a mutually-agreed-on kind of caring.

So for now, he'd continue to feign sleep long enough for her to slip from the bedroom undeterred. Continue to wish they didn't have a million things in the way of the two of them getting close enough to make love, and hence get close enough to potentially be really truly happy together. But even though mind-blowing passion wasn't in their immediate future, he could still do what had to be done to give his new wife—and the inadvertent mother of his children—the domestic assistance she needed.

Once they were past the Thanksgiving holiday, and their company left, their lives would settle down quickly. A daily rhythm would be established. And with it, hopefully, so would the closeness and sense of family they all wanted and needed to make their lives complete.

Chapter 5

When she slipped into the kitchen to make a quick cup of coffee, Merri found she wasn't the only one up. Addie was already sitting at the table, dressed, restless and ready to go.

"Trouble sleeping?" Merri asked sympathetically.

She dipped her head in acknowledgment. "Guess I slept too much on the flight home. Going out to take care of your herd?"

Reminded that Addie had grown up on a farm in Minnesota, she nodded. There was something about living the rural life that created a near instantaneous bond in people. "Yep…that's right."

"Want some help?"

Merri knew it would go a lot faster if she did have assistance. And given how much she had to do before they all headed to the community center for the annual

Thanksgiving dinner… "That would be great, thank you." She went into the mudroom, got out two pairs of Wellington boots, and handed a set to Addie. "Have you ever milked a cow?"

"I've done it the old-fashioned way—by hand."

Smiling, Merri went to the cupboard and pulled out an extra barn coat and work gloves. "We're a little more modern than that."

"Well, I'd love to see the operation. That is, if you don't mind me tagging along?"

It was easy to tell why Chase was so fond of Addie. Merri handed the other woman an insulated coffee mug. "I'd welcome the company."

As they drove out to the barns in the pickup truck, Merri filled Addie in on the specifics of the dairy operation. "Female calves are raised for two years before they produce milk, and milking is done twice a day—morning and late afternoon. Slim handles it most of the time, during the week, and I pick up a couple of shifts on weekends, when it's easier for me to get a sitter over to take care of the kids. Although I often take them to the barn with me, too."

Merri parked and got out of the truck.

As always, the herd was stabled in the adjacent barn at night, so it was easy to move them into the milking barn through the backing gates, and into the parlor. Addie helped Merri situate all twenty-four cows in their berths. Together they put out the feed and went up and down the aisles, sanitizing teats and hooking them up to the automated milking systems.

As they moved along, working nicely in tandem, Merri got the feeling that Addie was trying to work up the courage to talk to her about something. Merri hoped it wasn't more questions about how she and Chase had met.

Once everything was set, the two women stepped out to drink their coffee in the brisk November air, and admire the streaks of pink spreading across the horizon.

Finally, Addie spoke what was on her mind. Her cheeks a self-conscious pink, she blurted, "Don't worry about Starr when it comes to Chase."

Merri stiffened in alarm. Starr? The striking brunette who obviously had a big-time crush on Chase....

Addie lifted a hand. "It's obvious to everyone that she wants him to be a lot more than just her friend. She was hoping—since he's now out of the service—that she'd be able to make a play for him."

Merri ignored the sudden clenching of her abdomen. The idea that she and Chase had to prove themselves in family court, to Judge Roy, was stressful enough. Now she had to worry about someone trying to steal Chase from her?

She pulled in a breath and attempted to quell the sudden rise of anxiety within her. "You're telling me she hasn't made a move on him before?"

Addie shook her head soberly. "Starr knew she would crash and burn if she tried. Chase is a by-the-rules kind of guy. Fraternization within a unit is severely discouraged. Causes too many soap-opera-type problems, you know."

"So if you were to have a romance with a fellow soldier...one of you would have to be transferred out?"

"And Chase knows that and believes it's the right policy," Addie agreed. "It's why he never dated anyone within the unit, even on the sly. Plus, he was heartbroken by his previous fiancée."

Although Merri had been privy to that last bit of news, she'd never actually heard Chase's side of the story—just that he had fallen in love during his last years of medical school, and that the engagement was abruptly called off before he entered the military. True to form, he'd been tight-lipped about it ever since.

"Anyway, it's why we all came out here with Starr," Addie continued quietly. "'Cause we knew she was going to make a fool of herself over him. And we were hoping to sort of run interference—to keep things from getting too uncomfortable for either of them. Because at the end of the day, we think they both will still want to be friends."

Merri studied Addie's worried expression. "So you're telling me you think he's not interested in Starr that way."

She hesitated a second too long. "Well, obviously not, because he married you, didn't he?"

Yes. He had. For reasons Merri wasn't about to explain.

But would Chase have still married her if he'd known Starr was about to come after him, uninhibited by any military regulations that may have once stood in their path? Or would he have tried to solve the daddy dilemma another way in order to keep his options open?

Unfortunately, there was no way to know for sure.

No way she could ask Addie any of this.

"You all are so close," Merri said, instead.

"Crisis bonding." Addie walked through the wet grass and leaned against the pasture fence, her back to the beautiful Texas sunrise. She looked around, enjoying the sweet serenity of the morning. "Being thrown together in a field hospital forges quick, strong bonds.

And it's not just on the battlefield where this occurs. It happens to people in any kind of crisis situation."

Like mine and Chase's, Merri thought, keeping an eye on the milking operation, and finding all was still well. She paced away from the open doors. "So the lot of you will be friends for life."

Addie's expression grew uncertain. "As long as we're in the military together, we will be." Briefly, pain flashed in her eyes. "But once a person is back in civilian life, and the high-stakes camaraderie that keeps a unit together no longer exists, well…" She shrugged and looked Merri in the eye. "In those situations, friendships sometimes fade or disappear altogether, because the closeness wasn't based on anything enduring…."

Taking Addie's words to heart, Merri thought about the hospital grief group that had proved so important to her—in the months after her mother's death, as well as in the aftermath of her sister and brother-in-law's tragic accident. Both times, the support group had been a lifeline. But then, as everyone gradually healed and resumed their normal lives, the acute intensity of those friendships had faded.

They were all still friendly, of course. But not the way they had been while deep in mourning.

Merri swallowed. "Has the loss of this kind of friendship happened to you?" And more important, she thought nervously, would it happen to her and Chase? Not that they were all that close yet.

Addie nodded. "A few times, with people who have left our unit. But I'm still close to some individuals who left the army, too. So it depends."

Merri turned back to the fence, watching as the pale

yellow sun edged over the sagebrush that dotted the far horizon. "What do you predict will happen with Starr and Chase?"

Addie finished the rest of her coffee, and replaced the lid on the stainless-steel travel mug. "To date, they are just friends. Although, Starr's always believed where there's a will, there's a way."

And Starr clearly had a huge crush on Chase. Merri's stomach twisted with anxiety. "So what are you trying to tell me? That she might make a play for Chase while you all are here?"

Addie's expression sobered. "If she does, it isn't anything you should be mad at Chase about. Because he's married to you now, and he's an honorable guy. The kind who always does what's right in the end."

Like throw away his freedom to marry me, to give the kids the best possible life. Merri sighed.

It took another two hours to finish the milking, check the production information on the computer, turn the cows out to pasture and clean and disinfect the barns with high-pressure hoses.

By the time they got back to the ranch house it was nearly nine. Merri was in desperate need of a shower and shampoo. Aside from taking care of their company, she still had the casseroles to make. Or did she?

The aromatic smell of brown sugar and sweet potatoes hit her the moment she walked in the door. Was it possible Chase had been cooking? she wondered in shock.

She slipped off her boots in the mudroom and walked into the kitchen, Addie tagging along behind her. There, standing in front of the stove, wearing

Merri's favorite Williams-Sonoma apron, was a satin-pajama-and-slipper-clad Starr. Ovenproof gloves on her hands, she was lifting out four large casseroles. Four more sat, the picture of perfection, already baked. The last two were ready to be slid in to cook.

"Surprise!" Starr said.

"Look, Mommy!" Jessalyn called, from her perch on the counter next to Nissa and Davita. "Miss Starr cooked your sweet 'tatoes!"

Jeffrey nodded solemnly, clearly impressed. He beamed at Harmony and Polly, who'd been seated at the kitchen table, playing blocks with him, then pointed to the tattered piece of yellowed paper on the counter. "Just like the recipe said."

Addie looked as shocked as Merri felt, but not surprised. Clearly, Merri thought, this was stage one of Capture Chase's Heart. Complete with one button too many undone on Starr's satin pajama top.

"Wow," Addie said. She walked over to give a nicely dressed and showered Chase a friendly punch in the forearm. "You have been busy, soldier."

Merri nodded. Unable to vanquish the notion that she had just been upstaged in her own home, she forced a perfect hostess smile. "Wow is right. Thank you all so much! I hope you got breakfast…."

"Oh, yeah. Chase fixed us his famous eggs and tortillas."

"He makes a mean cup of joe, too."

"We saved some for both of you, though."

"Thanks." Ignoring the unprecedented jealousy roiling in her gut, Merri forced another smile. "But I'm going to head for the shower. In the meantime, carry on."

"Do you think she's mad?" she heard Starr say behind her departing back. "Chase, honey, I think she might be mad. Why would she be mad...?"

Why indeed, Merri fumed, heading for the stairs. A scant two minutes later, she was stepping into the shower. Only to discover the fifty-gallon tank had been drained of hot water. What was left was at best lukewarm. Deciding, what the heck, maybe a cold shower was what she needed right now, anyway, Merri turned off the hot spigot and stood under the freezing spray.

By the time she had finished a quick lather and rinse of her hair and body, her teeth were chattering and she was shaking from head to foot. But her temper had cooled. Until a knock sounded on the door and Chase said, "Merri, I need to talk to you."

Chase knew he was in trouble the moment Merri stepped out of the bathroom, wrapped in a thick terry-cloth robe. She smelled of lavender, but her lips were devoid of their usual luscious pink color.

Upon closer inspection, he saw the goose bumps on her fair skin...and the way she was shivering. "Did you take a cold shower?"

New color flooded her cheeks as she ran a towel over her hair, systematically blotting the dampness from it. "I didn't really have a choice. We're out of hot water."

He winced. "Sorry. All the gals were taking showers. Starr's headed there now."

"I hope she likes her water icy."

Okay, that had sounded very unhostesslike, which was in turn very unlike Merri. Aware that she had every right to be annoyed and stressed out, Chase took responsibility, too. "It's my fault. I had no idea we were short in that regard. I probably drained half the tank myself."

Merri regrouped and then flashed him a brief, purposeful smile. "I should have warned everyone." She shook her head, as if chastising herself for not thinking about it in advance. "When the old water heater went out last fall, I tried to conserve energy, and replaced it with a smaller model. With just the three of us here, we didn't need an eighty-gallon tank."

Chase leaned against the bureau, hands braced on either side of him, wondering what if anything she had on under that robe. Panties? A bra? Nothing at all?

He had to struggle to stay with the conversation. "If conservation is the goal, a heat-on-demand unit would be even better."

Merri tossed him a considering look over her slender shoulder, before starting to untangle her hair with a wide-toothed comb. "I considered it, but those models are a lot more expensive to purchase and install." She walked into the closet, hips swaying as she moved. "Right now I'm putting every penny I can spare into the expansion of the dairy, so it was out of my price range. At least for the moment..."

With his eyes on her sexy-as-hell legs, Chase followed her into the narrow space between the racks, speaking in a low, confidential tone. "It doesn't have to be, Merri." He watched as she searched through her wardrobe. The neckline of her robe gaped slightly, answering his earlier question. No bra, anyway. Just the soft, delicious curve of one plump breast.

He cleared his throat. "Now that we're married, I can help with things like that."

She kept her head averted, and focused on her mission—selecting the right thing to wear to the community event. As she held out a particular sweater, her teeth raked across her velvety soft lower lip. "I don't think we're going to run out of hot water very often. Unless you plan to have this many guests underfoot on a regular basis."

"You are ticked off that they're all here."

She grabbed a skirt, too, and a pair of matching suede heels, and then brushed past him. "On the contrary. I'm enjoying their company, as are the kids. And Addie was a great help with the milking this morning."

Chase watched Merri hang her outfit on the hook on the bathroom door. "Let's not forget that Starr pitched in to make all those sweet potato casseroles for the Thanksgiving buffet. Saving you a heck of a lot of time and work."

Merri returned to her dresser, pulled out a bra and panties and hose. "She certainly did."

Was that sarcasm underlying her low tone? Chase edged nearer. "I've heard of women being territorial about their kitchens…"

"Um-hmm." Lingerie in one hand, Merri pulled a pendant and earrings from her jewelry box. "Well, I'm not one of them."

But she certainly looked territorial about *something*.

"Mommy!" Jeffrey and Jessalyn burst into the bedroom. "That lady, the one in the apron, is screaming in the bathroom!"

Screeching was more like it, Chase thought, listening to the indignant, high-pitched sounds.

"Guess Starr just found out we're out of hot water," Merri said wryly. She made shooing motions toward the hallway. "Now if you'll excuse me, everyone, I've really got to get dressed and dry my hair."

"Kids," Chase murmured with outspread hands, ready to herd them downstairs. Once again, Jeffrey and Jessalyn looked at him as if he were persona non grata, and then fled in the opposite direction. Merri displayed the same intolerant attitude, which made it unanimous.

He was not yet an accepted member of this family, and at this rate, might not be for a very long while.

Chase rode with Merri and the two kids in her SUV. Addie and Starr took his pickup truck, while the other four women went in the van they had rented, all of them parking side by side in the community center lot. Chase opened the door for the twins, only to have them scoot over to the driver's side and wait for Merri to help them both out.

Give them time, he thought. *Closeness will happen.* He just had to remember not to push.

He shut the door and sauntered around to Merri.

He had never seen her looking prettier.

She had on a white cashmere sweater, a flowing, brown brushed-velvet skirt and suede heels. A silver pendant and matching earrings completed her holiday garb. "How are we going to do this?"

Jessalyn and Jeffrey tugged on Merri's hands, clearly wanting her to carry them.

"Honey, you're too big, you know that," she told Jeffrey. "You, too, Jessalyn."

No kidding. Chase thought. They were a good thirty-five pounds each.

Jeffrey argued, "You carry us sometimes."

"In emergencies," Merri allowed pleasantly, holding both their hands and walking around to open up the back of her SUV. "Like when you get really scared or have a boo-boo."

Jessalyn gripped Merri's skirt before she could reach for the foil-covered casseroles. "We're scared now, Mommy."

"Yep," Jeffrey angled in close. "We really really are."

No, they weren't, Chase thought. They were testing her, a fact Merri seemed to know very well. He could hardly blame the twins, though, for trying to figure out where the boundaries were. They'd had some pretty big changes happen in their lives in the past week. Changes no one had prepared them for.

The kids had a right to be ticked off.

Starr sauntered forward and laid a hand on Chase's arm, with Addie right beside her. The brunette smiled up at him, the look in her eyes reminding him that she had been a pediatric nurse before enlisting in the military to care for wounded soldiers.

Chase gave her an encouraging nod.

Starr knelt down at eye level with the twins. "I can carry you, Jessalyn," she offered, with open arms.

Addie hunkered down, too. "And I can carry you, Jeffrey."

The twins beamed in acquiescence.

"That is, if it's okay with Merri," Chase interjected, remembering that though he was technically their daddy now, when it came to the kids and the ranch, Merri was still the one in charge.

"Sure." She admonished the twins with a look. "As long as you behave."

"We will," they promised in unison.

Starr and Addie picked up the twins.

Merri turned back to the sweet potato casseroles. There were ten large pans and five adults. "I think we should all carry one at a time and then come back."

"I can carry two," Chase offered, figuring that would save at least one return trip.

She shook her head. "These pans are disposable. They really should be carried by the bottom rather than the sides."

Because this was her show, he acquiesced. A minute later, all of them had a casserole in hand, and the people started toward the community center, with Merri taking the lead.

Other people were moving toward the door, too. Including Liz Cartwright and her family, the Briscoes, and Judge Roy with her husband and four teenage daughters. The latter group was loaded down with gallon jugs of iced tea and lemonade. They reached the door well ahead of the others and stepped inside.

Tables that would seat hundreds of local residents were festooned with cornucopia centerpieces and covered with tablecloths in beautiful fall colors. A sumptuous-looking buffet was being set up. People were bustling to and fro and calling out cheery hellos.

Merri turned to Chase as they crossed the threshold into the banquet hall. Unfortunately, he turned to her at the exact same time.

Their casserole dishes collided. Chase kept a grip on his, but Merri was not so lucky. In her effort to keep from dropping it altogether, she wedged it against her chest. The foil covering slipped at the same time that the flimsy aluminum pan holding it bent into a V. And a big glob of the perfectly prepared confection squished out onto her sweater.

Around them, everyone gasped, Merri included. Chase steadied his own casserole with one arm and gallantly reached out to steady hers, in a gesture that was too little, too late. The slippery contents oozed over top of Merri's hands, causing her to lose her precarious grip.

Chase swore in frustration as the whole casserole fell to the tiled floor.

Merri didn't know what was worse, the wetness seeping into her beautiful white cashmere sweater, the ruined food all over the floor or the bright orange streaks splattered across her skirt and Chase's slacks. He set his dish down safely on a nearby table while a collective gasp sounded.

"Mommy, you're a mess!" Jessalyne declared. She turned and pointed at Chase. "So are you!"

"Yeah. A great big one!" Jeffrey concurred, aghast.

Thanks. Merri grimaced and lifted a reassuring hand. "I know, kiddos, but we'll clean it up." Her face flaming with embarrassment, she knelt to recover the crumpled aluminum container. Chase knelt at the same time.

They bumped heads.

"Ouch!" they said in unison.

Merri didn't know whether to laugh or cry, so she did a little of both while Starr took charge with laudable military efficiency. "Let's get the remaining casseroles to the buffet." The nurse picked up Chase's dish and marched off, clearly not willing to risk any more of her culinary effort than they'd already lost.

Several mothers from the preschool appeared, their own children in tow. They shot Merri understanding, empathetic glances. "We'll take charge of the twins while you deal with this," they promised.

"Thank you," Merri said.

Addie jumped into the fray. "I'll see if I can get paper towels and cleaner."

Another guest bent to whisper in Merri's ear. "It can be hard to get in sync physically with a new husband. Don't worry, dear. It will come in time." The elderly woman patted Merri's shoulder.

Would it? she wondered.

What would Judge Roy think? There was barely a hint of reaction on her face as she and her perfect family glanced their way from across the banquet hall. But as Merri looked down in horror at the icky, sticky mess, she could feel the other woman's disapproval. This was such a disaster!

Chase gripped her hand and helped her to her feet. "I don't suppose you have any clean clothes in the SUV."

"No." Merri sighed. "And if I drive all the way out to the ranch to get some—"

"You'll miss the dinner," Chase guessed.

She nodded, her mood no longer anything close to thankful.

"Looks like it's your lucky day." Merri's friend, Emily, suddenly appeared, waving a key in her hand. "Just so happens that Dylan and I have extra clothes at the Daybreak Café. They're in my office upstairs, behind the party room. And there's a bathroom, too. So—" she gestured to Merri and Chase "—help yourselves to whatever fits."

"I'm sorry," Merri apologized, still feeling hideously embarrassed as the two of them walked away.

"I ran into you," Chase said sheepishly.

"We ran into each other," Merri corrected in exasperation.

He shrugged and wrapped an arm about her shoulders. "Doesn't matter," he teased. "The end result is the same. We're both a big mess!" He gestured expansively. "Jeffrey and Jessalyn said so."

Not sure whether his response was for show or comfort, Merri leaned into him. "Do not make me laugh. This is so not funny."

His lips crooked up at one corner. "Tell me about it," he grumbled in return. "Do you know how long I spent picking out this ensemble?"

He had looked very handsome, Merri thought. Too gorgeous for his own good. Seeing him in a jacket and tie reminded her of their wedding day.

They walked past the closed sign and opened the door to the shuttered café. The empty restaurant was a peaceful oasis after the bustling community center.

Acutely aware of him, Merri led the way up the stairs, to Emily's private office. The closet in the corner was filled with clothes. Outfits for riding, for casual dinners in town, and fancy affairs. Merri began sorting through them.

Chase plucked up a sequined black dress with a plunging neckline. "This is nice," he quipped.

"Yeah. Like I'm going to show up in *that*."

His eyes gleamed as if he was imagining it.

Merri flushed. "You could wear a tuxedo."

Chase stepped into the bathroom and studied his reflection in the mirror. "Actually, I think I can get most of this out with a little water."

Merri eyed the stains on his pants, which started just below his crotch and fanned out in tiny splatters from the thigh down. "Lucky you."

He reached for a washcloth and dampened it beneath the spigot. While he dabbed at the spots on his dove-gray shirt, then began working on the charcoal fabric of his trousers, Merri continued rummaging through the options. Finally, she emerged with an ivory silk tank, a black wool skirt and a long cranberry cardigan. "Hope-fully, these will fit. Although my shoes aren't going to match at all." She lifted a trim ankle, showing off her brown suede pump.

Chase regarded her leg with mock solemnity. "Now, that's a crime."

Grinning, Merri aimed a fist at his sternum. "Cut it out."

Amber eyes lighting with mischief, he caught her forearm and held her hand over his thudding heart. "You cut it out."

Merri caught her breath at the intent in his gaze. "Chase…"

The next thing she knew his head was lowering, tilt-ing slightly to one side. And then his lips were on hers.

Chapter 6

Heaven help her, the man could kiss. And he wasn't just any man; he was her husband. If only the marriage was based on the kind of abiding love a couple should have for each other, Merri thought. But it wasn't. And she had to keep reminding herself of that. Otherwise, she'd think that the way he was kissing her and holding her was proof that he was falling in love with her.

And that couldn't be true.

They had a deal. This was a marriage made to support a family. To enable them to do best by the twins, and add another child to the mix. A child she would carry.

Meanwhile, he was pressed against her, deliciously warm and hard, his lips moving tenderly over hers. Desire swirled through her, making her pulse race, and turning up a fierce, thudding heat in the feminine heart of her.

The kiss was meant to curb frustration and restore humor to a situation that was fast getting out of control. At least that was what Chase had told himself when he ignored Merri's gasp of pleasure and took her into his arms.

But that was before she had slayed him with that look—the one that invited him to do what no one else had been able to accomplish—to try and tear down the barriers surrounding her heart, to find the soft vulnerable woman she tried so hard to shield from further hurt.

And, Chase thought with a rush of overwhelming want and need, damned if he wasn't determined to do just that.

Their lips meshed, more perfectly still. He plunged his tongue into her mouth, kissed the corners, realized she was kissing him back with a passionate resolve that wrenched a low groan from his throat.

Tightening his grip, he hauled her all the way against him and shifted her so her back was to the wall, the only sounds the rasp of their breathing and the low murmur of delight when he slid his hands beneath the hem of her cashmere sweater and cupped her breasts with his palms.

Her nipples pearled, and he slipped a thumb beneath the satin bra, basking in the feminine feel of her.

She leaned into his touch, her fingers finding their way beneath his shirt, the waistband of his slacks.

Wanting. Just as he wanted.

And that was when they heard it. The sound of footsteps coming up the stairs to the second floor of the café. A feminine voice calling out, "Chase! Merri? Are you up here?"

Chase and Merri broke apart, disheveled, and out of breath, right before Starr rounded the corner.

Chase's friend took one look at them and emotion flickered in her eyes, then disappeared.

"We were talking," he said.

Something less pleasant flickered across Starr's face. "I can see that," she said, her glance moving over his shirt, then Merri's sweater, and the proof that resided there.

Merri followed Starr's glance. Chase's shirt had barely been soiled before. Now, sweet potato casserole was smeared across the entire front of it. The creamy orange goop and flecks of chopped pecan were even more deeply embedded in the white cashmere.

Plus his shirttail was hanging out of the front of his pants.

While Chase seemed to have recovered from their passionate interlude, Merri was one guilty and embarrassed wreck.

"I'm sorry if I interrupted anything," Starr continued pleasantly with a poker face. "I just wanted to make sure everything was okay. And it occurred to me, Chase, that you probably had some clothes at the hospital, in your locker there, since you often go straight from office hours into surgery. I was going to offer to go and get them…"

Merri looked at Chase. Realized, to her further humiliation, that he had already thought about that, and had instead chosen to come here with her. To make sure she was okay, or use the opportunity to put the moves on her?

Not certain how she felt about consummating their marriage by indulging in some clandestine pre-Thanksgiving feast nooky on the sly, Merri drew a deep breath and said, "That's a really good idea, Starr. Actually, you can both go together."

Chase lifted a brow, obviously realizing she was trying to get rid of him, pronto. Merri lifted a palm before further protest could be made, and directed them to the door. "I'm fine here. Honestly. And dinner is set to start in another twenty minutes, so we all better get moving."

Once they departed, Merri took advantage of the privacy to pull herself together and deal with the fact that she had almost surrendered all her standards and had sex with Chase, then and there. Hadn't she told herself when she ended her last relationship that she would not let herself be used again or treated as less than she was? She deserved respect. So did Chase.

More important still, she wanted to harness her emotions and be in control of the situation. She wanted to act while thinking clearly, not while in the throes of uncontrollable lust. Because at the end of the day, there was no confusing lust with love.

"You want to tell me what's going on?" Liz asked Merri, a scant fifteen minutes later.

Breathless, and still glowing inwardly from having been thoroughly kissed, Merri scanned the room for the twins, saw them already seated at the table reserved for their age group. With relief, she noted the kids looked very happy as they colored their kiddie place mats.

She spotted Emily, too, all the way across the room.

Merri plucked at her borrowed clothing and mouthed a thank-you.

Emily smiled and waved back, mouthing *You're welcome.*

Aware that the attorney was still waiting for an explanation, Merri turned to Liz. "What do you mean, going on?" she asked, stalling for time while she tried to figure out just how much to reveal.

"You and Chase and the twins walk in with six of Chase's woman friends."

"Oh. That." Merri waved her concern away. "They're good friends. Medical personnel from the army unit Chase was in."

Liz eyed the group of attractive young women with an assessing gaze. "And they're all staying with you. While you're essentially still on your honeymoon."

Merri was acutely aware it had only been four days since the wedding. Four very eventful days. "It's a long story. But yes…Chase and I invited them."

"The twins seem to like them."

"As do I."

Liz considered that. "Where's Chase?"

To Merri's dismay, he chose that moment to walk into the community center, with Starr by his side, acting for all the world as if she, not Merri, were his wife.

Liz frowned as her glance cut to the Roys. The judge was eyeing Chase and Starr, too, and the attorney sighed. "This does not look good."

Tell me about it.

Frowning, Liz continued her summation with lawyerly calm. "First, you and Chase are about as uncoordinated and out of sync as any couple I have ever seen, bumping into each other and getting food all over both of you. Next, the two of you take off to change clothes, only to come back alone, looking…" She paused and shook her head. "And then fifteen minutes later, he shows up with that incredibly attractive shamelessly smitten brunette."

Her pulse racing, Merri lifted a palm. "I can explain."

Liz lifted a hand, too. "I don't need to hear it. I don't *want* to hear it. Just be aware that Judge Roy is privy to all this, too."

Their attorney had a point. "So what do you suggest I do?" Merri asked nervously.

"Demonstrate to everyone that what the two of you are proposing to the court is in the best interest of the twins. That there is every reason to put faith in you as a couple—and a family."

Chase didn't know what had gotten into Merri or Starr. All he knew was that he was sandwiched between them, and both were acting as if he were the most fantastic man on earth. Smiling at him, engaging him and each other in conversation, constantly touching his arms.

Addie kept trying to intervene, too, and divert all the attention to her, in a way that was unusual, to say the least. While Nissa, Davita, Harmony and Polly enjoyed their meal and looked on in bemusement.

Not that the twins were about to come in last, either. Jeffrey and Jessalyn sat nestled together on the other side of Merri. Demanding that she—and only she—cut their turkey, and take the offending green beans and sweet potato casserole off their plates.

Meanwhile, everyone they knew stopped by their

table on the way to and from the buffet table to congratulate Merri and Chase on their new marriage. And
each time it happened, she tensed.

Chase knew how she felt. Because it did seem a little insincere.

And that, he knew, was going to have to be rectified.

They couldn't go back into Judge Roy's court, swearing they were "family," when right now, anyway, they
were anything but that.

Maybe making love would help. That, and him finding a way to get close enough to the twins to become
the daddy they needed and deserved....

"Earth to Chase. Earth to Chase," Starr teased,
touching his arm again.

What was with all the physical possessiveness? He
turned to his former coworker, wondering how he could
get her to back off without hurting her feelings or making a scene. To his left, he heard Merri push back her
chair.

"Hurrah! We get to go play!" the twins shouted exu-
berantly, running off to the temporary children's center
set up in one corner of the banquet hall. Looking flustered, Merri rushed to catch up with them.

Starr kept right on talking, raving about the hospi-
tality of his home county, but Chase only had eyes for
the woman he had married.

Damn, but Merri was gorgeous, even in borrowed
clothes and shoes that didn't match.

Smiling, she settled the kids with the teenagers su-
pervising the indoor play area, then turned and plunged
back into the crowd of friends and neighbors, to his
surprise making made a beeline for every single, cute,
thirty-something man there. One by one, she patted

them on the biceps, whispered in their ear and urged them to tag along with her.

Within ten minutes, she had half a dozen guys surrounding her and was walking back to the table where Chase and his lady friends sat, enjoying their after-dinner coffees.

An unfamiliar pang of jealousy knotted Chase's gut. Was this some sort of payback for the onslaught of women around him?

Merri gestured magnanimously as they reached the table. "What we have here, fellas, are six ladies in need of the blue-ribbon tour of Laramie, Texas."

The men grinned, exchanging glances with each other as well as their feminine quarry. "I think we can handle that," one drawled.

"Particularly if all you ladies want to stay around for the band that's going to play later this evening, over at the dance hall."

"I don't know…." Starr demurred. "I'm not sure we should desert Chase or Merri, since we're all leaving tomorrow…."

He stood and nudged her gently, "You should go. It'll be fun. Besides…" He turned to his wife. "Merri and I will be busy with the kids this evening. 'Cause I don't think there's any way they're going to last that long."

Acting all wifely again, Merri confirmed, "They won't."

Starr wrinkled her nose. "You're really going to miss all the fun?"

Chase wrapped his arm around Merri's shoulders and gave her a playful buss on the temple. "Not all the fun." He winked salaciously and everyone laughed.

"Well," Addie murmured, looking straight at Starr, "they *are* newlyweds!"

* * *

Newlyweds indeed, Merri thought with a silent snort.

She didn't feel like Chase's wife. And he certainly wasn't acting like a husband to her, except that he was annoying her right now, the way she had seen almost every husband annoy his wife at one time or another. Unfortunately, for everyone's sake, Merri knew she had to follow their attorney's advice and demonstrate that she and Chase were a viable couple who would do right by their children.

"Can I have a word with you, hon?" Chase asked. "Privately?"

Not if it meant they would end up kissing again, here of all places. Merri gave him a look only he could see. "Can it wait? I've got to talk to Paige and Kurt...."

"Actually—" Chase began, tenderly tightening his grip and pulling her closer to his side.

At that precise moment, the hospital chaplain passed by, beaming. He gave Merri a thumbs-up. "Best sweet potato casserole I've ever eaten, bar none."

It figured, Merri thought dryly, the way her day was going....

"Don't know what you did to it, but the chaplain's right—it is fantastic," Deputy Rio Vasquez agreed enthusiastically as he passed by about the same time, another serving of casserole in hand. "Your mother's recipe never tasted so good in all the years you've been cooking it."

This would be the one time she would get wildly enthusiastic compliments.

"So good," a cowboy chimed in, "that it's now completely gone." He looked at Merri wistfully. "You did your mama proud."

"Thanks." Honor dictated that Merri give credit where it was due, no matter how embarrassed she felt. "But I didn't make it this year." Smiling self-consciously, she pointed at the stunning nurse on the other side of the room. "Starr did."

The men fell silent as they realized they had just put their foot in it.

"But I'll let her know you guys all really liked it," Merri promised, before turning to Chase. "In the meantime, I've got to let the twins know they're going to go home with Kurt and Paige and the triplets for a play date, while I tend to the herd back at the ranch and do the milking."

A mixture of surprise and hurt flashed across Chase's face. "I could have watched the kids," he said quietly. Realizing this was a private discussion, their companions drifted away.

Guiltily, Merri realized that she hadn't even thought to ask him if he wanted to do so. She was going to have to work on this co-parenting thing. "This is sort of our tradition," Merri explained, with an apologetic glance. "But if you want to go with them to Paige and Kurt's home, I'm sure it would be okay with them," she finished kindly.

Another wave of tension ran between them, as if he, too, knew how out of sync they were. Ready to do what he could to remedy that, he looked her in the eye. "How about I help you instead?"

Chase? Operating a milking machine? Cleaning out the barn? Merri shook her head. "Thanks, but Addie already offered to assist me again."

Chase aimed a thumb over his shoulder, his lips lifting in a grin. "Addie looks like she has her hands full with that cowboy."

Well, what do you know? Merri thought, watching Addie flirting shyly with her gentlemen companions. Good for her!

Merri turned back to Chase, still not able to see him assisting her. Like it or not, he belonged in a hospital, with a bevy of adoring assistants around him. She wrinkled her nose. "It's a dirty job."

He fixed her with a deadpan look. "I can get dirty."

Heaven help her, she was reading all sorts of things into that remark. Shrugging, Merri ignored the shimmer of sexual attraction between them. "Suit yourself."

Realizing he had gotten to her, upping the ante another notch, he chuckled. "Thanks, hon, I will."

She let her gaze rove over his tall, solidly built frame and powerful shoulders. "And stop calling me hon." When he came closer, she could feel his body heat. "Okay, sweetheart."

She put her hands on her hips and returned his smoldering gaze. "I don't like that endearment, either, cowboy."

He rubbed his jaw in a thoughtful manner, eyeing her thoughtfully. His gaze took her in, head to toe. "Babe?"

Her smile widened as the flirtatious mood between them deepened. "What do you think, hunk of burning love?"

He rocked back on his heels and squinted speculatively. "Sugar?"

Merri stifled her amusement and drew an indignant breath. "Doesn't really fit, either, honey bunch."

Chase laughed, the sound deep and flirtatious.

Awareness sifted through her as he shifted the fall of her hair away from her face and leaned forward to whisper in her ear, "Well, it's not going to be darling."

The warmth of his breath warmed her skin. Refusing to think about hauling him into her arms and kissing him again, she retorted, "Wise decision, hubby dear."

"Well, then—" He wrapped a possessive arm about her waist and gave her a decisive look meant to needle her even more. "Wifey it is, then."

Merri groaned at the thought, even as she let him guide her toward the door.

The facetious argument about what sort of endearments they could use for each other carried them all the way out to the ranch. Given the seriousness of the problems facing them—both in court and on the home front, it was a relief to talk about something utterly nonsensical. "Maybe I should just call you sheik," Merri decided, when they finally parked in front of the ranch house.

Chase got out of the SUV, glad they were finally going to have some time alone together. Their first real solitude since the afternoon they had decided to marry.

Grinning, he fell into step beside her. "Sheik?"

Merri paused to unlock the front door, then swept inside in a drift of lavender perfume. "You've already vetoed stud and honey, baby cakes and sweetie pie."

Merri carried their stained clothing into the laundry room and deposited it in a wicker basket marked Dry Cleaning. Whirling again, she slid past him and headed for the staircase.

Lazily, Chase followed. "But sheik?"

Inside their bedroom, Merri grabbed a clean set of work clothes and disappeared into the master bath.

"Kinds of fits with the 'harem,' don't you think?" she said, around the mostly closed door.

Chase began to strip down, too. "So you *are* jealous."

"I am not." Merri emerged, borrowed set of clothing in hand.

Chase admired the way she looked in her flannel shirt and faded, threadbare jeans. He strode to the closet and rummaged for his jeans. "I was," he admitted as he pulled out a thermal, long-sleeved T-shirt, too.

"Of what?" Merri sat down to pull on a pair of wool socks.

"You." Chase closed his fly. Tugged the shirt on over his head. "With all those guys you rounded up."

Merri slanted him a skeptical glance as he sat down next to her on the bed.

He shrugged, thinking about the way he'd felt when he'd seen her flirting with them. "I didn't know what you had in mind."

Her green eyes glimmering, Merri scoffed. "A sevensome?" She slapped her hand on his jean-clad thigh and bounded right back to her feet. "Seriously, Chase!"

He stood, too, locking eyes with her. "Well, okay, not that, but..." His mood turned deeply serious again as he admitted, "I think of you as mine."

He watched for her reaction.

To his frustration, she looked more wary than ever. "To a point," she said slowly, "I am."

He hooked his arms about her waist and pulled her close. "More than just a point," he said, wanting more than ever to take things to the next step.

Merri saw the desire in Chase's eyes. She splayed her hands across his chest and hitched in a bolstering breath. "Chase…" She moaned as his lips blazed a fiery path across her forehead, dipping down to the sensitive spot behind her ear.

"We're never going to feel married unless we behave like we're married," he coaxed, working his way down the slope of her throat.

Merri arched against him. Her fingers clutched his shirt, even as she struggled against the sensations coursing through her body. She closed her eyes, thinking maybe it wouldn't feel so erotic, so right, being here with him this way, if she couldn't see him.

"This isn't the way," she protested weakly.

He slid a hand beneath her chin and lifted her lips to his. "Tell me that in five minutes," he murmured, "and I'll believe you."

The next thing she knew they were kissing. Hotly. Tenderly. Merri shifted her hands to the nape of his neck and curled her fingers into his hair. Unable to help herself—the truth was she wanted to claim him, too—she surged against him, loving the taste and touch and wonder of him. He was everything she had ever wished for, and she could feel his arousal, pressing hard against her, summoning up her own blossoming need. She wanted him desperately and she let him know it with a sweet, searing kiss in return.

Chase knew it was medieval of him, but he wanted to put his stamp of possession on Merri. He wanted her with him, with absolutely nothing held back. Anchoring his arm around her waist, he guided her toward the bed. *Their* bed. Fell onto it with her, so she was beneath him. Her body was throbbing everywhere his was.

"Okay… You're convincing me," she gasped, slipping her palms beneath the hem of his shirt, running them across his skin. "But we've got chores to do, and kids to pick up later, so we have to make this fast."

Chase knew what she was thinking. As long as they kept this purely physical and matter-of-fact, their hearts would stay intact. He reached for the buttons on her shirt, uncovering her a few inches at a time. The swell of her breasts peeked out from the lace of her bra. He undid the clasp, revealing creamy skin and pink nipples. His lips followed where his eyes had gone. "Not too fast."

But again, she wanted to keep things casual, with all the caution their situation required, and none of the heart. Knowing that wouldn't work in the long run, not for her, Chase kissed her to remind her of what they could have, given half a chance. He kissed her to show her what he wanted them to have, in the end. He kissed her out of frustration for the way everything was evolving, and the way that it wasn't.

And she kissed him back, responding to his passion, meeting his need. Until he knew that what was happening had less to do with their marriage than the way she made him feel, as if he had to be part of her life, and she his. Not just for now...so they'd be more in sync as a married couple. But because there was something here. Something real and vital and worth exploring. Something they couldn't ignore.

He had no more time to contemplate that, however, because she surged against him, tugging and unzipping. "I can't wait...."

Needing, wanting her—and the closeness she offered—he tugged and unzipped, too, and it was like Christmas Day as they wiggled out of the rest of their clothes and climbed onto the bed. Their naked bodies pressed up against each other in the fading afternoon sunlight streaming through the blinds and he stroked her dewy softness. "Here?"

She yielded to him with the sure sense of a woman. "Yes. Oh…yes…there!" Arms wrapped around him, she kissed him again, trembling, clinging to him. He kissed her back, until she surrendered to him completely, the sweet whimpering sounds in her throat a counterpoint to the lower, fierce sounds in his.

"And here?" Chase asked, drifting lower, ready to take each moment as it came.

She caught his head in her hands. "Oh, yeah."

He parted her knees and his own pulse pounding, stroked the insides of her thighs. She arched to receive him, bringing him closer yet. "So. Very. Nice."

And then words deserted her as he made his next move, delved even deeper, and Merri came apart in his hands. Loving the way she looked at him then, as if he was her hero and she was his princess in waiting, he couldn't resist teasing, "Beginning to see my point?"

Her dreamy smile widened.

She wanted to keep things simple.

Yet he knew they were going to get complex.

Mischief sparkled in her green eyes. "As long as you see mine." Smiling sassily, Merri shifted and took control, her silky hair sliding over his chest. Downward she glided, wrapping her hand around him, using the same gentle rhythm he had used on her. Suddenly, he was the one on the edge. Her lips found him, loving him slowly and thoroughly. Chase groaned, desperate to have her. "Now I'm the one who can't wait."

She laughed, and the sound of her pleasure unleashed him. He shifted so Merri was beneath him.

Filled with the exquisite need that drove them both, he held her hands above her head, then kissed her again, long and hot, wet and deep, until he was pretty sure neither of them could have given their own name, and it felt so damn good their breath was rasping and their hearts were pounding. Until there was no doubt about what was coming next. "Tell me you want this," he commanded. *Tell me you want me.*

She gasped and bucked, near bursting. "You know I do."

A shudder racked him and then ran through her, as well. He entered her with one smooth stroke, lifting her, holding her close. Willing to play it her way for now, he murmured, "Tell me this is just the beginning."

Her eyes locked on his. She surged against him obediently and kissed him, unable to hold back. "It's just the beginning."

Her sweet compliance sent him further toward the edge. Satisfaction roared through him, perfect and all-encompassing. He moaned, and ground his hips against hers, touching his thumb to where they were joined. She murmured his name, pleading softly. He answered her by going even deeper. Sensation built upon sensation and the world fell away. Together, they spiraled into ecstasy and beyond.

Chapter 7

As soon as Merri caught her breath, the doubts starting creeping in. What had she done, except very possibly make the baby she wanted so much, with a husband she knew did not love her and probably never would? At least not in the way she had always wanted. Panicked, she began to ease from his embrace.

Chase tightened his hold on her. Pressed a kiss into her hair. And looked at her with his what-I-could-do-to-you-if-I-only-had-the-chance-to-make-love-to-you-again eyes. "Where are you going?"

That quickly, she found herself at the melting point. "The barns."

To her dismay, he saw right through her pragmatic reply. "No rest for the weary, hmm?" he murmured, calling her a liar with everything he didn't say.

Merri bit her lip. "You knew we had to do the milking when we stopped to…" She faltered, unsure what words to use.

His eyes tracked the sheet she held to her breasts. "Make love?"

Despite the fact they weren't in love with each other, that was what it had felt like. Merri nodded shyly.

Chase caught her wrist and pulled her back into bed. His amber eyes glimmering with suppressed devilry, he focused with laser accuracy on her mouth. "How could five minutes of cuddling be so wrong?"

Trying not to imagine what it would feel like to throw caution to the wind and have him buried deep inside her one more time, she stated as casually as she could, "I didn't think you were the type."

He shrugged. "I'm not," he told her. "At least in the past I haven't been."

"Then it's probably best we not change that," Merri retorted.

"Why not?" He stroked a hand down her back.

Resisting the urge to curl into the inviting hardness of his chest, she eased away for the second time. Caution was what she needed here. What they both needed. "I don't want us to be confused."

He lifted an eyebrow, a silent question.

"We may be married but we're hardly friends," she explained.

Those laugh lines appeared again at the corners of his eyes. "Getting to know each other better in the biblical sense might help speed things up."

Merri tossed her head. "Trust me, Chase. Events are going fast enough as it is."

His gaze turned compassionate. "Too fast?"

And then some, Merri thought. His understanding

attitude prompted her to admit, "I swore when I ended my relationship with Pierce that I wouldn't allow myself to indulge in any more whimsical thinking."

Chase studied her face, waiting for her to go on.

She sighed and perched on the edge of the bed, fingering the sheet tucked around her breasts. "When I moved in with Pierce, I knew he wasn't ready for marriage. He told me he wasn't going to be for a couple more years."

"But you got engaged nevertheless," Chase recalled.

Merri rose and began collecting her clothes, piece by piece. "He did that to meet me halfway."

Reluctantly, Chase rose and began to dress, too. "Only...?"

She tugged on her panties, then her jeans. "I'm pretty sure Pierce knew then that he was never going to want to get married to anyone. It just wasn't his thing." Quickly, she slipped on her bra, too. "But I couldn't accept that. I wanted it all back then. I wanted to have a husband and a family and the home that I had never had, growing up with a single mom. And I was sure if I was patient and loving and kind enough that I would eventually get what I wanted." She let out a wistful breath. "Allowing myself to hope that way almost destroyed me."

Chase sobered. "I get that you were hurt, but the two situations aren't the same. I want the same things you do. I've always wanted them."

Merri watched him zip up his fly. "Did you also want to be loved?"

Chase went still. He kept his eyes locked with hers for a long minute. Finally, he said, "I assumed that would be the case if I ever got there."

Merri stepped closer, guessing, "But it wasn't a necessary part of the equation."

He braced his hands on his hips, his eyes guarded now. "No."

Merri looked down, her fingers trembling slightly as she buttoned her flannel shirt. "It always was for me."

"Past tense," Chase observed.

"Fate and circumstances have conspired to make me lower my expectations."

He sat down to put on his boots. "Which is why you agreed to marry me, without love," he speculated.

She went to the bureau, picked up her brush and ran it through her hair. "I wanted to be fair to you, protect the kids—and give them a complete family, plus have another child."

Chase frowned, walking over to stand beside her. "That's all pretty cut-and-dried."

Slowly, Merri set her hairbrush down on the dresser and turned to face him. "If we're going to be successful, Chase, it has to be."

"So no cuddling."

She tilted her chin, affirming flatly, "No cuddling."

Because cuddling with Chase could tempt her to fall in love with him. Merri did not want to love another man who—in the end—did not love her in return.

"Maybe we should stay a few more days," Starr said the next morning. The gorgeous brunette looked at Chase from her place at the table, eager to be of assistance in any way she could.

Which would have been fine, Chase thought as he spooned coffee grounds into a filter, had it not been for her obvious crush on him. A crush that had seemed to be well under control—until his former coworker arrived in Texas, anyway.

"It seems like you-all are swamped," Starr continued, rising and carrying her plate to the dishwasher.

Chase put another pot of coffee on to brew, then moved to the breakfast room windows overlooking the play set in the backyard. Yesterday had been a great day, sunny, cool, crisp. Today, the typical November gloom was back. The temperature was hovering just above freezing, and rain was threatening.

"I don't have to be at work until eight this evening," Chase said. He had pulled nighttime duty at the E.R. the rest of the weekend, so he'd be sleeping at the hospital tonight.

Merri had been up at the crack of dawn. She had refused his help with the milking, going out with Addie instead, while he entertained their houseguests and watched the twins. As much as Jessalyn and Jeffrey would let him, anyway, given they preferred just about anyone to him.

Merri walked downstairs now, fresh from the shower.

Her hair still damp, she was wearing a pine-green corduroy shirt, denim jeans and boots. She helped herself to the breakfast casserole she had prepared the night before.

"You-all don't worry about that." Lounging against the counter, Merri forked up a bite. "I just have to do the milking this evening, and I've got a babysitter to help me with the kids during their dinner and bath. Slim will be back to take over the dairy operation tomorrow morning."

"We have a lot more people to see," Harmony pointed out.

Davita nodded. "My mother is expecting us in Shreveport tonight."

"And my folks want us in Nashville by Monday," Polly added.

"We don't want to let anyone down," Nissa interjected.

Chase provided further encouragement. "You-all should enjoy your road trip, as planned, before you split up to spend Christmas with your families."

Outvoted, Starr went to collect her suitcase.

Merri, Chase and the twins walked the women out. Watched as they loaded everything in their rented van. Hugs and goodbyes were exchanged all around and the kids waved enthusiastically until the servicewomen's vehicle left the drive and disappeared down the county road. Together, the four of them walked back into the house.

Chase barely had a chance to savor the sense of family before the twins pulled away. "Can we get our blocks out?"

"As long as you pick up your mess when you're done," Merri agreed.

"Hurrah!" They ran off to the play area in the sunroom.

"What next?" Chase asked.

Merri picked up the folded linens on the sofas and carried them to the laundry room, alongside the kitchen. She set them down next to the washing machine, glanced at her watch and sighed. Although they had just finished breakfast, the morning was nearly gone. "I'm not sure. I've got a lot to do…"

The overwhelmed expression on her face was all the invitation he needed. "What's most urgent?"

"The grocery store." Merri sorted clothes. "I really need to go. But I also have a lot to do here, and who knows how much I'll actually get done if the twins decide not to cooperate."

He moved back to give her room to work. "Then why not let me go, and take the kids with me?"

Merri poured detergent over the towels, shut the lid and turned the washer on. "I don't know if you've noticed, Chase, but the twins haven't exactly warmed to you."

He winced. Talk about hitting him where it hurt. "Exactly. Which is why we need to spend more time together, pronto."

Merri leaned against the dryer, arms folded in front of her. "Forced proximity?"

"It's been known to work. Besides, it will be fun."

Merri rolled her eyes and pushed past him in a drift of lavender perfume. "You wouldn't say that if you had ever taken them to the market."

Chase followed her into the kitchen. "Let me do this, Merri," he said quietly. "It's a first step toward becoming a family."

She stared at him a moment, then finally relented. "Okay," she said, waving a lecturing finger at him. "But don't say I didn't warn you."

An hour later, Chase was pulling into the grocery store parking lot, twins in tow. "I don't see why we had to go with you," Jeffrey grumbled.

"Yeah," Jessalyn said. "I wanted to stay with Mommy."

Chase put the list in his shirt pocket, then got out to assist the children. "You'll get to be with Mommy later. Right now she needs us to buy some groceries."

Jeffrey crossed his arms in front of him, making it difficult for Chase to get the safety harness off. "We don't want to share Mommy with you anymore," he said with a glare.

Well, at least I know what the problem is, Chase thought.

"Yeah," Jessalyn added, with equal seriousness. "Can you go home now? We decided we don't want you to be our daddy, after all."

Trying to hide his hurt feelings, Chase cast a look at the increasingly gray clouds overhead. Was it too much to hope that the rain would hold off till later? "We are going home as soon as we get the stuff."

"Not our house. *Your* house. We want you to go to your house," Jeffrey retorted.

"The Broken Arrow Ranch is my home now," Chase explained patiently.

Jeffrey scowled. "No, it's not. It's ours."

Jessalyn nodded in solidarity, then told Chase sternly, "You need to go away now."

Chase exhaled. Talk about running the gauntlet…

Figuring this discussion could wait until later, he took a calming breath and suggested mildly, "How about we do this? How about we all try cooperating for a change?"

Silence fell. The twins' expressions remained recalcitrant. And Chase knew for a fact how stubborn they could be.

When all else failed, there was always the carrot and the stick. It had worked on him when he was a kid. Heck, it still worked, when the stakes were high enough.

He straightened and rested one arm on top of the

SUV door. Casually, he announced, "There are cookies in it for anyone who is a big help to me in the store."

He knew they were hungry. They'd barely touched their breakfast or the peanut butter and jelly sandwiches Merri had insisted on making for them before they left the ranch.

Aware the children had finally stopped arguing with him, he upped the ante. "Any kind of cookies you want. You get to pick."

The ice in their demeanor thawed. Slightly mollified, the twins relaxed enough to allow him to unbuckle the straps and get them out of their safety seats, and out of Merri's SUV.

Chase held their hands as they entered the store. Merri had warned him not to let them roam free. He pointed to a shopping cart shaped like a car, with two side-by-side child seats, each sporting its own play steering wheel. "How about we ride in that?"

The twins readily agreed. Chase lifted them in and fastened their belts, and they were off. "You're not pushing very good," Jessalyn pointed out.

That was because the big, clunky thing was twice the size of the other shopping carts, nearly as wide as the aisles and had no turning radius to speak of. "I'm still getting the hang of it," Chase said.

He stopped in front of the Free Cookie display at the front of the store and got out one sugar cookie for each of them.

"I want two," Jeffrey announced.

"One each," Chase reminded the twins.

In search of the first few items on his list, he hit the produce aisle. It was crowded with other shoppers, most of them women. Everyone, it seemed, wanted to stop and congratulate him on his new job, and on moving back to the ranch with his beautiful now bride and those precious children.

The twins had finished their cookies. They were getting restless.

"Thanks so much. I've really got to go." Chase pushed on without the zucchini Merri had asked for. But the broccoli was handy, so he got that instead.

On to the meat aisle.

He scanned the packages, did not see top round, so bought sirloin steak.

"I'm still hungry!" Jeffrey said loudly.

"Yeah, I want another cookie, too!" Jessalyn announced.

"When we get home," Chase promised, rounding the corner as best he could, into the dairy and juice aisle.

There, in front of him, was Judge Roy. Like everyone else, she was dressed in jeans, shirt and a waterproof jacket, probably because the courts were closed for the Thanksgiving holiday. Beside her were two of her teenage daughters. The girls seemed perfectly behaved as they helped their mom get what was on her list.

Recalling what the judge had said about not trying to pull anything over on her, Chase nodded briefly in recognition, then hurriedly pushed on, catching a corner of the doughnut display in the center of the aisle. Several boxes tumbled to the floor.

Embarrassed, he bent to get them.

"I want those!" Jessalyn shouted.

Don't let them talk you into getting too much sugar, Merri had warned. *They'll want everything sweet that they see.*

"I think we'll just stick to cookies."

The twins opened their mouths to protest.

Aware of Judge Roy behind him, Chase leaned forward and promised very very quietly, "Remember? Be good, and you get to pick whatever kind of cookies you like."

As always, they drove a hard bargain. "Both of us?"

"Yes," Chase said, deciding it was only fair. "One kind of cookie for each of you."

"Hurrah!" The twins cheered so loudly every shopper in the aisle turned to look at them and smile.

Unfortunately, Chase couldn't find the next few items on the list.

The bread rack was ridiculously empty. There was every kind of jelly but grape. The kids were ornery and restless.

"I'm tired!" Jeffrey shouted.

"I'm hungry!" Jessalyn proclaimed, even louder.

Chase grabbed strawberry jam and headed down the cookie aisle.

With the judge in the store, the sooner he got out of there the better.

Jeffrey pointed to the extra-dark mocha biscotti. "I want those ones, up there."

Coffee flavored? Chase shook his head. "I don't think you're going to like them, buddy."

"I will, too!" Outraged, Jeffrey put a hand on the steering wheel and stood up in the cart.

When and how had he gotten his seat belt off? Chase wondered.

"And I want those." Jessalyn pointed to soft oatmeal raisin.

Anchoring one hand around Jeffrey's waist to steady the little boy so he wouldn't fall, Chase reached over to get the cookies his sister wanted, and dropped them in the cart. "Good choice."

"Now mine!" Jeffrey demanded.

Again, Chase refused. "Pick something else. Something that Mommy likes for you to have."

Wiggling out of Chase's light, easy grasp, Jeffrey folded his arms in front of him. "You said it could be my choice," he pouted.

Oh, great, was that Judge Roy coming down to the cookie aisle, too? Chase got hold of Jeffrey once again, anchoring him with one arm around his son's waist. "It can be, but…" Chase had to use his other hand to move the cart slightly to the right, so Judge Roy and her daughters could get by. Unfortunately, the wheels were stuck and the big cart wasn't budging. Chase set Jeffrey back in his seat so he could use both hands to maneuver the cart.

"Thanks," the judge said, pushing past.

"Then—" Jeffrey bounded out of his seat and jumped up onto the steering wheel on his side of the cart "—I'll get it myself." He lurched forward, losing his balance in the process. Chase caught him, but could do nothing about the half-dozen packages of cookies that were knocked down.

They clattered as they hit the floor. Judge Roy and her daughters swiveled to look, as did everyone else within earshot. Just that quickly, total chaos reigned.

"You broke my cookies!" Jeffrey wailed, and let out a sob of distress that echoed throughout the store.

Merri had just walked through the automatic doors of the grocery store when she heard a familiar sob that, once started, seemed to go on and on and on.

Picking up speed, she rounded the corner of the cookie aisle, so quickly she nearly mowed down the customers trying to get away from the piercing cries.

"Judge Roy!"

The woman nodded, her expression courtroom bland. "Seems like your son needs you."

"Mommy!" Jeffrey wailed. "Make Daddy go away!"

"Yeah, we don't like him!" Jessalyn sniffled between sobs.

It was a disaster. "Okay, you two," Merri soothed, gathering them into her arms. "Hush now. Hush."

The twins clung to her and their tears subsided.

Chase stood next to her, wearing that look of suppressed hurt and quiet disappointment she was beginning to know so well. A feeling that she was pretty sure he hadn't had much experience dealing with until now.

"I'm sorry," Merri said. "I knew this was a bad idea."

"Which is why you're here."

"I got to thinking, right after you left, that they're just too tired from all the activity of the past few days to handle any kind of shopping. So I got in the ranch pickup truck and drove here." Just in case.

Chase shot her a grateful look. "I'm glad you did." He rubbed the tense muscles at the back of his neck, admitting ruefully, "I could use the help. I've hardly gotten anything on the list."

"It's not a problem." Merri reached over and squeezed his arm. "We'll work together and wrap this up in no time."

An hour later, they were back at the ranch. Merri let the twins sit at the kitchen table and eat cookies and drink milk while she and Chase put the groceries away. When they'd finished, the children were led to the living room, where they settled on the sofa with their blankets and stuffed animals, and watched their favorite Thomas the Train movie.

Ten minutes into it, both were sound asleep. Merri switched the DVD off and returned to the kitchen, where Chase stood, breaking down some cardboard for the recyling bin.

"How do you do it?" he asked her, clearly discouraged. "It's like you have a magic touch."

Merri smiled wanly, her heart going out to him. "Not always."

He peered at her, sizing her up. "Most of the time."

She squeezed his hand. "You've got to stop trying so hard."

He caught her wrist before she could disengage. "Or in other words, I need to back off."

Merri nodded. "It's going to happen," she promised softly. "They will accept you as their father. But only when they're ready."

The two adults fell into a thoughtful silence. "And when will that be?" he asked eventually.

"I'm not sure." Merri moved closer. "You have to have faith."

His mouth took on a rueful twist and he rubbed a hand across the shadow of beard on his jaw. "I thought you didn't believe in wishful thinking."

"There's nothing magical about them needing a father." She turned to face him, squeezing his hand again. "Believe me, they are acutely aware they haven't had a daddy. They will love you, in time."

Chase anchored an arm about her waist and pulled her close. "You're sure?"

"Very," Merri said. She could see the desire in his

eyes, feel the heat in his body. Why pretend this wasn't happening when it was? In the past four and a half years, she had rarely thought about herself, and never done anything to tend to her own needs and desires. Being married to Chase made her want to change all that. He made her want to experience life—and pleasure—to the absolute fullest. Gazing up at him, she rose on tiptoe and wound her arms around his back. He threaded his hand through her hair, then fastened his lips on hers in a riveting kiss that stole her breath and weakened her knees. The hardness of his chest pressed against her breasts. Lower still, she could feel the proof of his desire. She arched against him, wanting, needing so much more. Yet knowing they weren't alone, this wasn't for show, and with the two children sleeping just a room away...

Merri splayed her hands across his chest, flummoxed by her reaction to him. "Chase."

She'd told herself she was going to wait. Get her feelings and fairy-tale fantasies under control again, before she pushed desire to the limit.

Reluctantly, he drew back. "I know. They might wake up."

That wasn't why she needed them to stop, but if he wanted to think it was...

It was better than telling him she was worried she might fall in love with him. Worried that her love would again not be returned.... Not in the same deeply romantic and passionate way, anyway....

Knowing this arrangement would work only if the playing field was level, and determined to do what was right and honorable for both of them, Merri marshaled her defenses.

She thought about the evening ahead, and the fact that she would be able to go to bed at a decent hour—albeit alone—while he was at the hospital, on duty. Her heart went out to him once more. "Do you want to take a nap, too, since you have to work all night?" she asked with concern.

The look he gave her said he would rather sleep with her. Now. Probably naked. Although it wasn't "resting" he had on his mind.

Yet as always, he was motivated by doing the right thing, for all of them. Frustration turned to acceptance. "Wake me in an hour?" he asked gruffly.

Merri nodded. "Sure thing." Then she watched, her heart breaking a little, as he walked off.

Chapter 8

Merri held the phone to her ear. "I understand," she said quietly, so as not to wake the still-napping twins.

Pacing to the window, she gazed at the ever deepening gray of the late-afternoon sky. "These things happen," she soothed. "You go rescue your brother before the storm hits. I'll take care of things here. Yes...give everyone in your family my best."

Lamenting the fact that yet again her life had just gotten more challenging than it needed to be, Merri headed up the stairs.

She walked down the hall toward the guest room.

Chase wasn't there.

She kept going to the master suite and found him fast asleep, sprawled out on top of her bed. Shirt unbuttoned, hands folded behind his head, he was the picture of sexy masculinity. And Merri felt her heart give a little jolt.

Why did he have to be so darn attractive? And why couldn't she stop thinking about how it had felt to make love with him?

More to the point, why was he in here instead of the guest room? Did this mean he intended to sleep with her from now on, even though their visitors had left?

Having him beside her all night would definitely make it easier to make love. It would also help them feel married, and would leave her more emotionally vulnerable. But maybe, Merri thought, given their very complicated circumstances, there was no way around that.

Maybe, she told herself sternly, she just needed to take things one day, one moment, at a time. And right now she had a task to complete.

Aware this was something a wife would do for her husband, Merri approached Chase and sat on the edge of the bed, touching the side of his face gently. "Oh, sheik?" she teased, doing her best to keep her tone light, playful. Unemotional.

Sleepy amber eyes opened. He sandwiched her hand between his palm and the roughness of his beard. "Hey." He flashed her that slow, sexy smile she loved so much, kissed the inside of his wrist. Another thrill went through her. Merri cleared her throat. "It's been an hour. Actually, a little over…"

Chase rubbed his eyes, then pushed himself up on his elbows. His expression ready-to-head-to-work sober, he listened intently, then asked, "Twins still asleep?"

Merri grinned at how much he already sounded like a doting dad. Seeing an opening to lighten the tension with a joke, she replied, "It's extremely quiet." She leaned closer, waggling her brows and inadvertently getting a whiff of his masculine scent. "So what do you think?"

Affection lit his gaze. "That they're still snoozing away."

Merri grinned back. "Correctamundo! You win the prize."

Chase sat all the way up and stretched his upper body. "Babysitter here yet?"

Merri tried not to notice how the smooth cotton fabric of his white T-shirt, visible beneath his shirt, molded to all that sinew. What the man could do for an underwear ad, should he ever be asked...

She pushed her desire aside long enough to answer his question. "Sadly, Amy, the babysitter, is not coming. Her younger brother was in a fender bender in San Angelo. Bobby just got his license a few months ago. He's freaking out. Neither of them have been able to get hold of her folks, and Amy isn't sure his truck is all that drivable, so she's going to rescue him."

Chase sat up against the headboard, his thigh nudging hers in the process. "I take it he wasn't hurt?"

Merri noticed Chase didn't move away. Nor did she.

Aware of the body-to-body heat, even through their jeans, she swallowed. "Not a scratch, luckily. Apparently his truck is another matter. Bobby drove up on the curb, so the axle may have some damage."

Chase groaned in sympathy. "That's an expensive repair."

"No kidding." Merri thought about how intimate it was, sitting here like this, just talking, sharing their day. Who would have thought this part of marriage would be so comforting and fun?

"Anyway," she continued, casting a glance at the

late-afternoon gloom outside the windows, "I hate to ask…but it's going to start raining any minute, and I've got to bring the herd in and do the milking."

He looked at her with none of the frustration he'd experienced earlier still evident. "You want me to watch the kids?"

She had to hand it to the man, he was resolved to be successful at whatever he did. And that went double in the daddy department. "Would you mind terribly? You said you didn't have to leave until eight, and I can wrap things up in around two hours."

He waved off her concern. "It's not a problem."

Merri stood, to let him up. She propped her hands on her hips. "You say that now," she warned, not purely in jest. "They weren't exactly cooperative earlier, and they're going to be even crankier when they wake up, because they're so off schedule." Which meant he'd have his work cut out for him.

Chase got to his feet in one smooth motion. "I wouldn't worry about it. They can't loathe me more than they already do." He paused humorously. "Can they?"

When she just looked at him, Chase ambled closer, towering over her. "I'm joking, Merri." He cupped her shoulders and the warmth of his touch was almost as soothing as the tenderness of his grip. "Of course I'll watch over them," he stated, searching her eyes. "I'm their dad. It's part of my job. Unless—" he narrowed his gaze "—you'd prefer I care for the herd instead?"

"No. It'll go a lot faster if I do it."

Chase picked up his boots and sat down to tug them on. "Are the Christmas decorations still kept in the attic?"

Reminded that he had once lived here, too, Merri nodded. "Same place as always." There were some things about the Armstrong ranch that never changed.

He stood and headed for the door. "What about my stuff? Is it still in the attic, too?"

Merri followed him into the hall, where she reverted to her the-kids-are-still-snoozing whisper. "You mean the belongings you left at the ranch when you went off to college?"

He nodded, his handsome face filled with purpose.

Curious as to what he was up to now, Merri smiled. "No one's touched the boxes since you put them there."

He looked surprised but pleased. "Can you give me ten minutes before you head out, to find what I need?"

It was fun being on his team, Merri decided. "Sure."

"Thanks." He patted her arm, more as a friend would than a husband, and headed off. Seconds later, she heard him milling around on the third floor.

Merri grabbed warm clothes. By the time she had her long underwear on under her jeans and shirt, he was tromping back down the stairs, several storage boxes in his arms.

She wrapped a washable cashmere scarf around her neck. "Want to tell me what this is all about?"

He grinned, as masculine and supremely determined as ever. "I'd rather surprise you."

Chase saw Merri off, then went into the living room, where the kids were still asleep. He set the boxes on the floor and opened them. A wave of nostalgia hit him as he lifted the first Lionel train car out of the box. Chase hadn't seen any of this in years.

Not since his dad had died, and he had considered

himself too grown-up to mess with toys. They'd been in the attic ever since.

No more.

He lifted out one piece after another. Tracks, engines, control box, cord. Then he heard the stirring behind him.

Recalling Merri's advice not to push, he kept his back to the kids while carefully dusting off each and every piece. There was a telltale thud as four small feet hit the wood floor in perfect unison and scooted closer.

One shadow fell to his right, the other his left.

The small, sleepy-eyed figures came even closer, dragging their blankets and stuffed animals in their wake.

"Where did you get that train?" Jeffrey finally asked from Chase's left.

Trying not to feel too encouraged, he responded casually, "It's mine. My mom and dad gave it to me for Christmas one year, when I was a kid. It's been in the attic."

Jessalyn came closer, too, flanking him on his right. "Does it have a name?"

Belatedly, Chase realized all the cars and engines in the Thomas the Train video the twins had watched before drifting off to sleep had names. He looked at the gold leaf lettering on the side of the black engine. "The train's name is Lionel."

Jessalyn pointed to a coal car. "What about this one?"

Chase read the identifying script decorating that one, too. "That's Pennsylvania."

Chase plugged the train in, hit the lever that would send it forward on the track. The train had juice; he could hear the engine going. Unfortunately, the wheels weren't turning. He switched it off.

The kids edged closer. "Is it broken?"

"Just a little rusty." Chase picked up the four cars he'd put on the track. "Let's see what we can do to make it work."

He headed for the kitchen.

As he had hoped, the kids trailed along after him.

"Whatcha doing?" Jessalyn asked curiously, climbing up onto a stool at the counter.

Chase rummaged around for some WD-40. Coming up empty, he reached for a bottle of cooking oil and plucked a basting brush out of the rack. "I'm going to try and oil the mechanisms on this thing."

Jessalyn wrinkled her brow in warning. "That's for cooking."

Desperate times called for desperate measures. "You're right—it is," Chase replied, appreciating her effort to keep him out of the doghouse with Merri. "But I think it will work on the train, as well."

"Cool," Jeffrey said.

Keenly aware that he had a captive audience, Chase got to work, carefully adding a little canola oil to all the moving parts.

When he had finished, he tried it out. Sure enough, the wheels and axels began to turn.

It was hard to know who was beaming more, him or the twins. He picked up all the toys. "Ready to see if it will work?"

Jessalyn and Jeffrey nodded enthusiastically.

Together, the three of them returned to the living room, where track pieces were spread out in the middle of the floor.

Chase went back to assembling them. By the time he had finished hooking everything up, the twins were as involved as he had hoped. "Okay," he said, on a wing and a prayer, "here goes."

He hit the switch. The train engine moved forward, smooth as silk. Jeffrey and Jessalyn's faces filled with wonder. Mesmerized, they cuddled even closer to him and watched the train go around, accepting him for the first time since he had come back to Texas.

Merri let herself into the ranch house, took off her boots and hung her rain slicker up to dry. Given how long she had been gone, she had half expected to hear crying or at least whining. Instead the place was amazingly quiet, except for…was that a *whistle?* And a *bell?* And her children—*their* children, she reminded herself sternly—laughing and talking excitedly?

Merri followed the sounds to the living room.

Her heart leaped at what she saw: Chase sitting on the floor in front of an old-fashioned electric train set, with a child on either side of him. Jessalyn had the bell and whistle. Jeffrey was manning the gear box.

"Okay, stop it," Chase said, "and reverse the train."

Jeffrey carefully did as ordered.

"Ring the bell!" Chase told Jessalyn.

She instantly complied.

Abruptly, the kids became aware of Merri. Their eyes shone with happiness. "Mommy, this is so much fun!"

"We get to play with Chase's trains."

"I see you all survived without me," Merri drawled.

Chase looked as content as she had felt the first time she'd held the children in her arms, as tiny babies. "We did." He smiled, obviously enjoying the simple domestic scene as much as she was.

Pleasure rushed through her. Was this what family life would eventually be like? Once adjustments were made? Still feeling a little chilled, she stepped closer to the hearth and stood with her back to the flames. "Want me to rustle up some dinner before you head off to the hospital?"

Chase shot her a grateful glance. "That'd be great," he said.

"We'll stay here and play, Mommy," Jeffrey said.

And they did. Right up until the moment they had to come to the table to eat. The only difficult part was afterward, when Chase had to leave for his shift. "But we don't want you to go," Jessalyn said, stamping her foot.

Jeffrey pouted. "Yeah, we like having you here!"

Chase hunkered down. "I'll be back tomorrow morning."

Since it was the weekend, there was no preschool. "You'll see him after breakfast," Merri promised.

The twins looked at him. For a moment, Merri thought they were going to launch themselves into his arms. Instead, they just smiled shyly and scampered away.

Merri turned to Chase. "Good work, champ."

He looked truly happy, hug or no hug. He reached for her, drawing her into his arms and bussing her cheek. "It's definitely a start."

"Mommy, you are not being fair!" Jeffrey said the next morning.

"Yeah," Jessalyn grumbled. "We want to play with Lionel and Pennsylvania!"

Merri glanced at the digital clock on the microwave. She had expected Chase home around eight-thirty. It was now nine, and there was no sign of him. "I told you before," she explained patiently. "The electric train belongs to Chase, and only he knows how to use it. So you're going to have to wait for him."

Jessalyn studied her suspiciously. "It's not that hard for grown-ups," she argued.

True, but Merri wasn't about to interrupt the fragile thread of cooperation and contentment that had sprung up between Chase and the twins over that heirloom toy.

She smiled again. "I'm sure Chase will let you play with the trains when he gets home from work. In the meantime, why don't we bake some Christmas cookies and surprise him?"

As expected, sugar was the magic potion that cut short all temper tantrums.

With the kids' help, Merri made the spritz dough and filled the cookie press. The kids took turns pushing the trigger that loaded them on the trays.

Merri turned the oven on to preheat, then handed the twins bottles of colored sprinkles.

Jessalyn decorated the miniature stars and Christmas trees on one tray, Jeffrey the other. When they were finished, Merri slid both trays into the oven to bake.

While they waited, Jessalyn propped her chin in her hands. "Mommy, is Chase really going to be our daddy now, and not just our uncle?"

Merri had an idea how confusing all this was for the kids. Trying to explain the complex adult reasons behind her marriage to Chase would have just made it more so. So she stuck to the facts, saying only, "He really is."

Silence fell as the twins exchanged looks. Finally, Jeffrey asked, "Is Chase going to be an army doc and go far away again?"

"No. I'm not," a deep reassuring voice said.

They all turned to see Chase walk into the room, several big shopping bags in hand. Joy flooded Merri as she savored the feeling of being there with him.

"What have you been up to?" she asked her new husband. On impulse, she stood on tiptoe and kissed him on the cheek.

Chase grinned. Wrapping an arm about her waist, he hauled her close and kissed her back, his lips briefly brushing her temple. He gave her waist another squeeze as he turned his attention back to the kids.

He set the shopping bags on the kitchen table. "I got to thinking last night that it's Christmastime, not just for us, but for Thomas the Train and all his friends."

When he started hitting the mark, he really hit it, Merri thought, impressed to see he wasn't wasting any time.

Jessalyn jumped up and down. "Like Percy and Rosie and Sodor?"

"Yes. So on the way home from work I stopped and got some stuff to help your trains celebrate, too."

The children's faces lit up with excitement. Chase shrugged out of his jacket. Still clad in surgical scrubs, he asked Merri, "Is it okay if we use the coffee table in the living room for now?"

"Go for it!" She beamed.

The timer dinged. Merri turned to take the cookies out of the oven, then joined the rest of the family.

"I didn't know if you'd ever had a Christmas village." Chase covered the table with a large rectangle of white felt. He pulled out four beautifully painted wooden pieces.

Merri admired the pharmacy, train station, grocery store and church. "We haven't. But it's a terrific idea."

Chase lifted miniature toy pine trees, lampposts and park benches from the bags. "Where do you think these should go?" he asked the kids.

While they were engrossed with the setup, Merri slipped from the room. She returned with a plastic storage bin of wooden train tracks and wooden trains and handed them over, then headed out again.

"You don't have to go," Chase called after her.

Not about to interrupt what this very special bonding between Chase and the kids, she called back, "Uh, yeah, I do, if we ever want to get the rest of those cookies baked!" There were approximately four dozen left to prepare.

Merri was just taking the last pan out of the oven when Jessalyn and Jeffrey came running in. "Mommy, come and see what we built! It's Christmas for our trains!" They took her hands, and she followed them into the living room. Chase was lounging on the floor next to the coffee table. A miniature village had been set up. He'd never looked more relaxed.

"It's beautiful," she said. "Did you say thank you?"

"Thank you!" the twins chorused shyly. They smiled at Chase broadly and sat down next to him to play.

Merri walked over. Golden-brown stubble rimmed his handsome jaw. He had circles of fatigue beneath his eyes. Reminded that he had been up nearly nonstop for almost twenty-eight hours, she said, "You doing okay?"

He shot a telling look at the kids, telegraphing his growing love for them. "Better than okay."

"Need breakfast?"

"I had something at the hospital cafeteria, about five."

"Need a bed?" Merri asked, beginning to get the hang of being his wife.

He exhaled. "Unfortunately, yes."

Merri continued to study him compassionately. "What time do you want me to wake you?"

"Four o'clock."

That was only five hours away. Merri wrinkled her nose. "Is that going to be enough rest?"

"Plenty. I want to have time to run another errand before I head back to the hospital this evening."

"Then four it is," she promised.

As it turned out, Merri didn't have to wake Chase up. He came down at three-thirty, freshly showered and shaven. "You-all up for an errand in town?"

The twins, who had been too excited to nap, scowled uncooperatively. "We want to play trains," Jessalyn declared.

"This is something for Christmas, to help us continue to get in the spirit of the holiday," Chase qualified casually,

All play stopped. "Is it going to be fun?" Jeffrey finally asked.

Chase shrugged. "Are the trains fun?"

The twins nodded. "Lots of fun," they said in unison.

"Then I think you'll like this, too." He walked over to the coat tree to get their light jackets.

The rain from the previous day had cleared up, and it was bright and sunny outside, although still a bit nippy. He helped the children on with their coats, then gallantly handed Merri hers.

"What about me?" she teased, enjoying their new-found family togetherness. "Will I like this, too?"

"Hmm." Chase tilted his head, studying her with impish eyes. "I guess we're going to have to find out."

Minutes later, they were in Merri's SUV, driving to town. Chase was behind the wheel; Christmas music was playing on the radio. "How about a little hint?" Merri asked curiously.

"Uh…" He chuckled. "No."

"But we want to know!" the kids chorused.

"Okay. I'll give you a few clues. It's big. And prickly," Chase said.

"A dinosaur?" Merri asked, playing along.

"Mommy! A dinosaur won't fit in the car!"

"It will if it's a toy dinosaur," she argued.

"But it's not a toy," Chase said.

"Hmm." Merri tapped her fingers against her lips in a parody of thoughtfulness.

Jessalyn bounced up and down. "What color is it?"

"Green." Chase smiled. "It's green and big and prickly…."

"I know!" Jeffrey shouted.

Jessalyn yelled, too. "It's a Christmas tree!"

"You all are so smart, you figured it out." Chase tossed Merri a warm glance. "I thought we would pick one out together, since it's for all four of us."

"Can we decorate it together?" Jessalyn asked.

Merri nodded. "I think we'll have time."

They arrived at the Laramie Rotary Club lot. It was brimming with beautiful Afghan pines of all shapes and sizes. "So the question is," Chase drawled, as they roamed up and down the aisles, "do we want a Charlie Brown Christmas tree? One that is little and needs lots of love? Or do we want a middle-size one, that isn't too tall or too short? Or a great big tree that's taller even than me?"

The twins looked at each other. "I want a little tiny one that needs lots of love," Jessalyn said.

"I want a great big one that is bigger than Da—uh, Chase," Jeffrey said.

Merri caught her breath. Jeffrey had almost called him "Daddy."

But not quite. She saw a flash of mixed joy and wistfulness in Chase's eyes. Again, her heart went out to him.

Chase went on cheerfully, "Okay. We have one vote for a tiny one, one vote for a big one. What does Mommy want?"

Merri propped her fists on her hips and played along. "Putting me on the spot here, aren't you, buddy?"

Chase spread his hands. "Everybody's got to vote."

"I noticed you haven't voted yet, Daddy." Merri deliberately used the moniker Chase coveted and deserved.

His eyes twinkled in response. "That's cause I'm waiting for you. Ladies first and all."

The children giggled. "Yeah. It's your turn, Mommy. You have to vote, too," Jeffrey told her.

"Then I want a medium-size one," Merri decreed.

"Your turn." The kids looked at Chase.

"I say…" he paused until he had them all waiting with bated breath "…there's only one way to break a three-way tie."

"Three trees," Merri murmured when they had finished securing the evergreens onto the roof of her SUV.

Chase tipped the teenage helpers handsomely, then

turned and pointed to the cargo area. "Don't forget the wreaths for the front and back doors."

Merri breathed in the fragrance of fresh-cut pine and man. He was so handsome and kind. "Don't you think it's a little excessive?"

"For our first Christmas together?" Chase murmured. "I think it's just right."

Merri warned, "You're going to spoil them."

"I'm going to spoil all of you." He took her chin in his hand and kissed her, right there in the parking lot.

A jolt of desire swept through her. Shocked but elated, Merri rose up on tiptoe and kissed him back. If today was any indication, she thought happily, they were going to have a very Merry Christmas indeed.

Chapter 9

"The current schedule must be killing you," Jackson McCabe said to Chase. "Working twelve-hour days, five days a week, and then some."

It was certainly wreaking havoc on the fragile bonds of his marriage, although as the new guy, he wasn't in any position to complain. Chase sat down opposite the silver-haired chief of surgery. "It's a lot easier than what I did in the military." There, he'd been on call literally twenty-four hours a day, seven days a week.

"Still, what works for the surgeons whose kids are grown and out of the nest probably doesn't work so well for you."

Over the past ten days, Chase *hadn't* been seeing as much of his family as he would have liked. "The day shift is okay. The twins get up at six most mornings, so I'm able to have breakfast with them before I have to leave for the hospital, at seven-thirty." In order to make the thirty-minute drive and arrive on time.

"And in the evenings?" Jackson pressed.

Chase did miss having dinner with them. "Merri's been trying to keep them up so I can see them when I get home at eight-thirty, and then tuck them in. Of course, when I've had the night shift, I'm home to have dinner with them and help with the bedtime routine *before* I head to work at the hospital."

"But you don't see them at all in the morning when you're on nights," the chief surgeon surmised.

Chase frowned. "Right, because they leave for pre-school at eight-thirty. Although sometimes we pass each other on the highway."

He winced. "That must be hard."

It was, particularly when the twins were upset because he wasn't around enough to play trains with them.

"How is Merri adapting to the new schedule?" Jackson asked with the compassion of a long-married man.

That, Chase thought, was hard to tell. Outwardly, she was pleasant and cheerful and cooperative, every inch the supportive wife and doting mother. Inwardly, was another matter entirely.

Now that their company was gone, she had fixed up the guest room again and suggested he sleep in there, to ensure he got enough rest.

That wasn't what he wanted, but he understood. Merri got up at five most mornings, even when she wasn't doing the milking, so she could shower and dress and have some time to herself before the twins awakened. To ensure she got enough rest, she usually went to bed by nine-thirty or ten.

"It's hard, being married to a doctor." Jackson continued, "Especially when you're a newlywed."

"Merri's been a trooper. And she's busy with her own business, too," Chase stated.

"Still, I imagine she'd like to see a lot more of you. So the other surgeons and I were talking, and we're going to make some changes to our shifts, moving the time from six to six, instead of eight to eight."

"Thanks. I appreciate that."

Jackson grinned. "And to precipitate the change, we're sending you home early today."

It was barely two in the afternoon! "I'm only halfway through my shift."

"I'll cover for you. You just go home and enjoy that new wife and those kids of yours. Let 'em know how much they mean to you."

Gratitude welled within him. "I will," Chase said with a smile.

Figuring that as long as he was going to surprise Merri, he might as well bring home dinner, too, Chase changed out of his scrubs and stopped by the Daybreak Café. The restaurant, which served only breakfast and lunch, was closing. But Emily was there, along with her husband.

"Got anything I could just put in the oven for dinner tonight?" Chase asked.

She pointed to the specials listed on the blackboard. "King Ranch casserole, for the adults. Macaroni and cheese for the kids. Plus a couple of salads and some grilled vegetables?"

"Sounds great." Chase shared the twins' sweet tooth. "Dessert?"

"How about a fresh apple pie and some vanilla ice

cream?" Emily winked. "Got to celebrate while you can, you know." She disappeared into the kitchen.

Huh? Chase looked at Dylan. "Any idea what your lovely wife was hinting at just now?"

Dylan scoffed. "C'mon, Chase. The whole town knows."

"Knows what?"

"That Merri was in the obstetrician's office this morning. One of the other pregnant ladies said that she had that special glow...." He paused. "You didn't know she had an appointment?"

"She probably wanted to surprise me." Was Merri pregnant? They'd kissed numerous times, but made love only that once, roughly two weeks before. So she couldn't be very far along, if she was in fact pregnant. Was that why she hadn't wanted to continue sleeping with him? Because she had sensed the deed was done and she had been successfully impregnated the first time out of the gate? Or was it simply because she was still trying to get used to being married to him, before they leaped into bed again? The only thing Chase knew for sure was that he didn't want to rush her, any more than he already had. Because Lord knew she deserved some kind of courtship and a get-to-know-each-other-better period.

"Hey." Dylan dragged him out of his fog. "We didn't mean to upset you. It is good news, isn't it?"

"If that's what the news is," Chase said.

Was that what he wanted? How did he really feel? Besides completely stunned—and once again, disappointed at being inadvertently shut out in the whole baby-making process.

"You are the daddy, right? I mean, tell me I didn't

put my foot in my mouth—that you didn't marry Merri so suddenly because she found herself in a situation courtesy of someone else?"

Chase scowled at his friend. "Of course not. If Merri's pregnant, I'm definitely the father."

Emily walked back out, carrying two big bags of takeout. The stricken look on her face said she had heard enough to realize what was going on. "I'm sorry, Chase. We just figured that, being a doctor and her husband, you would know."

Was that why Jackson had given him the rest of the day off and gotten the other surgeons to adjust their schedules? Had the chief of surgery heard the latest on the rumor mill?

"Of course, it's none of our business if Merri is pregnant," Emily continued kindly. "We're sorry. We didn't mean to overstep."

Get a grip. Chase held up a hand. "It's okay. It's no secret that Merri and I are trying to, um, expand our family. So…" He shrugged and smiled. Maybe it was all happening sooner than they had ever imagined it could.

Merri was sitting in the kitchen, in front of her laptop computer, when, to her surprise Chase strode in, carrying two large bags from the Daybreak Café. He smiled at her and set the food inside the fridge, clearly a man on a mission. "Where are the kids?"

"At a playdate." Battling a self-conscious flush, she pushed back her chair and stood. "What are you doing home?"

He closed the distance between them and wrapped his arms around her, as had become his habit when coming and going. "I got the afternoon off for good behavior."

Merri sank into the comforting warmth of his tall, strong body. He smelled and felt so good. "That's nice," she murmured against his chest.

"The chief of staff has also changed my hours to make them a little more family friendly."

Merri listened while Chase explained. She pulled in a stabilizing breath, then stepped back as casually as she could. "That's really nice."

"You look like you've been busy." He helped himself to a Christmas cookie from the trays cooling on the counter.

Merri swallowed. "I got a notice that a few of the gifts I ordered in early November are not going to be arriving before the twenty-fourth, after all, so I'm getting a few more things on the internet, for the kids, with overnight delivery."

He looked at her assessingly. "Anything else?"

"What do you mean?"

He held her gaze for a long time. "Maybe something you want to tell me?"

Merri tensed. "Like what?"

He caught her hand and reeled her in close. "Like the fact you were seen coming out of the obstetrician's office this morning."

Heat flooded Merri's face. Pressing a palm to his chest, she stepped back a pace. "How do you know that?"

He lounged against the counter and folded his arms. "People were talking about it at the café over lunch. Emily overheard and told Dylan. By then, the word was you were pregnant, so he congratulated me."

"Wow." Knees wobbling, Merri sat down on a kitchen stool. "Like a real-life version of the telephone game."

Chase lifted an eyebrow. "You're not answering the question."

"I wasn't aware there was a question," she protested weakly.

He came toward her, then stood with his hands braced on the counter edge on either side of her, lowering his face till they were nose-to-nose. "Are you pregnant?"

Merri hitched in a stabilizing breath. "No."

He fell silent. She saw the disappointment in his eyes. "Did you think you were?" he finally asked.

"No. I mean, there's still a chance, but I figured the odds weren't all that good, since we only did the deed that once…" She finished breathlessly.

To her surprise, he looked a little embarrassed. "Then why were you there?" he asked her calmly.

Merri shrugged. "I wanted to make sure all systems were go if and when we ever got around to…"

"Making love again."

She exhaled in relief. "Yes."

"And…?"

"I'm definitely healthy," Merri announced. "Definitely midcycle."

"Definitely ovulating," Chase presumed.

She turned bright pink.

Crinkly lines appeared at the corners of his eyes. "You are, aren't you?"

He didn't have to smile so widely. "Yes," she admitted reluctantly, knowing it would do no good to fib to a man with M.D. at the end of his name. "I'm at my prime for the next twenty-four to forty-eight hours."

He chuckled, obviously raring to go. "Were you going to tell me?"

Merri made a face. "I was thinking about it."

He made a face right back.

"I don't want you to feel like you're a stud on call or anything," Merri hurriedly said. "I mean, we may live on a ranch, but things don't work that way between you and me."

"They sure haven't lately."

She pushed herself off the stool. He took her place and tugged her onto his lap. "Do you still want a baby?" he asked, hugging her close. "*My* baby?"

Like, who else's would she want? "Yes," Merri said soberly, deciding a serious question deserved a serious answer. "I still want your baby, Chase. Very much. And…" She wreathed her arms about his neck.

"And what?"

"I want you."

Merri's confession wasn't what Chase expected to hear, but it was what he needed. "I want you, too," he whispered, laying claim to her with a kiss.

Trembling, Merri kissed him back with hot, open-mouthed kisses that invited even as they incited. There was only one problem. Chase lifted his head. "When are the kids coming home?"

Merri smiled. "They aren't. I have to pick them up in town at four-thirty."

"Which means we've got less than an hour."

Her soft, sexy laughter was music to his ears. "Think we can get it done?"

He chuckled back. "I reckon." He set her down, stood and then swung her back up into his arms. "As long as we get started right away." Holding her against his chest, he strode toward the stairs. She kissed his neck, the underside of his chin, the corner of his lips, as he moved. With every touch of her mouth, blood pooled, low and strong. By the time they reached the bed, they were both breathing erratically.

He set her down and tipped her face up to his. The way she looked at him then, all soft and wanting, prodded him to risk even more—not just his body, but his heart. He tugged Merri closer and slanted his lips over hers, taking everything she had to give. And she gave him everything…

Chase inhaled the sweet fragrance of her skin and the lingering scent of her perfume, and knew he'd been welcomed into her world, fully and completely, at long last. He threaded his hands through her hair, totally immersed in the here and now, in the way her soft sweater dress clung to her slim body, the way her nipples pressed against the fabric, the way her legs parted, ever so slightly.

"Chase."

Needing more, he slipped his hands beneath her dress, shifting it higher. Sliding his palms across her tummy, he hooked his thumbs into the elastic of her tights and peeled them down. Then, kneeling, he followed their path with his lips.

She gasped and held his head in her hands. He wrapped his arms around her thighs, basking in her warmth, the silk of her skin, the way she shuddered, when he hadn't even touched her yet.

He kissed her again, loving the way she opened herself up to him, with a purity and innocence that rocked him to his core. "You're so soft," he whispered. "So sweet."

"And needy," she teased, lifting her dress and pulling it up over her head. Smiling down at him, she undid the clasp of her bra. Lust poured through him at the sight of her pink, jutting nipples, along with the need to possess more than just her body.

With a low moan of pleasure, she drew him to his feet. His mouth found her breasts, the slope of her neck, the vulnerable hollow of her throat and then her mouth.

She kissed him again and again, already reaching for the buttons on his shirt, his fly. A short time later, they were both naked, both on the bed. She was climbing astride him. Their gazes locked. And then she was kissing him again, with a sweet deliberation. She caressed his abdomen, his thighs, touching…tempting. Until he could stand it no more, and shifted her onto her back.

Grabbing a pillow, he slid it beneath her hips. Brought her knees up and pushed her heels back, to rest against her derriere. Eyes widening, she gasped again as Chase climbed between her thighs and they slowly, deliberately became one.

Self-control evaporating, she cried out as his hands moved over her, finding every pleasure point, loving and possessing. She arched up into him, surrendering willingly. Raw need gripped them both and then they were climbing. Higher, higher still. Until they crested together and clung there, hearts pounding in unison before coming slowly, slowly back down again, to the most wonderful peace Chase had ever known in his life.

For long moments, Merri held him tightly.

Finally, she whispered, "Chase?"

"Hmm?"

"Do you think we made a baby?"

He kissed her cheek, then leaned back to gaze into her eyes. "I hope so." Because there was nothing he wanted more than another child with her, one they created on their own this time. "But if not—" he bent and kissed her again, feeling connected to her in a very fundamental way "—we'll just have to keep trying." Sighing with pure male satisfaction, he lowered his head and fused his lips to hers in a long, sensual kiss.

"A hard job, hmm?" Merri teased, the look in her eyes saying she already wanted him again.

He grinned back. "But since somebody's got to do it, it might as well be us." And then to make sure they gave it their all, he set about making love to her again.

Chapter 10

Close to suppertime, Paige welcomed Merri and Chase into her restored Victorian home. "Don't you-all look happy. The two of you are positively glowing."

And why not, given the way she and Chase had just made love? Merri thought. As if they were in love… and always would be. Although nothing of the kind had been said, as per their earlier agreement to keep theirs a practical family arrangement, instead of a conventional romance.

"So is it true?" Paige pressed. "Or is the hospital grapevine just working overtime?"

Aware that people were still trying to figure out why she and Chase had gotten together, Merri pursed her lips. "The rumor mill is wrong. I'm not pregnant."

Chase took the gossip in stride. "We're trying, though. That's no secret."

Paige studied Chase's smile. "Sounds like fun."

It had been. Maybe too much? Wanting to steer the conversation away from their complicated relationship, Merri asked, "How have the kids been?"

"Good." Her friend smiled in turn. "They're out in the sunroom. They played with our wooden train set earlier. They couldn't stop talking about the electric one Chase set up for them."

He nodded fondly. "My old Lionel."

"It made quite an impression on Jessalyn and Jeffrey. As have you, Chase. They couldn't stop talking about how much fun it is to have a father around."

Joy lit Chase's face. "They said that?"

Paige led the way to the rear of the house. "Not in so many words. But it was 'Chase this' and 'Chase that.' Clearly, they adore you, which again is no surprise," she declared. "Kurt and I always knew you would make a great dad someday. And, of course, Merri's always been a great mom to them."

As the adults moved through the kitchen, they heard the voices of three-year-old Lindsay, Lori and Lucille, as well as those of the twins. Jeffrey was speaking loudly and authoritatively as they approached—*maybe because he was the only male in the group?* Merri wondered. "The daddy does not sleep in the same bed as the mommy. The mommy sleeps here." Jeffrey pointed to the pink bedroom in the dollhouse. "And the daddy doll sleeps here." He put the boy doll in another bedroom, on the other side of the hall.

Jessalyn was nodding in agreement. "And the twin babies sleep here," she said, putting two infant dolls in yet another bedroom.

"No," Lindsay argued, joining the melee with her

two dolls clutched firmly in her little hands. "The mommy and daddy sleep together in the same bed. Like this." The other triplets nodded vigorously in support.

Jessalyn rushed to her brother's defense, saying emphatically, "The mommy and daddy do *not* sleep in the same bed. They sleep in different beds."

Merri felt her cheeks grow hot. Chase squinted. Paige managed not to look at either of them. "Hey, kids," she said with a pediatrician's gentleness, "look who's here!"

"Chase!" Jeffrey and Jessalyn exclaimed in unison. They rushed over to greet him, wrapping their arms around his legs. He hugged them back with a forearm arm around each one's shoulders.

Jeffrey gazed up at Chase with utter hero worship. "Tell them you do not sleep in the same bed as our mommy!"

Could this get any worse? Merri wondered miserably.

"Yeah," Jessalyn insisted. "Tell 'em, Chase!"

"I think the mommy and daddy dolls can sleep wherever they want to," he answered smoothly. "Together or apart."

"And I think," Paige interjected, studiously ignoring what had just been revealed by adroitly changing the subject, "that it's time for everyone to put the toys away and say goodbye."

A chorus of groans went up from all five kids as they reluctantly complied. "Do they hafta go?" Lindsay whined.

"We want to play more," Lucille said with a stomp of her ballet-slipper-clad foot.

"Maybe you can come to our house next week," Merri offered.

"Sounds like a great idea, doesn't it, girls?" Paige concurred. Mollified, the kids smiled in assent.

Merri held out her hands to the twins. "Say thank you to your hosts for having you over," she said. Dutifully, they did. Coats, caps and mittens were gathered. With promises to see each other soon, Chase and Merri escorted the twins out the door.

They stopped at the Dairy Barn for a quick bite, then headed back to the Broken Arrow. Baths and bedtime followed.

Chase met up with Merri downstairs.

He took one look at her face and knew the direction of her thoughts. "Paige isn't going to say anything."

Merri knew her friend would never knowingly hurt them. "It's humiliating enough that she heard."

Chase took her into his arms. "I think we'll get over it."

Merri exhaled slowly. "That's not the point." She looked up at him. "What are the kids saying to everyone else, at preschool?"

Once again, all that raw male power was focused on her. "You want me to ask their teacher?"

Merri flushed. "No. Of course not." She stepped away.

He shrugged and shoved his hands in the pockets of his jeans. "Then don't worry about it."

His laissez-faire attitude was driving her crazy. "How can I not? We thought the talk and speculation after I was seen at the obstetrician's office was bad. What's it going to be like when word gets around that

I'm trying to get pregnant and we're not even sleeping in the same bed?"

He strolled closer, his eyes intent. Even in a rumpled shirt and jeans, with a day's growth of beard rimming his face, he looked raskishly sexy. "There's only one way to fix this. We sleep together...in the same bed and the same room from now on."

Her mouth went dry. "Chase...I..."

"I mean it, Merri." He clasped her shoulders with his big hands. "It's time we stop testing the waters and got all the way into this marriage."

Basking in the warm familiarity of his gaze, Merri realized he made a valid point. Besides, she couldn't risk the kids coming out with anything else.

"This way," Chase continued smoothly, "whatever the kids do say will only add credence to the fact that we're serious about this marriage and have been from the first."

Merri swallowed, aware this still wasn't love. Nor was it ever likely to be except in the most casual way. "All right," she said finally. "I'll do this for you."

"For us."

Heart pounding, Merri nodded. "But there's something else we have to do, too," she stipulated in return. "Go and see Liz first thing tomorrow, and talk to her about our concerns."

Fortunately, their attorney made time to see them shortly after they dropped the twins at preschool the next morning. "So what's up?" she asked.

Merri wrung her hands nervously. "I'm really worried about the public perception of our marriage, and how that might impact Judge Roy's decision."

Liz looked at Chase, to see how he was feeling. "I can understand where Merri is coming from."

Merri went on, "First, there were all the raised eyebrows when Chase's army friends showed up without warning, just a couple days after we got married. Then our awkwardness as a couple at the Thanksgiving dinner at the community center. The scene in the grocery store with the twins…"

Briefly, Chase jumped in to explain what had happened the first time he had taken the twins out on his own.

"And now," Merri continued, her misery mounting, "we just found out the twins are saying things to their preschool friends that could be misconstrued."

Liz squinted. "Such as…?"

"That there have been nights, because of Chase's schedule at the hospital, where we've been sleeping in different rooms."

Liz listened sympathetically.

"And now, because I was seen at the obstetrician's office yesterday, there are rumors that I'm pregnant."

"Are you?" the attorney asked, poker-faced.

"Not yet." Merri flushed.

Chase added seriously, "For the record—we're trying."

Liz shrugged and said nothing about the wisdom of that, either way. "Okay."

"But then I got to thinking that maybe the judge wouldn't approve of that, either." Unable to sit still a moment longer, Merri vaulted out of her chair. "What if Judge Roy decides that neither of us are good enough parents? And that I shouldn't have guardianship of the twins myself? I mean, I see on the surface that none of what we've done here makes sense to outsiders." She began to pace. "And yet Chase and I agree we're not going to rectify that by making his true paternity part of the public record. Because we think that would hurt the kids...."

Liz interjected gently, "You're in a difficult situation."

"An understatement." Chase grumbled, shoving his hands through his hair.

The lawyer regarded them both solemnly. "I understand your concerns, but the judge doesn't make a decision based on gossip, or even anything that happens around town. She rules by using the facts and data that have been submitted to the court—the financial records and employment history of both of you, your marriage license, Merri's history of guardianship to date, the wishes of the late parents and, finally, Merri's wishes to now share guardianship duties with you, Chase."

Liz paused to let her words sink in. "Judge Roy *cannot rule* based on rumors and innuendo, or even any unfortunate scenes she may have seen in the grocery store, because none of this is legally relevant to your petition."

That all sounded good. And yet... "But the judge is human and she's a parent, and by all standards, a very good parent." Practically a perfect one, Merri thought dourly.

Liz nodded. "Which is probably going to make her more understanding because she does have children."

"Then why didn't she say anything to us at the time?" Chase asked quietly, moving to stand next to Merri. "Or at least crack an understanding smile, if that was the case?"

The lawyer rocked back in her chair. "Because she didn't want to do anything that would taint the case and have it overturned on appeal."

"Oh," Merri said, catching Chase's eye. He put his hand in hers and clasped it firmly.

"The facts are," Liz continued, "you are both upstanding citizens. You've done a good job as guardian to the twins for the last four-plus years, Merri. You've managed the estate well, and the children are thriving. Everyone can see Chase is trying, and that things are getting better as time goes on. Right?"

Merri and Chase both nodded. The twins weren't calling him Daddy yet, Merri reflected silently, but they were growing more emotionally attached to him, more so every day. That much was clear.

"You're both family to these twins. You're married. And this isn't about the ranch."

"Not at all," Chase and Merri confirmed in unison.

Silence fell for several moments.

"So does this mean you think Judge Roy will rule in our favor?" Merri asked at last.

Liz leaned forward. "I can't promise you that you are going to have a good outcome."

No lawyer could, Merri knew. That would equate to having a crystal ball.

"Judge Roy has the information she requested, and I guarantee she will look it over very carefully. Meanwhile, the two of you are going to continue to do everything you can, between now and the hearing on January 3, to demonstrate that you are serious in your intent, and devoted to each other and the kids."

"Beyond that?" Chase asked, with furrowed brow.

Liz shrugged. "We all wait it out and hope for the best."

That suddenly seemed like too little, too late in the offense department. "What happens if Judge Roy denies the request?" Merri asked, needing to know—and prepare for—the worst-case scenario for her own peace of mind.

"You can appeal," Liz stated bluntly, lifting her hand. "But let's not go there, Merri. We'll cross that bridge if and when we come to it."

"What else can we do?" Chase asked, squeezing Merri's hand.

"Nothing. You have to be patient." Liz smiled gently. "I know it's hard. But it's the only thing you can do. Just keep doing the best you can by the kids, and see what happens."

Merri left their attorney's office more distraught than when she'd entered. "Well, that didn't help!"

Chase put his hands on her shoulders. "It's going to be okay."

She ignored the comforting warmth radiating from his palms. "I don't know how you can say that."

He tightened his grip protectively and leaned in close. "I say it because I believe in us." Before she could do more than haul in a breath, he lowered his head and kissed her full on the mouth, not caring that they were standing in the middle of Main Street. Merri had never been one for public displays of affection, but there was no denying that the steamy embrace was working its magic and making her feel so alive.

Finally, he lifted his head. She looked up at him, dazed and aroused. And comforted, too.

"Better?" he murmured softly.

He didn't know the half of it. But she was not about to encourage him, lest he think it was okay to do this on a regular basis, especially when they had a court case coming up.

Merri cleared her throat. "You make me want to believe in dreams coming true…" And a marriage that had started out all wrong, but was beginning to feel, despite the odds, all right.…

He looked deep into her eyes. "And Christmas cheer?"

Merri sighed, meeting his compelling gaze. "Definitely Christmas cheer," she murmured back.

So far this had been her best holiday season ever, despite the difficulties.

"And speaking of holiday spirit, I think we should attend the hospital staff Christmas party tomorrow evening, as a family."

Merri pulled up the calendar on her phone. "Don't you have to work?"

He nodded. "I get off at six. I'll meet you and the kids in my office. We'll go to the party together."

"Sounds good."

Unfortunately, things didn't work out as they had planned.

When Merri and the twins got to the hospital Saturday evening, Chase was not in his office. Kate Marten, the head of grief counseling, was. Merri took one look at the mixture of apology and regret on her face and said, "Let me guess…Chase isn't coming." So much for their plans to present a united front to the community at large.

"He's with a patient. It will be a while. I told him I'd escort you and the twins to the party in the meantime."

This was all part of being a surgeon's wife, Merri told herself sternly. She pushed her disappointment aside and smiled with all the graciousness she could muster. "Sounds good. Thank you." She gathered the twins, who had been looking around curiously, close to her side.

The four of them went back out into the hall that led from the annex of doctor's offices to the main hospital. Merri couldn't help but think about the last time she had seen Kate there. It had been shortly after she and Chase had said their vows, in the LCH chapel. The psychologist had offered her services, on behalf of the hospital, in any way they needed. Neither of them had taken her up on her offer.

"So how have you been?" Kate asked casually.

"Very busy." *Falling hard for my handsome husband.* Merri slanted the older woman a look. "You?"

"The holidays are always busy for our department."

"I imagine so," Merri murmured. "Grief can hit you pretty hard around the Christmas season. It did me for several years after—" mindful of the twins, she chose her words carefully "—our loss."

"But it's better now?" the counselor asked gently.

With joy welling up inside her, Merri admitted, "I have a lot to look forward to these days. A lot to be thankful for, too."

"That's good to hear." Kate paused at the door of the staff lounge, which had been converted into a winter wonderland. Snowflakes hung from the ceiling. Garlands of white decorated the walls. A thronelike chair sat next to the beautifully decorated Christmas tree.

Festively dressed children and adults were already enjoying the sumptuous holiday buffet that had been set out.

Merri's friend Emily came over to say hello, and Kate eased away into the crowd of partygoers.

"I didn't realize you were going to be here tonight," Merri said.

"My café is catering the event. Dylan was tapped to play a very important role, too. You know. Lots of ho, ho, ho and Christmas cheer and all that." Emily inclined her head slightly toward the Saint Nicholas throne.

"Oh." Merri grinned.

"He's a little nervous." Emily chuckled and continued speaking in code. "He's never done it before. But the staff thought it would be better to have someone largely unrecognizable to the tiny folk."

Merri chuckled, too. "Good thinking."

Jessalyn tugged on her hand. "Mommy, where's our daddy?"

"Yeah," Jeffrey said, pulling on her other hand. "You told us Chase was going to be here tonight!"

"I know," Merri commiserated gently, wishing she did not have to be the bearer of bad news on such a happy occcassion. "But—"

"Hey! There he is!" Jessalyn bounced up and down. "There's our daddy!"

She pulled free of Merri at the same time her brother did. The two raced for Chase, who was still clad in blue surgical scrubs and a white coat. "Chase! Chase!" they both shouted, as a few eyebrows rose.

Merri knew what the adults were thinking.

Shouldn't the twins be addressing Chase as "Daddy" now, instead of by his given name?

He hoisted a child in each arm and lifted them up against his broad chest. "Jessalyn! Jeffrey!" he teased, in the same excited tone.

The kids beamed up at him just as bells jingled in the hallway. Seconds later, a bearded Santa Claus strode in, clad in the traditional red velvet garb. "Ho, ho, ho!" Dylan Reeves boomed, eyes twinkling behind the wire-rimmed glasses. "And Merry Christmas!" He set down his pack and stood, hands on his hips, gazing at all the wide-eyed children gathered around him. "Who wants to be first to tell Santa Claus what you want more than anything in this world?"

Dylan pointed at Jessalyn and Jeffrey. "How about you?" He sat down and held out his arms.

For a moment, Merri didn't think the children were going to approach him. Then Chase bent his head and whispered something in their ears. They grinned, and wriggled to be let down. When Chase set them on the floor they marched over to Santa Claus, one by one whispering something in his ear.

Dylan looked surprised. "That's what you want?" he asked.

Jessalyn and Jeffrey glanced at each other and nodded vigorously.

"Well, that's a mighty fine wish," Dylan boomed, with a wink and a nod. "I'll see what I can do to make it happen."

"Dylan wouldn't tell you, either?" Merri asked Chase hours later, as they got ready for bed.

"He said, and I quote, 'I think that's the kind of thing you want to hear straight from them.'"

"But the twins wouldn't tell us what they told 'Santa'!" Merri protested, hand over her heart.

Clad in a pair of low-slung pajama pants, Chase picked up his toothbrush. "Dylan is sure it will come out eventually, when the time is right. Say, on Christmas morning."

Merri tore her eyes from the sculpted contours of his bare chest. "Then it will be too late. We won't have gotten them whatever it is that their little hearts desire more than anything in this world."

He handed her the toothpaste tube. "Dylan said it's not the kind of thing you can buy."

Together, they brushed and rinsed. Merri straightened, wiping her mouth on a towel. "Then how are we going to get it for them?"

"Good question." Chase dabbed a bit of paste from the corner of her lip with his fingertip. Silence fell and then he shook his head. "I thought parenting was supposed to be easy."

Merri switched off the light and followed him out of the bathroom. "According to what book?"

Together, they walked over to the bed. Chase shrugged. "The good parents make it look easy."

Merri climbed beneath the covers. "Don't sell yourself short, Chase. You've been an amazing dad to the twins."

He shrugged and joined her, leaning against the pillows. "You think so?"

"I know so." She snuggled closer, insinuating her leg between his. "They love having you around. They were really disappointed when they thought you weren't going to make it to the party tonight."

He wrapped his arms around her and sighed deeply.

"I was disappointed, too. But I got there."

"You sure did."

Silence fell again. He continued stroking her hair, then pressed a kiss on top of her head. Much lower, she felt him stirring.

"You know, chances are you're still ovulating," he murmured.

Merri's pulse picked up. They'd made love every day since she'd visited the doctor. And though she had heard that sometimes men grew weary of the baby-making routine, Chase seemed no more tired of her than she was of him. In fact...

She let her fingers caress the flat, silky expanse of his abdomen. "You really want to...?"

He caught her by the waist and shifted her upward, until she was cozily ensconced over him. "I do," he whispered tenderly, kissing her.

Merri smiled and returned the caress with all she had. "Well, then, it's settled," she said, slipping her arms about his neck. "Because I do, too."

Chapter 11

The twins barreled into the kitchen just as Merri took the last blueberry pancake off the griddle. "Mommy, how come our daddy is yelling?" Jeffrey demanded.

Merri wrinkled her brow. "What do you mean, yelling?"

"Like this!" He looked at his sister, and they yelped in unison. "Do you think he got a boo-boo in the shower?"

A faint trickle of alarm went through Merri. "Did it sound like he did?"

The two shrugged. "I dunno," Jeffrey said.

"Was the water running?"

They nodded affirmatively.

"Then what happened?" Merri turned off the griddle. "Did Chase stop yelling?"

"Yes, but first he said some of the words we're not supposed to say."

"And then what?"

Jessalyn blinked. "It was real real quiet."

"Except for the water," Jeffrey added seriously. "'Cause it was still on."

Merri knelt down to their eye level. "Did you ask Chase if he was okay?"

Jessalyn scoffed. "You told us not to bother a grown-up in the bathroom 'less it was an emergency. And we didn't have an emergency!"

Did Chase have an emergency? Merri hoped not. Bathroom accidents could be lethal, and if he wasn't talking, that could mean he had fallen and hit his head…. Feigning calm, she guided the twins into their chairs. "You two sit down and eat your pancakes. I'll go check on your daddy."

"Should you take him a Band-Aid?" Jeffrey called after her.

"I have some upstairs. I'm sure it will be fine." Merri walked as far as the hall, then dashed on up the stairs, silenting berating herself all the way. This was what she got for allowing Chase, who had clearly been dead on his feet after an eighteen-hour shift to get cleaned up and try to stay awake long enough to have break-fast with the twins before they went off to preschool.

She should have told him his health was more important, and sent him straight to bed. The kids would have understood.

Merri burst into the master bedroom, raced through it and threw open the bathroom door.

The shower had stopped, she realized belatedly. Chase was standing there, naked as could be, drip-ping wet.

"What happened?" He stepped out of the glass door.

Merri was hit with a blast of cool air. And the impact of gazing at her sexy-as-could-be mate in the altogether. Flushing and terribly aroused, she explained, "The twins said you were yelping in distress!"

Chase looked embarrassed. "They heard that?"

She imitated the sounds the twins had made.

He chuckled. "That was me, all right." He lazily rubbed himself down with a towel. His flat male nipples were erect, as the rest of him was beginning to be, she noted, despite the goose bumps standing out on his arms and legs.

Reluctantly, Merri dragged her gaze back to his face. "Did you run out of hot water?"

"Yes. And then no." He ran a towel over the day's growth of beard on his face. "And then yes. And then no."

She smacked her forehead with the flat of her hand. "Oh, no."

"Oh, yes…" Towel around his waist, Chase closed the distance and hauled her against him. He smelled good. Like soap. And mint. And man.

Merri apologized with a wince. "I forgot I had the washer on! I always put in a load first thing, before I start breakfast."

His eyes roved her face appreciatively. "I could tell it was something like that." He ran a hand down her spine, drawing her closer still.

"I'm not used to having a man around." Merri's breasts pressed against the hard, damp muscles of his chest.

"I could tell that, too." Chase's hands slid lower and cupped her derriere. "Although I can't say I'm sorry about that." He kissed her temple, her cheek, her ear. "I like being your one and only."

And I like being yours. Much more of this and she would really fall in love with him....

Merri swallowed, noting the sudden parched feeling in her throat. "Forgive me?" she asked.

"Depends." His wicked grin widened as he pulled her up on tiptoe, so she was pressed even more intimately against him. "Are you going to kiss me and make it all better?"

"Well," she whispered playfully, "when you put it that way..." She linked her arms around his shoulders, closed her eyes.

"Mommy!"

"What are you doing, and where is Chase's boo-boo?" The twins' voices echoed loudly and impatiently behind her.

Merri knew what part needed to be eased. It was pressed up against her and hidden beneath the towel. Busted by the most diligent and effective of chaperones, she dropped her arms and turned carefully, so her back was against his chest, her hips nestled against the proof of his desire.

Chase wrapped his arms around her waist, holding her close. He lowered his head and pressed his lips to her hair. "We were going to kiss," he explained.

"Yuck!" the twins said in unison.

"I know." Chase regarded them solemnly. "So it's a good thing you came up here and interrupted us, otherwise who knows what might have happened?"

The children wrinkled their noses, clearly perplexed while Merri stifled her laughter.

"Did you get an owie?" Jessalyn demanded eventually, coming closer.

"No," Chase told them sincerely. "I'm sorry if it sounded like I did."

"We ran out of hot water again," Merri explained. "Everything is fine."

"Oh."

She shepherded the twins toward the door. "Our breakfasts are getting cold. Daddy—" she cast a look over her shoulder, making no effort to hide her affection "—we'll see you downstairs, okay?"

Chase nodded and gave her a look that said he intended to finish what they had started. Jovially, he called, "Be right there, kids! As soon as I get dressed."

"Bye! Have a great day at school!"

"We'll see you later!"

Merri and Chase waved as the car carrying the preschoolers drove off.

He walked back inside with her. "So," he concluded huskily, "you were worried about me."

Merri shut and locked the door behind them. "Of course I was worried." She made a comical face. "The twins made it sound like you had fallen and couldn't get up."

His belly laugh electrified the air. "So naturally," he concluded, deadpan, "you told them to stay put, and came to my rescue."

"Well." Merri shrugged and met his eyes. "You are my husband." More so every day.

He ran his palm over his unshaved jaw. "Speaking of marital duties…'"

Merri quirked her lips. "Were we?"

"We're about to." His expression innocent, he swung her up onto the kitchen counter and moved in, trapping her with his arms.

Merri's heart began a slow, heavy beat. Chase smiled. "Now, where were we earlier, when we were interrupted?" He undid one button on her blouse, then another. Gazed down at her cleavage. "Oh. I think I remember...."

"Chase..."

He undid several more buttons. "We haven't had nearly enough time alone." Easing the blouse from her body, he whispered, "I vote we take advantage of this...."

The kiss that followed ramped up her desire and curled her toes. Eventually, he lifted his head. "So what do you say?"

Merri sucked in a breath, aware she had zero willpower where her husband was concerned. She rubbed the moisture from his lips. "That you're a hard man to say no to."

His next smile was even more devastating. Chase took her hand, and pressed it over his manhood. "I'm a hard man, period. And I have been since you walked in on me."

Merri checked him out. "That's not good."

He shifted his weight. "It can be. At times like now."

Oh, my. "Chase."

"Merri..."

She smiled, knowing that he knew he had turned her on in a major way. She kissed the tip of his nose, his cheek, his jaw. Ran her free hand down his chest. "We should go upstairs."

His eyes turned opaque. He lifted her hand from

the most masculine part of him and kissed the back of it. "We'll get there. Eventually." His eyes darkened all the more. "But first…"

Chase undid the clasp of her bra, which went the way of her blouse. She trembled, watching as he ran his fingers across the smooth skin of her abdomen, over her ribs, then palmed her breasts. He groaned at her responsiveness.

Merri rested her forearms on his shoulders and gazed up at him. "You make me feel so good."

His lids lowered to half-mast. "At last, you've discovered my plan," he teased, covering her mouth with his once again. Merri's pulse skipped ahead, into a fast, hard rhythm as he kissed her, his body unyielding. No longer willing to wait for a bed, she palmed his shoulders, the corded muscles of his back, the smooth curve of his buttocks.

Chase moaned. Smiling, she brought her hands around to the front of his soft gray sweats and slid her fingers beneath the waistband. He moaned again as she pushed it down, caught the band of his briefs and slid her fingers beneath that, too. His skin there was warm and covered with crisp hair. Lower still was the satin hardness she had admired earlier. She closed her fingers around him, wanting, needing.

"Not yet." He caught her wrist, his voice hoarse and unsteady.

She clutched at him, already spiraling. "Yes.…" *Yes! Yes!*

"You're not ready."

Merri felt the throbbing deep within her, the slipperiness between her thighs. "I beg to differ with you there, pardner…" she argued, her voice soft and thick.

Smiling with lascivious intent, Chase eased open the front of her jeans, lowered the zipper. "But you will be," he promised, lifting her long enough to push the denim down and then off.

Cool air assaulted Merri's skin. She trembled as he set her down again, positioning her legs so they were wrapped around his waist. He kissed her once more, stroking her with his hands, ever so tenderly. Merri shuddered in response and opened even more, desire sweeping through her in powerful waves.

Chase lifted her partially off the counter, murmuring encouragement all the while. Just when she thought she couldn't stand it anymore, he ended the passionate kiss and lowered his head to her breasts. Excitement surged through her as his lips became as busy as his hands, laving, adoring, inciting. Deliberately, he moved her against him, shifting her back and forth, driving her out of her mind, even with his clothes between them. Need overcame her, and everything in her tightened and peaked. She finally let out an exultant cry and trembled in release.

Chase's eyes were hot and his smile was tight when she slowly came back down to earth. Transfixed at the sight of him, so hard and hot and ready, she reached for the hem of his T-shirt, dragged it up over his head and tossed it to the floor. He watched her, clearly liking her plan, when she drew his sweatpants and briefs the rest of the way down his thighs. He kicked them off, away.

Merri caught him by the shoulders and brought him close, wrapping her legs around him until she was straddling him, and he was... right where she wanted him. This time she let herself look into his eyes as he slid home, going deep, going slow. Emotion shimmered through her.

She wasn't sure she had felt married before.

She did now.

She wasn't sure she had felt loved before.

She did now.

She wasn't sure he'd felt loved, either.

But the way he was looking at her, so avidly, so openly, told her that in this moment, he did. And really, Merri thought as she took his head in her hands and brought her mouth to his, that was all they needed.

"Don't go." Chase caught Merri's hand before she could leave the bed, and pulled her back into his arms. He kissed her neck, behind her ear, leaving trails of fire and need in his wake.

Merri shut her eyes, basking briefly in the erotic glow the two of them created every time they were together like this. "Believe me." She sighed, absorbing his warmth and strength. "I would like nothing better than to stay, but I have to go."

He slid his hands down her hips. "Why?"

Much more and he'd have her begging. Merri tried—unsuccessfully—to wriggle free. "Because if I don't I'll stay here all day."

He smiled as if he'd won a prize. "So?"

"And you won't get any sleep. And as your wife," she continued archly, tingling even as she slipped from his light, easy grip, "one of my duties is to make sure you get the rest you need. So people won't be saying things like, 'Have you seen Chase Armstrong? Boy, that fella sure isn't getting any shut-eye.'"

Chase threw back his head and let out a raucous

laugh. "They'd probably just figure it was because I was on my honeymoon with my very hot and lovely wife."

Merri grinned despite herself at the image that conjured up. She sat beside him and stroked the crisp, curling hair on his chest. "You can be really ornery, you know that?"

He ran his eyes over her possessively, admiring her naked form. "Someone currently in this room brings it out in me." Then he bent to kiss her knee. "And speaking of that person—you still haven't told me what you want for Christmas."

Selecting the right gift was hard under normal circumstances. In this instance…? She shook off the question, letting him know that he didn't have to give her a present. "I have everything I want and need." *Well, almost,* she amended silently.

He studied her eyes. "Except a baby."

Merri smiled. "I think we just worked on that." Although from what she knew, the ovulation period was either well over or fading fast. She looked at him, knowing generosity should go both ways. "What do you want for Christmas?"

Devilry lit his eyes. "Besides more lovemaking?"

"There must be something you want and don't have."

"I really can't think of anything, now that I've got you and the twins."

"Except…"

His expression turned wistful.

"…the fact they aren't yet calling you Daddy," Merri guessed.

He exhaled. "At least they've accepted that I *am* their daddy."

Merri gathered up her clothes. "It would be nice to have them call you something other than Chase."

Arms folded behind his head, he lay back on the pillows and watched her dress. "I asked Kate Marten about that. I figured she would know, since she's had a lot of experience dealing with kids, moving out of one situation and into another, so to speak."

Merri came closer, still buttoning. "And?"

He shifted over so she could sit down and put on her socks. "She said it will happen when the kids are ready, and not before."

Merri turned, concluding, "So we have to be patient."

Chase nodded. He took her face in his hands and gave her another sweet and loving kiss. "Which, as it turns out, is not such a bad thing. As long as we're together."

Chapter 12

Chase had just sat down to go over the chart of a patient he had operated on, when his cell phone vibrated.

"Going to be one of those days, hmm?" Paige commented, from the other side of the conference table.

Luckily for him, it wasn't anything that would take him back to the O.R. He showed the screen to his colleague.

Wordlessly, Paige checked out the photo of his six vacationing army friends, who'd been visiting the Grand Ole Opry in Tennessee. All were decked out in Santa hats and grinning broadly, next to a hand-lettered sign, held by Starr, that said Hi, Chase!

Having just come out of surgery herself, Paige paused to make a notation on a chart. "You still getting those?"

He nodded. "Every time the ladies hit a particularly exciting landmark or destination."

His colleague got up, walked to the fridge in the corner of the staff lounge and took out two bottles of sparkling water. Returning, she handed one to him. "Merri okay with that?"

Chase wondered if Paige was thinking about what the twins had said—about him and Merri sleeping in separate beds. Something in her inscrutable expression hinted that she was. Not about to go there, he sat back and uncapped the bottle. "Sure." He lifted it and took a long drink. "Why wouldn't she be?"

The pediatrician shrugged, her concern for her long-time friend evident. "They're all awfully pretty."

Chase was growing tired of everyone telling him how to manage his marriage. He didn't need or want their advice, well-meant or not. "Merri understands they're just good friends."

Another silence fell, followed by a lift of Paige's brow.

Chase had never been one to explain himself to others. In this case, to protect Merri, he made an exception. "Relationships in field hospitals can get pretty intense."

Paige took another look at the photo on the screen and relaxed slightly. "And just like when you're out of medical school or residency, they fade."

"Merri knows that, too." Chase picked up his pen.

"Still, that kind of thing can be easily misinterpreted."

Did she think that was why he and Merri had been sleeping apart in the beginning? Not that it mattered, since he wasn't about to kiss and tell.

"Merri knows it's only temporary. They're all headed back overseas a few days after Christmas."

"And Merri's not jealous."

Chase thought about the passionate, unrestrained way the two of them had been making love, the happiness they had found. "She understands how I feel about her."

"Good." Paige inclined her head toward the picture on his smart phone. "'Cause if she didn't, pal, you might be in trouble."

With Chase tied up in surgery all day, Merri decided to get a little shopping done. So, after she picked the kids up at preschool, she took them to the Dairy Barn for lunch and a talk. "Now that you're older, it's time you realized that Christmas isn't just about getting presents," she said seriously, acutely aware there were only ten shopping days left. "It's about giving something, too."

"We know that, Mommy!" Jessalyn dipped her chicken tender into barbecue sauce. "That's how come we already made you something at school."

"Want us to tell you what it is?" Jeffrey asked eagerly. "Because—"

"Uh, no." Merri reached over and playfully covered their mouths with her hand. "You need to surprise me." She dropped her arm and sat back.

The twins nodded seriously. "Okay," Jessalyn replied.

Then Jeffrey added, "We won't tell you we made you a flowerpot and a picture frame that says I Love You, Mommy."

Not about to let on he had just unwittingly given everything way, Merri kept herself from cracking a smile. "Good. Anyway, back to what I was saying. Now that

Chase is your daddy, you need to do something nice for him, too."

"We can't," Jessalyn said.

"Yeah." Jeffrey muched on a fry. "We're all done making presents at school."

"Well, that doesn't mean you can't make him something just as nice at home, while he's at work," Merri countered.

"Okay, then, we'll make him a new Lionel train, because he really likes them."

"That's a little complicated."

They looked at her expectantly. "You can help us," Jeffrey said.

Merri finished chewing her burger. "I meant complicated for me, too."

Jessalyn leaned forward importantly. "But we have to get him a new train, because he likes trains and that's what he wants."

There was no faulting that logic. "How about this?" Merri paused to make sure she had their attention. "After we finish our lunch, we'll go over to the arts and crafts store and pick out a couple of those wooden trains that need decorating, and you two can paint them. Then Daddy can take the trains to work and put them on his desk so he'll have a reminder of you there."

"Okay," they replied happily.

Merri drew a breath, ready to tackle something much more sensitive. "And as long as we're on the subject of Daddy…don't you think it's time you started calling him Daddy?"

More frowns appeared. "That's not his name. His name is Chase," Jeffrey argued.

Patience. "I know you've always called him that."

They'd never even wanted to say Uncle. "But now it's different."

Their frowns deepened. "No, it's not. That's still his name. Everybody calls him that," Jessalyn stated.

Merri inhaled and tried again. "My name is Merri, but you call me Mommy."

"Because you are our mommy."

"And Chase is your daddy," Merri reminded them gently.

"But that's not his name...."

Eventually, finally, Merri decided not to make an issue of it. Maybe Kate was right. It would happen when the twins were ready. And not one day before.

"You can't be serious!" Emily said the following afternoon, stopping by their table in the café, where Chase and Dylan sat poring over the sales literature Dylan had picked up for the busy physician. "You can't give Merri that for Christmas!"

Chase had to give her something. And judging by all the whispering the twins had been doing, and the way Merri was constantly and humorously shushing them, everyone else had a jump on him in that department.

"It's a good gift," he argued. Given how happy Merri and the kids had made him, he wanted to make sure Merri had something she would really like.

"Maybe for a non-occasion..." Dylan reluctantly agreed with his wife.

"But for your first Christmas together?" Emily topped off each of their coffees. "You've got to get her something that says how you feel about her."

A little offended, Chase pointed to the picture in front of him. "This *does* say how I feel."

Merri's friend rolled her eyes. "Maybe about the ranch, and her not doing a good enough job taking care of it."

Chase's spirits fell. He took another look. "Oh." He swore silently. "I see your point."

"I think you should still get it, given what you've told me about the issue," Dylan advised. "Just not as your primary gift, but as, um, a stocking stuffer."

"In that sense it would be okay," Emily agreed, after thinking about it for a second. "In fact, I'm sure Merri would appreciate it, if it was given in humor."

"Well, it's not like I was going to present it with all the fanfare of a new car," Chase retorted mildly.

"Cars are out, too. It's such a guy gift. No woman wants to get a car." Emily patted her husband's shoulder affectionately, then sashayed off to serve another customer.

Admiring the easy way husband and wife interacted, Chase turned back to his friend. "What are you getting Emily for Christmas?"

Dylan cut into his chicken-fried steak. "A new custommade saddle with her name engraved on it."

Chase blinked. "You call that romantic?"

He grinned. "For a woman who likes to ride mustangs as much as I do, it's a darn good gift. But I'm throwing in a little perfume and a negligee and stuff like that, too, that shall go unmentioned to anyone but the two of us. Just make sure whatever you give Merri says ROMANCE in capital letters."

Chase left the Daybreak Café and returned to the hospital, thinking about his friend's advice.

There was no doubt Emily and Dylan were happily

married. Three years in and the two still acted like newlyweds.

Chase wanted the same result. Which got him thinking. Maybe there was a way to give Merri the romance she had been deprived of, after all.

"What do you mean I have to meet you at your office in the hospital annex promptly at six-thirty?" Merri said four days later. The truth was, she was feeling a little out of sorts. Unusually tired. Bloated. *Pregnant...?* Pushing the wishful thinking aside—she was not going to count her chickens before they hatched—she drew a deep breath and waited for Chase to go on.

"I thought we'd go out for dinner this evening."

Merri would like nothing better than to have a meal in a candlelit restaurant, seated across from her handsome new husband. Especially since they'd never actually been on a real date.

It was all either family time or hot wild sex in bed.

"I appreciate the idea, but the kids just had their last day of preschool before the holiday break. They're pretty tired. I don't think they'll be able to handle a dinner out without melting down."

"I figured as much, but I've seen to that, too. Paige and Kurt said they'd take the twins. All you have to do is drop them off at their house in town on the way to meet me."

Again, Merri yearned for a real date. With adult conversation. A relaxing dinner, where she didn't have to cut up anyone else's food. She'd also like time to get ready at leisure. Maybe take a bubble bath, go to the salon, get her hair done. "You're sure we can't do this some other night?" *When I have time to prepare and can really knock your socks off?*

"You know what they say. Never put off till tomorrow what you can do today... I'll see you in a little bit, okay?"

Merri sighed and put down the phone. Luckily for her, the kids were surprisingly cooperative about getting ready to go back out. Forty-five minutes later she had dropped them off and was headed into Chase's office.

The waiting room was empty. No surprise, since his staff had gone home for the day. It was, Merri soon discovered, just the two of them. And Chase was wearing a suit and tie. The same dark suit and tie he had worn when they got married in the hospital chapel, as it happened.

She looked down at her casual jeans and sweater with regret. "You didn't tell me we were dressing up. I assumed we were going to one of the restaurants in town."

"We are, but I thought it would be nice, since tonight is our first-month anniversary, to put forth a little extra effort."

Oh, no! Merri pressed her fingers to her lips, aghast. "I totally forgot."

Those crinkles appeared at the corners of his eyes. "You're surprised I remembered."

"Well, yes, I—I guess I am." When did she start stammering? She hadn't been this nervous around him since he'd come back to town. But he hadn't looked so inscrutably mysterious since then, either.

Chase smiled wryly and scratched his head. "I guess

I'm going to have to do better in the romance department."

"Trust me. You've been doing just fine." Merri had never been so head-over-heels for any man. The fact she was married to him just made it so much better.

He held up a hand. "Not to worry. I brought something from your closet…" He produced the tea-length navy dress and delicate white cardigan she had worn when they'd said their vows.

"You know what that is."

"I do. And for the record, I love the way you look in it."

He hadn't said he loved *her,* just the way she looked. Still, it was something. Merri shook her head. "You really are full of surprises this evening."

"Need help changing?"

If he helped they might end up making love on his office floor. And while that could be incredibly sexy, it wouldn't be appropriate. Merri didn't want to have to worry about a janitor walking in on them. Besides, Kurt and Paige could watch the kids for only so long before bedtime, so they better get a move on.

Merri shook her head and smiled. "I'll just be a minute."

When she walked back out, Chase was waiting for her. He had a medium-size silver gift box in his hand.

"What's that?"

He sat on the edge of his desk and pulled her toward him. "An early Christmas present."

Merri struggled with another stab of regret as she perched on his inner thigh. "I haven't gotten you anything yet."

"It's okay." He looked at her affectionately. "I want you to open this."

Merri's heart skipped a beat. "Now?"

"Yep." The sexy smile reached his eyes. "Right here. Right now."

Swallowing against the building ache in her throat, Merri undid the bow and lifted the lid. She blinked in surprise when she discovered a small, red velvet box surrounded by shiny gold tissue paper. "What is it?"

Innocence glimmered in his eyes. "Don't know. You'll have to look and see."

Merri gingerly opened the jewelry box. Inside was a diamond solitaire ring that was a perfect match for the platinum wedding rings she and Chase already wore.

The affection in his eyes deepened. "I thought you should have an engagement ring."

Tears filled Merri's eyes at the unexpected and truly lavish gesture. "Oh, Chase," she whispered, studying the sparkling diamond. "It's beautiful."

Relief mingled with the happiness on his face. "I didn't want to wait one more day."

With his help, Merri slipped it on. And for the first time, she felt married in the way she had always wanted—in the romantic sense. Emotion welled. The tears she'd been holding back spilled over her lashes, and she stood up to hug him fiercely. "You've made me so happy," Merri whispered thickly.

He hugged her back. "That goes both ways."

They paused to kiss, deeply and tenderly. Reluctantly, he drew back. "Much as I hate to say it, we'd better get moving if you want to have time to show that off," he teased.

She slanted him a curious look. "Where are we going?"

Chase led her toward the door. "Somewhere I can hold you in my arms."

They fell into step companionably. "The bed-and-breakfast just outside of town?"

He chuckled. "Good idea. But no."

As it turned out, they only had to walk down Main Street.

"The Lone Star Dance Hall?" Merri paused in front of the popular restaurant, which looked crowded. Vehicles spilled out of the lot, and onto the street. Inside, it appeared as if people were standing shoulder to shoulder.

Chase tucked a strand of hair behind her ear. "I remember it being one of your favorites when you were younger."

Merri loved to two-step and line-dance. She just hadn't done it in forever. "It is. It's sweet of you to remember."

Chase smiled and took her hand in his. Together, they walked in, and Merri got her second big shock of the night when the country and western band struck up a lively Texas version of the Wedding March.

"Surprise!" Chase murmured in her ear. "You've just been gifted with a reception."

And then on cue, all their close friends and their very nicely garbed twins shouted, "Congratulations, Chase and Merri!"

Chapter 13

"You know, you don't have to keep looking at me that way," Merri murmured a bit later.

Chase took her hand in his and led her onto the floor for the first dance of the evening. And their first official dance as husband and wife. "What way?" he murmured sexily.

Joy bubbled up inside her. "Like this is the best night of your entire life."

Chase held her even closer. "It *is* the best night of my entire life." He smiled. "So far."

"Meaning what?" Merri teased, enjoying having her body pressed intimately against his. "You expect things to get even better?" How was that even possible?

He looked deep into her eyes. "I do. I think every day we spend together is going to be happier and more fulfilling than the last."

Merri grinned up at him. "Ever the optimist, aren't you?"

Chase kissed her temple. "When it comes to you and me, I have every reason to have hope and faith." And, as it turned out, he wasn't the only one who thought the two of them had only good days ahead. Everyone in the packed dance hall stopped by throughout the evening to offer similar sentiments. But what meant the most to them were the words from the hospital's chief counselor.

"I'd like to offer my congratulations, as well as an apology for my earlier misinterpretation of the situation," Kate said when the party had finally wound down and Merri and Chase were in the process of packing up and getting ready to go home.

Kate sent a fond glance toward Chase, who was corralling the still-energetic twins into their coats and hats, while Merri organized their mountain of wedding gifts. "I was wrong to think your marriage might be ill-advised. It's obvious the two of you are very much in love."

Merri paused, not sure how to respond to that. Thanks to Chase and the effort he'd put into their belated wedding reception, the night had been wildly romantic, with a professional photographer documenting it all. A sumptuous dinner had been followed by champagne toasts and wedding cake, laughter and dancing, and even the occasional surprisingly passionate kiss.

Chase had given Merri the reception of her dreams, and memories of their evening together would last a lifetime. But as for actual love? That was something she and Chase hadn't sought or even begun to discuss.

As Kate's husband, computer technology mogul

Sam McCabe, joined them, Kate continued stacking gifts into neat piles, for easier transporting, "I just want you and Chase to know that we could not be happier for you."

Merri smiled as she loaded presents onto a cart. Appreciating the candor, she replied, "I realize our wedding may have seemed very quick and untraditional."

Kate smiled up at her husband of many years. "Yes, well, once upon a time, Sam and I were a surprise to everyone, too."

He laughed and squeezed her hand. "Including, as it happens, the two of us."

Merri identified with that notion, all right. She hadn't expected to have a hot, wild, passionate relationship with Chase, never mind start to fall in love with him. But both were happening....

"The point is," Kate continued, "the foundation of every happy family is the strong love and enduring relationship between the parents."

Her husband nodded in agreement. "You can't have a successful family without that."

The couple helped Merri steer the loaded carts toward the door. "It's obvious you and Chase have something very special and unique," Kate said.

But was it love? Merri wondered. She knew how she was beginning to feel. She knew Chase desired her and enjoyed being with her and the kids. That he loved the twins was also evident. But did he love her—in the way that Kate and Sam had been talking about?

Would Chase ever care for her that way? And what would happen in the long run if he didn't? Would a one-sided emotion be enough to sustain them?

* * *

"What were you talking about with Kate and her husband this evening?" Chase asked later, after they had put the very sleepy twins to bed.

Merri closed their bedroom door and filled him in on the conversation.

He couldn't say he was surprised. "I figured she'd come around," he admitted with a great deal of satisfaction. "Everyone would, given a little time. When they realized we weren't behaving recklessly..."

Merri nodded, looking comforted, too, by the outpouring of love and good wishes they had received. "It felt good, having the community support us that way."

Chase knew now how sensitive she was to the opinion of others. He was glad the wedding reception had made her feel better about their situation.

Merri unknotted his tie and pulled it off. "I don't know where to begin to thank you," she whispered emotionally. "It really was an incredible party."

And she'd been an incredible bride.

She looked so beautiful. Even more so than she had on their wedding day. And that was saying something.

"And the ring," she said softly. "It just makes our union all the more official."

Was that why she thought he had given it to her? Chase wondered in alarm. For appearances sake?

To his disappointment, it seemed so.

Wary of pushing her too hard, too fast, Chase reined in his quickly escalating feelings. The two of them had made a deal—to have a union based on friendship, co-parenting and sex. He had to stick to that. At least for now. Maybe in time more would be possible, but for right now they both needed to be grateful for all they had, which was a lot.

He cleared his throat. "You deserve it, Merri, and so much more." He watched as she took off her cardigan, then her dress. She slipped into the bathroom, returned in just a robe. "You've been a great wife to me. A *great* wife. And a great mother to our kids."

Merri smiled and glided closer. Their gazes meshed and she searched his eyes. "Thank you. You've been a great husband, and a great dad."

Silence stretched between them. Chase had no idea if she was ever going to want anything more than what they had right now. But he knew what he wanted to have happen. And to get there, he would need to do a lot more work on his half of the relationship.

Smiling, he toyed with the belt on her robe. "Technically, it's not our wedding night."

She undid the knot then ever so slowly released the ends. "I guess it's not."

Damn, he was hard already. "But we are still on our honeymoon." He opened her robe all the way.

She was naked. Incredibly beautiful and hot. And waiting. For him. To catch up.

She let him go and moved back, to lounge against the bureau, hands braced on either side of her, robe open.

More than ready to join her, he held her eyes as he stripped off his shirt, kicked off his shoes and shucked his pants.

Naked, too, he sauntered toward her.

Eyes glittering mischievously, she tilted her head and picked up the threads of their conversation. "I don't know, Doc, if we can still be on our honeymoon after a month."

He slid his hands inside her robe. Her skin was as hot as he was. He kissed his way down her throat, to the sensitive spot at the base of her neck. "Maybe we'll always be on our honeymoon."

She sighed and leaned closer, her nipples beading against his chest. She turned her head so their lips met, and kissed him back, until both of them were trembling. "I think I could live with that," she whispered.

"So could I." Chase carried her to the vanity and sat down with her on his lap. "Ever feel like it's Christmas already?" he asked, as he finished unwrapping her.

Merri smiled. "Every day."

Aware that she needed some serious loving—they both did—after the momentous month they'd had, Chase set about claiming her as his. She did the same for him, rocking against him, and urging him on, even as he surged into her, entering and withdrawing in shallow strokes that had them both panting and moaning for more.

They drew it out as long as possible, savoring every second, and when they'd finally reached their peak and were drifting slowly, inevitably down again, he held her while she cuddled against him.

An unimaginable tenderness swept through him. Chase knew it had been only a matter of weeks that they'd been together, but he could no longer imagine his life without her.

He sensed she felt the same.

Whether she knew it yet or not, it was a lot more than simple honor, or a desire to do the right thing, keeping him with her and the kids.

Some unions were just meant to be.

Theirs was one of them.

* * *

The day after their reception was challenging, to say the least. With Chase at the hospital, Merri had her hands full.

"You said our daddy was going to be home for dinner!" Jeffrey grumbled.

Merri helped her son on with his coat and knelt to zip up the front. The extra excitement and late hours the evening before, and an unusually short nap that afternoon, had turned both twins cranky. Merri hoped an afternoon ride on their tricycles would help get their endorphins going and calm them down.

"He was supposed to be home in a little bit. But another surgeon got sick, so Daddy has to stay at the hospital and take her shift this evening."

"I don't care!" Jessalyn crossed her arms sulkily. "I. Want. My. Daddy. Now."

Feeling a little overtired and overwrought herself, Merri turned to Jessalyn and assisted her into her jacket. "Well, unfortunately, that is not going to happen."

"Why not?" the twins chorused in perfect unison.

Merri sighed and gave up trying to explain. Hands on their shoulders, she ushered both out the door and onto the front porch. "Because it just isn't." She held their hands as they climbed down the steps. The fresh air and cold winter sunshine had to help. "You two wait right here while I get your tricycles out of the garage." Merri punched in the code and watched as the electric door rose.

By the time she had stepped inside, grabbed the bikes and walked back out, Jeffrey was no longer where he was supposed to be.

Jessalyn, meanwhile, had sunk down on the driveway and was pulling at the Velcro strap of her athletic shoe. "Mommy!" she whined. "Fix this!"

Merri set the bikes down. "What's wrong with it?" She scanned the area for Jeffrey and found him, to her utter dismay, climbing on the stacked firewood, a short distance from the house.

"Oh, my...Jeffrey! Get down from there right now!"

He glared at her with all the pugnacity a four-and-a-half-year-old could muster. Merri knew he was testing her. On days like this, it seemed as if all the twins did was test their limits in one way or another. "I mean it, Jeffrey. You could get hurt!"

Jessalyn continued to wail indignantly, demanding her share of attention, too. "Mommy! My shoe!"

Who said Christmas was a happy time? Merri wondered irritably as she started toward Jeffrey. "I'm counting." If she made it to three, there would be a time-out. A fact her son very well knew.

He picked up a splintery piece of kindling and threw it to the ground as hard as he could.

"One." Merri kept going. Jessalyn kept screaming. Jeffrey threw another piece of wood.

"Two." Merri picked up speed. Another stick went flying, this one so heavy that throwing it nearly rocked Jeffrey off his feet. Merri rushed forward. "That's it, then. Thr—" She had to dodge hard to avoid another as the last piece of split firewood came tumbling toward her.

Jeffrey screamed again. This time not in rage, but in pain.

Thirty minutes later, with the cacophony in the car still at earsplitting levels, Merri was nearly at the hospital. "Jeffrey, Jessalyn, please calm down. It is *just a splinter.*"

"It hurts!" Jeffrey wailed. Beside him, Jessalyn sobbed in sympathy.

Merri knew this was not exactly life or death. She also knew there was no way she was going to be able to get the offending piece of wood out on her own. So here they were, about to make an hysterical entrance into the E.R. that no one would soon forget.

Merri could only imagine what Priscilla Roy would make of this calamity, if and when the esteemed judge heard about it, which she most surely would. Merri eased into a parking space reserved for patients, and cut the motor. She turned to face the twins. "Listen to me," she said in her most stern but soothing voice. "We are going to go in the hospital and—"

"See our daddy!" Jessalyn stopped crying momentarily.

Merri hoped they would. But wary of making another promise that might not come true, especially if Chase was currently in surgery, she said, "We're going to get one of the nurses or the doctors to help us fix Jeffrey's hand. But to do that, we first have got to be quiet, because there are sick people in there. And we don't want to hurt their ears with all this crying."

Amazingly enough—maybe because they had exhausted themselves on the thirty-minute drive to town—the twins fell silent, nodding in assent. There was nothing Merri could do about their red and tear-swollen faces, however, as she got them out of their car seats and guided them into the E.R.

Brianna, one of the triage nurses, came forward. "Hey, Merri."

When Jeffrey burst into tears, Jessalyn teared up, too—out of sympathy.

"What have we got here?" Brianna asked gently.

"A splinter," Merri said, pointing at Jeffrey's hand, which he promptly clasped against his chest.

Merri asked, "I don't suppose Chase...?"

Brianna shook her head. "He's been in surgery. But I heard—"

The elevator doors opened. A big, handsome man in blue scrubs stepped out.

"Daddy!" Jessalyn shouted in joy.

"Daddy!" Jeffrey wiggled out of Merri's arms and ran toward Chase. "Daddy, I got a splinter!" He burst into fresh tears, and Jessalyn joined in. Both hurled themselves into his arms.

And it was only as Chase picked them both up and cuddled them close that Merri realized what the twins had just said.

"They called you Daddy," Merri said, after the splinter had been taken out with one swift, sure, painless pluck of the tweezers, and the tiny hand disinfected, then wrapped with a Scooby-Doo Band-Aid.

"I know." Chase's smile was as big as all Texas. "I heard." He kissed Merri tenderly. "Who said Christmas doesn't come early?"

She and the kids stayed long enough to have a quick dinner with him in the hospital cafeteria, then headed home. Merri skipped baths and put the kids in their pajamas, then in bed. They were asleep before their heads hit the pillow.

The next morning, Chase hit the shower as soon as he got home from the hospital, and she gave the twins bubble baths before breakfast. When her turn came, there was once again no hot water.

Chase grinned, looking surprisingly pleased when she told him she was going to wait an hour or so until the tank had filled again.

"Actually, you may have to delay a little longer than that today," he said, rubbing his jaw.

Merri wasn't surprised he wanted to make love. He often took advantage of the time they were alone, when the kids were at preschool. But he didn't kiss her or lead her toward the bedroom.

Instead, he led her toward a front window.

Two utility trucks were rumbling down the driveway to the ranch house. Merri read the writing on one. "You called a plumber?"

"And an electrician. And someone from the gas company." The trucks parked side by side.

She blinked. "Why?"

Chase hugged her close and grinned. "It's time for your next gift."

"So you liked the tankless water heater?" Emily asked the following day, when she dropped by the ranch house for coffee.

Merri eased away from the kitchen table, where the twins were busy painting the wooden trains they had selected as Christmas gifts for their daddy.

"It's great." She walked Emily out to the garage to show her the new appliance mounted against the wall. "You can see how little space it takes up. And there's no limit on how much hot water is available, since it literally makes it on demand before it goes through the pipes. It can supply three different spigots at once, without any disruption in service." She beamed. "Which means we can have the shower going and still be running the dishwasher and the washing machine, and be okay. The best part is that it's energy and cost efficient."

"You are besotted," Emily teased as they walked back into the house.

Merri cast her friend an amused glance over her shoulder. She moved to the stove to put on the teakettle, thinking about how much fun it had been when she and Chase had christened the new water heater the previous afternoon, after the workmen had left, and again this morning, before the twins woke up. "Besotted by a water heater?" she asked innocently.

As at home in Merri's kitchen as her own, Emily got down two mugs. "I was thinking more about the husband who gave it to you."

Was it that evident? Merri brought out a selection of tea bags and shrugged. "I am still on my honeymoon, as everyone keeps pointing out to me."

"Uh-huh." Emily plucked a peppermint tea out of the mix and ripped open the seal. "Then what is bothering you? Because I could tell the moment I walked in that something was on your mind."

Merri kept her voice low to avoid alerting the twins, who proved daily they couldn't keep a secret. No matter how hard they tried, they always divulged it in about five seconds. "I haven't been able to figure out what to get Chase," she whispered, dropping a blackberry tea bag into her cup. "Christmas isn't even here and he's already given me a diamond ring, a wedding reception and, as you just saw—" Merri wrinkled her nose playfully "—the water heater of my dreams."

Emily's eyes danced. "Maybe he's the one besotted."

They both were, Merri thought. At least sexually. Romantically? Well, that was still up in the air, and would be until—or if—he fell all the way in love with her.

Because if he didn't, they'd be left with a lopsided arrangement, with her caring more about him than he did about her—and Merri had vowed, after her breakup with Pierce, that she would never put herself in that situation again. But she had, and the weird thing was, she loved Chase so very much, she wasn't even all that sure she minded. He made her so darn happy! Every single day. She could live with loving him more than he loved her. But that wasn't the primary problem today.

Sobering, Merri dragged her attention back to her dilemma. "I know this sounds stupid and frivolous, but I'm serious. Christmas Eve is *tomorrow,* and I want to do something extra special for Chase. Yet I'm still coming up blank."

Everything she looked at, everything she considered, seemed just plain wrong. Lifting the whistling kettle off the stove, Merri admitted, "The only thing I have gotten him so far is a framed photo of him and the kids."

Emily glanced at her. "Not one of the two of you?"

Carefully, Merri filled both their mugs. Reluctant to admit she was still trying not to jinx it, she said, "We're waiting for the proofs from the party photographer. Chase wants to use one of those for his office."

Which made sense, of course, since they were both in their wedding finery.

Emily added sugar to her tea. "Have you asked him what he wants?"

"Yes." Merri removed her tea bag and took a sip.

"He says the same thing I always say—that I already have everything I want."

And, Merri realized dreamily, for the first time in her life, it was true. Or would be, if Chase would only fall in love with her the way she was falling in love with him.

"Surely you must have some ideas."

Merri savored the peppermint on her tongue. "That's just it. I don't."

Her friend furrowed her brow. "That isn't like you. You always know what to get, in terms of gifts. What's different about this?"

Merri looked over the counter at the twins, who were so engrossed in decorating the train cars, they were oblivious to the adult conversation. "It's our first Christmas as man and wife," she whispered.

Emily waited.

She drew an enervating breath. Might as well get it all out. "I'm afraid I'll disappoint him."

Emily helped herself to one of the spritz cookies on the counter. "And if you do, then what?"

Merri took her friend's elbow and guided her into the formal dining room. "Then people will see it as proof that we aren't as in sync as a couple should be."

"Ah, yes," Emily retorted gravely, "the Thanksgiving sweet potato casserole travesty."

Abruptly, Merri felt as cranky and out of sorts as the kids had before Jeffrey got the splinter. She looked at the beautifully decorated tree, and the elaborate Christmas village, complete with working Lionel train, which Chase and the kids had added to nearly every day.

"It's not funny." She stalked to the mantel, where four stockings, embroidered with their names, had been hung in a row. Abruptly, although she couldn't say why, she felt near tears. "I'm in crisis here."

Emily walked over to comfort her. "I know you are, and for no reason. Chase adores you. You adore him."

Her friend made it all sound so simple. It wasn't. Not when there was biology, and legalities, and the demands of personal honor involved.

Frustration mounting, Merri turned back to Emily and challenged, "Then why can't I think of something that will demonstrate that to Chase, the way he already has to me?" *Why do I continue to feel at such a loss?* She thought she had put any inadequacy in a relationship behind her.

"You'll come up with a great idea." Emily patted her shoulder encouragingly. "As soon as you calm down and take a breath, and summon up the information and ideas you already have in here." She pointed to Merri's head. "And here." She pointed to her heart. "Just have a little hope and faith, and I promise you it will all work out."

Chapter 14

Pleased that she had finally solved the dilemma that had been plaguing her for weeks, Merri walked down Main Street, Chase's Christmas present in hand. Halfway to her SUV, she encountered their attorney, who also appeared to be taking the afternoon off to do a little last-minute shopping.

Liz smiled as the BlackBerry in her pocket began to hum. "I don't have to ask how things are going," she remarked. "You look happier than I've ever seen you."

Merri stepped back to let another pedestrian pass. "Thanks. I am."

Liz shifted the packages in her arms to be able to check the message on the screen. "The impromptu wedding reception the other night was a very smart move, too."

Shock rendered Merri momentarily speechless. "We didn't do it to prove a point."

"I know that." Liz slid her phone back in her pocket. "I get that it was romantic in origin, and something you and Chase wanted to do." Sobering, she went on, "But it was a very good maneuver to let everyone in town see how you and Chase feel about each other." Her voice dropped a notch. "When you add that to what happened in the emergency room the other night—"

Merri looked at her in surprise. "You heard about that, too?" she whispered.

Liz led her into an alley between two historic brick buildings, so they could talk privately. "The kids calling Chase Daddy and launching themselves into his arms? Yeah. I heard about it. At least a dozen times, if not more. Apparently, there wasn't a dry eye in the house."

Merri gulped, feeling a wave of emotion. Talk about joy and newfound love! This sure was the season... "It was pretty touching," she admitted, trying not to become teary.

Liz's expression gentled. "My point is, when we talked ten days ago, you and Chase were worried about the public perception of your marriage, and the fact the kids didn't seem to be accepting him. Now, thanks to recent events—some scripted, some not—word on the street is that has changed. So much that the four of you could be the poster happy family."

Merri couldn't help but feel pleased about that, especially given the inept start she and Chase had experienced, trying to acclimate to each other and orient the kids to all the sudden changes.

She breathed in the yuletide fragrance of freshly baked gingerbread cookies from the bakery two doors down. "You think it will get back to Judge Roy?"

"Please!" Liz silenced her phone when it went off

again. "In a community as close-knit as this? Of course it will."

Relief flowed through Merri. It certainly would help to replace the initial impressions she and Chase and the kids had made with something a lot more positive.

"I still can't guarantee results," Liz reminded her. "No attorney can do that. But thanks to recent events, your chances for the outcome you want are a whole lot better than they were initially. So…" She grinned. "…merry Christmas!"

Merri beamed. "Merry Christmas to you, too!"

"What's got you feeling so chipper?" Chase asked Merri after they had put the kids in bed that evening.

Happy to finally have a moment alone with her husband, Merri told him about her conversation with Liz.

Chase didn't look as surprised as she had been. "I was hoping that would help," he murmured, following her into the laundry room.

A shimmer of unease slid down Merri's spine. She paused in front of the clothes dryer. "That wasn't why you threw the party and gave me the diamond ring, was it?" she asked in a soft, wary tone. "To make our marriage seem more legitimate, and therefore help us in court?"

If that was the case, it took all the joy out of both events. It also made her a romantic fool, because she'd thought—hoped—that his actions had been motivated by their newfound passion and growing feelings for each other.

He reassured her with a sober glance. "No. Of course not. I gave you the ring and the party because our new bond deserves to be celebrated. I'm honored that you agreed to share your life with me and be my wife, and I want everyone to know how much you mean to me."

Merri wanted to shout out her love to the whole world, too. The only problem was, Chase had never mentioned love. Or even infatuation.

She studied him, knowing him well enough to realize there was more there, just beneath the surface. "And yet you're not unhappy it's apparently had this result, are you?"

He shrugged. "I want this matter settled as soon as possible, Merri. I want us to be a complete family, the two of us co-guardians of the kids." He put his hands on her shoulders and intimately searched her face. "I thought that was what you wanted, too."

"Of course it is," she declared hotly, wondering how they had taken something happy and turned it into conflict. Tomorrow was Christmas Eve. She didn't want to argue with Chase.

His hands slid down her arms to her wrists. "Then?"

She leaned back against the washer and forced herself to go on. "It occurs to me now that this could backfire. Particularly if Judge Roy were to perceive it as an attempt by us to put something over on the court." The woman had certainly warned them…

Chase settled next to Merri. His back to the dryer, he laced a protective arm about her shoulders, drawing her in close to his side. "I don't think she will take that view. I think at the end of the day she'll know we're sincere."

Merri hoped Chase wasn't just telling her what he thought she wanted to hear. She resisted the urge to rest her cheek against his shoulder, and forced herself to play the part of devil's advocate. "And if Judge Roy doesn't?" *What then?*

Chase intwined their fingers, squeezed. His gaze never left her face. "Then we keep on trying, because you and I know the truth. That our intentions have always been honorable." He brushed a strand of hair from her cheek, and his low voice was as soothing as his touch. "Everything we've done here has been to protect the kids and build a strong and loving family for them." He paused to let his words sink in. "And as Kate pointed out to us, our relationship with each other is the foundation for that."

Which meant they had to be fully married, so if asked, they could swear under oath that theirs was a real marriage in every way.

Chase misunderstood the reason behind her anxiety. "I know there's still a lot up in the air, Merri, but it's all going to work out for us. You'll see."

Merri spent the night in Chase's arms and woke up feeling much better. It was silly to worry about things they had no control of in the end. What mattered now was the twins' first Christmas with a mommy and a daddy.

As if to drive home that fact, the first thing Merri saw that morning when she opened up her email was an electronic holiday card for the entire family.

"Look, Mommy," Jessalyn cried excitedly when Merri showed the photo greeting to the twins. "It's Addie and Nissa and Davita and Harmony and Polly and Starr!"

All were wearing their Santa hats again. All were

holding signs naming their various hometowns, with the message, "Next Stop, Christmas!" beneath.

Chase, who was manning the griddle, making pancakes, came over to see, too. He grinned at the holiday greeting.

"What's that?" Jeffrey asked, pointing to a digital clock sign that said 84:22.

"I think it's how much time is left before they have to catch their flight overseas, to go back to work in the field hospital."

"Sorry you're not going?" The words slipped out before Merri could stop herself.

Chase held her eyes and shook his head. "I'm right where I'm supposed to be." He gazed at her contentedly, then reeled her in and kissed her soundly.

"Ooh" the twins said in unison. "You're kissing!"

They sure were, Merri thought, her spirits rising and her knees wobbling. It was times like this, when he was holding her in his arms, that it felt as if the barriers around their hearts had completely fallen away. She reveled in the feeling of hard male muscle pressed up against her, and the longing she saw in his eyes.

Fortunately, the kids had already moved on. "Does Santa Claus kiss anybody?" Jessalyn asked, propping her hand on her chin. She watched as Chase went back to the griddle to flip the pancakes, which were a perfect golden-brown.

Jeffrey traced the label on the syrup bottle already on the table. He scowled thoughtfully. "Maybe his reindeer," he suggested finally.

Merri grinned at the mental image. "And Mrs. Claus," she said.

Chase carried two plates of silver-dollar pancakes to

the table and set them in front of the kids. "Speaking of Santa—" he flashed Merri a look, then returned to the griddle "—is there anything you little ones forgot to tell him that you want?"

Jeffrey and Jessalyn looked at each other and seemed to communicate without saying a word. "No," they said finally, in unison.

"You sure?" Merri asked.

"He knows. We already told him. At the hospital Christmas party, remember?" Jessalyn stated.

But whatever they'd said remained a mystery to their parents. "You can always tell us, too," Merri said.

"No, we can't," Jeffrey argued stubbornly. "You can't tell anyone your wish or it won't come true. Remember what you said when we blew out the candles on our cake?"

The logic of a four-and-a-half-year-old! "I think that's just birthday wishes," Merri told him, adding butter and syrup to both stacks.

"Nuh-uh! All wishes are secret," Jessalyn declared, "if you want them to come true." She and Jeffrey stared into each other's eyes yet again, in that magical way they had. "And we really really do."

"You can't tell anyone but Santa what you want for Christmas, and we already did," Jeffrey explained.

Merri looked at Chase. He looked at her. This was not the kind of thing they were going to be able to reason with the kids about.

So they did the only thing they could do, and called Dylan, who'd played Santa, when the twins were out of earshot.

"Trust me," Dylan reiterated, "it's the kind of thing you'd much rather hear from them. I'm sure they'll tell you tomorrow, when they wake up and get what they've been wanting for weeks now." He exhaled sharply. "You *are* going to be off, aren't you, Chase? You wouldn't miss this?"

"I've got today and tomorrow off," he assured him. The other surgeons in rotation, who didn't have small children anymore, had seen to that.

"Well, then," Dylan said mysteriously before hanging up the phone, "you're all set."

Ten hours later, the kids were finally asleep. The cookies and milk they'd set out for "Santa" had been consumed, the presents arranged beneath the tree. Blissfully, Chase and Merri settled down for some quiet time in front of the fire.

Chase's eyes sparkled. "Was that home pregnancy test kit in the bathroom yours?"

Aware this was the most exciting Christmas Eve she'd ever had, and that Christmas Day promised to be better yet, Merri flushed. She tucked her hand in his larger, callused palm. "You weren't supposed to see that!"

His heated gaze trailed over her features before returning with slow deliberation to her eyes. "I probably wouldn't have, if I hadn't been looking for a new blade for my razor." He paused, his expression becoming even more hopeful and intent. "Are you pregnant?"

Glad she had him beside her, Merri gripped his hand all the tighter. "I don't know yet. I'm not supposed to take the test until I'm at least a week late, and that won't be until the twenty-seventh." Three days from now...

Tenderly, he kissed the back of her hand. "But you think there's a good chance."

She looked deep into his eyes. "Usually, I'm like clockwork, and this cycle I'm not."

He grinned like a proud papa-to-be. "Well, then, congratulations." He shifted her onto his lap and delivered a long, sexy kiss.

She leaned back, appreciating the excited gleam in his eyes, knowing what a great daddy he already was, and would be to another child, too. "Congratulations to you, too," she replied softly. "But let's not tempt fate by talking about it too much." It scared her to want something—or someone—this much. And she did want Chase, so very much.

He hugged her close. "Agreed. We'll have plenty of time for that later. In the meantime," he murmured, drawing back to look into her eyes once again, "since I think we might be just a little busy tomorrow morning, making Christmas dinner and setting up the new set of train tracks, I'd like to give you your last gift this evening, if that's okay."

Merri bounded off his lap. "More than okay." She turned around with a wink and a curtsy. "Since I've got something for you, too."

Moments later, they settled on the floor in front of the beautifully lit and decorated tree, presents on their laps. "Ladies first," he said, smiling.

Achingly aware of just how much she had come to depend on him, Merri opened with trembling fingers the gift box he handed her. Inside was a platinum charm necklace, with the birthstones of all four of them set inside intricately intertwined hearts. He couldn't have picked a more meaningful present. Aware he'd come close to her heart, as always, Merri sighed with pleasure. "Oh, Chase. It's gorgeous! Thank you!"

She paused to kiss him, reveling in the minty taste of him, then handed him a long, slender box that contained the gift she had spent so much time picking out. She beamed at him, hoping he would like his present as much as she liked hers. "Your turn."

He waggled his eyebrows teasingly, then tore open the wrapping. Inside was a thick envelope bearing the local travel agency's logo. Curiosity piqued, he turned back the flap and saw the itinerary. A grin as big as Texas spread across his rugged features. "A cross-country train trip to Disneyland!"

Eager for him to see, Merri pointed out the rest. "And a plane flight back." She'd attended to every detail of the dream vacation. "It'll be the twins' first time on a train and a plane and at Disneyland. And their first big family vacation, too."

Chase laughed in delight. "They're going to love it. I love it." He gathered her close in a hug, then drew back, looking handsome and at ease in the soft twinkling lights of the tree. "Thank you." He paused to look deep into her eyes. "This is an incredible gift."

"I'm glad you like it," Merri said softly. Glad she understood what was in his heart, as surely as he did hers.

Contentedly, they lingered before the fire, enjoying each other's company, then went upstairs to further celebrate their first Christmas together. Feeling the connection between them deepening, they made tender, exquisite love, and Merri fell asleep wrapped in Chase's arms, dreaming of the baby she was sure they had made.

They woke at just past five the next morning. Jessalyn and Jeffrey were standing beside their bed, the two preschoolers jumping up and down with glee.

"Mommy! Daddy! Is it time yet?" Jeffrey tugged on Chase's arm.

Jessalyn tugged on Merri's. "Can we go downstairs? And see if Santa came?"

Chuckling, Chase and Merri sat up, and rubbed the sleep from their eyes. "Absolutely," Chase said in his gravelly voice. Grinning, the four of them clasped hands and went downstairs.

The tree with all its colored lights sparkled in the semidarkness. At the sight of the presents beneath it, the kids let out whoops of delight. Mad, happy chaos followed. Gifts were opened, one after another, and exclaimed over. Pleased that she and Chase had done well in selecting presents for the twins, because all she really wanted was for them to be happy, especially today, Merri smiled at them affectionately.

"So, did you get everything you wanted?" Chase asked finally, still curious about their secret request to Dylan Reeves, aka Santa Claus. "Everything you asked Santa for?"

"Of course." The twins looked at Chase and smiled even more mysteriously. Then they went back to examining their new trains.

Merri and Chase exchanged baffled glances. "You want to tell us what it was?" Merri asked, as she helped to take a new doll baby out of its box.

The twins shrugged, as if the answer was obvious. They dropped what they were doing and ambled over to Chase. "For Daddy to still be here and not go away," Jessalyn said. "And see?" She pointed at him for proof. "He's right here. Just like we asked Santa."

Dumbfounded, Merri and Chase stared at each other. No wonder Dylan hadn't wanted to divulge their wish.

Chase gathered the kids onto his lap, then took Merri's hand and reeled her in close, too, so they were all sitting on the sofa, snuggling together. Gently he smoothed a hand down the twins' spines, and asked, "Why would you think I was leaving?"

Beginning to look a little worried, Jessalyn confided, "Because all the grown-ups said so."

"When?" Merri asked in alarm.

The little girl frowned. "At the welcome-home party. Everyone talked about how long you were gone away, Daddy, and how they never figured you'd stay in Laramie County, if you ever came home again."

To her distress, Merri remembered something like that being said. Countless times. She should have known the precocious, ultra-observant duo would pick up on it and internalize it.

Jeffrey leaned forward to confide, "The army ladies were sad you were leaving *them,* too. Especially Miss Starr. But Miss Addie and Miss Harmony said *they* weren't surprised. They always knew you'd go back to Texas someday and that you had to leave them, whether any of them liked it or not!"

"We didn't want you to leave *us,* too," Jessalyn allowed defiantly, tears of anguish beginning to shimmer in her eyes.

"Yeah! 'Cause—" Jeffrey hiccupped and wrapped his arms around Chase's neck "—we like having you around."

"And we love you, Daddy," they finished in unison.

Cuddling them close, Chase said thickly, "I love you both, too."

"So you won't ever leave us?" Jeffrey asked, while Merri swallowed around the lump in her throat.

"I won't ever leave you," he promised the kids gently, kissing them on the tops of their heads. Grinning, he ruffled their hair. "So we don't need to worry about that, okay?"

They beamed, the last traces of sadness leaving their faces. "Okay." They hugged Chase one more time, then raced off to play with their toys again.

"That was some Christmas present you just got," Merri told Chase, still feeling a little choked up by the revelation of just how much they adored their new daddy. They'd come to count on him almost as much as she did!

He nodded, then gave her a steady look that set her pulse pounding. "It sure was." He drew her close and kissed her, his hand drifting to her tummy, hovering protectively over the baby that just might be inside her.

"And the best thing, Merri," he whispered, "is that for us, this is just the beginning."

The day after Christmas, Merri woke before dawn. Still so happy over the way the holiday had gone, she expected to be bursting with energy. Instead, she felt achy and out of sorts. Attributing it to all the activity of the past few days, she shook off her lethargy.

Chase studied her sluggish movements with concern. "You sure you don't want me to do the milking?" he asked gently, getting up, too.

Merri appreciated his offer, even as she refused with a shake of her head. The dairy farming was her thing; she wasn't about to push it off on him.

"It's my responsibility." Because Slim had come in on Christmas Eve and Christmas Day, she was handling both morning and evening chores for the next several days.

She sauntered toward him, loving the way he looked in low-slung pajama pants and a day's growth of beard, and she ran a palm over his warm, bare chest. "And you have to work this evening."

He kissed her as if rest was the last thing on his mind, then promised, "I'll have breakfast ready for you when you come back in." He kissed her one more time before heading downstairs.

Merri went into the bathroom to get dressed and to her dismay, quickly realized why she felt so icky.

Chase knew something was up the moment he saw her face. He stopped filling her stainless-steel thermos and put the coffee decanter back on the warmer. "What's wrong?" he asked gruffly.

Regret at having spoken too eagerly, too soon, filled her cheeks with heat. "I'm not pregnant," Merri admitted with embarrassment.

His face fell, and somehow it helped to know that he was disappointed, too. He came toward her, arms outstretched, and held her tightly. "Ah, Merri, I'm sorry."

His tenderness melting her heart all the more, Merri fought back a sudden rush of tears. "I'm the one who's sorry," she said, hoarse with disappointment. How could she have been so foolish? So hopeful? Knowing what the odds were that she would conceive during the first menstrual cycle of trying, whether they'd known when she was ovulating or not?

Merri gulped. "I—"

"Hey. Hush…" Chase stroked a hand down her back, then hugged her again. "You're going to get pregnant."

His deep voice rumbled in her ear. "Probably sooner than you think." He drew back and, hooking his thumbs beneath her chin, lifted her face to his. Grinned in the familiar, unrepentant bad-boy way he employed whenever he wanted to make wild, passionate love with her. "In the meantime," he murmured with a wicked gleam in his eyes, "think of all the fun we're going to have trying."

He was ready now. Feeling his erection pressed against her, Merri ran her palms down his back to his buttocks. "You're such a great guy." She fitted her lower half to his, knowing another bout of lovemaking would make them both feel better.

But right now, the herd was waiting....

She rose on tiptoe and kissed the underside of his jaw. "Rain check?"

"An extra special rain check. Whenever you feel up to it," he promised huskily. "Until then...my offer to do the milking this morning is still good."

"No." Knowing she needed the time to herself, to think about—and accept—the disappointment not being pregnant had brought, she channeled her inner sassiness. "But I look forward to that breakfast you're going to fix me when I return."

Chase grinned and promised, "I'll make sure it's an extra special one, too." They kissed again, and he swatted her playfully. "Hurry back."

So glad he was in her life, Merri dutifully agreed.

Unfortunately, when she returned to the ranch house, she quickly realized their first holiday together had taken another unplanned turn.

A rental car with out-of-state license plates sat in

the driveway, a lone suitcase and Santa hat in the back-seat, a single coffee cup in the holder. Unexpected company? Again?

Merri had a sinking feeling she knew exactly who it was.

Chapter 15

Chase stared at Starr, glad that the twins were still upstairs, sound asleep, and that Merri was out in the barn. The last thing she needed was to find him with a woman hell-bent on making a pass at him. "You have to leave," he told Starr grimly.

She ignored his attempts to politely show her to the door, and stalked past him to the kitchen. "Not until I save you from yourself."

This, Chase thought, did not sound good. He tried to head her off. "We've been friends a long time." Which was the only reason he was being as circumspect as he was.

Moisture brimmed in the young nurse's eyes. "And I've loved you forever," she said thickly.

"I'm sorry, Starr." Everyone had hinted that this was the case. He had figured he could avert confrontation by pretending not to notice his former coworker's crush. As firmly and kindly as possible, he said, "I don't feel that way about you. I never have. I never will."

Tears spilled down her face. "You don't know what you feel! If you did, you never would have married Merri after being back in Texas for just a few days!"

There was a certain truth to that observation, Chase admitted ruefully to himself. When he'd first become involved with Merri, he'd had no idea how hard and fast he would fall, or how mind-blowingly happy she—and the kids—would make him. But now he did have a family, and he was determined to protect them.

He sent Starr a warning glance. "You don't know anything about that."

The nurse scoffed and stomped closer. "I know this. You haven't let yourself be serious about anyone since your engagement ended."

Chase shrugged. Nothing complicated about that. "I didn't want to date."

Starr glared at him. "And now suddenly, out of the blue, you want to marry someone—*just like that?* Be honest." She balled her hands in frustration. "This is all about honor. You're with Merri out of some cock-eyed notion of responsibility for your brother's kids."

It had started out that way. Now? "It's complicated," Chase finally allowed. About so much more than just the twins and his inability to legally claim them as his own without defaming the Armstrong family name. "I don't expect you to understand," he said grimly. Nor would anyone else. Chase knew he was doing what was best for everyone.

Starr paced back and forth, years of emotion spilling out. "I understand this. You can't build happiness out of a need to behave with integrity."

He'd done pretty well so far. Because the truth was, the past five weeks with Merri and the kids had been the happiest of his life.

"Standing by family and behaving honorably will take you only so far. If anything, your work in the field hospital should have shown you how short and precious our lives are! You have to stop worrying about everyone else and start seeing to your own needs." Starr grabbed a tissue and wiped the moisture from her cheeks. "You're such a good guy, Chase…" She held out her hands beseechingly. "You deserve so much more than a dutiful marriage to Merri can give you."

"It's true," a familiar voice said from the doorway.

Swearing inwardly, Chase turned to find his wife standing there, ashen-faced, regarding him with icy eyes.

Merri continued into the kitchen, stepping carefully. "Chase is a great guy." She looked at Starr and continued in a low, flat tone, "He deserves everything life has to offer. We all do."

"Which is why—" Chase said firmly, taking Starr by the arm "—you are leaving." He marched their uninvited guest through the foyer. "I wish you all the best. I really do." He opened the door wide and guided her onto the porch, his expression stern. "It's not here. It's not with me. And it never will be."

Starr dug in her heels and glared back at Merri. "I don't know what this hold is that you have on him, but if you have any heart at all, you'll let him go, because you're never going to make him happy. Duty isn't the same as love." Tear streamed from her eyes. "I get that you need a man to help you bring up the twins, but it doesn't have to be him."

Actually, Chase thought, given that they were his, it kind of did.

"And it doesn't mean he has to marry you!" Starr spat out.

Chase caught the door with his hand before she could slam it shut. He closed it quietly, so as not to wake the children still sleeping upstairs.

As always, when returning from working in the dairy barn, Merri appeared to want nothing more than a hot shower and a set of clean clothes. She walked back through the hall to the kitchen, set her thermos on the counter.

"I'm sorry that happened," Chase said, eyeing her pink cheeks and pale lips. "Sorry you had to hear that."

Merri's shoulders slumped in defeat. "I'm not. Because Starr's right." She gazed at him, her expression twisted with remorse. "We shouldn't be together. Not like this. Not for the long haul."

"There's even a term for it," Merri murmured wearily, reflecting on the conversation she'd had with Addie weeks before. "Crisis bonding."

"There's no question that the situation we have found ourselves in with the kids did turn both our lives upside down."

"No kidding." She'd been so full of guilt about not going to Chase sooner with what she knew—and so fearful about what the emotional fallout would be—that she'd allowed herself to think only in the short-term.

"We did the right thing, Merri, getting married."

Had they? "I thought so at the time."

Looking back, she wondered how she could have been so reckless. Letting herself believe that everything would work out the way she wanted, over time.

That Chase could give the kids the security and love they deserved, and her the baby she wanted. And then, when one thing led to another, and their blinding passion seduced her into letting her guard down further, she had convinced herself that their marriage could be real and lasting because her love was strong enough for both of them.

Never thinking about how much she was taking from him.

Now she knew better.

Because now she understood what it was like to love someone completely. The problem was, Chase didn't feel that way about her.

To not have that—ever—because you were tied to someone else out of duty or obligation was just plain wrong. Starr was right about that.

Chase edged closer. "And now you think our marriage was a mistake."

"For the long haul? Yes. It was."

His jaw set. "How can you say that?"

Tears welled in her eyes, but Merri stayed strong. "Because it's true," she said quietly, wishing with all her heart that it wasn't. "We're through the bulk of the crisis now. The twins have accepted you as their daddy in a way that will never be undone."

His lips formed a sober downward curve. "So you're dumping me."

"Suggesting we take a step back now, while we still can, and reevaluate. Because Starr is right to be concerned, even if she doesn't know all the details behind our marriage."

"Like the fact I want you and you want me…and that's not going to change, no matter what label you put on it?"

He was talking about the purely physical again. "That particular turn in our relationship was born out of extreme stress and pressure to do the right thing by you and the kids. Our desire for each other was fueled by all the emotion and potential heartache we were facing. And those are factors no one else but us can ever possibly understand, because they didn't live through this the way we have."

"It seems to me that's all the more reason we should stay together," he argued.

If only he had said he loved her, or could love her…

"Because we're bound to get closer, over time."

"Or grow apart, as people sometimes do, once the crisis that brought them together ends," she countered.

Chase studied her, legs braced apart, hands on his waist. "This is because you found out you aren't pregnant, isn't it?"

Merri flushed under his steady regard. "That has nothing to do with it."

"Really?" He released a short breath and came even closer. "If the situation was reversed, if you were pregnant right now, would you be standing here, telling me we made a mistake and needed to end this?"

Misery engulfed her anew. "The point is I'm not pregnant." And that was a good thing. Wasn't it?

He turned a disillusioned glance her way, his hurt and dismay evident. "And you won't give me a chance to remedy that."

Merri hurt, too, but she knew the pain they felt now was only a fraction of what they would feel if they continued recklessly down this path. "You deserve love, Chase. I do, too."

He recoiled as if she had slapped him. "Or in other words," he said bitterly, "just like my ex, the minute things don't go your way, you're out of here. There is no compromise. No meeting each other halfway. No putting each other's needs and desires, dreams and goals, above our own."

He didn't know how much Merri wanted to forget being noble, forget doing the honorable thing, and welcome him back into her arms and her bed. She swallowed hard, forcing herself to go on. "You heard what Kate said. To have a successful family, we need a strong and loving relationship, as foundation." *Love* being the operative word.

He braced himself as if for battle. "We have that."

Merri shook her head sadly. "Not in the way she meant. We need to be soul mates, just like every other happily married couple we know. Like Paige and Kurt. Emily and Dylan. And we're not, Chase." She cut him off with a lift of her hand. "Given how we rushed into this, there's no way we could be."

"I disagree. Sure, the beginning was a little rocky, but lately it's been great."

She held her head high. They had managed to become effective co-parents and even friends with benefits. "But what happens if you do fall in love with someone else one day?" she challenged, her heart breaking at the thought. *What then?*

"I told you. I don't feel that way about Starr."

"But you might feel that way about some woman

eventually, Chase." *You certainly haven't intimated you feel that way about me.*

He reached for her tenderly. "I have everything I need with you."

Except love, Merri thought. And love was what he needed most of all. Splaying her hand across his chest, she pushed him away, determined to do what was right. "Look. We'll figure this out. We'll find a way to go forward as co-guardians of the kids."

"And until then?" he asked, his resentment obvious.

Disappointment stabbed her heart, even as she forced herself to be practical. "We disrupt the twins' lives as little as possible, and go back to the way it was when you first moved in with us."

His expression closed. "Separate bedrooms."

Merri nodded, her heart now officially broken. "And a marital relationship that is anchored by friendship, nothing more."

Chase paused in the doorway of Kate Marten's office. "Got a minute?"

The grief counselor stood and motioned him in, then shut the door for privacy. "What's on your mind?"

Chase had never been the kind of guy who went to others for advice on his personal life. It was what it was. He dealt with his problems on his own. But this was different. It wasn't just him. Or Merri. Regardless of what had happened in their marriage, they still had to protect the kids. And right now, he had no idea how to do that.

"When I first came back, and Merri and I got married, you thought it might be some sort of stress reaction to being back home, after years doing trauma surgeries in a military field hospital."

Kate interrupted with a lift of her hand. "Obviously, I was wrong about that."

"Actually, your instincts were right on. There were extenuating circumstances behind our rush to the altar."

Kate looked at him curiously.

"And as you guessed, some things I do need to talk about." *With someone I can trust to give me rock-solid advice.* "So if I ask for doctor-patient confidentiality—"

"You've got it," Kate promised. "What you say here will go no farther than this office."

Relieved to be able to speak to someone with perspective, Chase took a seat on the sofa. While she listened, occasionally taking notes, he told her about the deception his late brother and sister-in-law had perpetuated, and the necessary decisions that had followed.

"So it was a marriage of convenience."

Chase nodded, realizing now how unromantic that sounded. "It started out that way."

"And then changed into something much more viable."

His gut knotted. Had he ever been what Merri needed? Wanted? "I thought it had."

Kate smiled sympathetically. "So did everyone else."

Chase slumped back on the sofa. "Apparently everyone—including me—was wrong." He scrubbed a hand over his face and scowled. "Merri told me yesterday that she doesn't think we should continue trying to make our marriage a real union. She wants a more platonic arrangement."

Kate pursed her lips. "And you agreed."

Slowly, Chase released a breath. "I made a commitment to be a father to the twins. To provide the most normal, loving environment possible for them."

She nodded in approval. "And you're keeping that promise."

"Yes." Even though he'd had the faith and hope kicked out of him, it was the only honorable way to proceed.

Kate gave him a long, probing look. "Can you do that?"

Chase paused, giving the question the consideration it deserved. "Technically, yes. Merri and I have enough willpower to adhere to whatever restrictions we agree upon." At least in terms of their physical relationship. Emotionally, well, his feelings were going to be a lot harder to corral. Especially when it came to putting her back in the friend category, and nothing more.

Kate tapped her pen on her notepad. "Then what's the problem?"

For starters? "The kids. They're pretty sensitive to what goes on around them." Chase explained the twins' wish that he still be there on Christmas Day.

"You think if you and Merri are no longer intimate the twins will figure out something is amiss?"

"Given what they've already been able to observe and surmise? I know they will." Chase leaned forward, hands clasped between his knees. "And the thing is, I don't want them hurt." And because he was selfish....

"I don't want to give them up," he admitted. "I've already missed almost five years of their lives." The thought of losing even more time with them was unbearable. "I don't want to turn into a three-days-a-week, every-other-holiday dad." Which was the kind of arrangement an eventual divorce would bring.

"And that's why you're determined to stay married to Merri."

"Yes," he said gruffly. Even though the thought of never being *with* her again—after all that spectacular lovemaking they'd shared—was like having his heart crushed in a vise. There wasn't going to be a part of him that didn't miss her desperately.

"Hmm."

"What?" Chase demanded when the counselor said nothing more.

Kate lifted an eyebrow. "I think you might want to ask yourself why the two of you are still so amenable to the idea of living under the same roof—when there are so many other options available."

"Is there any way to delay the hearing with Judge Roy without jeopardizing Chase's request for co-guardianship?" Merri asked their attorney early the following day. Another night sleeping down the hall from Chase had left her restless and upset. Worse, despite her Oscar-worthy performance at breakfast, the kids were beginning to pick up on it. Chase had noticed, too.

Liz ushered her into the conference room.

"Why would we want to request that? What's going on?"

Merri swallowed, feeling abruptly near tears. Why had she allowed herself to be so reckless and make such a mess of things? Especially when she knew better than to take anything on faith! "I made a mistake, marrying Chase."

Liz patted her shoulder. "And you came to that conclusion because…?"

Her guilt intensifying, Merri slumped into a chair. "He deserves to love and be loved…."

"Isn't that what's been going on with the two of you?" the lawyer asked.

Merri pushed aside the memory of the hurt and confusion in Chase's eyes when she'd told him their physical relationship was over. "Maybe for me," she allowed softly, realizing how different life would be if her feelings were returned.

"Not for him."

Merri shrugged. "He does love the kids with all his heart. And they love him, too, so very much."

"What do you think he feels for you?"

Did she even want to answer that?

Liz pressed on. "Pretend we're under oath here. Pretend I'm Judge Roy. Answer the question. What do you think he feels for you?"

Realizing their attorney was only doing her job, Merri forced herself to reply. "I think Chase feels lust for me." There was no doubt their passion was incredible. "And friendship." To the point he made her feel she could talk to him about practically anything. Except anything that would put him on the spot and make them both uncomfortable. "And a close bond because we both share a biological connection to the kids, and want to parent them."

Liz sat back in her chair, a bemused look on her face.

"What are you thinking?" Merri asked impatiently.

She flashed a wry smile. "How ironic it is that just when all the speculation has completely died down, and everyone believes that you and Chase and the kids absolutely belong together, the two of you want out."

"I didn't say we wanted this."

"Of course not," Liz murmured, unconvinced.

Merri threw up her hands in frustration. "But it's the only sensible way to proceed. Naively, I had hoped otherwise, but let's get real—Chase and I are not going to be happy staying under the same roof if we are not sleeping together as man and wife."

"Of course not."

"That kind of proximity... well, you've seen Chase. You know how incredibly handsome he is." *In bed. And out. The truth was, all he had to do was breathe and...*

"And he thinks you're easy on the eyes, too, I gather?" they lawyer asked dryly.

Merri frowned. "I'm being serious here, Liz."

Her attorney's eyes gleamed. "I can see that."

Merri drew a breath and forced herself to go on, even more frankly, "Anyway, I was thinking that maybe if we delayed, we could use the time to figure out a way to convince Judge Roy and the court to allow Chase to live on the property—perhaps in a separate dwelling—and continue to be a dad to the kids."

"As a co-guardian?"

"Yes. Since he loves the twins and they love him. So they wouldn't lose any time with each other, the way people do in a normal divorce or legal separation."

"And you'd be okay with that?"

"I'm okay with anything that makes him and the kids happy."

And keeps him a safe distance away. So that my constant lusting after him won't be an issue for either of us.

Liz played with her pen. "What does Chase think about this?"

"I haven't spoken to him yet. I wanted to make sure

it would work, that his rights were protected, before proceeding."

The attorney set down her pen and speculated for a moment in silence. "I see," she said finally.

"You look like you do," Merri allowed nervously, "and you don't." Was her blunt honesty about to get them in even more trouble? It felt as if their lives were already screwed up enough.

"Maybe because you're acting like you care more about Chase's needs than your own. Which, I have to tell you, is not usually the case in proposed divorce action. And I have to ask you, Merri." Liz paused to give her a long, searching glance. "Why is that?"

Merri thought for the rest of the day about what Liz had asked her.

By evening, she knew what she had to do. But Chase was at the hospital and not due home until noon the following day. Which was okay. It gave Merri time to arrange for the kids to be elsewhere, and figure out what she was going to say.

Unfortunately, Chase didn't walk in at twelve-thirty, as scheduled. Nor was he there at one o'clock, or two.

Her spirits sinking, Merri was just reaching for the cord to unplug the Christmas tree lights when she heard the front door open and close.

Her heart racing with anticipation, she straightened.

Chase strode in.

He looked as tired as she would have expected after an eighteen hour-plus shift.

He was also freshly showered, shaved, wearing a neatly pressed shirt and slacks. Looking more ready for a date than bed, he shrugged out of his coat, dropped it on the arm of the chair and kept right on coming toward her. He pulled her into his arms and pressed his body against hers, his mouth against her hair.

It was the kind of casual, wordless greeting two longtime lovers gave each other, and despite herself, she melted into him.

He felt so damn good. So warm and strong and male. Beneath his shirt, she could feel the beating of his heart. Briefly, Merri closed her eyes, breathing in the tantalizingly familiar fragrance of soap and man. He kissed the top of her head, the gesture casual and tender, then ever so reluctantly released her and stepped back.

Merri tilted her chin and gazed into his eyes. Unbelievably, he looked as if he had missed her as much as she had missed him. And it had only been forty-eight hours since they'd stopped behaving as man and wife. Forty-eight long, lonely, unbearably miserable hours.

"Hey," Merri said softly, joy mingling with the longing deep inside her.

He was here. He was happy to see her. It wasn't the answer to all their problems, but it was a good first step, she realized, as courage flooded her anew.

His gaze drifted over her, as if he was drinking in and memorizing every detail. He reached up and tucked a strand of hair behind her ear, with a look of forgiveness she hadn't expected to see in his eyes. "Where are the kids?" he asked softly.

The lump in her throat was back, as another wave of anxiety slid through her. "Playing with the triplets, at Paige and Kurt's."

Chase covered Merri's hand with his and locked eyes with her. "They're due to be picked up when?"

"Six this evening." Her throat tightened even more,

making it difficult to swallow. She consulted her watch. "Which gives us about three and a half hours." *To work things out and find a holiday miracle of our very own, before the New Year.*

Chase's gaze intensified, the silence reinforcing all that was at stake. "Good." He ran a thumb over her knuckles. "'Cause there's a lot I want to say."

Glad she hadn't unplugged the Christmas tree, after all, since it gave a much needed element of cheer to the wintry stillness of the living room, Merri drew a bolstering breath. Ready to make whatever sacrifices were required, she looked deep into his eyes and said, "Okay."

He gazed down at her with the quiet intensity she loved so much. "I talked to Kate Marten yesterday."

Ignoring the sudden wobbliness of her knees, Merri tried to figure out where all this was going. The same place she wanted, she hoped. Blinking back a mist of emotion, she confided, "I talked to Liz Cartwright."

He came closer. "There's not going to be any divorce." His voice was a sexy rumble. "I won't agree to it."

Merri splayed her hands across his chest. "Okay."

He wrapped his arms around her and held fast. "No more pretending for all the world to be married, either. Because we *are* married, Merri." He tightened his grip on her affectionately. "I don't know how or when it became so much more..." He let the words sink in, then flashed the sexy grin she loved so much. "The realness of it sort of snuck up on me." He lowered his head and kissed her sweetly.

Merri slipped her arms about his neck and kissed him back, then admitted, "It took me by surprise, too."

They shared another kiss, even more ardent and persuasive. "I've been trying not to rush you, but sometimes there's just no slowing down what's in your heart."

"No kidding." Merri laughed shakily, as she realized all her dreams were about to come true. "It's like a freight train, going full speed."

He nodded in agreement, then forged on, the words coming from deep in his soul. "That being the case, you might as well know. I love you, Merri." She let out an exultant laugh, and he soldiered on. "And I'm pretty sure if you really think about it, you'll realize that you love me, too."

His confidence was as contagious as his bravery. "I don't have to think about it—I know how I feel. I've loved you for some time, Chase Armstrong." Relieved to finally be able to admit what was in her heart, Merri went up on tiptoe and kissed him with every bit of passion and joy she possessed. "I'm head over heels in love with you," she whispered.

He pulled her nearer, still, until they were pressed intimately together. "So no more talk about what we have not being enough."

Merri cuddled close, ready—finally—to open up her heart and take all the risks required. "None."

His gaze was steady and sincere. "It's not just about doing what's right for the kids anymore. It's about doing what is right for us, too."

"And that is?" Their kiss was long and slow, soft and sweet, as Merri prepared to take that final leap of faith with him.

"Loving each other every day for the rest of our lives."

Epilogue

"His eyes are all squinty." Six-year-old Jessalyn scowled.

"Yeah. And he doesn't have much hair and he's all red and wrinkly," Jeffrey complained.

Merri and Chase were prepared for this. They'd taken the hospital's class on sibling and newborn bonding. "That's because all babies look like this when they are born," Chase told the rising first-graders calmly.

"Want to see the pictures we took of you on your first day in the hospital?" Merri asked.

The pair nodded and climbed closer to her on the bed.

Chase took baby Andrew and handed Merri the little book of photographs they had prepared. The twins studied the portraits carefully. "Which one am I?" Jessalyn asked finally.

Merri pointed her out. "You're the one in pink, be-cause you're a girl."

"And I'm the one in blue because I'm a boy," Jeffrey deduced.

The adults exchanged tender looks.

"That's right," Merri said, wrapping her arms around the two and folding them close. She breathed in their sweet, familiar scents. "And you were both incredi-bly cute, even with red, wrinkly skin, fuzzy hair and squinty eyes."

They both grinned, pleased. "Can he play with us now?" Jessalyn asked.

"Maybe get in the stroller and go outside?" Jeffrey suggested.

Chase and Merri exchanged amused glances this time. "He's not ready for that yet," Chase told the kids affectionately, "but he can hang out with all of us now, right here."

The twins sighed. Each snuck a look at baby An-drew and smiled again, broadly this time.

"They seemed to take the introduction well," Chase remarked twenty minutes later, when they'd gone off with Paige and Kurt and the triplets for some cafete-ria ice cream.

Merri relished her time alone with Chase. She clasped his hand and squeezed it. "I thought so."

"In fact, this whole last year and a half has gone really well." He sat on the bed next to her, facing her. Together, they admired their new baby. Andrew was healthy and strong. He had Chase's nose and her eyes, the twins cherubic lips and stubborn chin.

Love filled Merri's heart. Every one of her dreams had come true. "I know it's July…"

Chase stroked her cheek and gazed deep into her eyes. "But it kind of feels like Christmas, doesn't it?"

Merri nodded emotionally. What had started out as a point of honor had become so much more. She and Chase had found love. The wrongs of the past had been righted, on the home front and in court. The twins had a daddy and a mommy, as well as a new baby brother. And most of all, Merri and Chase knew the utter joy that faith and hope could bring to a family and each other. "We're just so blessed," she whispered, tears of happiness filling her eyes.

His own eyes gleaming, Chase kissed her tenderly. "I couldn't agree with you more."

* * * * *

We hope you enjoyed reading

THE GROOM WHO (ALMOST) GOT AWAY

by *New York Times* bestselling author
CARLA NEGGERS and
THE TEXAS RANCHER'S MARRIAGE

by reader-favorite bestselling author
CATHY GILLEN THACKER

Both were originally Harlequin® series stories!

Discover more heartwarming contemporary tales
of everyday women finding love and becoming
part of a family or community from the
Harlequin® American Romance® series.
Featuring small-town settings and irresistible cowboys,
Harlequin American Romance stories are must-reads.

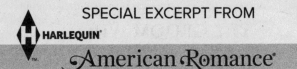

SPECIAL EXCERPT FROM

HARLEQUIN®

American Romance®

*Rose McCabe wants to use Clint McCulloch's newly
acquired ranch for blackberry farming, but the sexy
cowboy wants it for pastureland for his herd. Can the
two come to a temporary agreement?*

Read on for a sneak preview of
LONE STAR DADDY
by ***Cathy Gillen Thacker**,*
part of her **MCCABE MULTIPLES** miniseries.

"You can ignore me as long as you want. I am not going
away." Rose McCabe followed Clint McCulloch around the
big farm tractor.

Wrench in one hand, a grimy cloth in another, the rodeo
cowboy turned rancher paused to give her a hostile glare.
"Suit yourself," he muttered beneath his breath. Then went
right back to working on the engine that had clearly seen
better days.

Aware she was taking a tiger by the tail, Rose stomped
closer. "Sooner or later you're going to have to hear me out."

"Actually, I won't." Sweat glistened on the suntanned
skin of his broad shoulders and muscular back, dripped
down the strip of dark hair that covered his chest, and
arrowed down into the fly of his faded jeans.

Still ignoring her, he moved around the wheel to turn the
key in the ignition.

It clicked. But did not catch.

He strode back to the engine once more, giving Rose
a good view of his ruggedly handsome face and the thick

chestnut hair that fell onto his brow and curled damply against the nape of his neck. At six foot four, there was no doubt Clint was every bit as much as stubborn—and breathtakingly masculine—as he had been when they were growing up.

"The point is—" he said "—I'm not interested in being a berry farmer. I'm a rancher. I want to restore the Double Creek Ranch to the way it was when my dad was alive. Run cattle and breed and train cutting horses here." He pointed to the blackberry patch up for debate. "And those thorn- and weed-infested bushes are sitting on the most fertile land on the entire ranch."

Rose's expression turned pleading. "Just let me help you out."

"No." He refused to be swayed by a sweet-talking woman, no matter how persuasive and beguiling. He had gone down that road once before, with a heartbreaking result.

A silence fell and Rose blinked. "No?" she repeated, as if she were sure she had heard wrong.

"No," he reiterated flatly. His days of being seduced or pressured into anything were long over. Then he picked up his wrench. "And now, if you don't mind, I really need to get back to work…"

Don't miss LONE STAR DADDY
by Cathy Gillen Thacker,
available June 2015 wherever
Harlequin® American Romance®
books and ebooks are sold.

www.Harlequin.com

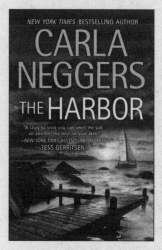

HARLEQUIN®

A *Romance* FOR EVERY MOOD™

JUST CAN'T GET ENOUGH?

Join our social communities
and talk to us online.

You will have access to the latest
news on upcoming titles and special
promotions, but most importantly,
you can talk to other fans about your
favorite Harlequin reads.

Harlequin.com/Community

 Facebook.com/HarlequinBooks

 Twitter.com/HarlequinBooks

Pinterest.com/HarlequinBooks

THE WORLD IS BETTER
WITH
Romance

Harlequin has everything from contemporary, passionate and heartwarming to suspenseful and inspirational stories.

Whatever your mood, we have a romance just for you!

Connect with us to find your next great read, special offers and more.

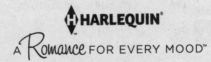